IRISH SAVIOR

M. JAMES

Copyright © 2022 by M. James

All rights reserved.

No part of this book may be reproduced in any form or by any electronic or mechanical means, including information storage and retrieval systems, without written permission from the author, except for the use of brief quotations in a book review.

This is a work of fiction. Names, characters, businesses, places, events and incidents are either the products of the author's imagination or used in a fictitious manner. Any resemblance to actual persons, living or dead, or actual events is purely coincidental.

AUTHOR'S NOTE

This will be one of those books you have to discuss! Join my Facebook reader group here https://www.facebook.com/groups/531527334227005!

ANA

*P*ain. *All I know is pain, half-sensible, twisted into a position that no one should hold for this long, every muscle in my body aching.*

Voices, someone's saying my name in an accent that I don't recognize, that doesn't sound like anyone I know.

A stranger.

Hands, undoing the ropes. Bringing me down, the blessed feeling of being free, and then the rush of blood to all the places where my circulation couldn't reach, sending new waves of pain over me, through me, until I would scream with it if I could make a sound. Something inside of me is screaming, but that's nothing new. I feel as if I've been screaming for months now, so long that I can't remember what it's like not to hear it in my head, ever since Franco took that knife to my feet, shredding the soles and burning the wounds.

What Alexei has done almost feels like child's play compared to that. Just another man, profiting off of the suffering of others. The whole world is full of them. I see that now.

More hands, lifting me, carrying me. The feel of cool leather under my cheek, the smell of an expensive car. Cold air, and then the car's moving, around corners and over bumpy roads until I want to be sick, but I don't have the strength.

I don't think I'll have the strength ever again.

I wish I could just die.

The hands again, lifting me out of the car. Up, up stairs, more leather against my arms and legs, those hands settling me into a seat. My eyes focusing just long enough to see a strange, handsome face hovering over mine and a rich, thick accent speaking to me. He's so attractive that it startles me, because I haven't seen anyone like that in a long time. Someone whose good looks aren't overshadowed by the evil in their soul that I can see so clearly, because they don't bother to hide it.

Franco was like that.

Alexei was like that.

Who is this man? Why is he looking at me like that, as if he's worried for me? Doesn't he know that Alexei will be back any minute, and he'll be in trouble? I'll be in trouble.

"We'll be home soon," he says, in that same voice, that strange accent. It sounds French.

But no one working for Alexei is French, as far as I know.

I don't know how to tell him that I no longer have a home. My apartment is gone. My life is gone. But my lips and tongue still aren't working, my body paralyzed, and I slump back into the seat as someone pulls a soft blanket over me. It feels better than anything has in a long time, soft and warm like cashmere, and I want to tell whoever it is that they shouldn't, that he'll be angry.

Alexei.

I don't want to make him angry.

The roar of an engine, the feeling of lifting, soaring, and then the exhaustion of it all creeps over me, and my head falls to one side as my eyelids slide shut again.

Am I falling asleep, or am I dying?

I can't bring myself to care.

* * *

THE SOUND of birds is what wakes me. I open my eyes slowly, blinking away the last of sleep as I struggle to wake up all the way. My face feels puffy, my eyes dry and sticky, and my tongue is stuck to the roof of my mouth, which feels as if it's been stuffed with cotton.

I don't know where I am.

There were no birds at the mountain chalet. At least, I'm pretty sure that there weren't. Alexei didn't let us out to see.

Alexei. Fear rises up in me, hot and sharp, and I feel like I'm going to throw up. I push myself upright, feeling pain shoot through me as I wrap my arms around my stomach, trying not to be sick. I'm not even sure if I can stand up, and I don't want to be sick all over the bed.

My eyes focus a little more, taking in more of my surroundings, anything to distract myself. *This is nothing like the room at the chalet*, I realize, reaching out with one hand to smooth it over the bedspread. It's a floral chintz, blue and white, and there are pillows to match, tossed on a wing chair by the window. I turn slowly, pressing my hand against the pillow I'd slept on, and my hand sinks into it.

Down. Luxurious and soft. Another one next to it, as if I might need two.

There was nothing like this in the room that Alexei kept us in–me, Caterina, Sofia, Sasha, and Caterina's two stepdaughters. My heart squeezes in my chest as I wonder what's happened to them, if they were sold, if Viktor ever showed up as Caterina had so stubbornly believed that he would.

If he had—if he and Liam and the others had come to our rescue, it was too late for me.

That's not his fault, but it hurts all the same.

Liam. Something in my chest squeezes painfully again at the thought of the handsome Irishman who was, even if very briefly, my friend. There was never any future for us, but I can't let myself think for very long about how he looked at me, the way he kissed my hand, how he seemed to actually listen to me when we talked. The way he'd lean forward, eyes bright and interested, as if what I was saying mattered. As if he didn't have anywhere else he wanted to be.

I'd let myself fantasize about it just a little. What it would be like to have a man like Liam in love with me. It was a ridiculous fantasy; I'd known that even then. Liam is one of the Irish Kings, *the* Irish King, the man at the head of his organization's table. A man like Luca and Viktor, except kinder somehow, a bit softer. Younger than either of them, so the world hasn't had a chance to make him hard.

Even before what Franco had done to me, even before Alexei, before *I'd* become broken and a shell of the girl I'd once been, I wouldn't have been an appropriate match for someone like Liam. I used to be a party girl, reckless and fearless, the one who would drag Sofia out away from her violin and her studies and make her go out on the town with me. I was the reason we ended up in the club that night that she was taken by the Bratva, the reason Luca swept in to save her.

I'm not the kind of girl that men like Liam marry. My family name was disgraced a long time ago, and I'm not rich. I don't even have a home of my own anymore. I'm not a virgin—far from it. I don't have connections, money, or innocence to bring to the table. And now, after everything that's been done to me—I don't think I have anything at all.

I barely remember what it felt like to be that girl.

And now—I'm not even sure where I am, let alone *who* I am.

Slowly, I take in the rest of the room. There is a wide bay window open to let in a warm spring breeze and birdsong. Sheer lace curtains flutter at the windows, a soft throw blanket that looks like cashmere over the back of the wing chair. On the other wall, I see a wooden wardrobe that looks antique; the surface is worn down to a dark sheen with brass hardware. Everything in the smallish room looks old, but in a way that seems intentional, rather than shabby, down to the framing around the door and the antique knob. There's another door directly across from the bed, and as I lean forward, I can peer around it just enough to see that it's a small bathroom with an iron clawfoot tub. Behind the wing chair, there's a proliferation of houseplants, some of them doing their best to trail their leaves out of the open window. Nothing about it feels particularly masculine. If anything, it's a room meant to feel soft and cozy, like a haven. A nest.

Where the fuck am I? My heart starts to pound in my chest, anxiety rising up hot and thick, and I clutch the blankets around my hips, trying not to panic. I can feel a spiral coming on, the fear clutching at my throat, and I force myself to push back the blankets, swinging my legs over the edge of the bed. Somehow being in this place that feels meant to comfort, to shelter, feels even more terrifying than the clear danger of Alexei's mountain chalet. I don't understand it. None of it makes sense, and it feels like a trap.

I wish I could remember more of what happened. I know that Alexei was having a party—elite guests coming to see if they would want to purchase the women he had for sale. Caterina, Sofia, Sasha, the two little girls, Anika and Yelena. He'd told me—I squeeze my eyes tightly shut, trying to remember, even though I don't want to.

You're too damaged to sell. No one will buy a washed-up ballerina with ruined feet. And even if I could find the type of man who would, the type who likes a girl who can't run, you're a disaster in here as well. He'd flicked the side of my head, hard, a stinging pain against my temple. *You start crying hysterically when anyone touches you, spiral into a panic at the slightest provocation.*

He'd laughed then, but his expression hadn't looked humorous. *If I had the time, I'd find the right man to buy you. One who likes broken, crying little girls who can't get away. But I don't have the time for that. So instead, you'll serve a different purpose, my pretty little ballerina. You'll make a lovely centerpiece for my party.*

I'd tried to struggle, terrified of what he meant, already crying. But there'd been no chance of escape. A needle was already sliding into my arm, the drugs that made it so that I don't remember anything about the party after that. I vaguely recall him rigging me up, twisting my body into some sort of grotesque dancer's pose. Still, everything after that is a blur of shapes and sounds and smells, without any form or sense to them.

It's difficult to get up. After being forced into the pointe shoes that Alexei had made me wear, my feet are even more painful than usual. They cramp the instant I try to stand up on them, but I force myself to do it anyway, holding onto the bedside table and then the wall as I move towards the window, suddenly desperate to see out of it.

I'll know where I am then, maybe. There will be some clue. And if nothing else, at least I'll feel the sunshine on my face. We were only at Alexei's for a week or so, maybe a little more, but it feels as if it's been so long.

The breeze coming in is warm, nothing like the bitingly cold wind in the mountains of Russia. I'm far from there, wherever I am, and I breathe in for a moment, the smells of a city reaching my nose. It's not the scent of an American city, though, thick with exhaust and smog. Instead, I just smell sunshine, fresh bread, coffee wafting from somewhere below. My stomach rumbles, and I press my hand to it, looking out across the rows of apartment buildings that look hundreds of years old, like something out of a history book, like nothing I've ever seen before. There are people walking on the sidewalk below, chattering happily in a quick, rapid foreign language that takes me a moment to place, but when I do, I realize that it's French.

The man on the plane. He had a French accent.

And in the distance, faintly, the shape of the Eiffel Tower.

I blink, once, and then once more. *I'm hallucinating. I'm dreaming.* I pinch my cheeks, slap my face, anything to wake myself up. But when I look again, it's still there.

What the fuck is happening?

The sound of the doorknob turning jolts me out of my freshly spiraling thoughts. I spin as quickly as I can, gripping the edge of the windowsill to steady myself as the door opens, terrified that it's going to be Alexei on the other side of it, even though I know that makes no sense at all.

But it's not.

It's a man I've never seen before, strikingly handsome, with messy dark hair and piercing blue eyes, wearing silk pajama pants and a silk dressing gown over that. He looks at me as if it's not at all surprising that I'm here or that he is. I realize with a start that he has a breakfast tray in his hands with a covered plate on it, a glass of orange juice that looks freshly squeezed, and small glass pots of jam and syrup. It looks so good, so perfectly out of some kind of fantasy, that I can't quite believe that it's real.

Maybe whatever Alexei did to me really completely broke my mind. Or perhaps I'm still drugged at the party, and this is some kind of lucid dream.

The smell wafts towards me, eggs and something made of sweet batter, and my stomach rumbles again, turning over painfully. I don't let go of the windowsill, though, shrinking back as he sets the tray on the bed and turns to face me.

"Good morning," the man says casually in English, but his voice is so thickly accented that there's no doubt that he's as French as the city outside my window.

This isn't real. It can't be real.

"Did you sleep well, Anastasia?"

I stare at him, my stomach dropping to my toes as my mind races, trying to make sense of it all. *How the fuck does he know my name?* It has to be a dream. But do things hurt in dreams? My body is aching in every part, pain ranging from a dull ache to a sharp burning, and it should wake me up, it should—

Maybe I'm just too drugged.

"Who are you?" I blurt out, feeling the windowsill biting into my hands, the pain in my feet shooting up into my calves. But I don't move. I can't. I'm frozen in place with panic, my eyes flicking to the door as a possible means of escape, even though I know I'll never make it. And if it is a dream, it won't matter. I'll just end up right back here.

The man smiles at me. "Of course," he says, his voice smooth and rich as melted chocolate. "How rude of me." He makes a small bow at the waist with a flourish, and I stare at him, certain now that I've gone entirely insane.

"My name is Alexandre Sartre," he says as he looks up at me, straightening.

"A—Alexandre?" I can't wrap my mouth around his last name, not right now.

"Yes, that's right." He smiles pleasantly. "Alexandre Sartre." He says it again, as if I didn't hear him the first time.

"What am I doing here?" My voice is shaking, and I swallow hard. "I want to go home." *As if I still had a home. As if that could ever happen again.*

His smile falters a little. "I'm afraid that's quite impossible, Anastasia."

I blink at him, feeling my hands start to tremble too. "Why—why is that?"

"Well, Anastasia, it's quite simple." The smile returns to Alexandre's face, his lips parting to show gleaming white teeth.

"You're here because I bought you, Anastasia Ivanova." He steps away from the bed and walks towards me, his fingers slipping under my chin and tilting it up so that I'm forced to look into his brilliant blue eyes.

"You're very beautiful," he murmurs. "And you're mine now."

LIAM

"So we're back to making an alliance with the Russians again? Are ye fecking kidding me? After ye're father nearly got us all slaughtered by the Italians and Russians both, for double-dealing?"

Colin O'Flaherty is leaning across the table, green eyes flashing at me as he brings his fist down on the heavy oak table that serves as the meeting place for the Irish Kings, our symbol carved into the center of it. A hum of agreement follows his outraged words. Though, there's one voice notably absent, the man who should be at the opposite end of the table from me, denoting his position as the second-highest ranking family in the hierarchy of the Kings.

Graham O'Sullivan.

His absence is a statement in and of itself and one that I know I'll have to deal with quickly. Graham himself isn't the problem—I like Graham O'Sullivan well enough, even if he can be a stubborn and hardheaded old man at times. But they all are, to an extent, anyone over the age of fifty, and that's most of the men around this table. Most of them are at least thirty years my senior, which makes leading them difficult.

Hard to give men orders when they see me as still wet behind the ears. Hard to have them respect me when I wasn't even the one they expected to take the seat at the head of the table after my father's death.

Hell, I didn't fucking *want* it.

It was supposed to go to my brother, Connor McGregor. But he's off god knows where, dead or gallivanting around the homeland, and fuck if I care which it is anymore. Or at least that's what I tell myself because the only other two options are anger or grief—anger that he left me with this mess after the shite that our father pulled, or grief that my brother is certainly all but lost to our family forever.

Anger is a distraction I can't afford, and grief weakens a man.

Weakness is another thing I can't afford, not when the other Kings are waiting for an opportunity to prove that I'm not fit to lead us, so that they can insert one of themselves or their sons into my place.

Which brings me back to Graham O'Sullivan and the reason why his absence is both problematic and the last fucking thing on this earth I want to deal with.

I'm meant to marry his daughter, Saoirse O'Sullivan. I know well enough that not a man at this table understands why I haven't signed the betrothal contract in my own damn blood, if that's what it would take to marry her. Saoirse is a rare beauty, raised to be the wife of a high-ranking member of our families, a perfect match for me in every way. *Too* good for me, if you ask her father, but he's offered me her hand anyway because it benefits us both.

Marriage to Saoirse would solidify my place at the head of the Kings, ensure an alliance with the only other family that no one here would dare to defy, and give the O'Sullivan family a permanent connection to the throne, as it were. My heir will bear my name, but he'll have O'Sullivan blood in his veins, and that matters.

If I marry Saoirse, that is.

Graham's absence means that arrangement is in danger. And I know I should be more worried about it than I am.

I certainly shouldn't be thinking about a girl half a world away, a girl who I should never have had more than a passing interest in to begin with—a girl whose whereabouts I don't even know now.

Anastasia Ivanova.

"I went to Russia to see what could be done to mend things with Viktor Andreyev," I say firmly, placing my hands on the table and looking around the gathered men, my gaze landing finally on Colin O'Flaherty. "He made an alliance with the Italians. He and Luca Romano broke bread and agreed on a truce, the lynchpin of which was Viktor Andreyev's marriage to the Bianchi widow, Caterina Rossi-Bianchi. Now Caterina Andreyva." I narrow my eyes. "Would you have the Kings barred from a table where the Italians and the Russians feast?"

O'Flaherty looks flustered. "Of course not. But for the Bratva *pakhan* to agree to such a thing, after your father—"

"I'm well aware of what my father did and his foolishness," I say icily. "There's no need to remind me of it every time we sit down at this table. He thought he could take it all for himself and rule all of the Northeast territories with my half-brother and me at his side."

Well, I suppose I can guess where Alexei got the idea. My father and Franco's treachery has had longer-reaching consequences than even he could likely have imagined. He certainly would never have guessed that one of Viktor's brigadiers would take up the idea and try to claim it for himself.

A fresh wave of bitterness washes over me. It's a stretch to blame my father's betrayal for the fact that Ana is the property of some French billionaire. Possibly lost beyond my reach, but it's not hard for me to make that leap, given my anger.

There's a great deal of it pent up in me these days, more than ever before. My father's plot, the discovery that a man I'd met a handful of times was, in fact, my half-brother, a man who turned out to be a monster. My father's rightful execution at the hands of Viktor Andreyev, my ascension to a place that I'd never planned on being. The unjust loss of a girl I'd only just been getting to know, a girl that I shouldn't care so much about.

The idea of anyone being sold, handed over to another person to be treated like a possession, is enough to make me blisteringly angry. But the fact that it's *Ana*, who has already been through so much, more than even I know—it makes my blood boil. And I don't know where to start to make it right, or even if I should, which makes me feel that much worse.

"Viktor Andreyev is a forgiving man when it is justified," I say firmly. "He knows that the sins of the father are not those of the son, nor are the sins of one brother a reflection on the other. He sees this mutual friendship as a way forward for our families, a way for us all to prosper."

"Prospering on the backs of women sold to lie on them, ye mean." Finn O'Leary speaks up then, his iron-grey brows drawing together. "We all know what Viktor Andreyev traffics in, or rather *who*. And I'm not here to be a part of it."

"That's the second part of what I'm bringing to you." I look around the table, taking a breath. "Viktor Andreyev has removed himself from the business of human trafficking. I have it on good authority that no more women will pass through his hands for sale."

O'Leary snorts. "And we're meant to believe this? It's a lucrative business, aye, if one that makes my very skin crawl. What will the great and mighty *pakhan* do for his riches now?"

"That's yet to be entirely determined," I tell him calmly. "There are other ways to make money involving sex that are consensual. And there's some talk of him partnering with a syndicate in Russia that trains spies and assassins for various—jobs. But I believe—"

"You *believe*." Finn O'Leary shakes his head in disgust, and I can see O'Flaherty nodding along. "Why should we agree with what you believe, boy—"

I'm on my feet before I entirely know what I'm doing, my hands slamming against the hard wood of the table. "We sit at this table because the King who leads our families has always valued the input of the others. But *I* lead the Kings. Not you, Colin O'Flaherty, or you, Finn O'Leary, or any of you others who might agree with them but are too cowardly to speak up. *I* sit in this chair, at the head of this table. *I* say that we will make an alliance with the Bratva, conjoining with their truce with Luca Romano and the Italian mafia, so that *all* of us may eat at the table where the great families of this city feast. When I tell you that I believe Viktor Andreyev, that I believe the friendship he has offered me and the terms of that, you *will* listen and heed me." I clench my jaw, my gaze meeting every man in turn. "I am not my father, but I *will* rule here in his stead. *Ní éilíonn mé go nglúine tú, ach iarrfaidh mé ort bogha.*"

I do not demand that you kneel, but I will ask that you bow.

A heavy silence falls over the table.

"Aye, lad," Connor O'Flaherty says finally. "You've a little of your father in you after all, I see that. But a great many of us would like to hear the O'Sullivan's words on the matter. And he is not here today. I wonder why that is?"

"I hear Saoirse O'Sullivan waits to hear your response to her father's offer," O'Leary says, his eyes narrowing. "A man who wishes to lead us would not falter at marrying an Irish princess and making her our Queen, now would he?"

"Saoirse O'Sullivan is a fine choice." Denis Mahoney speaks up then, his ice-blue eyes fixed on mine. I feel a quaver in my gut at the expression on his face because I know well enough how close Mahoney and my father were. I know, too, that he sees me as a pale shadow of what my father once was. "Royalty among us, and a beauty to boot. Sign the betrothal contract, lad, and you'll find us all a great deal more amenable to your plots and plans for the future of the Kings."

A silence falls again, and Denis Mahoney stands up, looking around the table. "I think we've discussed all we can today, lads. I know I've had all I can stomach."

His gaze locks with mine again, bright and defiant, and then he turns and strides out of the room. There's a rumbling around the table, but each of the other men slowly stand as well, glancing at me as they file out.

A cold feeling settles in my belly as they do. I can feel how fragile the reins of power are, how quickly they could snap in my fingers, and I remember something I once heard my father say to my brother—my *real* brother, Connor McGregor. His namesake, the one who was meant to rule after him. The one he forgot when he embraced his bastard son in his treachery.

I was always forgotten by my father, even when I stood at his side. And now I see that has farther-reaching implications than even I might have seen.

"They shouldn't be able to do that."

Niall Flanagan's voice comes from behind me, and I turn slowly to look at him. He'd been standing there silently throughout the entire meeting, steadfast and ready to defend me physically if need be—which would never happen here. No man sitting at this table would resort to blows. But Niall is my right hand, my enforcer—and in many ways, even though he works for me now as he once worked for my father, like an older brother to me, seven years my senior.

"No man at this table should walk out on you. You are the King, the head of these families—"

"I know, Niall. I know." I rub a hand over my face, letting out a long breath, my shoulders sagging with exhaustion now that it's only he and I. "But what should I have done? Thrown the table over and pitched a fit like a wee wean? Threatened violence?"

"Your father was feared—"

"Aye, and look where that led us." I lean forward, letting my head drop into my hands. "Connor should be here. It was him that was meant to lead, not me. He was raised for it—"

"Aye." Niall comes around my left side, dropping into the nearest seat. "But it's you that sits here now, Liam. There's no use looking back and thinking of what might have been. It's unfair, aye, but that's life. And there's plenty right here in front of you that needs your attention."

I groan, not looking up. "You're talking about Saoirse."

"Aye, I am." Niall's gaze rests heavily on me. "You've been gone some weeks, Liam, but while you were in Russia, things didn't stop here. The O'Sullivans are restless. Your hesitance to sign the betrothal contract is on the verge of being seen as an insult to them. Saoirse is young, beautiful, well-connected, and rich. There's not a man alive who wouldn't leap at the chance to wed and bed her, and yet here you are, dithering over it like a lad."

"If you think so highly of her, marry her yourself," I growl into my hands. "Relieve me of this burden."

Niall snorts. "As if a woman like Saoirse would ever look twice at a man like me. No, it's a King she's meant to marry, and you specifically, Liam McGregor. She's not even a shrew—for all I hear, she's a pleasant lass despite being a wee bit spoiled. So what—"

I raise one eyebrow, looking at him sideways over my fingers, and Niall winces.

"It's the ballerina, isn't it?" Niall asks with a sigh.

I don't want to tell him that yes, it is Ana. I know what his response will be.

But it's the truth.

Anastasia Ivanov.

I haven't been able to stop thinking about her since I set eyes on her at Viktor's safe house. I don't know exactly what it was that came over me when I'd set eyes on the pretty, petite blonde in the wheelchair, but in the days since, it's felt almost as if I'm a different man—as if there was the Liam McGregor who didn't know Ana Ivanova, and the one who does now.

The process of arranging my marriage with Saoirse O'Sullivan predates my meeting Ana. And up until recently, I'd been alright with the idea. I hadn't been thrilled with the prospect of giving up my bachelorhood—most men of my status keep mistresses or sleep around on their wives, but I've never felt comfortable with that idea—but Saoirse is beautiful and pleasant enough, from the few occasions I've met her. A wife that I would find tolerable, perhaps even come to love in time.

It's not what I'd expected for myself, not having been meant to be my father's heir—but it wouldn't be the worst fate. Everything Niall and the others have said about Saoirse is true. She's beautiful, rich, elegant, and well-suited to me and my station.

It wouldn't be the worst fate—if it didn't mean giving up Ana.

The truth is, I don't even know for sure how Ana feels about me. She was sweet and funny when we spoke at Viktor's safe house in the garden, but it was clear that she had many walls up. I could feel how guarded she was, how unsure she felt about why I was even talking to her. I have no idea what happened to her, but from the little I'd gathered from Sofia, Caterina, Viktor, and particularly Luca's warnings to me, something traumatizing had happened to Ana to put her in that wheelchair. She'd lost her career as a ballerina, that much was plain. As for the rest of it—all I know is that it must have been something awful.

And now, something worse still has happened to her.

She's been sold to a man whose name none of us know. The only clues we have are his French accent, and he's clearly obscenely rich. I'm meant to go to Manhattan next week, and Viktor plans to allow me to go through his former client files. It might give me some further clue to go off of. But what then?

Chasing after Ana means leaving behind my duties here, my responsibilities, and more importantly at the moment, putting off making a decision about Saoirse.

Which in and of itself puts everything in danger that I've tried to hang onto, for my father's sake. Traitor or not, he was my father. And I'm doing my best to repair his legacy.

"No answer is an answer in and of itself, ya know," Niall says with an exaggerated Gaelic drawl.

"And if I say yes?" I eye him, dropping my hands. "I know what you're going to say to me."

"You said she was sold." Niall raises an eyebrow. "It's a hell of a fate for a girl like that, to be sure. And I can understand wanting to go after her. But surely that's Viktor's responsibility? Not yours, to put so much at risk for a lass ya barely know."

"I have—feelings for her," I say tersely. "I can't leave this alone. I wouldn't be able to live with myself—"

"And will ya be able to live with yourself if your seat falls to one of the others? O'Flaherty, maybe? Graham O'Sullivan might get tired of waiting and marry his lass off to one of the other men. Your position isn't so strong that you can afford to risk it, Liam. We Irish have fought too many squabbles and wars to see blood as the be-all and end-all rights to rule. Ya have to earn it. And your father didn't leave you in the best spot for that."

"I know." I rub my hand over my mouth again, feeling exhausted. I haven't had a decent night's sleep since Alexei broke into Viktor's safe house, not even since getting back to Boston. They're all full of Ana, most of them nightmares about what could be happening to her while I try to find the first lead to where she might be.

No man who buys an unwilling woman could be a good man.

I push myself up from the table, needing desperately to think about something else. "I'm heading to the ring to blow off some steam." I glance at Niall. "Come along with me? I could use a good sparring partner."

"Aye, and I'm the best." Niall stands up, grinning. But his smile falters as he looks squarely at me. "Think about it, Liam. You weren't opposed to the O'Sullivan match before you left for Russia. That lass changed things, and not for the better. She won't be accepted by the other Kings as a proper bride for you. Best put her out of your head, and the responsibility on Andreyev to find her. Make it a condition of the alliance, if you want. But don't go yourself."

"I'll take what you've said under advisement," I say flatly, but I can see from the expression on Niall's face that he doesn't believe me. "Come on now. Let's go get a workout in."

The boxing ring has always been a good place to clear my head. Sweat and a good old-fashioned fight are good for the soul, and it's where I feel most at home these days. Certainly not at the Kings' meeting table, where I was never meant to sit at all, and since coming back to Boston, not in my own apartment either. My resting hours were already occupied with thoughts of my late father and my missing brother more often than not, but now they're full of thoughts of Ana, too, waking or sleeping.

I'm going to find you, I tell her again silently, as if she can hear me, wherever she is. As if the words could travel that far and find her for me.

I just hope that it's a promise I can keep.

ANA

You're very beautiful. And you're mine now.
Mine now.
Mine.
Mine.

The words echo through my head as the Frenchman—Alexandre—drops his hand from my chin and takes a step back, gesturing towards the tray of food. "You need to eat, *petit poupée*." He smiles at me, that same gleaming smile that is somehow all the more unsettling for how genuine it seems. "I do not know how long it has been since *Monsieur* Egorov fed you, and you certainly have not eaten since I took you away. You must be very hungry."

I am—my stomach is rumbling painfully—but I can't seem to pry myself away from the windowsill. My feet are starting to hurt badly, pain shooting from my soles up through my ankles and calves. Yet, I feel frozen to the spot, whether from fear or shock or both—or maybe something else altogether—I don't know.

"Do you remember the party, *petit?*" Alexandre frowns, two small lines drawing together in the middle of his forehead, but it doesn't take away from his looks. He's still extraordinarily handsome, with a face as elegant and nearly perfectly sculpted like a statue in a museum, except for the slight bump in his aquiline nose. But it doesn't take away from his beauty either—because that's what he is, truly, a beautiful man. There's something almost faintly feminine in the way he moves, graceful and catlike, and it reminds me of something that makes my chest tighten painfully, as if the memory hurts.

The male ballerinas at Juilliard. I remember then. Most of them were Russian, but a few French and American students were among them. All of the men were lithe and muscled, graceful and somehow both masculine and feminine all at once. Alexandre reminds me of those men, in his manner and his movement, and the thought both cuts me to the bone and feels oddly comforting at the same time.

"No," I whisper, struggling to speak past the lump in my throat and the dry cotton of my mouth. "I don't remember much of anything. Just him drugging me—a needle in my arm. A little bit of them putting me on the stage—and then nothing really after that." I press my lips tightly together, trying not to cry. "Everything after that—it feels like a dream. A nightmare, really. I don't know what was real and what wasn't."

"Why don't you tell me what you dreamed, then?" Alexandre seems to have forgotten the tray of food. Instead, he sinks down onto the edge of the bed, watching me intently.

I blink at him. I don't really want to remember it, but something in his voice makes it sound as if he's not asking, exactly—or rather, that he's asking to be polite, but that he will require an answer.

"It's all bits and pieces," I manage in a whisper. "I remember someone taking me down and what felt like being in a car. And then I was being carried somewhere else—a face that I didn't recognize, and being warm again—and then I was asleep. I woke up here." I lick my lips nervously, looking at his handsome, still face. "I don't—I'm sorry. I don't really remember anything else—ah!"

I cry out softly as the pain in my feet intensifies and my knees buckle, the windowsill digging painfully into my palms as I struggle to keep myself upright. I feel like I'm going to fall, and then I *am* falling, my legs no longer able to hold me up. Since my injury, I've been too depressed to do more than a little of the physical therapy the doctors assigned me, missing most of my appointments and failing to keep up with it at home. I relied on the wheelchair long past when I should have still been using it. Now it's gone—but the result is that the muscle I'd once carefully cultivated as a dancer, remaining lithe and slender while still strong, is also gone. I'm not the capable, fit ballerina I once was. Instead, I'm frail and thin.

I'm nothing like what I once was.

I close my eyes as I crumple towards the floor, wishing it would open up and swallow me. But just as I can feel the edge of the sill and the wall scraping against my back, my body falling to one side, strong arms go around me, lifting me up. One under my head, the other beneath my legs, sweeping me into the air and close to a chest that smells strongly of lemon and herbs, and underneath that, a warm and masculine scent.

It stirs something in me that I haven't felt in a long time—what feels like a different lifetime ago now. I'd forgotten what it was like to be held close to a man's chest in arms meant to hold and not hurt, to breathe in the scent of a man's skin and find it pleasant.

He did *hurt you, though,* I remind myself, my eyes still squeezed tightly shut. *He* bought *you.* It doesn't matter that he hasn't hit me, hurt me, or raped me yet. It's coming. I know it is. If there's one thing I've learned since Franco, it's that there are so many more terrible men out there, waiting to hurt me, take advantage of me, than I ever knew.

Not Liam. He wouldn't hurt you like that. You know it's true.

I push away the thought as quickly as it enters my mind. I don't want to think of Liam here, in this place, certainly not that chilly afternoon when he'd sat in the garden and laughed with me by the firepit. I'd felt the closest to myself that I'd been able to in a very, very long time.

I feel something soft underneath me, the creak of the bed as Alexandre sets me down, and my heart starts hammering in my chest. *This is it,* I think to myself, my stomach twisting in knots. *This is where he takes what he bought.*

"Here." There's the clink of metal on china, and I open my eyes a sliver to see Alexandre taking the cover off of the plate of now-cooling food. "Eat what you can. I'll be back in a moment."

What is he doing? I watch him go with confusion, my stomach rumbling at the freshly wafting smells of fresh food. He disappears into the bathroom at the far end of the room, and as I examine what's on the tray, I hear the sound of taps being turned on.

But now that I *see* the food, I can't focus on anything else. There are scrambled eggs on the plate, light and fluffy and a deep yellow, mixed with flecks of herbs and some kind of soft cheese. Next to them are two fragile, delicately folded crepes, with fruit peeking from inside, likely what's meant to be eaten with either the syrup or the jam in small pots next to the plate. There's orange juice too, and a glass of water, and I can feel my hands shaking as I look at it, unsure what to eat first.

"Don't eat too fast," I hear Alexandre's voice from the bathroom. "You'll make yourself sick if you do. Small bites, and slowly."

I don't understand him at all. He seems genuinely concerned for me, which makes no sense. *Or does it?* He'd paid money for me, how much I don't know. Alexei had seemed insistent that I was worthless except to a very certain type of man who enjoyed the pain and fear of injured, helpless women. Alexandre doesn't seem to be that sort of man.

He could be toying with you. Lulling you into a false sense of security, so it's that much worse when he does hurt you. The thought worms its way into my head, bone-chillingly terrifying, and my hands start to shake so badly that I'm not sure if I can pick up the fork to eat.

If not that, though, he must not have paid very much for me. If Alexei thought I was worthless, he would likely have taken any offer. Which begs the question—why is Alexandre treating me so kindly, if I'm worthless, just a cheap distraction he picked up at a party?

I manage to take a small bite of the eggs, and the flavor drives every other thought out of my head. "Did you cook this yourself?" I blurt out before thinking better of it, staring down at the plate. I taste garlic and thyme and rosemary, all savory and then combined with the sweet tartness of goat cheese, combined with the unusual richness of the eggs.

"I did." Alexandre comes to the door, his robe gone and the sleeves of his silk pajama shirt rolled up to his elbows, revealing leanly muscular forearms furred with dark hair, the unbuttoned vee of the shirt showing more dark hair on a hard chest. "A single man must learn to cook for himself, no? Without that, he will be either broke or very hungry." He smirks, but it's not the cruel expression I remember from Alexei's face, just a humorous one. "Come now, eat a little more, *petit poupée*. I know you are hungry."

I manage another bite of the eggs and then use the fork to cut off a delicate bite of the crepe, dipping it in the red jam. The flavors of sweet batter, fresh berries, and strawberry preserves burst over my tongue, and I almost want to cry. I can't remember the last time I ate something this good. We ate well at Viktor's safe house, but it was what could be preserved at the house or gotten quickly to a compound that deep in the mountains—certainly nothing this fresh or flavorful. Before that, I'd been subsisting off of what I could feed myself—mostly microwaved meals and food from boxes, nothing like what I'd once eaten on my ballerina's diet. And Alexei certainly hadn't fed us well.

"It's good, *petit?*" Alexandre is looking at me with worried concern as I eat a few more small bites of the crepes and another of the eggs, washing it down with the orange juice, which tastes, quite frankly, like what I imagine sunlight would.

"It's delicious," I manage, swallowing hard as he strides towards me. My heart immediately stutters in my chest, the forgotten fears rising up sharply again. "Thank you, I—"

"We put a great deal of stock in our food; the French do." He smiles at me pleasantly. "It's a matter of national pride. None of that processed bagged and boxed garbage that Americans love so dearly. You are American, aren't you? I can hear it in your accent."

"Ah—yes." I force myself not to scramble backward on the bed as he comes closer, my fingers gripping the edge of the mattress to keep them from shaking. "My parents immigrated from Russia. Or my mother did, rather—I—"

Without another word, he scoops me up from the bed the same way he had from the floor, sweeping me into his arms. "Russian, American, a little of both? It does not matter to me, *petit*. But we must get you feeling better."

For what? I want to ask, but I don't. I feel like I can't breathe as he carries me towards the bathroom, my chest so tight that it hurts and my stomach in knots of anxiety that makes me feel as if I could throw up everything I just ate.

The bathroom is almost stiflingly humid, the claw-foot tub full of hot water with tendrils of steam rising from it and pools of oil floating on the surface. I can't speak as Alexandre sets me down on a small stool in the center of the room, his hands going to my shoulders.

"Let's get this nonsense off of you," he says, his fingers sliding under the straps of the ballet leotard I'm still wearing. The ridiculous tutu and the pointe shoes are long gone, but I'm still wearing the flesh-colored leotard that Alexei had me dressed in—and nothing else. There's nothing beneath it, and now Alexandre is about to undress me.

I can feel myself tense, every muscle going painfully stiff as Alexandre peels the stretchy material off of my shoulders and down my arms. I wait for him to run his hands over my bare breasts as he slides the leotard down, remark on the way my nipples are stiffening even in the warmth of the room, caress my waist and hips, slide his hand between my legs. But he does none of those things. He's almost methodical in the way he takes it off, peeling it down to my hips and then coming around in front of me to pull it off the rest of the way. His gaze doesn't linger either, not on my small breasts or my concave stomach or the apex of my thighs, nor does he comment on anything else.

Alexandre merely tosses the leotard to one side as if it's something filthy, then picks me up carefully, almost as if he's being cautious not to graze any spots that might be considered inappropriate. And then, as carefully as he lifted me, he deposits me in the water of the bath, which is so hot it momentarily takes my breath away.

As soon as I have a chance to acclimate to it, though, it feels so wonderful that I could cry. I can smell the floral scent of the bath oil that he added, the hot water and soft oils sinking into my skin in a way that feels as if it goes down to my very muscles and bones, loosening everything until I feel as formless and liquid as the bath itself, like I could slither down into it and disappear.

"Is it too hot?" Alexandre asks, his brow furrowing again as he opens a cabinet. "A hot bath is good for nearly everything that can ail a person, I think."

"No, it's—" *It's perfect,* I want to say, but it feels like too much. "It's quite good," I manage. "Thank you."

"You are mine to care for." He strides back to the side of the tub, a sea sponge and a bar of some pale pink soap in hand. "I could hardly let you stay in those old clothes, unfed and unwashed, now could I? And besides, it's clear that you have not been cared for in some time. Perhaps not even by yourself, no?"

The quick way that he cut to the heart of it stops me from answering. I look away, but Alexandre just pulls the stool to the edge of the tub, reaching for another bottle and pouring a thick white liquid into his hand. "Dip your hair into the water, *petit*," he says, nodding at me. "So that I can wash your hair."

"I can—" I start to say, but he fixes me with his sharp gaze—he has hazel eyes, I see now, eyes a greenish-brown and flecked with gold, bright beneath his shock of messy dark hair. The words die on my tongue, and I remember who I am, who he is, and why I'm here.

Mine.

Mine now.

Mine to care for.

He might not be hurting me, but he does have the ability to command me, and I need to remember that. I tilt my head back, sliding down in the tub to get my hair wet, and when I come back up, Alexandre turns me so that my back is to him, his strong hands sliding into my hair as he begins to wash it.

Somehow, that's enough to momentarily make me forget all over again who he is and why I'm here. No one has touched me like this in so long, and it feels so fucking good, his long fingers against my scalp, scrubbing and massaging, like the best hairdresser you've ever had but then better than that still. I bite my lip to keep from letting out a moan, not wanting to give him the wrong idea, and that thought is enough to snap me back to reality.

There's no giving him the wrong idea. *If he wants you, he'll take you. You're* his.

But the strangest thing out of all of this is that there's nothing he's done yet that could even really be construed as sexual. He undressed me, but he didn't so much as look at me in a sexual way, let alone touch me. He's washing my hair, but it's not a sexual touch either, more a strong and utilitarian one. He's efficient at it, scrubbing deeply and getting every strand of my long blonde hair, then reaching for my shoulders and turning me again in the tub so that I can slide down and rinse it out.

When I come up again, my arms wrapped over my breasts protectively, Alexandre is soaping up the sea sponge, the scent of almonds and rose filling the air and mingling with the floral aromas of the bath oils and shampoo. I tense as he reaches for me, waiting for the moment when his touch will linger a little too long in the wrong spots.

But it doesn't. He washes me with the same quick efficiency, not giving me a chance to do it but also not touching me in any way that feels even the slightest bit erotic. He reaches for my arm to pull it away from my breasts, and when I tense, the expression in his hazel eyes turns stern, almost scolding.

"I need to be able to wash you everywhere, *petit poupée*," Alexandre says firmly, and I swallow hard as I let my arms fall to my sides, trying not to panic.

Petit poupée. I took French in high school, and I remember enough of it to pick up a little here and there. *Little doll.* I feel just as helpless as he reaches up to wash my breasts, the panic coiling in my stomach and rising up into my chest, making me shiver despite the warmth of the water.

But the sponge merely glides over my skin, catching briefly on my nipples before he moves it lower, down my stomach. He reaches down to lift my legs up over the edge of the tub, nudging my thighs apart so that he can run the sponge between them. Still, even that is as methodical as every other thing that he's done so far. He doesn't linger or even look overly long at any part of my body. If anything, it's me that's affected, both because of how strange it all is and the unfamiliar intimacy of his touch, even if he's not trying to make it so.

It *feels* intimate, the handsome man in the steam-wreathed bathroom, his hand between my legs as the sponge trails over my labia, brushing against my clit as he moves it up again, over my inner thigh. My nipples are diamond-hard, a sudden pulse of warmth between my thighs. I suddenly want him to bring the sponge there again, to rub it over that spot that's unexpectedly warm and aching in a way that I'd almost forgotten it could.

The sponge slides up my thigh, my calf, trailing sweet-smelling soap over my skin, washing away the days of captivity at Alexei's and leaving me feeling soft and clean, warm and liquified. I feel almost safe for the first time in months.

And then his hand's pause, his fingers pressing against the top of my foot, and I see his expression change.

And I remember where I am.

Who I am.

Who *he* is.

What the fuck are you thinking, Ana? I feel hot and embarrassed, my skin flushing even redder, ashamed of the pulsing between my thighs and the slick wetness there that I know has nothing to do with the oiled bath water, just my own weakness after being touched gently for the first time in ages. I want to jerk away from his touch, but instead, I just go very still, remembering that a man who would buy another human is not someone to pull away from. Remembering all over again that I'm still in danger, however slowly it is creeping up on me.

Alexandre holds my foot in his hand, reaching for the other as he lets the sponge fall to the tile. His eyes darken as he runs his fingers over the thick scars on my soles, and I wince, starting to pull away despite myself.

"It hurts?" he asks, his accent thickening, and I nod. I can't speak. I'm on the verge of tears, on the verge of a full-blown panic attack, and it's all I can do not to tear away from him and huddle in the furthest corner of the tub.

"So this is why he said you were broken," he murmurs, his fingers still tracing the scars. "These feet in those shoes, what exquisite torture that must have been—"

I shudder, biting my lip until I think it might bleed, a fine tremor starting to run through me. Alexandre seems to be caught in a trance, his hands holding my feet as if transfixed by them, and then he shakes his head as if snapping out of it, his gaze flicking up to mine.

"Who did this?" Alexandre demands, his tone deepening. "What happened to you, Anastasia?"

I shake my head, my hands curling into fists. I feel cold again despite the lingering heat of the water, tense and afraid, and I try to pull my feet back, but his hands tighten on them.

"Tell me what happened," he insists.

"I don't want to talk about it," I whisper. "It's over now. I don't want to—I *can't*—"

Alexandre's face hardens, the handsome and elegant lines turning stern and cold. "You're mine, Anastasia," he reminds me. "My *petit poupée*, my broken ballerina. You're not to keep anything from me. As your master, I demand you tell me—"

"I can't!" The words come out choked, my body starts to tremble, and I know I won't be able to stop myself from melting down much longer. "I can't talk about it, I can't, I can't—"

Alexandre stands up suddenly, shoving my legs back into the bath with a force that sends some of the water splashing up over the tiles. *"Ingrate!"* he shouts, his eyes suddenly furious. "And what do you think would have happened to you if I'd left you at *monsieur* Egorov's, eh? Would you have said no to him? Would you, *mon petit cher?*"

"I—" I can feel the tears welling up, dripping over my lashes. "Please, I'm sorry, I just can't talk about it—"

"Can't." Alexandre shakes his head in disgust. "Disappointing. *Décevante!*" He clenches his jaw, and I start to cry in earnest, the fear taking over as I pull my knees to my chest, curling into as tight of a ball as I can. I don't know what he'll do next, what the consequences will be, and for one terrifying moment, I think he's going to lunge forward and haul me out of the bath.

But instead, he steps back, his hand running through his hair until it sticks up wildly, his eyes full of a bright and angry confusion. And then he spins on his heel, stalking out of the bathroom and slamming the door behind him so hard that the room shakes, more water slopping out of the bath.

I'm alone.

So very, very alone.

Bending my forehead to my knees, I start to sob.

LIAM

The flight to Manhattan, although technically short, feels interminably long. Niall is sitting across from me on the private plane, his face set and emotionless. Still, I know what he's thinking—that I haven't agreed to the marriage yet, that Saoirse and her family will be at the wedding as well, that I'm neglecting my responsibilities. And the worst of it is that I know he's right. I *am* putting my near-obsessive worry for Ana ahead of everything I *should* be worrying about back in Boston. But I can't shake it.

Since our last conversation, Niall has mostly kept silent about it. He *is* my employee, after all, at the end of the day, but it doesn't mean that I don't know what he's thinking anyway. I can read the disapproval on him, no matter how hard he tries to hide it. We've been close for far too long.

All of the major families will be at this wedding, which is as much a reaffirmation of Viktor and Caterina's bond as a sign of the new peace between the Russians, Italians, and Irish. It's meant to be for them, a symbol of a commitment that was once arranged and now is chosen, but it's also about something more—a peace like none of our families have seen in decades.

The fact that two of the bloodiest families in the Northeast are the ones orchestrating it is nothing short of a miracle.

I should be thinking of how I can use this to my advantage, how the Kings can rise in their fortunes along with the Andreyevs and the Romanos, along with all of the families beneath them. But instead, I'm thinking about the meeting I have with Viktor this afternoon, before the wedding tomorrow.

A driver is waiting for Niall and me at the hangar. He takes us directly to Viktor's offices downtown, where Viktor and Levin are waiting for me. Viktor gets up from his desk as soon as I walk in, a pleasant smile on his face. I hold out my hand to shake his, but he pulls me into a strong, one-armed hug instead, grasping my forearm as he embraces me.

"I'm glad you're here, Liam," he says firmly, once he steps back. "Tomorrow is an important day for our families. That you will be a part of it, as well as the other Kings, is a huge step forward."

Especially after your father's treachery.

That Viktor doesn't say it aloud is a testament to how far we've come, I know that. The mistrust that existed between us earlier on has eased, and the fact that there are boxes of files around the office, waiting for me to pore through them, is a further sign of his trust. There's a great deal of personal information in those boxes that Viktor Andreyev is entrusting me with.

It's for Ana's sake, I know, to ease his own guilt and for the sake of his wife and Sofia Romano as well, but it doesn't change the fact that this is huge.

"It will take time to go through the files," Viktor says, gesturing towards the boxes. "I've already pored over some of them, as has Levin. So far, we've found nothing helpful."

"Did Caterina or Sofia mention anything else that might give us a clue?" I frown. "Sasha, maybe?"

"Only that he spoke French and that he dressed very eccentrically." Viktor rubs one hand over his mouth as Niall and Levin move another stack of boxes closer to where we stand. "Caterina also mentioned that he paid a huge sum for Ana. He seemed to like that she was—flawed."

I can't help but seethe inwardly at the use of the word *flawed* to describe Ana—I don't think of her as such. Wounded, perhaps. In need of care and tenderness, certainly. But *flawed* is the last word I would use for the beautiful, delicate former ballerina.

"How much?" I ask as I reach to open one of the boxes. That in and of itself could be a clue if we could find a pattern of a client who spent a similar amount each time if it were notable in some way.

"A hundred million," Viktor says, and I freeze in place.

"Excuse me?" I turn slowly, looking at him with disbelief. Behind me, I can see that Niall and Levin have gone very still as well. "A hundred thousand, you mean." A low price, but maybe fitting, considering Ana's injuries and mental health. Alexei probably wouldn't have been able to fetch a high price for her—

"No." Viktor shakes his head. "I couldn't believe it at first either, but Caterina was very firm that she'd heard correctly. Sasha and Sofia backed up the information as well. Apparently, there was some argument between Alexei and this Frenchman over it. Alexei didn't want to be seen as fleecing the Frenchman by selling him a girl for a price so over her value. But the man insisted on it. He seemed quite convinced that Ana was worth the sum."

I grit my teeth, a flood of conflicting emotions washing over me. On the one hand, a man who would pay that high of a price for Ana might treat her well, meaning she could be safer than I had expected until she can be found and rescued. On the other, the fact that he had paid so high a price could mean he had specific plans for her—which could encompass things I can barely stand to think about.

"So we're looking for a high roller." I force the speculation out of my head in an effort to focus on what we know. "French, obscenely rich, eccentric. It's not much to go on."

"It's not," Viktor agrees. "And I've rarely had dealings with French clients that I know of. Some don't contact me directly, it's true, and their bank accounts are always offshore. Sometimes they go to lengths to conceal information such as their actual nationality, names, etcetera. Understandably."

"Of course. We have clients who do the same." No matter how

detestable I might find Viktor's former trade, it's true that illegal goods are illegal goods, no matter what is being dealt with or to whom. The Irish have long trafficked in weapons, and there have been plenty of clients who have made sure to conceal anything that could be used to give away their identity. "That makes it more difficult, though."

"Exactly." Viktor frowns. "The files might give us some clue, but we're unlikely to find a clear match."

"We'll start with the clients you've dealt with that you know are French," I say decisively. "And then go through the anonymous ones looking for a pattern of high sales or large amounts spent."

If my thoughts had been full of Ana before, they're even more so as we comb through Viktor's files. With each name, each list of women purchased, and dollar amount spent, all I can think of is her—somewhere in the world, in a country that I can't put my finger on, with someone whose face I can't picture, being…what, exactly? Hurt? Tortured? Violated? Kept locked in a room or chained in a basement? My forehead creases tightly as I flip through page after page, my teeth gritted so tightly that my jaw begins to ache.

"I know you're concerned for her," Viktor says gently as I set another file down, letting out a sharp sigh of frustration. "We all are. I harbor a great deal of guilt that she was lost before we could rescue her. Luca does as well. But if it helps—" he hesitates. "The men who purchased from me in the past rarely are cruel. Some have their predilections, of course, and I can't say that I followed up on the women after they changed hands. But men who spend such a high sum rarely treat their acquisitions poorly. Whatever terrible things you're imagining, Ana is likely not enduring them."

"She's a possession," I grind out, slamming down another file. "A woman sold for the purpose of satisfying a man. It doesn't matter if she's clothed in silks and eating caviar with a palace of her own; another man is forcing himself on her. Another man owns her. And that alone is intolerable."

"I understand." Viktor nods to Levin, who takes away a stack of boxes that we've deemed unusable. "I thought it might help to know that at the very least, she's likely not in pain or suffering privations."

"It helps," I tell him, not meeting his eyes as I open another file. "But not enough."

* * *

WE SPEND hours combing through Viktor's records, but it offers up almost nothing of value. The few French clients he's dealt with in the past aren't high rollers—they bought lower-priced girls, still large sums but nothing approaching a hundred million or even in that ballpark. The anonymous clients *are* high spenders, but even they have never spent so high an amount. And the girls that Viktor sold to them were all immaculate—virgins, eighteen or nineteen years old, physically perfect in every way. There's no indication that any of them would have paid a high price for a girl not in "perfect condition," a term that makes me physically sick to think, but is a fact of the business that Viktor used to engage in.

I'm grateful that he no longer does. Particularly after seeing the terms of it so clearly, in black and white written out in front of me, I'm not sure I could have participated in an alliance with him if he still had. It unsettles me that it even occurred in the past, but if Viktor can look past the treachery of my family, I can make allowances for him as well.

Particularly if it helps me at all to find Ana.

"Luca and Sofia will be at my house for dinner this evening," Viktor says, as we set aside the last of the boxes. "I'd like it if you would come as well. It would be good for us all to sit down together before the wedding."

"Of course." I nod. "I'd be glad to see everyone."

I've only been to Viktor's home once before, prior to his marriage to Caterina and everything that unfolded with Alexei. It's much changed since then—some parts of it still closed off to renovations due to the damage that Alexei did, and other parts redecorated more to what I assume is Caterina's taste. The décor before was rich to the point of almost being gaudy, but Caterina has given it an understated elegance that I can appreciate. It feels warmer, almost more homelike, despite the stone floors and exposed wood throughout the house.

"Liam!" Caterina gives me an equally warm welcome, embracing me and kissing me on both cheeks. "I'm glad that you're here. Viktor said you might come for dinner."

"I'm glad to be here as well. And to see that you're looking better." She does look much improved from the last time I saw her, her cheeks flushed pinker, and her figure filled out slightly, as if she's put on a bit of weight. More than that, she looks happy, and it's the first time I've ever seen her so at ease. Whatever happened between her and Viktor after we rescued her and the others from the chalet, it's made a marked difference.

It's even more evident in the way she lights up when Viktor enters the room behind us, walking directly towards her and giving his wife a quick, firm kiss on the mouth, which she returns with equal fervor. It's clear that they're in their honeymoon stage, behaving like newlyweds at last, and it makes my chest ache a little.

If I marry Saoirse, this won't be the relationship that we have. And there's no point in even imagining what it might be like to marry Ana. Just the task of saving her is far from being a foregone conclusion—anything beyond that might as well be an impossible fantasy.

"The others are sitting down already," Caterina says, motioning towards the dining room. "Tell Levin to come sit with us too, and—" she glances behind me. "Who else is here with you?"

"Ah, I apologize. This is Niall Flanagan, my right hand." I motion for him to step forward, and he does so, inclining his head respectfully to Caterina.

"It's a pleasure to meet you, Mrs. Andreyva," he says, and she blushes lightly. I manage to keep the smirk off of my face just barely—Niall often has that effect on women. It's amusing to see that he has it even on a woman as happily married now as Caterina and to a man like Viktor.

"It's nice to meet you as well, Mr. Flanagan. Let's all go sit, shall we? Hannah will be very disappointed if the food gets cold."

There's a roast dinner already assembled on the long dining table, the scents rising tantalizingly into the air as I take a seat on the left side of Viktor, Luca and Sofia to his right on the other side of Caterina. Max is seated next to me, and a little further down the table, Sasha is next to Anika and Yelena, both of whom look to be in much better health than the last time I saw them as well. Caterina seats Niall and Levin at the very end and then slips into her chair next to her husband, her cheeks glowing as she looks at him.

"We're still in the process of replacing much of the staff," Caterina explains as she picks up a dish and hands it down. "But Hannah is an excellent cook, and I think we can all manage to serve ourselves tonight."

"Of course." I'm not used to having as much staff as the Andreyevs and Romanos are. Even a family as high-ranking as mine rarely employs more than a housekeeper and cook, not the full staff that Italian or Bratva families are accustomed to. The Irish are independent and stubborn to a fault, even when blessed with the riches that the families of the Kings have acquired.

We're always prepared for it to be gone in an instant and teach our children self-sufficiency as a result. I was always raised to depend only on myself—a trait that has come in handy, with my father dead and my brother lost.

"How have the children been?" I ask Caterina and Viktor quietly, when I see that they're occupied with Sasha serving them their food. "They look well."

"Anika is healing remarkably well," Viktor says, a pleased look on his face. "Particularly now that we're home with our own doctors. Her wound will scar, but there's no permanent internal damage."

"Both of them have been seeing a child psychologist," Caterina says softly. "I insisted on it. They're coping well, I think, considering. Yelena doesn't fully understand what was happening or what Alexei's plans were. Anika understands a little more, but not the scope of what he intended, I don't think. Which is for the best," she adds firmly. "They have nightmares still, particularly Yelena. But they're doing well, considering how short a time it's been. And Sasha has been a lifesaver in helping with them."

I glance down the table at the pretty, slender strawberry blonde who is busily convincing Yelena to eat her green beans, occasionally glancing up to sneak glimpses in the direction of my side of the table. I know it's not me that she's looking at though, but Max, who is studiously slicing his roast into pieces and avoiding that end of the table entirely.

"They're resilient." I look back at Viktor and Caterina. "Like their parents, I think. And you?" I nod towards Sofia. "Are you recovering well?"

Sofia nods. She still looks paler than I recall, but she manages to smile. "I've been on bed rest for a couple of weeks while the doctors made sure that there was no damage to the baby. But we both seem to be fine. I haven't been sleeping as well as before, but that's to be expected, I think. I've been through plenty before this, and I'll get through this, too."

"*We* will," Luca says firmly, squeezing his wife's hand. "And this alliance among our three families is the beginning of that." He looks between Viktor and me. "With a strong bond among us, men like Alexei will think twice before they try to overtake our territory again."

I nod. "I intend to make sure that the Kings are in agreement with that."

"Let's not talk business," Caterina says firmly. "A peaceful family dinner is what we all need, I think."

The conversation turns to other things then—the wedding tomorrow, where Viktor and Caterina will go afterward, the happy news of Caterina's pregnancy. After dinner, while Caterina, Sofia, and Sasha take the girls upstairs to get them ready for bed, Luca, Viktor, and I head towards his study with Max, Levin, and Niall following behind.

"You said the Kings will be on board with the peace?" Viktor goes to the bar at the far side of his study as we all take seats by the large, crackling fireplace. He pours glasses of vodka for himself and Levin, handing Luca a brandy and whiskey for Max, Niall, and myself. "I've heard rumors that there are some rumblings of unrest among them."

"There has been, since my father's execution," I say tersely as I take a sip of the whiskey. "But it's nothing to worry about. I'll bring them in line. It will merely take some time and the building of trust. I haven't held my father's seat for long."

"And for some weeks of it, you were in Russia." Viktor takes a sip of his vodka, settling into his own seat. "And now, I expect that you plan to go after Ana. Wherever that might take you. Is there no marriage arranged for you already?"

I tense, taking another deep slug of my drink. The whiskey heats me all the way down, a welcome burn, and a much-needed moment before I have to answer.

"There could be," I say carefully, feeling Niall's eyes on me. "She'll be on my arm at the wedding tomorrow. Saoirse O'Sullivan. But nothing has been signed."

"And you think to marry Ana instead of this girl, if you can find her?"

"I haven't said that." I finish the drink, and Viktor holds out his hand, getting up to refill it. "I don't know what Ana's feelings are for me."

"You're aware that the Kings would likely not accept her as your wife." Luca glances at me, swirling the brandy in his glass. "She's not—well. And she's a former ballerina, no one of note—"

"That's not exactly true." Viktor hands me a second glass of whiskey. "The Ivanov family is well known in Russia—because Anastasia's father was a traitor. A Bratva man who turned on his brothers and ratted to avoid a sentence in prison. His wife and daughter fled to the States, and he was hunted down and killed. Her name is dirt among the Bratva families, and I'm sure the Kings are aware of that too."

"If her father was a Bratva traitor, what does that mean to me?" I shrug. "Her name will be McGregor, not Ivanova if I marry her. But like I said, marriage isn't what's on my mind at the moment. It's finding her. Everything else can come later."

It's not strictly true, but it's not a lie either. I've certainly thought of marrying Ana. I'm not the kind of man to keep a mistress, and to suggest something like that to her would be insulting. Neither is she the sort of woman I can see myself fucking for a little while and then getting out of my system. Anatasia Ivanova has been very firmly *in* my system since I saw her at Viktor's safe house, and I haven't been able to get her out of my thoughts. Knowing how near-unreachable she is hasn't dimmed my desire for her, either.

If anything, it's made it all the more obsessive. But that's not something any man in this room needs to know.

"You're leaving a power vacuum at a bad time if you go after her," Luca cautions. "The power of the alliance that we're all making relies on the leaders of it being here. Without you, it's possible another might step up. O'Sullivan, perhaps, especially if he can make another match for his daughter."

"If you're insisting on going after Anastasia," Viktor says thoughtfully, "it might be worth signing the betrothal before you go. That would help to solidify your position, at least. Frame it as a business trip that you're going on, whatever you need to. But if the O'Sullivans have a betrothal contract, it will show good faith."

I pause, taking another long drink of the whiskey. The idea of signing the contract sets my teeth on edge. It all but makes it impossible for me to marry Ana if such a possibility ever did exist, since breaking a contract with *any* family, particularly one as well-connected as the O'Sullivans, would have serious consequences for my position at the head of the Kings.

It could go so far as to start a civil war among the Irish.

But I also know that Viktor is right.

Agreeing to marry Saoirse with pen to paper is a way to buy me time to find Ana without risking my position significantly more than I already have. It's not the option I would choose, but mine are narrowing.

"When are you planning to set out to look for her?" Luca asks, finishing his brandy. "Sofia has been worried for her. Even if it's not the wisest choice on your part, it will set her mind more at ease to know that you're searching."

"The morning after the wedding," I say firmly. "I know that I can't shirk my duty to appear tomorrow, nor would I want to miss it," I add, glancing at Viktor. "But I won't wait a moment longer after that." I look at Max then, who is sitting pensively with his whiskey barely drank in his hand. "You handled yourself well in the fight at Alexei's," I tell him. "If you'd be willing to come with me, I could use the assistance."

Max glances at me, surprised. "Certainly," he says, with less hesitation than I'd expected. "I think some time away would be good for me, anyway."

Likely has something to do with Sasha. I glance away from the former priest back to Viktor, watching the exchange blankly. "I'd also ask that I could borrow Levin, at least for a little while. You said earlier that you felt some guilt for what happened to Ana under your watch. If you'd like to do some penance for that, allowing me to take Levin with me would be helpful. His syndicate connections could come in handy."

Viktor frowns. "I'll need him soon to help with setting up my new business," he says, considering. "The syndicate will be sending students for him to train soon. But I think I can spare him for a little while, at least. As you said, I bear some responsibility. I can't go myself, but Levin will do well in my stead. I'll let you know if I need him to return at any point."

"Thank you." I glance towards Levin. "I assume you're fine with it?"

Levin nods. "I'm glad to help. I'll reach out tonight and see what contacts I might be able to make useful."

The conversation turns to other things then, Viktor refilling my glass and handing it back to me. But as I look into the fire, all I can see are blue eyes looking back at me, sweet and lost, eyes that I'd felt myself lost in too, that day in the garden.

I feel as if I'd do anything to find her. Anything to save her and bring her home, to make her whole again.

I just don't know yet what that will require of me—or what I might have to sacrifice to do so.

ANA

When Alexandre comes back, I haven't moved a muscle. I feel frozen in place, too exhausted from the rush of emotion and adrenaline to even cry any longer. I'm just curled into as tight of a ball as I can in the cooling bath, my knees pulled to my chest as I try to calm my body's shaking and wait to see what will happen next, what the consequences will be.

He doesn't look angry any longer, though. His face is smooth and calm, even concerned, and he dips his fingers into the bathwater, ignoring how I flinch away from him without meaning to.

"It's getting cold," Alexandre says decisively. "Come on, *petit*, let's get you out and dried off."

What? I look up at him, confused, unable to quite process the sudden change in his mood. He's gone from being furious at me to kind again, which is only further underscored by the way he carefully lifts me up out of the bathtub, wrapping me in a thick fluffy towel as he seats me on the stool and begins to methodically dry me off.

I can't make sense of it. He makes sure every inch of me is dry, but as before, he doesn't linger in any specific spot. He dries my hair last, squeezing it with the towel and then wrapping it in a smaller one as he leaves the large thick towel wrapped around me, disappearing back into the bedroom for a moment before reappearing with fresh, clean clothes.

"You'll want to get some more rest," he says, and I reach for the clothes, eager to be dressed. I feel too vulnerable like this, frail and naked on the stool, but Alexandre pushes my hands away.

"Sit still, *petit poupée*," he insists, and I swallow hard, freezing in place obediently. Not so much from a desire to obey, as I'm sure he thinks, but out of sheer fear of what might happen if I don't. I've seen now that he has an angry side to him, and I'm afraid to draw it out again. I don't know what might set him off.

His hands are careful as he dresses me, though, in pink silk pajama pants and a matching button-down pajama shirt, like the doll that he keeps calling me. He buttons it one at a time, his fingers grazing my flesh but never lingering as I sit there trembling, and then Alexandre circles around me, reaching for a comb.

I feel like I can't move. *He's so strange,* I think as he starts to run the comb through my hair, humming to himself under his breath as he gets every knot out of my long blonde strands, as if this were normal. As if me sitting on a stool in pink silk pajamas while a man who purchased me from a Russian sex trafficker combs my wet hair were just another night of the week.

Where did he even get the clothes? Were they just in a dresser somewhere? *Have there been other girls like me?* That's an even more frightening thought because I haven't heard any sounds to indicate that there's anyone in the apartment other than Alexandre and me. Which means, if there were other girls, they're gone now.

What happened to them then, these supposed girls, if they even existed? Did they run away? Sold again? Dead? A chill runs over my skin, and I shiver despite the warmth and steam in the bathroom, and Alexandre notices it.

"Are you cold, *petit?*"

"A little," I whisper, even though I'm not exactly. But Alexandre still sets the comb aside, scooping me up into his arms and carrying me to the bed. He sets me down gently against the stacked pillows, peeling back the duvet and sheets and tugging them over me, almost as if he's tucking me in.

"I'll bring you food and tea," he says, and I don't protest, even though I'm not sure if I can eat. It's late afternoon outside by now, the sounds on the street quieting in that space between the midday activity and people going out for the night. It's peaceful, and I'm exhausted, but I'm also too keyed up and confused to sleep.

I wish I could remember the party and the events that led to Alexandre buying me and bringing me here. It's all a blur of half-remembered feelings and sensations, which leaves me feeling more lost than ever before.

A deep, intense feeling of longing washes over me—longing for not just my old life, the old me, but everything else along with it. My friends—*Sofia*. Caterina. My heart aches in my chest as I wonder all over again what happened to them, if they were sold too, if they're somewhere else in the world now, experiencing something similar. Maybe something worse. And those two poor little girls, Anika and Yelena—I squeeze my eyes tightly shut, fighting back more tears.

I'd known there were monsters in the world, especially after my encounter with Franco, but I'd never imagined that they were anything like Alexei. His evil, his depravity, is beyond anything I could have seen, even in my darkest nightmares. And now—

Alexandre is no Alexei, but there's something off about him, too. Something that I can't quite put my finger on, but that leaves me on edge, waiting for the other shoe to drop.

Something other than the fact that he bought *you?* A small, mocking voice in my head reminds me of that fact, making my heart sink even lower. And it's true. No matter how gentle Alexandre is with me or how well he cares for me, the fact remains that that's the truth— Alexandre owns me. He bought me, paid another man money for a human being, and that alone should be irredeemable.

It shouldn't matter that having someone touch me gently, with kindness, feels so good that I want to forgive anything, just to feel it again.

It's been so long. So long since I've felt happiness, or comfort, or

IRISH SAVIOR

pleasure. I'd clung to that afternoon in the garden with Liam for exactly that reason, because it had given me a sliver of happiness, a glimpse at the woman I used to be.

And then I'd lost it, just as quickly.

I can't rely on Alexandre for those things. And yet—

What if he's all I'll ever have? What if this—a man who is gentle with me even if he's odd and mercurial, a man who doesn't seem to want to harm me, is all the future I have to rely on? I could try to run away, but not anytime soon. I'm physically unfit to try to get away, and I have no money, no means of getting a ticket anywhere or even sustaining myself, in a country where I speak a fraction of the language.

The door opens and my eyes fly open as Alexandre walks in with a fresh tray. This time there's the scent of sausage, and I see some sort of flaky pastry embedded with herbs wrapped around a slice of dark-colored meat, with a cup of tea and a glass of water. Alexandre sets the tray down over my lap, seating himself on the bed near my feet as he looks at me pointedly.

"You need to eat and get your strength up, *petit*. Take a bite. It's very good. One of my favorites, from a café near here. Perhaps I'll take you some time."

He says it so casually, as if it were a given that he might take me to a café, like a date. It sounds so ridiculous that I want to laugh, but I don't. I don't want to make him angry again, and besides, my stomach is rumbling. The food smells delicious, and I pick up the utensils, noticing how heavy they are.

"Real silverware." Alexandre notices me weighing it in my palm. "None of that cheap shit you Americans are used to." He smirks when he sees my face. "Nothing against Americans, of course," he adds in a voice that suggests he does, in fact, have something against them.

"All of my friends are Americans," I say quietly as I cut off a piece of the sausage-stuffed pastry. "They're all lovely people."

"In a sense." Alexandre shrugs. "I would say a woman like that Italian girl on the other stage—she was your friend?—was more a product of her family's traditions than the country she lived in. The same goes for you. You might have lived and gone to school in America, but a part of you will always be Russian. Just as I, to my core, am French. No matter where I live, *Vive la France* will always be deep in my soul."

"Sofia." I grab on to his first statement, clinging to it like a raft. "The Italian girl—her name was Sofia, and the other girl was Sasha. And the two children—do you know what happened to them? Did someone buy them, too?"

Alexandre pauses for a moment, then shakes his head. "No, sadly, I cannot tell you, *ma petit*. I had purchased you and left before any other transactions took place. There was a couple looking at the Italian girl —a Greek shipping magnate and his wife, I believe. But I do not know what came of it. As for the children—" His eyes narrow, his expression darkening. "It is a poor choice on *monsieur* Egorov's part to traffic in children like that. I have certainly made a note of it, myself."

I blink at him. "So you think that's bad?"

"*Merde!*" Alexandre exclaims, startling me so that I stop with a bite halfway to my mouth. "The sale of children? Particularly as Alexei wished to sell them? Of course. It is pure evil. The man ought not to breathe the same air as any sophisticated individual. For anyone else, I would not have given him my money in sheer protest of such a thing. But for you—"

His blue eyes flick upwards to mine, searching my face, and I can see something lingering there, some deep and dark emotion that I'm afraid to see too clearly. Instead, I bring the bite of food to my mouth, looking down at my plate. The flavor explodes over my tongue, something rich and gamey, and I try to focus on that. But my heart is racing in my chest, and I can still feel Alexandre's eyes resting heavily on me.

"For you, I could not resist," he says quietly, his voice dropping an octave, deep and rough, his accent thickening over the syllables. It sends a rush through me, my skin prickling, and I stab the pastry again, forcing myself not to look at him. His gaze on me feels magnetic, as if he's pulling mine upwards, drawing me towards him.

"This is good," I say quickly. "What is it? It doesn't taste like any sausage I've ever had."

IRISH SAVIOR

Alexandre sits back, and when I look up, I see a frown flickering over his face, as if my changing the subject displeased him. "Boar," he says finally. "It's boar sausage in an herbed pastry. One of my favorite dishes."

I nod, taking another bite. "It's really good," I repeat, swallowing hard. I don't know what to say, how to make small talk with this strange man as he watches me eat. However, I'm equally at a loss about how to endure his weighted gaze on me, full of emotions that I don't feel capable of handling right now.

The man *bought* me, for fuck's sake. What emotions could he possibly have about it?

"Tell me about what you used to do," Alexandre says suddenly. "Back in the States. Before—this." He gestures at my feet, and I feel my chest tighten again.

"I don't—it's not very interesting." I lick my lips nervously. "I don't know if there's anything to tell, really." *Why the hell does he want to know?*

"I know that you used to be a ballerina," Alexandre says it smoothly as if it's nothing. Still, the words send a rush of emotion through me until my throat feels choked with it, my chest hot and tight, and I feel like I won't be able to speak.

Used to be a ballerina. Used to be. Used to be.

Not anymore. The thing that was most important to me, more than anything else in the world, is gone. I hadn't said that out loud to myself yet, not in those terms, that I *used to be*. Not even the one time I actually went to the therapist my doctor referred me to. I couldn't.

And yet Alexandre has said it aloud, as if it's a given. As if I should think of myself that way, in those terms. *Used to be.*

"Yes," I manage past the lump in my throat, not wanting to let the silence stretch out for too long and make him angry. "I was a ballerina at Juilliard." The words slip out, hanging in the air between us. *Was.*

And then I burst into tears.

They're not pretty tears. They're hot, angry tears, tears of pain, tears that make my face screw up and my eyes squeeze tight, my hands fisting in the bedspread beside me as I drop my fork, my shoulders shuddering and shaking. Tears of hurt that I've lost so much that I'm still losing, that with every minute that ticks by, I'm getting further and further away from myself. Tears of anger towards Franco, Alexei, and Alexandre—towards every man who has contributed to this. Even irrationally towards Liam, because he wasn't there. He didn't save me, and I'd hoped he would. Caterina had pinned her hopes on her husband and Sofia on hers, but I'd had no one to hope for.

No one other than a handsome, red-haired, sunny Irishman who once had kissed my hand and called me *lass*, told me how beautiful I was, and listened to me talk in a cold Russian garden by a firepit.

It was nothing to go on. I have no right to be angry. But I am, if for no reason other than I need to be angry as much as possible, so that I don't hurt as badly. Anger is easier than loss, easier than grief. Anger can be directed outwards instead of slithering inside of you, wrapping itself around your soul until it crushes everything you have left.

Vaguely I feel the tray being taken away, the silverware scooped up, and then suddenly the weight of someone in bed next to me. I flinch away, but Alexandre's hands on me are insistent, pulling mine away from my face, moving me so that I'm lying in bed on my side facing him. He's on his side, too, watching me as his eyes search my face and his hands wrap around my clenched fists.

"Cry it out if you need to, *petit*," he says soothingly. "It's hard to lose things. Hard to let them go, *ma petit poupée casée*. You can cry as long as you like."

"What do you want from me?" I whisper it through my sobs, and I don't know if he can understand me because he says nothing. He just holds onto my clenched hands, listening to me sob as he hums under his breath, that same song that he'd hummed while he brushed my hair.

Alexandre is a strange man. Deep down, I know that some of his eccentricities should terrify me because he could be anything. He could be a serial killer for all I know, toying with me like a mouse, luring me into a false sense of security before he takes me apart piece by piece. It wouldn't be a stretch for his oddities to point towards such a thing. But after facing Alexei, I can't bring myself to feel as terrified as I should.

I cry for a long time, lying there, feeling it all pour out of me. Alexandre lays there too, silently, and when I finally open my eyes, he's watching me, as if he hasn't looked away from my face all this time.

I don't know if I should feel comforted or creeped out, or maybe a little of both. I'm too exhausted to feel anything at all if I'm being honest.

Alexandre rolls off of the bed then, letting go of my hands and getting up in one of those lithe, graceful movements that remind me of the male ballerinas back at Juilliard. He gets the cup of tea and leaves the room, coming back a few minutes later with a fresh, hot one that he pushes into my hands.

"Drink it," he instructs. "It will make you feel better."

I nod, raising the steaming cup to my lips. It tastes like rose and chamomile with honey, and it is soothing, the heat slipping down my throat and the steam clearing my sinuses. "I was going to be the prima," I whisper as I take another sip of the tea, finally looking up to meet his eyes. "I had an audition with the New York Ballet, not long before what happened—" I break off, unable to talk about Franco yet, about what had happened to my feet. "All my instructors at Juilliard were sure that I was going to be the next prima. It would have taken some time, of course, but they were so sure I would get there, that I'd be the best—" my voice breaks, and I go back to drinking the tea, fighting back more tears. "It's all gone now. That's why I don't want to talk about it. There's nothing left to tell, and it hurts too much."

He can drag it out of me if he wants, I know. No amount of kindness or concern can change the fact that he owns me, that I have no home or money or resources of my own, that everyone who cares about me is so far away or lost altogether that I might as well be all alone in the world. If he insists on knowing it all, now, I will have to tell him.

But I don't want to. I don't want to talk about it, and Alexandre must see something in my face that convinces him not to push, because he doesn't. He simply sits there as I finish the tea and takes the cup out of my hands when I'm finished, his long fingers wrapping delicately around the fine, flower-painted china.

I notice, for the first time as he takes it away, that there's a chip in the porcelain.

And then, as he sets it aside, I feel a sudden, intense sleepiness, so deep that it feels like a wave pulling me under, and I realize with a thrill of fear that there must have been something in the tea.

I look up at Alexandre fearfully, but his face is smooth and calm as he leans down, pulling the covers up over me and tucking me in. "*Va te coucher, ma petit poupée,*" he says softly, his accent soft and caressing the syllables as he leans down, pressing his lips against my forehead.

He says something else, but I don't catch it. I'm already falling asleep, and I can't resist the exhaustion pulling me under.

If I'm being honest, I don't want to.

LIAM

Viktor and Caterina's second wedding is as grand an affair as the first. And, as expected, Saoirse is here as my date. She's waiting for me in the car when I come down, dressed elegantly in an emerald green silk gown that's gathered at the breasts to show off her cleavage to its best advantage, thin straps holding it up over her pale, slender shoulders. Her reddish-blonde hair is done up in some elaborate updo and secured with gold and emerald pins, and her makeup is flawless. She smiles sweetly at me when I slide into the car, adjusting my tailored jacket, and I know the message that her father is sending through her is clear.

She's an Irish vision, a shamrock princess dressed in green. Graham O'Sullivan couldn't have been less subtle about it if he'd hit me over the head with the Catholic catechism and poured a pint of ale over me to follow it while singing Galway Girl. And she's beautiful tonight, I can't pretend otherwise. The dress makes her already green eyes even brighter, a match for mine, and she's glowing, radiant as a candle on a windowsill.

Niall's words come back to haunt me. *Any man would be lucky to wed her.* Any man *would* be grateful to be handed a lass like Saoirse O'Sullivan—any man except me, apparently. Because despite how lovely she looks, how prettily she smiles, or how soft her hand is in mine when I raise it to my lips, I can't feel anything for her. No affection and no arousal. It's been months now since I've taken a woman to bed. I should be at half-mast just from the sight of her breasts wrapped mouth-wateringly in that silk dress, but I don't feel so much as a twitch downstairs. My cock is well and truly asleep, and not even her soft intake of breath when my lips brush over the back of her hand is enough to wake him from his slumber.

"It's sweet, don't you think?" Saoirse asks, her voice light and musical, and I look at her quizzically.

"What is?"

She blinks at me as if I'm a bit slow. "The wedding, of course. Their second wedding, now that they're in love." She puts some emphasis on the last word, and I wonder what she means by it. Is it her acknowledging that the union her father is trying to arrange for us isn't a love match, and that she doesn't expect it to be one? Or is it her hinting that she wants more from me, some sign of affection and romance?

I hope it's not the latter because even if I accept the betrothal contract the way Luca and Viktor have urged me to, I can't love Saoirse. Maybe in time, if I wed her, I'd come to feel the warm affection that I imagine any decent man must feel for the woman who warms his bed, keeps his house, and gives him children. But passionate love, the kind that burns hot and bright and pushes men and women to make choices that they might not otherwise make, the kind that drives a person mad with need, the kind that makes a man burn down the world to get to the woman he loves—I can't give her that. I can't picture it with her, not ever.

She's been raised to be a good daughter of the Kings, an Irish princess, the closest thing to royalty we have left. I don't think she'd expect it. And yet—I can see out of the corner of my eye the way her breathing quickens as she pulls her hand respectably away from mine, folding them together in her lap as she looks out of the window at the scenery passing by.

I know she wants me. I'm not so modest as to not be aware that

I'm a handsome man. I'm far from the playboy Luca once was, but I've had my fair share of women pass through my bed, and not a single one of them has been coerced there or left unsatisfied. I've never had any trouble finding a woman eager to bed me.

I'm sure Saoirse would be no different. And if I married her, I'd do my best to please her. But I know that my heart wouldn't be in it, perhaps even less so than the other women I've had sex with.

Because now, there's someone else on my mind—a specific woman, one that I can't shake. And I know, deep down, that would hurt Saoirse far more than simple detachment on my part. A husband that doesn't love her—every high-born crime lord's daughter knows that's likely her fate. A husband in love with—even obsessed with—a woman he knew for only a few days? That would cut more deeply, I know.

But it's where my thoughts are lingering as I open the door for Saoirse, taking her hand as we walk up the steps of the Russian Orthodox church where Viktor and Caterina first exchanged their vows and now will do so again. Vows that Caterina was coerced into taking the first time and does so willingly now. It's all very sweet and romantic, just as Saoirse said, and I'm happy for them.

I'm glad that they've found their peace with each other. But I've never been further from feeling peaceful.

I sit next to Saoirse as the ceremony starts, Luca and Sofia on the other side of me. Viktor and Caterina have skipped playing out *every* part of the wedding over again, opting out of a wedding party, for which I'm grateful if only because it means I have someone to carry on a conversation with besides Saoirse.

"Oh, she looks lovely," Saoirse breathes rapturously, and I turn my head in time for us all to stand for the bride's entrance.

I'm not one to know much about wedding dresses, but Caterina does, in fact, look beautiful, if only because she's practically glowing in the lacy gown that she chose. It has soft, flowing sleeves off her shoulders, letting her skin glow in the candlelight, but with enough coverage that her scars are pointedly hidden. From what Viktor has said, I know that she's self-conscious of them still, but no one in the candlelit church would have noticed if she'd worn a strapless gown with plunging cleavage. She looks too beautiful, her dark hair loose over her shoulders, her eyes only for Viktor.

It's incredible to me to see the change in them. I remember seeing her stiff and frightened at their first wedding, Viktor tense and cold, how clearly it had been a marriage of convenience, a means to stop the bloodshed between the Italians and the Russians. Now Viktor is looking at her with a soft, warm gaze, the desire and love for his wife plain in his face. And it stirs something in me, something that I know I can't have with Saoirse.

Something that makes me all the more eager to leave tonight and go after Ana.

It's a stupid decision. I know that, down to my bones. The wise choice—the one my father and brother and Niall and every man whose advice I've ever listened to or would want to take into consideration—would be to stay here. Let Viktor and Levin use their connections to send someone else to find her. Or, alternatively, to trust that a man who paid a hundred million dollars of good money for a woman would treat her with some kindness and gentleness, more, perhaps, than Ana has experienced recently at the hands of others. To marry Saoirse, cement my place at the head of the Kings, and carry on with the life that I'd begun to settle into before the day that I met Anastasia Ivanov.

And yet, I know just as deeply that I *can't*. It's irrational and reckless, the kind of romantic, passionate choice that makes fools of men like me, but I can't let her go. I can't forget about her, and I can't abandon her.

For her, I'm willing to lay everything on the line, no matter what it means.

I want something that I've never wanted before, up until now.

I want to feel the kind of love, the kind of passion, the kind of *devotion* that makes a man like Viktor look at his wife the way he's looking at Caterina now, as they exchange new vows.

I vow to hold you close to me always, to love you for who you are, to always see the best in you. To give you my body, my heart, and my soul—

These aren't the traditional vows. I hear Saoirse sigh next to me, hear her sniff a little as she dabs a handkerchief to her eyes carefully. They're romantic, passionate, written by Viktor and Caterina themselves.

They're the kind of vows a couple truly in love makes.

I've never felt that. I'd never expected to. But now?

Now I want to know what that could be like. To experience a kind of devotion that would send a man across the world searching for the woman he loves. That would make a man wreak the sort of violence that I watched Viktor exert when he cut Alexei apart.

I'd helped too, a little. But Viktor had done the bulk of it. Not for his business, not for the loss of profit that Alexei had cost him. He'd taken Alexei apart piece by piece, exacting a slow and horrible death, because Alexei had dared to touch his children and his wife. Because he'd wanted to avenge what he loved.

Now it's my turn. I can't say that what I feel for Ana is love in the truest sense, not yet. But it's enough to make me set everything aside in search of her. What would that be called?

Obsession? Infatuation? Desire?

I don't know, and I'm past caring.

The reception is elegant and beautiful, held at the Plaza Hotel in downtown Manhattan, but I have a hard time taking pleasure in any part of it. My thoughts are firmly on Ana, so much so that it's hard to focus on anything else, including what Saoirse is saying to me. As the main course for dinner is passed out—delicately braised lamb with a pairing of garlic potatoes and fresh greens—Saoirse lays her hand on my arm, clearly trying to get my attention.

Her nails are painted a shade darker than her skin tone. Elegant and simple. In keeping with what Saoirse was raised to be—a lady fit for a man of my status to marry. Out of my league, really, since I was never meant to be the heir. It should be my brother Connor sitting here with Saoirse's hand on his arm, her green eyes fixed on him. Then I'd be a free man.

Free to look for Ana. Free to do whatever I like with her—sleep with her, marry her, anything I please.

If you weren't the leader of the Kings, you wouldn't have been there to meet her in the first place. Connor would have gone to Russia, and you would have stayed behind.

I'm not in the mood for what makes sense just now, though.

"Liam." Saoirse's soft voice drifts towards me. "You seem very far away."

"I'm just distracted." I cut into the buttery lamb, which falls apart under my fork, but it tastes like cardboard on my tongue even though it's cooked by a five-star chef. *What is Ana eating? Is she being fed well? Is the man who bought her taking care of her, or is he starving her, taking pleasure in making her rely on him? Would a man who paid a hundred million dollars for a woman starve her?*

I grit my teeth, forcing the obsessive thoughts back. This does no one any good, and I know it. I feel as if I'm going mad, and that won't help Ana or myself or anyone connected with this. I need to keep my wits about me, however difficult that might be just now.

Saoirse picks at her food too, but I think it's more from anxiety about my mood than a desire to seem dainty. At least, I hope so. The thought that she might be eating lightly in an effort to seem ladylike and delicate irritates me even more, and I focus on my own meal, doing my best to engage in the conversation with Luca. Sofia seems to notice my mood and manages to divert Saoirse's attention, for which I'm grateful.

I barely make it through the dessert course before I start to feel claustrophobic, the tie at my throat too tight, the air too thick. As the music increases in volume, Viktor and Caterina getting up from their table to dance, I push myself to my feet. Saoirse looks up at me hopefully, and I know that she's thinking that I plan to ask her to dance as well when the floor opens up, but nothing could be further from my mind right now.

"I just need some air," I say quickly, ignoring the hurt expression on her face as I turn sharply on my heel, striding out towards the nearest balcony.

It's blessedly empty, and I go to the railing, clenching my fists around it as I look out over the city. It's glowing in the darkness, the usual glorious Manhattan view. I'd always appreciated it, more expansive and voluminous than Boston ever is. There's a small country's worth of people down there, living their lives, going about their business, unaware of the man standing several floors up, contemplating the reckless decision he's on the cusp of making.

It's almost soothing in a way to think of how many people are just beyond me in this city, with their own joys and angers and griefs and hurts, their own wins and losses, a million and a half people with their own complex lives. People who think their problems are every bit as important as I do, and it puts it a bit in perspective somehow, making all that I have weighing on my mind feel smaller.

Still, I wonder what any of them would do if they faced what I am right now. I've known Ana for a matter of days, for hours within those days, if I'm being honest. But something about her has sunk into me, slipped into my blood and bones, and wrapped its fingers around my heart, and I can't let her go. I want her to be saved, and I want to be the man who does it.

It can't be anyone else. It has to be me. I feel that down to the depths of my soul, in a way that I know I'll regret it to my deathbed if I leave this to someone else. Even if I come back and have to marry Saoirse, even if Ana wants no part of me, I can't let someone else do this.

I have to be the one who finds her.

"Liam?" Niall's voice carries across the balcony towards me, and I tense automatically, turning slightly to see my right hand coming to join me at the balcony railing. "Feeling a bit under the weather, lad?"

"Just a lot on my mind." I look back out over the city as Niall digs in his trouser pocket for a pack of cigarettes, lighting one and holding it out to me. I shake my head, and he shrugs, flicking the lighter and breathing in the smoke before blowing it out away from me.

"I've never smoked, you know that." I glance at him as he puffs on it once more, leaning his elbow on the railing.

"Never a bad time to start, lad." Niall grins. "Ah, I take that back. Ye're father would have my hide for saying such a thing, God rest his traitorous soul." His face goes serious then, settling into lines as he looks at me pensively. "There's a lovely lass out there looking a bit hurt that ya haven't asked her to dance yet."

I press my lips together thinly, looking away from Niall. "You know, at thirty-one, you're not so old as to be acting like my father; for all that, I don't have one any longer."

"Nah, not your father, lad. Ye're older brother, I think, since that one's faffed off as well." Niall doesn't look away from me, his amber gaze steady. It's a thing I've often appreciated about him, how he doesn't fear me, nor did he ever fear my father or brother. He has strong values and sticks to them, a man of fierce loyalty and commitment. But just now, it's getting a bit irritating.

"I don't need you to talk to me about Saoirse. I've heard enough on that count."

"Have you, lad?" Niall puffs once more on the cigarette and then flicks it over the railing, leaning hard on one elbow as he laces his fingers in front of him. "Because what I see is a perfectly lovely girl being comforted by a woman she hardly knows, because the man who ought to be her fiancé is off mooning over some girl he's barely met."

"I've barely met Saoirse," I retort. "I don't know her any better than I know Ana. And yet you'd tell me to marry *her*."

"Aye, lad," Niall says quietly. "I'd tell you that because it's what's best for the family, for the Kings, for all that your father and brother and all the others have worked so hard for, for generations." He goes silent for a moment, and I can feel his gaze resting heavily on me, taking in how tense and irritable I clearly am.

"It's a fuckin' sin what happened to that girl," Niall says finally, his voice low and gruff. "I don't fault you for wanting to go after her. Any decent man would want to do so. Mary, Jesus, and Joseph, I want to do the same. But the best I can do is tell you what I have before. Make it a stipulation of the peace for Viktor to use all his resources to find her. Let him exorcise his guilt that way. It's his doing and not yours that put that poor lass into those hands."

"I know it's not my fault!" I slam my fist down on the railing, turning to face him. "It's got nothing to do with that, don't you see?"

"Sure, lad." Niall looks at me pityingly. "You've got it bad for the

IRISH SAVIOR

lass. Any man with eyes can see that. But who's to say you can't feel the same for Saoirse? She's beautiful. A true Irish rose, made for you in every way. Raised to be the wife of a man like you—"

"Oh fuck off." I shake my head, turning away again. "I'd half think you were carrying a torch for her, the way you carry on."

Niall goes quiet, and I hear the flick of the lighter as he lights another cigarette. "Saoirse is no lass for me," he finally says in a low tone. "She's an O'Sullivan, aye, and meant for a man of good birth and money. She'd never sully herself with the likes of me, and I'd be ashamed to let her do so."

I glance over at him then, surprised. His expression is pensive, and I realize then what I should have realized before, that my right-hand man is pushing me towards a woman that he himself has, perhaps, the same sorts of feelings for that I have for Ana.

But of course, he's right. A man like Niall and a woman like Saoirse would be like oil and water, from two entirely different walks of life. Not to mention her father would be as likely to pitch her off the roof of their mansion as see her marry a man like Niall. And besides, it would cause no end of trouble among the families, even threatening my position.

"You'd best go ahead with it," Niall says quietly. "Come back to Boston, man, and sign the contract. Stop putting off what ya know must be done. There's no getting around it, and ye'd be a fool not to."

His Gaelic accent is thickening as he speaks, a clear sign that he's growing irritated with me, and truth be told, I can hardly blame him. But I'm angry too—angry with him for pushing me, at my father for being a traitorous bastard who pushed me into this position in the first place, at my brother for being gone.

"Go back to Boston yourself," I say sharply, turning away. "I'll call you when I have news. Until then, don't bother me again."

"Liam—"

"Go!" I don't look at him, though I know deep down I'm only hurting one of the few people left who still care for me. "That's an order, Niall. Or would you disobey me, too?"

There's a moment of silence, and then I see Niall flick what remains of his second cigarette, turning away from me as well. "Of course not," he says quietly. *"Ní ghéillim ach do d'ordú."*

I obey only your command.

His footsteps recede into the distance, leaving me alone with my thoughts again, on the balcony with only the warm breeze of early summer to keep me company. I should go back inside, I know, but I don't want to just yet. I want to stay out here a little longer, with the silence and the thoughts of Ana that both tear at me and bring me a sense of purpose.

The sound of a door opening and footsteps pulls me out of my thoughts, and I tense, clenching my jaw with irritation. "Niall, I thought I told you--"

"It's not Niall," a woman says, and for one insane moment, I think that it's Ana, and she has come back and that she's found me out here.

But then I turn, and see that it's Sofia.

LIAM

Her face is soft and faintly concerned as she walks towards me, and I struggle not to let my irritation overwhelm me. "Is this about Saoirse?" I ask bluntly, turning to face her. "Because if it is, I told Niall already—"

"It's not about her." Sofia walks towards me, joining me at the railing, looking out over the city. "It's about Ana. I wanted to talk to you before—well, Luca said you were leaving tomorrow. To try to find her."

"That's the plan." I look at Sofia curiously. "With Max and Levin, if all goes according to plan. You haven't come out here to tell me not to go?"

Sofia laughs softly. "Why would I do that? Ana is my best friend. If there's a chance in hell of anyone finding her, I'd do all I could to encourage them."

I can't help but chuckle at that. "Everyone else, your husband included, seems hell-bent on keeping me in Boston and getting me to marry Saoirse."

Sofia shrugs. "She's a nice enough girl, I think. But I don't even really know her. If you're meant to marry her, that's your own duty and burden to figure out, but I'm hardly going to tell you not to try to find Ana on account of it. I'm selfish enough to want my best friend back, no matter what it might cost you—if you're willing to go after her."

Her blunt honesty shocks me, but I appreciate it. "You're very forthright," I observe, watching her curiously. "It fits with what Luca has said about you, though. I suppose I don't know you all that well, despite what we've all been through in the past weeks."

"You don't know Ana well either." Sofia looks at me appraisingly. "Yet you're willing to put your engagement and position on the line to go after her. Why?"

I open my mouth to answer the question, but she's still speaking. "An arranged marriage is nothing new for a man like you. My marriage to Luca was arranged, and he wasn't pleased about it, but he did it anyway. Viktor actively arranged his with Caterina, and her husband before that was arranged for her. Love doesn't often factor into weddings among crime families; I know that well enough. Caterina and I have been lucky, in the end, despite what it took to get there. So why?"

The question should have a serious answer, and I pause a moment to give it the weight it deserves. "I feel as though I love her," I say bluntly, giving Sofia the same honesty she gave me. "I know that's ridiculous. No one can love someone they've known as briefly as I've known Ana. But I can't shake her. She's in my head constantly. I feel, down to my bones, that I have the responsibility of going after her. And all I have to go off of is that one afternoon when I talked to her in the garden. But there was something about her—"

"You're obsessed with her." Sofia looks at me flatly. "Men love to think they're saving women, don't they? It drives you all to insanity. And I can't lie and say that it's not sexy. Luca had this kind of possessive desire with me—" she shakes her head, flushing slightly. "He still does. I see it in Viktor, and I can see it with you. But you need to understand, Liam, if you're going to do this—", she pauses, her eyes wide and cautious. "The Ana that you're going after—the Ana that you met—is a very different person from who she used to be."

I blink at her, unsure of what Sofia is trying to get across to me. "I

IRISH SAVIOR

know she's been hurt, physically and emotionally," I say finally. "Luca and Viktor have been quite effusive about that, in fact. They've told me repeatedly that she's—" I hesitate, disliking the word. "Broken. And I have eyes, I could see that she was in a wheelchair. But when I talked to her, I didn't see a broken girl. I saw someone who had been hurt, who needed care, but I—"

"Still saw someone very different," Sofia says, interrupting me. "Look." She fishes her phone out of her clutch purse, turning her back to the railing so that I can see the screen. She flips through pictures from months ago, and then a year or more, well before her marriage to Luca.

She's right. "That's Ana?" I ask, pointing to the blonde girl with her posing in the photos, usually taking the selfies.

Sofia nods. "See what I mean?" She keeps flipping through the photos, and I breathe in deeply.

The girl in the photos isn't the Ana I recognize, Sofia is right about that. This girl is on her feet, her hair dark instead of blonde the way it was when I met her, flying around her cheeks, a bright smile on her face. She's poured into short shorts and tight jeans and crop tops, short dresses and miniskirts, wearing makeup. She's in a ballet costume and pointe shoes, her eyes glowing, ready for the stage. There's a photo of her and Sofia together, Ana *en pointe*, Sofia holding her violin.

Sofia flicks a few photos further to a video clip and presses play. "Watch," she says quietly. "And then there's another I'd like for you to see."

The first video is of Sofia and Ana out at a bar. Ana is clearly filming, trying to convince Sofia to stay out later. "Just another drink," she pleads, laughing as Sofia shakes her head amusedly, trying to push the camera out of her face. "Come on, I won't even go home with that guy who got my number if you stay out with me! You didn't like him, right?"

"Of course, I didn't," Sofia says firmly, her mouth twitching. "He wasn't good enough for you."

"You don't think *anyone* is good enough. That's why you're still a virgin." Ana flips the camera so that she's the one looking into it, her blue eyes bright and a little glazed from drinking. "This is our last night of the semester, and Sofia wants to go home and *sleep*. But tonight is about making memories, right? Memories *together.*" She flips the camera again, now so that both she and Sofia are in the frame, her arm thrown around Sofia's shoulders as she tilts it down. "Best friends forever, right? From roommates to best friends in the whole world. Three months, and I can't live without you. That's why you're staying in the city this summer with me!"

"Where else would I go?" Sofia rolls her eyes affectionately. "I've lived in this city my whole life, Ana. I'm obviously staying for the summer."

"But with *me*. In *our* apartment."

"*My* apartment, that you pay like…barely a quarter of the rent for."

"Because we're best friends! Right?"

"Yes," Sofia finally gives in, laughing as she tilts her head against Ana's. Sofia is blonde in the video, as dyed platinum as Ana is naturally honey blonde. "Best friends. I'm glad you answered my post for a roommate. I wouldn't have wanted anyone else. And I'll have another drink, *if* you promise not to go out with that guy if he calls you."

"Yes!" Ana fist-pumps, waving for the bartender. "Two more drinks?"

The video goes black then, and I glance at Sofia's face to see that she's crying softly, tears trickling down her cheeks. "She was a mess," she says softly. "But she was *my* mess. My best friend, when I had no one in the entire world. My parents were dead. I had a mysterious benefactor giving me money and no one left to care about me, except for Ana. She was wild and crazy and reckless, but she loved me when no one else did. She was my everything for a long time."

Sofia swallows hard and flips to the next video, pressing play without a word.

It's a very different video. The strains of Tchaikovsky's *Swan Lake* fill the air, and a tall, slender, graceful girl in black with her honey blonde hair pulled back in a tight ballerina bun enters from stage left.

She's entrancing. There's no other word for it. The Ana I met in Russia at Viktor's safe house was beautiful and sweet and sad. The Ana in the first video Sofia showed me was gorgeous and fun and sexy, but this girl is something else altogether. She's radiant, elegant, every step graceful and perfect, flowing through the steps of the ballet as if it were written specifically for her. It's as if she *becomes* the music, overshadowing everyone around her, so that it's impossible to look at anyone other than her.

I've never seen anything like it. If I'd thought I was in love with Ana before, the girl in the video captures my heart in a way that I couldn't have imagined I could feel. And if I'd wanted to save her before, knowing that this elegant, graceful, perfect creature has been caged somewhere by a man who doesn't deserve her makes me just this side of murderous.

"She's beautiful," I whisper, but the word doesn't do her justice. There's no word in the English language, or any other, that could describe Anastasia Ivanova dancing.

"That's what she lost," Sofia says softly. "It was everything to her. More, even, than my violin was to me. She gave everything to it. She would have given so much more, would have *been* so much more, and then—"

"What happened?" I look at Sofia, feeling a fierce, intense anger rise up in me. "What happened to her?"

"That's not for me to tell you." Sofia bites her lower lip, wiping away her tears with her free hand as her makeup smudges. "Ana needs to tell you that if you find her. Which—you *will* find her, won't you? Please. Out of everyone, I can tell that you care the most. Luca—he wants to find her for her sake as well as mine, but he can't leave now. And Viktor can't either. I know that you're risking just as much, but you—" she shakes her head, squeezing her eyes tightly shut for a moment. "I think you love her, as ridiculous as that sounds. And so maybe you're the best one to go, no matter what."

I'd already been committed to finding her. But if I'd been certain of it before, I'm even more so now. I have to find her, that girl in the videos, and I have to put her back together, somehow. I want her beyond all reasoning, but most of all, I want to be something *to* her. Her savior, most of all.

"I'm going to find her," I tell Sofia firmly, my gaze fixed on hers. "I swear to you—"

"Liam?"

The door opens, and Saoirse steps out, her long emerald green dress blowing around her ankles in the breeze. She looks beautiful and faintly sad, and part of me feels guilty for the instant irritation that flares up in me at the sight of her. It's not her fault that I've become obsessed with another woman in a way that I never can be with her, but she'll bear the brunt of it anyway.

"Saoirse, now isn't a good time—" I start to say, but she shakes her head firmly, walking towards me with her gold clutch purse gripped firmly in one hand.

"Sofia, I need to speak with Liam, please. If you'll give us a moment."

Sofia's eyes widen a little, but she nods, giving me one more pleading look before hurrying back inside, leaving Saoirse and me alone.

"Liam, we need to talk." She looks at me, her delicate chin lifted, and I can tell that she's not about to be swayed. Still, I try anyway.

"I agree," I tell her quickly. "But maybe now isn't the best time." I start to turn away from the railing, but Saoirse stops me with her hand on mine, her green eyes fixing mine with a look that says she's not going to back down.

Even if I don't want to deal with it, I can respect it. So I stop, letting out a long breath as I turn back to face her.

"Alright, Saoirse," I say quietly. "What is it?"

LIAM

*S*aoirse looks a little hurt at my tone. "You act like talking to me is such a terrible thing." She pauses, looking up at me with those soft green eyes that seem made to weigh me down with guilt. "Is talking to me really so bad?"

"No," I tell her honestly. "I just have a lot on my mind." Unlike Niall, Saoirse should have no reason to pick up on what that thing is, thankfully. I can't imagine her reaction if she knew that another woman is on my mind.

"Business?" Saoirse's voice is quiet and even, nonplussed by my answer.

"Yes." I glance away from her, over the city. "I'm supposed to leave on a business trip in the morning, and I'm concerned about it." I look back at her with a tight smile. "It's nothing for you to worry about, though. I'll be back soon." *Hopefully, that's true. And I'll deal with the consequences then.*

"Before you leave—" Saoirse hesitates. "Liam, my father wants to meet at St. Patrick's tonight. The three of us and his brother."

"What?" I blink at her, startled. "Why the fuck would he want that?"

Saoirse flinches slightly at the curse, but she remains where she is.

"To sign the betrothal contract, Liam. You've put it off this long, but my father—"

"Your father doesn't run the Kings. I do. He particularly doesn't run me—"

"He's a powerful man, Liam. It wouldn't be wise—"

"I don't need you to lecture me or advise me!"

Saoirse drops her gaze at that, clearly wounded. "I'm sorry," she starts to say, but I interrupt her, feeling chagrined.

"No, I'm sorry." I take a deep breath. "I'm stressed, but that's no reason to take it out on you."

I turn away from her then, facing out towards the city as I rub a hand over my mouth. I'd shaved for the wedding, and I oddly miss the growth of beard that I'd started to accumulate while in Russia. It had made me feel older somehow, more in control.

Luca and Viktor's advice last night comes back to me, urging me to sign the contract before I leave to find Ana. I know, deep down, that they're right. If I run off half-cocked with the betrothal up in the air and my position hanging, I'm likely to come back to find a theoretical noose tied for me by the same men I'm meant to lead.

If I sign the contract, it will prove that I'm taking my position seriously and pacify Graham O'Sullivan until I can return home. It will keep an outright uprising from breaking out while I'm gone, that's for certain.

It will also lead Saoirse on, a thing that I know she doesn't deserve, and make marrying Ana incredibly difficult, if not downright impossible.

Long-term, it's both the best and worst thing I could do. And I can't seem to focus on anything for very long that isn't the short-term goal of finding Ana.

Sign the contract, I tell myself. *Sort it all out later.*

It's a bad idea, I know it. But I don't know what else to do that still allows me to go and look for the woman I can't get out of my head.

"We'd be a good match," Saoirse says suddenly, interrupting my thoughts. She touches my arm gently, and I catch a whiff of her perfume, something soft and rose-like. "Liam, look at me, please."

Reluctantly, I turn to face her, my entire body tense. I don't know what she takes it as—maybe me trying to hold myself back from leaping on her with desire, which couldn't be further from the truth. But she steps very close to me, raising her hand to lay her palm against my fresh-shaven cheek as she looks up at me with something dangerously approaching desire in her wide green eyes.

"We could be happy," she whispers, and she goes up on her toes, her mouth moving towards mine.

For a moment, I consider letting it happen. I can feel the warmth of her lips, soft and plush, nearly touching mine. Her body is warm and supple; it would be slender under my hands but with gentle curves a bit more full than Ana's. I imagine touching her breasts, feeling the curve of them in my hands, the nipples stiffening through the silk as she kisses me. I imagine her arching against me, and I know I should feel the same pulse of desire, should feel my cock starting to rise in response.

But there's nothing. Saoirse doesn't arouse me, and I can't force it. It's another reason to question the wisdom of the betrothal because few things would threaten my standing in the Kings as much as actually marrying Saoirse and then being unable to consummate the damned union.

"Liam." Her warm, sweet breath is against my lips, her mouth nearly touching mine. "Liam, please."

I don't know what she's asking for—for me to kiss her or to sign the contract, but at the moment, I'm not sure that I can do either. I reach out to grip her upper arms gently in my hands, and I feel the shiver of desire that goes through her. She looks up at me, her eyes wide and glazed with arousal, and I can feel her reaction to me, feel how much she wants me. This isn't just Graham O'Sullivan acting through his daughter. Saoirse *wants* me. She wants this marriage, and she's going to fight for it just as much as her father is.

Her face falls when I move her gently away from me, taking a step back as well to put some physical distance between us.

"You can kiss me, you know," she says, her voice slightly petulant. "You're not going to take my virginity with a kiss."

"I know how it works, Saoirse," I say sharply, and regret it instantly. The look on her face tells me the last thing in the world she wants to think about are the other women I've fucked, especially when I won't even kiss her. I run my hand through my hair, letting out a frustrated sigh.

Every time I open my mouth around her, I seem to say the wrong thing. It's just another reason to believe the marriage wouldn't work well, even if Ana weren't in the picture.

Of course, if I didn't have another woman on my mind, I might not be so resistant to kissing the beautiful one in front of me.

I've never before had a woman so lovely practically begging me to lay one on her and felt not the slightest desire to do so.

It's a good thing Niall can't see this. I run my hand through my hair again, turning away from Saoirse. I can't look at her soft, hurt face a second longer. She's making me feel like a right piece of shit, and frustration wells up in me as I hear her voice pierce the air behind me again.

"Liam, you don't want to make my father angry. He's already starting to test the waters to see who might agree with him that you don't deserve your seat at the head of the Kings. You need to sign the contract. If not for me, then for yourself—for your family's legacy." Saoirse pauses, her voice cool and clear again. "My father and I will be at St. Patrick's tonight. It would be a wise decision if you were there as well."

She starts to turn away, and I should let her go, if only to get the much-needed peace that I came out here for in the first place. But instead, without turning around, I call her name.

"Saoirse."

I hear her stop and her soft intake of breath before she speaks again. "Yes, Liam?"

Now I do turn around, and I see her facing away from me, her slender shoulders rising and falling as she clearly struggles to control her emotions. The back of her gown is open, displaying her pale back, and I wonder what it would be like to want to run my fingers down

IRISH SAVIOR

the length of her spine to unzip that dress and find out what lies beneath it.

Everything would be so much easier if I did.

"We don't need to play this game, you know," I say tiredly.

She tenses. "No, I don't know," Saoirse says finally. "What are you talking about?"

"The game where you pretend you want me to get me to sign it, like you just did."

Saoirse's hands slowly clench at her sides, and I blink, startled. It's the most emotion I've seen from her so far that isn't sadness, and it makes me respect her a little more as she slowly turns to face me, her face set in tense lines.

"I'm not pretending, Liam," she says quietly. "I do want you. It's embarrassing to admit, really, because you so clearly don't feel the same. I don't know why, or what's making you drag your heels, and I'm not sure I want to know. But I'm not faking it to convince you to do anything."

I let out a long sigh, shaking my head. "Saoirse, this will be easier if we're honest with each other. You can't tell me that if it weren't Connor standing here instead, you wouldn't be saying and doing the same things. It's him you would have been meant to marry if he hadn't disappeared. It's the position and marriage you and your father want, not me. Your father, in particular, would be a hell of a lot happier to have married you off to Connor, and not to me."

Saoirse purses her lips, irritation coloring her pretty features. "Liam," she says calmly, her fingers tightening on her clutch purse. "I'd thank you to not tell me what I do and do not feel, as if you knew me better than I know myself. You're right that Connor would have been my husband if he'd stayed to take your father's seat, and you're right that I would have done as my father wished and married him if that had been the case. But as far as what *I* want—" she lets out a sigh, her shoulders slumping a little as she looks at me.

"We grew up together, Liam," she says quietly. "Not closely, no. I doubt you ever paid much attention to me, not even when we were teenagers. I didn't have a lot of friends because my father kept me so sheltered. A girl of my rank is a precious thing, you know. No chance can be taken with her innocence." Her voice changes slightly, the words mocking. "But that doesn't mean I didn't notice you, Liam. You and Connor, with Niall acting like an older brother to the both of you, and Connor always the serious one." She shakes her head, her lips trembling slightly, and I can see that she's holding back tears.

It makes me feel like an asshole.

"I knew back then Connor would probably be my husband one day. My mother said it often enough. But he wasn't the one I wanted. I used to daydream about *you*, Liam. The cocky, funny, reckless younger brother who got away with everything because he wasn't the one meant to inherit. The one that your father never paid much attention to and let you run wild. I didn't want the serious, stern, arrogant older brother. I wanted the one who made me feel like he might be an adventure. Something different than what I'd grown up with all my life."

Saoirse reaches up then, pushing a strand of hair out of her face that's blown loose in the breeze. "I see now that's not the man you are. But the fact remains, Liam, that I was overjoyed when my da came to me and said you'd be the man I was marrying. It's not a burden for me to marry you, but I see quite plainly that it is for you. So I'll say this—you can think whatever you like. But don't you *dare* tell me how I feel ever again, Liam McGregor, because you don't know." Her chin trembles, but she keeps it up, green eyes flashing as she stares me down. "You don't know."

I feel my own shoulders slump as I look at her, exhaustion filling every part of me. "I'm sorry, Saoirse—"

"I'll be at St. Patrick's tonight," she says, turning away. "Be there or don't. But my father will be calling a meeting of the Kings tomorrow if you're not."

I let out a breath I hadn't known I was holding as she stalks back towards the door to go back inside, her spine stiff and straight.

Saoirse O'Sullivan will make some man a hell of a bride.

It's a shame that I wish it didn't have to be me.

ANA

When I wake up the next morning, it's to the scent of brewing coffee and a breakfast tray on a side table next to me. I open my eyes slowly, only to jolt awake when I see that Alexandre is sitting in the wing chair, waiting for me to wake up.

"Were you watching me sleep?" I ask defensively before I can stop myself, pushing myself slightly upright in bed. That, coupled with the drugged tea last night, has me on edge, but he clearly didn't drug me in order to do anything to hurt me. My clothes are all still on just as he left me, and I'm unhurt so far as I can tell. It seems like he just wanted me to get a good night's sleep, which somehow feels stranger than if he'd actually violated or harmed me.

"I was waiting for you to wake up," Alexandre says smoothly, as if that answers the question. "Go on, Ana, eat. It's still warm."

Groggily, I reach for the breakfast tray, uncovering the plate. It's the same as yesterday—the herbed and scrambled eggs with goat cheese, the thin crepes, and my stomach growls with anticipation.

Seemingly satisfied that I'm going to eat, Alexandre stands up gracefully and crosses to the wardrobe, where he flips through several hangers with clothes that I can't quite make out. I eat with a bit more gusto than yesterday as he does—I feel like I'm starving. My stomach seems to have settled enough to actually have a real appetite. Despite the fact that Alexandre is hardly someone I can trust, my body at least seems to feel as if it's safe enough to have normal physical reactions again.

I'd been so depressed at home in New York that I'd barely eaten in months, leaving me skinny and frail. I don't think my mental health has hugely improved in the last two days since I was *sold*, but somehow being a world away from New York seems to have made the fears and trauma that I'd experienced there feel less—immediate somehow. *Maybe it's just the change in scenery,* I think as I dig into the food.

As long as I'm able to eat, I know I should. There's no telling when I'll lose my appetite again, when the sudden uprooting won't be enough to trick my brain and body into wanting to care for itself, or when Alexandre will turn cruel. I know better than to let myself relax and feel safe here when I barely know this man who now owns me.

As I finish eating, Alexandre lays something out on the bed, and I blink at it, unable to fully believe what I'm seeing at first.

It's clothes—but not really. It's a maid's outfit, and my first reaction is for my heart to plummet as I shrink backward. *Here we go,* I think, my pulse speeding up. *This is his fetish. He's going to cram me into this maid's outfit and have me—what, exactly? Dust the chandeliers while he fucks me?*

But then I look at it more closely, and it becomes somehow even more confusing.

It's not a maid's outfit in the sexual sense at all. In fact, it is so far as I can tell, a very historically accurate Victorian-style maid's outfit, which while possibly appealing to a certain subset of men—perhaps ones who have the letters p, h, and d after their names and work in an office with tenure, isn't exactly fetish-wear.

Does he really want me to just—clean his apartment?

I guess if he didn't pay much for me, maybe he just wanted a maid. It would not be the most outlandish thing if he'd seen a girl in a bad situation and paid for her so that he could have her work in his home. *Like a rescued puppy.* I'm hard-pressed to believe he's that altruistic, though. And it doesn't explain some of the other things, like the way he calls me *doll* in French and handles me like one, or how he's brushed my hair and watched me sleep.

Not to mention the fact that it's a bit odd in the first place to put me in a costume to clean the apartment.

"Here," Alexandre holds out a pair of flats, interrupting my train of thought. "I thought that being on your feet cleaning might hurt them after a while. Please sit whenever you need to, but in the meantime, these may help."

I blink at him, startled as I take the shoes. It takes me a moment to realize what's different about them, but I realize that they're padded with some kind of thick, special insole that should help cushion my feet. I still won't be able to stay on them for long periods of time, but it won't be painful to walk at all.

"Thank you," I say, glancing up. "Um—what do you want me to do, exactly?"

Alexandre shrugs. "Just clean while I'm out. I'll show you around once you're dressed. Dust, vacuum, mop the floors, that sort of thing. Nothing too terribly strenuous, and please, as I said, rest whenever you feel the need."

He motions for me to stand up then, and I do, feeling a bit dizzy all over again as if I'm in a dream. Nothing feels like it makes sense. I'm too dazed to protest when Alexandre starts to undo the buttons on my pajama top. Once again, he doesn't touch me inappropriately. He undresses me like a mannequin in a storefront window—or a doll— laying the silk pajamas neatly aside on the bed as he reaches for the maid uniform.

I'm viscerally aware that I'm naked as he steps away from me. Not just partially nude, but entirely bare, from my toes to the top of my head. Alexei had demanded I shave myself completely bare just as he'd ordered the others to before the party, but the stubble is beginning to grow back, and I wonder if Alexandre will want me shaved. He doesn't seem to be taking any sexual interest in me, but still—

I swallow hard as he holds up a pair of black satin panties with a frilled waist that seems to match the maid's uniform, and he has me step into them as he pulls them up over my hips. It's as matter-of-fact as everything else, and he does the same with the maid's uniform, letting me step into it and then buttoning it up the back, tying on the apron, and then reaching for a silver-backed hairbrush on the vanity. Alexandre runs it through my hair before carefully pinning it up in a bun and fixing the maid's cap atop it, setting the shoes on the floor last of all for me to step into.

When I look in the mirror, I don't look sexy. I look pretty enough, I guess, if you're into very pale, too skinny blonde girls in historical wear. Still, I look as if I'm off to some reenactment, or maybe a community play. *The Crucible*, perhaps.

I definitely don't look like anything remotely approaching anyone's fetish, which should be a relief. And it is, in a way. I'd have had a complete, spiraling panic attack if Alexandre had put me in lingerie with the intent to force me to fuck him. As it is, it's hard to tamp down the rising feeling of panic because it still doesn't make sense.

And it's all still very strange.

Alexandre waves me towards the door, opening it for me. "Ladies first," he says politely, following me out as I step into the hall and see the rest of the apartment for the first time.

It both is and isn't what I'd expected. It's clearly very old, if well-kept. The walls are wood-paneled, with knots and whorls telling me it's real wood. The floors are hardwood planks as well, with thick and well-worn rugs along them that I don't doubt are Turkish and Persian, probably worth as much as several months' rent in Manhattan, if not more. There's another bathroom in the hall, which ends in an expansive living room with a huge stone fireplace on one side, bookcases lining the walls, and art hanging from them in nearly every available space, along with more rugs covering the hardwood floors.

Alexandre is the furthest thing from a minimalist I've ever encountered. There's not a speck of available wall, floor, or table space that doesn't have some rug, book, antique, art, or doily covering it. Nevertheless, it somehow all comes together in a sort of art-history, eccentric collector's aesthetic rather than looking like an episode of *Hoarders*. It's all clearly authentic and expensive, too, likely the result of years and years of collecting.

"Just through there is the dining room and the kitchen," Alexei says, pointing towards the north end of the living room. "And to the left there, is my study. It, and my bedroom, are the only rooms you are not permitted to go into. Do you understand me?"

I nod, swallowing hard at the sudden, harsher change in his tone. "Of course," I say quietly. "Ah—where is your bedroom?"

"Upstairs." He points towards a wrought-iron and wood spiral staircase that leads up to a second floor. "There are two rooms up there, my bedroom suite and the room that serves at the library. You may go into the library and clean it, but do not go into my room." He pauses, his blue eyes fixing mine with a sternness that I haven't seen before from him. "I'm very serious, Anastasia. My study and my bedroom suite are off-limits."

"Okay." I nod again, licking my suddenly dry lips nervously. "You just want me to clean?"

"Yes, as well as you are able. As I mentioned earlier, there are dishes to be done and dusting, vacuuming, and mopping. I'll be out for some time, so please don't rush. I'll come back this afternoon and we can go out to shop for food."

We're going out grocery shopping? It's not any stranger than anything else he's said, but I'm still slightly taken aback, so much so that I don't even flinch when he kisses my forehead gently, patting the top of my head and telling me he'll be back soon. I stay frozen to the spot, feeling like nothing so much as a puppy left to my own devices, patted and told to be a good girl until her master comes home.

I—should hate it. The old Ana *would* have hated it. But he hasn't hurt me. He hasn't done anything except treat me a bit strangely. He's fed, clothed, and left me alone in his house without any restrictions other than a couple of rooms I've been told not to go into. He didn't tie me to the bed or chain me to a radiator. He hasn't starved, hurt, or assaulted me.

He *patted me on the head.*

I feel like I'm losing my mind.

Maybe I lost it a long time ago.

I look around the room, trying to decide what to do first. Cleaning isn't the worst thing in the world—I always hated chores back home, but it will give me something to do. Back then, all I wanted to do was goof off or sleep after a grueling week of dance classes, practice, and choreography, but I have none of that now. All I have are endless hours with nothing to fill them, nothing but my own thoughts eating away at my brain. *Maybe it will do me some good to keep busy*, I think, heading decisively towards the kitchen. *And besides, his apartment is interesting. It might be fun to explore.*

The dishes are easy enough, although it makes me nervous to handle them. There are no cheap IKEA plates and cups here. Everything is fine china and heavy silver, which I know enough to know you're supposed to polish it, though it takes me a while to find the silver polish. What I notice, though, as I had when he'd given me the tea, is that most of the dishes are slightly damaged in some way. A chip here, a flawed design there, a deep patina to some of the silver that can't be polished away. And the dishes aren't the end of it.

The furniture in the dining room is gorgeous, heavy antique wood and likely very old, but there are flaws—scratches, dings, water stains. The expensive rugs are frayed in places or spotted in the designs from age, and the collectibles are the same. They're all beautiful and, to my amateur eye, appear authentic and not just damaged junk—but they *are* damaged. Dented or scratched frames, chipped paint, a torn page or broken spine or missing gilt lettering on the books, cracks in the antiques. There's a beautiful Japanese vase with gold poured in the cracks, and I remember hearing about that technique somewhere, though I can't remember the name.

As I make my way through the rooms in the apartment, I can feel myself tensing, on edge with each door I open and each new thing I pick up to clean. I can feel myself waiting to unearth something terrible, to find something that tells me what's wrong with Alexandre, what horrible fate is waiting for me—or for him to come back in suddenly, for him to have tricked me into doing all of this, touching his things, and then punish me for it.

I can't understand why he's being so kind to me when he purchased me—the two things seem diametrically opposed to each other. I can't help but feel as if I'm holding my breath, waiting for the trap to spring.

But it doesn't. All I find is room after room filled with beautiful items that are expensive-looking but faintly flawed, and something begins to dawn on me.

It's not hard to piece together. I sit down on the couch halfway through dusting the seemingly endless art on the living room walls after I come back downstairs from the library and take off my shoe, looking at the ridged scar tissue on the soles of my bent feet.

Everything in this apartment is damaged in some way. Not enough to take away from its beauty, not even enough to be noticeable at first, until you get up close. But it's all flawed somehow.

Just like me.

I don't know how to feel about it, and I certainly don't think it's something I should point out to Alexandre. Something inside of me, some instinct, says that he won't want me to realize it, to know anything about this odd predilection of his. And truthfully, picking up on it doesn't mean I understand it. It's one thing to collect flawed art, but a *person*? It's vaguely creepy, but also in a way...sweet?

I don't understand it. I don't understand *him*, and as curious as the apartment has made me, I'm not sure I want to. He seems complex, certainly, a man with layers. But I'm afraid of what I might find if those layers were ever peeled back—or how he might react if I tried.

The sound of the front door opening comes a few hours later, when I've cleaned just about everything I can. I'm dusting off a few small statues on a side table when Alexandre comes down the entryway, a pleasant smile on his face as he walks into the living room and looks around.

"You've done a lovely job, Anastasia," he says, and I can't help but feel a warm burst of pleasure at his praise. It feels *good* to have someone be happy with me, to tell me that I've done well, even if it is the man who owns me.

"Come with me," he says then, motioning towards the hall that leads to my room, and my stomach clenches.

"Don't you want to look at the rest of it?" I ask haltingly, suddenly nervous. *Maybe it's now. Perhaps he's going to take advantage. I'm tired. I can't fight back, as if I ever could anyway.*

"I'm sure it's all just as excellent," Alexandre says pleasantly. "Come along, *petit*. We have errands to run."

I know better than to argue with him. I follow him mutely down the hall back to my room, leaving the feather duster abandoned on the couch as he opens the door and gestures for me to come in.

He leaves me standing in the middle of the room as he flings open the wardrobe again, combing through it and one of the dresser drawers before turning back to me with an armful of clothing and laying it on the bed. He steps up very close behind me then, and I freeze, going tense and rigid all over before I realize he's simply unpinning the maid's cap from my hair.

"I can undress myself," I say quickly, feeling a sudden burst of bravery. "You don't have to do it every time."

"Ah, but I want to, *petit*." His voice is firm, and I close my mouth instantly against any further argument.

His touch is gentle, but I'm afraid to anger him. I stay very still as he begins to undo the buttons of the maid costume one by one, getting me out of it until I'm standing naked in the center of the room again, even the panties gone so that I'm bare except for the shoes on my feet.

"Can you walk around town, *petit*?" Alexandre asks, as casually as if I weren't standing entirely naked in the middle of the room right in front of him. "Or are your poor feet too tired?"

I don't think he's mocking me, and they *are* sore, but I decide that I shouldn't opt to stay home just in case. It could be a test, and I don't want to fail.

"No, I'm fine," I say bravely. "I can walk. It wasn't that hard to clean. My feet are doing much better."

Alexandre peers at me as if he's trying to decide if I'm lying, but finally shrugs and motions for me to step into the fresh pair of underwear he's holding, this time a pair of light blue cotton panties with small white flowers on them. It's on the tip of my tongue to ask him why he has so much women's underwear in his apartment, but something tells me that I either wouldn't like the answer, or he won't want to say—or maybe both.

The dress that he puts me in for our errands is breathtakingly lovely—a wrap dress made of raw silk in a light blue that brings out my eyes. It hangs on me a little, the v-neck coming down low enough that my cleavage would be all too visible if I had any, but I've always been remarkably small-breasted, and as thin as I am, I'm mostly sternum and ribs. Something about the way the dress hangs looks elegant, though, flowing over my pale skin like I'm a marble statue, instead of hanging off of me like a clothes hanger. Alexandre runs his fingers through my hair so that it spreads out over my shoulders in a thick blonde waterfall and makes a pleased noise deep in his throat.

Something about that sound of pleasure ripples through me, making my bare nipples spring up hard under the silk, pressing against the fabric in a pleasant way that sends shivers over my skin. I have the sudden urge to turn towards him, rise up on my tiptoes and press a kiss to his cheek, but I force back the impulse. It makes no sense—why would I want to do something like that? Alexandre isn't a *good* man, no matter how nicely he touches me. *He isn't a good man just because he hasn't beaten me or violated me,* I tell myself, repeating it over and over as Alexandre crosses the room to a small jewelry box sitting on the vanity. But as I watch him, moving through the room with that same graceful elegance that makes my heart ache with nostalgia, I can feel the words becoming harder and harder to cling to. They feel slippery as the silk of my dress beneath my hands, and I clench my fingers in my skirt as he flips up the lid of the jewelry box.

A few faint notes of a familiar song trail out from the box, a plastic ballerina turning on one foot, and the room suddenly tilts.

Every girl has had one of those jewelry boxes, hasn't she? The one with pink silk glued to the inside and the ballerina with her tiny stiff tutu twirling slowly, the one that you could wind up over and over until it stopped working?

The one that Alexei thought it would be fun to make a mockery of, rigging me up in the same pose for his guests at the party.

The party where Alexandre bought me.

I feel the room spinning, my stomach clenching until I think I'm going to be sick, my breath coming sharp and fast until I can feel myself starting to hyperventilate. I don't realize I'm falling until my knees hit the floor hard enough to bruise, and I catch myself with the heels of my hands, gasping as I try to get my bearings.

"Anastasia?" Alexandre's voice comes through the fog of panic that seems to have risen up all around me, thick and choking, and I try to focus on it, but I can't. I know how ridiculous it seems that I would focus on his voice of all things, this man who is at least partially responsible for my situation, for why I'm not home in my own bed, in my own apartment, far away from all of this.

Except I never was far away from it. It's always been right here, ever since Franco, waiting for me in the worst moments. Waking or sleeping, it's always there.

I can feel my toes curling in the shoes, my feet trying to bend away from the phantom pains that shoot through them, the cutting and burning that I keep reliving, and now there's Alexei's torment on top of it, the marks from the belt and the pain from the rigging, and that goddamned song—

It keeps playing, the ballerina keeps turning, and I hear myself starting to scream, gasping, shrieking sobs as I clap my hands over my ears and rock back and forth.

Make it stop, make it stop, make it stop, make it stopppppp---

"Anastasia! Anastasia!" Alexandre shouts my name, and I feel his long-fingered hands on my shoulders, gripping tightly as he shakes me. "What the fuck is wrong with you, *petit*? Snap out of it! What the fuck—Anastasia!"

I'm crying now, thick gasping sobs that leave my eyes and nose streaming onto the expensive rug underneath me. Alexandre stands up, shaking his head with an expression of what could be disgust as he steps back, looking down at me.

"*Monsieur* Egorov mentioned this," he murmurs, watching me

shake and sob on the rug. "These...panic attacks." He waves his hand as if he's unsure if that's what he should call it. "These *fits*."

The music is slowing, and I can hear his words more clearly now. As the music stops, I struggle to breathe, shaking all over as I slowly drop my hands from my ears to the rug, bracing myself as I try to stop crying. *He's getting angry,* I think fearfully, looking up at him through tear-blurred eyes. And then, immediately after—

Why does he have one of those jewelry boxes?

It seems like a strange thing to have. I blink slowly, licking my dry, salty lips as I look up at Alexandre, whose expression is now a mixture of confusion and concern. He squats down slowly, reaching for me with his hands tight on my upper arms as he pulls me, wobbling, to my feet.

"Anastasia," he says slowly. "What is wrong?"

I squeeze my eyes tight, swallowing hard as I try to get my bearings. "The jewelry box," I manage past the lump in my throat, my voice shaking. "The jewelry box—"

Alexandre's brow furrows, and he looks even more concerned and slightly irritated. "What about it?" he asks, his voice edging on impatient.

"It—" I blink, looking towards the box on the vanity. "It—"

I'd seen it. I *know* I had. The small cheap jewelry box I'd had as a child, that so many girls had back then, lined with pink satin with a small, spinning ballerina that danced to tinny music as you opened it. The ballerina that Alexei had made me play the role of at his party.

But that's not what's on the dresser. There is a jewelry box, but it's a deep cherry wood with black velvet lining and a mirror on the back of the lid. Antique and elegant, like everything else in Alexandre's house.

Everything except me, apparently.

Because what I'd seen hadn't been there at all.

LIAM

I go to St. Patrick's.

I spent the rest of Viktor and Caterina's wedding reception trying to make up my mind. I know that signing the contract is no small thing. If I go back on it when I return to Boston, for any reason, the consequences could—and almost certainly will be—dire.

But by the time the happy couple is on their way out of the ballroom, I know that there's really no choice. Whatever the consequences of this decision turn out to be—whether I'm forced to go ahead with marrying Saoirse in the end or whether I break the contract, those are problems for the Liam of the future to contend with.

Right now, if I want to keep the peace and maintain my hold over the Kings while I go and search for Ana, I have to do this. If not, I have no doubt that the threat Saoirse made on the balcony wasn't an empty one.

If I leave in the morning without the contract signed, Graham O'Sullivan will call a meeting of the Kings without me, and I very well could come back to a civil war.

So while most of the other guests go off to enjoy afterparties in downtown Manhattan, Luca and Sofia go back home. Sasha returns to

IRISH SAVIOR

watch the kids while Viktor and Caterina enjoy a second—ostensibly better—wedding night than their first. I call my driver for a much less entertaining reason. Saoirse is nowhere to be seen and hasn't been for some time—I assume she and her father are already at the church.

"Where are you off to? Early morning tomorrow, isn't it?"

Max's voice comes from behind me as I wait at the curb, and I glance over as the tall Italian comes to stand next to me. He's dressed neatly in a black suit, the glimmer of a silver chain at his neck, his handsome features casual and easy as if there were nothing on his mind this fine night.

Knowing what I do of Max, that's unlikely to be the case. But he's excellent at hiding his emotions.

Truthfully, there's not a man I know who isn't.

"It is," I confirm. "I've got some business at St. Patrick's first, though."

Max smirks. "Off to church? I didn't think you were a particularly religious man, Liam McGregor."

"I'm not." I frown. "It's Kings' business."

"Ah." He nods, as if it makes more sense to him now. "Makes sense why Father Donahue canceled my meeting with him tonight, then."

"Sorry about that." I glance at him, entirely serious. "Trust me, I'd rather you have had your meeting, and I didn't have to deal with this."

Max shrugs. "I'll speak with him when we get back. If anything, Viktor will just owe me yet another favor for helping you." He gives me a wry grin. "That is, if I'm still welcome on this mission of yours."

"Of course. I need all the help I can get." I rub my hand over my mouth as the driver pulls up to the curb. "See you in the morning. At Viktor's private hangar, bright and early."

"Will do." Max lifts a hand as I slide into the car. "Good luck."

I grin at him with a humor that I don't feel. "I'm Irish, man. I've got all the luck I need already."

If only I really believed that. As the car begins to wind through the streets towards the cathedral, I don't feel lucky. The woman I want, a woman that I feel I'd started to fall in love with, was sold perhaps half an hour before I could have saved her. Now she's somewhere in the world, going through god knows what, possibly even beyond my reach. I'm minutes from signing a contract that almost certainly will have far-reaching consequences, no matter whether I keep it or break it.

Except for Niall, I'm alone in the world. My relationships with Luca and Viktor are, at their roots, business relationships—there's no denying that. We are friends, to an extent, but that doesn't mean we'll never be at odds again. There's a burgeoning friendship with Max, but he has his own demons, his own ghosts that haunt him.

I can't help but laugh. My enforcer and a defrocked priest are the two men I feel that I can trust most, and aside from that, the one woman I'd like to have at my side I might never be able to reach. Even if I do, there's no guarantee she'll want me or that she won't be so broken that she's beyond saving.

No, I don't feel that the fabled luck of the Irish is with me at all, if I'm being honest.

The cathedral is glowing with a dim, low light as I walk into the nave. I see Father Donahue at the foot of the altar, talking quietly with a man who I can tell even from the back is Graham O'Sullivan, if only because Saoirse is next to him. She's still wearing that same emerald green gown, her skin glowing nearly translucent, and she looks ethereally beautiful, like an angel or a saint.

This is the woman you're supposed to marry. I can hear Niall's voice as if he were next to me, murmuring in my ear. *And you're going to run halfway across the world for some other lass that you hardly know, who might already have forgotten about you?*

I'm basing everything off of one chilly afternoon in a garden, a light in Ana's eyes when she looked at me that I can't shake, and those videos that Sofia showed me. I can't stop thinking about the laughing girl with the dyed dark hair in the bar or the graceful ballerina who had captured my heart in a few seconds of watching her glide across that stage.

Whoever hurt her in the first place, whoever broke her spirit and put her in that wheelchair, I want to destroy them myself, piece by piece, as brutally as Viktor did to Alexei. And then I want to do the same to whoever is holding her captive now.

It doesn't matter if he's being cruel or kind to her; no man who buys another human being is worth anything but the bullet I'd put in his head to send him beneath the dirt where he belongs.

And if what I have to do to secure my position here while I accomplish that is sign this goddamn contract, then that's what I'll do.

Saoirse smiles at me as I approach, her rosy mouth curving upwards. She looks happy to see me, and I don't know if it's actually my presence or that I'm here doing what I'm supposed to be doing, but it's better than anger, I suppose.

"Liam." She leans up as I come to stand next to her, brushing her lips over my cheek. "I'm glad you're here."

"As am I, lad." Graham O'Sullivan turns to look at me, his voice gruff in his bearded face. "I'd started to think that you planned to dishonor my daughter and myself by shirking your duty to the Kings."

"Not at all." I force myself to smile pleasantly at him. "Just had to do a bit of housekeeping first, that's all."

Graham doesn't look as if he entirely believes me, but he doesn't argue. "Do you have a ring with you for my daughter, lad?"

Ah, fuck. I hadn't thought of buying an engagement ring for Saoirse, mostly because I'd been doing my damndest to avoid the betrothal altogether.

His mouth twitches with irritation. "I'd expected as much. Here you are, lad." Graham holds out a black velvet box, and I take it reluctantly, as if it might burn me.

I can tell from his expression that he's not at all thrilled to be marrying Saoirse to me. If he had a son, I expect he'd be pushing for an uprising among the Kings to seat his son in my place instead. But since all he has is a daughter, this is his power play. I know he'd have rather married her to Connor, if nothing else.

There's a small, bitter pleasure in knowing that Graham O'Sullivan's hand is in a way being as forced as mine. But it doesn't change the facts of what is happening here tonight.

Nor does it change that I can't take pleasure in making a false vow. I've always believed strongly in keeping my word. My father turned traitor, and that will make my own betrayal if I break this contract, all the worse. But even if there weren't a single consequence to breaking the promise I'll be making tonight, I would still feel guilty about it, down to my bones.

Niall was right about one thing, Saoirse deserves better than a false vow and empty words. But that's all I can offer her tonight. The alternative—leaving Ana to her fate or letting someone else be the one to go after her—is even more unthinkable to me.

I open the velvet box Graham hands me. It's a little rough around the edges, clearly having been kept in a drawer for some time. Inside is an oval diamond set in heavy gold, with a round emerald on either side.

"It's was Saoirse's grandmother's ring, and then her mother's," Graham says stiffly. "She'll be proud to wear it."

"Aye," Saoirse says softly, her slight accent peeking through. A generation removed from our homeland, she sounds more American than anything else. But growing up around a generation of proud Irishmen and women means that it can't be escaped entirely, and the sound of the faint accent coloring her syllables is almost charming.

There's a great deal about her that could be charming, if only she were the woman I wanted.

Father Donahue clears his throat. I can see from his expression that he's aware of the tension and that not everyone here is thrilled with the proceedings. However, he's been party to enough mafia dealings over the years—Italian, Russian, and Irish—to know when to turn a blind eye and when to speak up. This is a time for the former, and he steps up to the altar, the two of us following with Graham O'Sullivan just behind me like a glaring gargoyle.

"Liam Aidan McGregor," Father Donahue begins, his eyes fixed on me uncomfortably. It makes me feel like he can see something even I can't, something down into my soul. "Is it your intention tonight to pledge your hand to this woman, Saoirse O'Sullivan, with the intent that you will bind yourself to her in holy matrimony?"

My mouth feels dry as cotton, and I'm not sure I'll be able to speak.

Saoirse's hand is light and slender in mine, and I cast a sideways glance at her. She looks ethereal in the light, and I feel like a shite and a cad for not wanting her. A month ago, perhaps I would have, even in a superficial sense.

The heart wants what the heart wants.

Everyone I know, who I trust, would say it's romantic drivel—except, maybe, the men who are going along with me on this mission to rescue Ana. They, at least, see some value in what I'm doing, even if they don't know what I hope for at the end of it. And Sofia—

Sofia is depending on me too, to bring her best friend back to her. She'd had no problem playing on the emotions I have for Ana, even encouraging them. But then again, what wouldn't someone do to rescue someone they love, especially when she can't go herself?

Graham clears his throat behind me, and I know my time is up.

"I do," I say clearly, turning to face Saoirse in front of the priest.

"And do you, Saoirse Margaret O'Sullivan, pledge your hand to Liam McGregor, with the intent to give yourself to him in holy matrimony?"

She smiles softly at me and nods. "I do," she whispers, and I feel my palm starting to sweat around the ring I'm clenching in my other fist.

"Then Liam, you may place the ring on your betrothed's hand to signify this bond and solemn promise."

My hands are shakier than Saoirse's, though I manage to hide it. I slip the heavy gold ring over her slender finger, and I see her small, sharp intake of breath as it settles on her hand, as if she were expecting I might bolt at the last moment.

It's taken everything in me not to.

I feel numb afterward, as if the ring were the most solid part of the ceremony, though there's more to it. Father Donahue gives us both communion as we kneel in front of the altar, Graham still at our backs, and then the contract is presented to the three of us to sign. Me first, and then Graham, and Saoirse last of all. She signs quickly, without hesitation, and I feel a pang of sympathy for her.

Even if I never touch her over the course of our engagement—and I have no plans to—it will be difficult for her father to marry her off if

M. JAMES

I break the contract. There's a stigma to it, even if the girl is still virginal when the contract is broken. It's just one of the many reasons that Graham O'Sullivan won't take it lightly, and one of the reasons that I feel so much guilt for letting it go this far at all.

But what choice do I have?

"It's done then," Graham says gruffly. "Come along, Saoirse, there's a flight back to Boston waiting for us. I expect we'll see you back at the head of the table sooner rather than later, Liam?"

"I'll be gone for a little while, starting tomorrow." I force myself to meet his eyes, so that it doesn't seem shady. "Business. It shouldn't take too long." *I hope that it doesn't.* Niall can only stall for me for so long, and the longer I'm gone, the less the contract I've signed will hold weight. Graham will expect a wedding before the year is out, and I have no doubt that Saoirse will begin planning as soon as she's back home.

Meanwhile, I'm setting off to find Ana.

"Be safe, Liam," Saoirse says softly, pausing as her father starts off down the aisle of the church. "Come back soon."

"I'll do my best," I promise her, feeling my stomach clench with the burning guilt of it all. She smiles at me, turning to follow her father with a sweep of her gown, and I stand there, feeling as if I could crumble into dust.

"You don't look like a man about to be happily wed," Father Donahue observes from behind me. "I've seen many couples pass through this church, some happier than others, but I've never seen a man look so conflicted about marrying a lass like Saoirse O'Sullivan."

"Not you, too." I rub a hand over my face, groaning. "I've got a lot on my mind, Father."

"Another woman?"

The priest, as always, is far too perceptive. "It's more complicated than that."

"Aye, it always is." Father Donahue crosses over to one of the front pews, patting the wood next to him as he looks at the altar, the glowing lamp hanging just behind it. "Come and sit for a spell, lad."

"I've got an early morning—"

The priest gives me a piercing look, and I sigh, coming to take a seat at the pew behind him instead, for a quicker escape if need be.

"Is there something you need to confess?"

"Not as of yet," I say defensively and then let out a long breath, running a hand through my hair. If there were anyone I could talk to without fear of it getting out, Father Donahue is the one, even more so than Max. He's bound by his own vows to keep it confidential, and Father Donahue is even more trustworthy than most. He's been the priest to too many men of the mafia not to know when it's in his best interests to keep silent. It's kept him alive through regime changes when many others might not have managed the same.

"You know Anastasia Ivanova?"

The question appears to take Father Donahue aback for a moment.

"Yes," he says finally. "Not well, but I know of her. Through Sofia Romano, mostly—she brought the girl to me for counsel a few times, after—"

"After what?" I narrow my eyes. "I know she was hurt. Can you tell me more about that?"

Father Donahue shakes his head. "You're asking a priest to break the vow of the confessional? Shame on you, lad. But then again, your father was no stranger to broken vows and lies."

"I'm not my father." I grit my teeth. "I don't need you to tell me who he was, either. I'm well aware that he was a traitor, from the minute he put that bastard son in Francesca Bianchi's womb to the moment he tried double-dealing with the Italians and Russians. He was nearly the ruin of us all."

"And you're setting yourself up to finish the job if you don't keep the vow you made just there." Father Donahue nods to the altar. "Don't think I can't see through you, son. I'm too old, and I've seen far too much not to know what's spinning inside that head of yours. Your heart is with another woman, or you think it is—Anastasia Ivanova—and you've been thinking about how to get out of that betrothal contract before you even signed your name to it."

"It's not that simple."

"So you keep saying."

"She's a captive." I rub my hand over my mouth, letting out a frustrated sigh. "She was kidnapped in Russia, along with Sofia, Caterina, and some others."

"Aye, I've heard about what happened."

"She was the only one we weren't in time to save. Alexei—the man responsible—sold her before we managed to break in. I don't know where she is, but—"

"But you intend to find her. And what, marry her?"

"I don't know," I say sharply, the defensiveness returning to my voice. "Finding her is the first part."

"And the betrothal a way to secure your position until you make up your mind."

"Aye." I look away, feeling exhaustion start to overwhelm me. "It's not an easy thing to grapple with, Father. I don't wish to break Saoirse's heart or break my word. But I have two things pulling at me. The legacy my own father left me—"

"—and your feelings for this woman."

"I don't think you're an expert on affairs of the heart. No offense, Father."

Father Donahue smirks, an odd expression to see on the old priest's face. "It's not the first time I've heard that said to me, son. But I don't need to have felt the fires of lust myself or have entered into the bonds of marriage to know the struggles that it makes other men grapple with. And as for love—" he shrugs. "There are other loves than just the kind between a man and a woman or the love for a partner. Family, friends—I've felt love and loss too, son. I've lived a long life, and loss is a part of that."

"I can't—" *I can't lose her,* I want to say, no matter how ridiculous it sounds. "I can't abandon her. But I can't abandon all of my responsibilities here, either."

"You've put yourself in a hard position, lad," Father Donahue says. "I don't have much in the way of advice to offer you, only compassion. But I caution you to think of the weight of a vow before you take it." He pauses, his flinty gaze meeting mine.

"Your father didn't."

* * *

THOSE WORDS HANG over me as I return to my hotel, alone and weighed down with a dozen burdens that threaten to crush me underneath their weight. *Your father didn't.*

He's right, of course. My father didn't think of the weight of a vow, or rather he only thought of his own profit, and now he's beneath dirt and concrete, executed by Viktor Andreyev.

But it's not profit I'm concerned with. My father's goals were mercenary, but mine is different. Mine has to do with emotions, with the heart, and while I know it won't change the consequences, surely it makes what I'm doing all the more justified.

Ana. I can't get her out of my head. As I loosen my tie, unbuttoning my shirt, I can't help but think of what it would be like to have her here, in my room with me. I'd clung to that memory of the afternoon in the garden, but now I have more of her, thanks to Sofia. I have a picture not just of a broken girl in a wheelchair, but of who she was before that. I think of the laughing girl in the bar and imagine what it might have been like to run into her somewhere like that—how different things might have been for us both. Or if I'd seen her at a performance if she'd made it to the New York Ballet, and how I might have been entranced by her. How I might have pursued her, tried to make myself her patron, started a romance with none of the complications I'm currently facing.

It's a foolish thing to imagine. Ana was never an appropriate match for me—a ballerina, particularly one with her last name, is no more a suitable wife for the head of the Kings than she is now. But I can't help but linger on the thought of it, a fantasy of going to her dressing room with roses, asking her out for the night, taking her back home.

I wanted to kiss her that day in the garden, as inappropriate as I'd known it would have been. She'd smiled at me in the cold light, and I'd wanted to get up from the bench where I'd been sitting, cup her delicate face in my hands, and press my lips to hers. I'd thought about her reaction, the way she might breathe in sharply with surprise, and even now thinking about it makes me hard, my cock stiffening in my suit trousers as I slip off my shirt.

Fuck. My gut feels twisted with guilt, but the rest of me is flooded with desire, my skin tingling with it as I finish undressing and stride towards the shower, my cock hard and aching, visions of Ana filling my head. The image in my head flickers between the sweet, shy, nervous girl in the garden who had looked at me as if I were the first good thing she'd seen in a long time and the vivacious, boisterous girl in the bar, the elegant ballerina on the stage. I know that the girl in those videos is the *real* Ana, the girl that she'd been before the world broke her down, and I want to know that girl too. I want to know all of her, every part of her, every facet.

Everything that ever happened to her to make her who she is, the good and the bad, the beautiful and the ugly. I can take it and still love her.

I know I can.

But first I have to find her. And then I have to convince her of that fact, that I want her, damage and all. Scars and all.

I bend my head under the hot water of the shower, bracing my hands against the wall as I squeeze my eyes tightly shut. The desire for her tears through me, hot and insistent, overtaking my good sense. *I could have kissed her that day in the garden. Giving her something to hold onto.*

But I'd had no idea of what was coming next.

I hear it, over and over, the soft, sharp intake of breath she might have made as I kissed her, the way she might have tilted her chin up, leaning into the kiss. My mind takes it further, to me lifting her off of the bench, sweeping her into my arms, and carrying her upstairs, forgetting about the obligations I'd had that afternoon. Laying her down in my bed in the guest room, gently stripping away the layers of clothes, the soft sweater she'd worn and the shirt underneath, revealing the inches of skin to my gaze as I dragged my lips over her body, showing her what it would feel like to be adored, desired, loved.

It mingles with all the other fantasies that have become jumbled up with that one since Sofia showed me the photos and videos on her phone, and my cock throbs insistently, so hard that it's nearly touching the smooth ridged muscle of my belly as a tumult of images of Ana flood thorough my mind. Ana in her ballerina's outfit, Ana in the bar, Ana in the garden. My hands on her face and my mouth on her lips, pulling her into a cab after meeting her at the bar, backing her into her dressing table after following her backstage post-show. Her body under my hands, smooth and lithe and graceful, and it's the Ana that Sofia showed me that takes over, laughing under my touch, arching into it, her hands tangling in my hair as she rises up to kiss me.

Before I know it, my fist is around my cock, sliding across my taut, straining flesh under the hot spray of water, a grunt of pleasure and need escaping my lips as I start to stroke myself, slowly and first and then faster. There's nothing but thoughts of Ana in my head, pushing her back against her dressing table as I fall to my knees and pull the edge of her leotard aside, pressing my lips to her hot, drenched flesh as I lick her pussy until she screams with pleasure. I want to know how she would taste, how she would feel, the muscles of her thighs leaping under my hands as I lick her to climax after climax, lifting her up onto the table while she's still quivering, freeing my aching cock, and thrusting into her.

I gasp as I squeeze the length of it, my thumb rubbing over the slick head as I thrust into my fist, imagining that it's her, her legs wrapped around my hips, her head tilted back as she moans with pleasure, her long bare throat exposed for my lips to trail down, biting and sucking as I fuck her.

It doesn't matter that none of that is a reality now, that the Ana who danced so beautifully on the stage is gone, that the fantasy filling my head will never happen. It makes me want her all the more, the girl she once was and the girl she is now, and I grit my teeth, groaning with lust as I push myself towards the release that I so desperately need. I want her here, with me now, drenched and wet in this shower as I push her up against the tiles, kiss her mouth, her neck, her jaw, lift her up so that her legs wrap themselves around my waist as I slide into her. That new image fills my head, the steam wreathing around us as I clutch her head in the back of my hand, her wet hair tangling around my fingers, and my hips pump harder and faster into my fist, imagining that it's her, that I can hear her cries of pleasure as she comes, as I—

"*Fuck!*" I snarl the word aloud as I feel the tingling rising up from my toes, my balls tight and aching between my legs as I feel the first rush of my climax, every muscle in my thighs rigid as I stroke myself hard and fast, groaning with pleasure.

It feels so fucking good. Not as good as being buried inside Ana would, but something about the fantasy intensifies all of it, making my cock throb with a sensation that makes my toes curl against the warm tile floor of the shower, my breath coming in hard, fast gasps as I paint the wall of the shower with my cum, groaning out Ana's name between gritted teeth as the flashes of fantasy keep pouring through my brain until every last shudder of my climax has passed through me.

I lean forward, panting, my body still twitching as I let go of my pulsing cock, letting it begin to soften under the hot spray of the water as I try to catch my breath. Even after the intense orgasm, I don't feel as if I have any more clarity than I did before. I still feel consumed by her, by the need to find her, to see her again.

I can't rest until I do. I can't go back to Boston until I do. I made two promises, and there's one thing I know, down to my very bones.

I'll be damned if I'm going to break both of them.

ANA

Despite my outburst, Alexandre and I still wind up going out.

Without a word, as I'd stood there numbly in the middle of the room staring at the jewelry box, he'd gone to the bathroom and gotten a hot washcloth. He'd returned and tilted my chin up with one hand, wiping away my snot and tears until my skin was clean and pink, and then disappeared back into the bathroom again. When he'd reemerged, he'd come to stand in front of me, his fingers under my chin as he'd looked almost disapprovingly into my eyes.

"That's enough of that, *petit*," he'd said firmly and then gestured for me to follow him, whatever he'd been about to get out of the jewelry box forgotten.

Outside, away from the confines of the room and the shuddering fear I'd felt at the imagined music, I feel foolish. I can't believe I'd panicked over something so clearly imagined. Beyond that, it feels like magic to be outside again. I haven't felt the sun on my face since Alexei kidnapped us, and the Paris sunshine in late spring is something else altogether. I tilt my face up, feeling it warm my cheeks as the scents of flowers and fresh bread and restaurants cooking food for the evening dinner crowd fill my nose. I feel a sudden rush of happiness that I haven't in what feels like an eternity.

I forget for a moment where I am and who I'm with and the circumstances that have brought me here and just soak in the sound of birds chirping in the late afternoon, the warmth of the sun and the cool breeze, the feeling of being warm again after the bone-deep chill of Viktor's safe house and the mountain chalet.

"You look happy, *petit*," Alexandre observes. "Very different than a moment ago. What happened back there?"

"Nothing," I mumble, feeling abruptly pulled out of my happy moment and slightly resentful of it and him. "I just had a flashback, that's all. It happens sometimes."

Monsieur Egorov warned me about this. These...fits.

Alexandre stops on the cobblestone street, reaching to slide his fingers under my chin so that I'm forced to face him. "You need to learn to control it, *petit*. It's embarrassing, such—emotion."

You try going through the shit I've had to deal with and not having "fits." I want to snap it at him, to lash out, but I don't. Something in his expression tells me that he would be even less tolerant of a public scene, and so I keep my mouth clamped tightly shut. I just nod, and he reaches up, stroking my hair as we start to walk again.

"That's my good girl," he says, but I don't feel the same flush of pleasure that I'd felt earlier when he'd complimented my cleaning, and the afternoon feels as if it's fallen flat. I'm reminded all over again that he owns me, that if my panic attacks and emotional outbursts upset him, I'll have to find a way to force myself to control it, no matter what.

We walk slowly, Alexandre clearly still mindful of my feet, and I'm grateful for it because they hurt, though I don't let on. The cushion in the flats helps somewhat, but I haven't spent this much time on my feet since I'd recovered enough to begin walking and physical therapy. I'd stayed in the wheelchair whenever possible, too depressed to even try, and now I'm paying for it.

"How are your feet, *petit*?" Alexandre asks suddenly, as if reading my mind. I pause, glancing over at him as I wonder how honest I should answer.

"They're alright," I finally say hesitantly. "A little sore. I haven't been on them this much in a while. But I feel better, overall, than I have in a while." It's true, even despite my outburst and Alexandre's reaction.

"It's Paris," Alexandre says with a grin. "The good sleep and fresh air does wonders for a person. It's not as good as the countryside, of course, but even here can heal a great many wounds."

A great many wounds. I go quiet for a moment, and Alexandre notices it.

"I think you have a great many, *petit poupée*," he says softly. "But that doesn't mean that you can't still have a good and happy life if you try."

And how does you owning me figure into that? I want to ask, but I don't. I remember his irritation with my emotions earlier, and I don't want to spoil his pleasant attitude now.

Even with the earlier blow to my mood bringing me down slightly, it's still pleasant to walk through the farmer's market, Alexandre guiding me as he stops at stall after stall, purchasing items and slipping them into the fabric bag he gave me to carry. He buys fresh eggs and an array of vegetables, fruit and cheese, and a baguette as long as my arm that smells so freshly of yeast and dough that I could cry.

I'd thought, at Alexei's, that there was a chance I'd never experience anything like this again—walking through a city, breathing in good smells, feeling something closer to happiness than I've felt in a long time. Even before Alexei, when Franco destroyed my feet, I'd wondered if I'd ever feel even a flicker of something to bring me happiness again.

When I'd met Liam, when his eyes met mine, and he'd kissed my hand, it had been the first real time I'd felt it since Franco kidnapped me.

That afternoon in the garden had been the second.

The memory gives me a flush of pleasure, my skin heating as I remember how he'd looked at me, his eyes lighting up with interest and—attraction? I hadn't dared to think that someone like him could really have been attracted to me, not this version of me, but what I'd seen in his face had said something different.

I push the thoughts away as we leave the farmer's market. It feels wrong to think about Liam while out with Alexandre, as if I'm betraying one or the other, and I'm not sure which it is. I barely know either man, and one of them owns me. The other I know it does no good to think about. He's half a world away from me now, and I'm sure he's given up. He's back in Boston, and if he thinks of me at all, it's certainly not with anything but pity.

That last stings, making my chest ache. *Pity* isn't what I would have wanted from him. But thinking about anything else is ridiculous. Just foolish hope that will only hurt me more in the end.

Alexandre leads me to a small street-side café, and when we stop at one of the tables, I realize with a start that there's a woman already sitting there. She looks quintessentially French, tall and model-thin with dark hair cut in a stylish bob and large sunglasses, wearing skinny jeans and a striped t-shirt with perfectly applied red lipstick, some of which is on the end of the cigarette she's lazily smoking. There's a small cup of coffee and a pastry in front of her, and it takes a moment for her to see us.

The moment she does, I can see the difference in her body language as she stands up, going from relaxed and careless to attentive. "Alexandre!" she cries out in a thick French accent, her voice caressing the syllables of his name as tenderly as a lover. *"Mon cher,* I'm so glad you came! I was afraid you might cancel on me."

"On you, Yvette? Never." He smiles, but it's tighter than the smile on her face, more reserved. He reaches for her, though, pulling her into an embrace. As she kisses him on each cheek, lingering a bit longer than strictly necessary, I feel a strange flash of jealousy.

I'd felt pretty in the silk dress he'd put me in, with my hair loose, even with my face pink and eyes slightly swollen from crying. But now, next to this elegant woman, I feel young and frumpy, out of place. She looks like the very picture of French beauty, cool and classic, effortlessly put together. There was a time when I might have felt that way about myself, usually when I was in my ballerina costume, ready to go on stage. But I haven't felt that way in a very long time, and next to Yvette, I feel even worse.

"You've canceled on me more than once," she says, wagging her finger teasingly. "But it's a beautiful day, and you're here, so let us enjoy it, *oui*? I have coffee already; I'll have the waiter bring more."

Alexandre pulls out a chair for me, and it's only then that Yvette seems to notice my presence. Her nose wrinkles slightly as she looks me up and down.

"Is this your pet?" she asks lightly, smirking. "I didn't know you'd acquired a new one, Alexandre."

A new one. Something about that cuts deep, the fears I'd had before rising up again. I think of the women's clothing mysteriously in his apartment, the way he'd been so effortlessly prepared to have me there, and I feel the knotting anxiety in my stomach again. *If there have been others, where are they now?*

Maybe she just means an actual pet, like a dog or a cat. It would be dehumanizing, but it's a less terrifying option than the thought that I'm just another one in a line of girls in Alexandre's possession, none of whom are there now.

Alexandre narrows his eyes at her, and Yvette gives a delicate huff, taking her own seat as Alexandre and I both sit down. "I didn't mean any harm," she insists, glancing back at me. "She's a pretty little thing. I think you ought to have a collar and leash on her, so she doesn't get away. Out here like this, she could run off at any second." She takes a drag on her cigarette, puffing the smoke out as she taps it with one long, manicured fingernail.

"She won't run away," Alexandre says it with such absolute certainty that it startles me, as if he's thought about this on his own time and decided that my running away wasn't something he needed to worry about.

Truthfully it's not, though. I've already gone over it in my own head—I don't speak much of the language, I have no money and no way to contact anyone. Trying to run would only either get me kidnapped by someone much worse or serve to piss Alexandre off, ending my time of comfort and relative ease at his home.

I have no doubt that he could make things much worse for me if he wanted to. And Yvette's words make me shiver. *A collar and leash.* If there were other girls, did he treat them like that? Is that my future if I disobey him? Just the thought makes me want to claw at my neck, my throat tightening as if there were already something around it.

Alexandre and Yvette are talking about something else, and I try to focus, blinking rapidly as I shove down the mounting panic. I know Alexandre won't appreciate it if I have another spiral out here in public and in front of his friend. But I quickly realize that they're speaking in French so rapidly that it would be impossible for me to follow even if I understood more of it. It makes me feel small and invisible, as unimportant as a lap dog brought along to the café.

Just breathe. Don't think about it.

"Come back to the apartment for dinner," Alexandre offers, this time in English, and my heart skips a beat in my chest.

No, I want to say, that flush of jealousy rising up again. I picture Alexandre cooking dinner for Yvette in the kitchen that I cleaned, and I grit my teeth, my blood heating. I have no right to feel jealous—it doesn't even make any sense. But I can feel the shift in the air when she's near, the way he acts differently, the way she's so attentive to him. I don't know if they're lovers, but there's something there, and it makes me feel a way that I know I have no right to.

A way that I shouldn't even feel towards a man who purchased me, who owns me like property.

"I like the sound of that," Yvette says, smiling sweetly as she blows out another puff of cigarette smoke. "You always were such a good cook, Alexandre. I'd love to. Shall we start walking back now?"

"We haven't had coffee yet." Alexandre waves to a passing waiter. "Two cappuccinos, please, and whatever fresh pastry you have."

I'm surprised by the order. I hadn't thought he would get anything for me—in fact, I wasn't entirely sure that he remembered I was still there at all. I see Yvette narrow her eyes, and I feel a small burst of pleasure at her irritation, as well as the fact that Alexandre thought to order for me.

My emotions feel like they're on a roller coaster, one that I don't entirely understand. The doctor I'd been seeing in Manhattan had suggested antidepressants, which I hadn't taken for more than a day, and which I certainly can't access now. The fact that I'd hallucinated the jewelry box earlier in the throes of a panic attack has left me feeling shaky and off-kilter, and now Yvette is making me feel even worse. Somewhere in the past couple of days, I realize, I'd started thinking of Alexandre as *mine*. My captor, my owner—but still mine. And now I'm seeing the life he has outside of his possession of me and the confines of the apartment, and it's affecting me in ways that make me feel just this side of insane.

Maybe Alexei was right when he said I was too broken. Maybe I'm worse off than I'd thought I was.

The waiter delivers the cappuccinos, a chocolate croissant between them on a small china plate, the flaky pastry glistening in the sunlight. I reach for it without thinking, and Alexandre raps me smartly on the back of my hand like he's punishing an errant puppy.

"Bad girl," he says sharply. "Don't reach for things until I tell you you can have them."

"She needs training," Yvette observes lazily, puffing out more smoke. "You're getting lax, Alexandre."

"This one is different," he says sharply, tearing off a piece of the croissant and holding it out to me.

It takes me a moment to realize he wants me to eat it from his fingers. He wants to feed me, and in the apartment, I might not have minded, but out here, it's different. There are people walking past, and I can feel Yvette's eyes on me, watching. It makes me feel embarrassed, my cheeks flushing hotly red, and I look at Alexandre plaintively, hoping he'll understand without my saying that I don't want to.

"*Petit.*" He says the word warningly, and my heart skips in my chest. *I'm going to make him mad*, I realize, and the panic starts to rise up again thickly, making my breath come short until I'm not sure I can eat at all.

Yvette's nails tap against the table, and I feel a shudder run down my spine.

Obediently, I open my mouth, leaning forward so that Alexandre can feed me the bite of croissant. His fingers brush my lips, the most intimate touch so far, and a shiver runs over my skin, making it prickle with—anticipation? Fear? I don't know which, but as the flavors of butter and chocolate burst over my tongue, I feel as if I could cry with the convoluted mess of emotions rising up inside of me, pleasure and fear and need and uncertainty, made so much worse by Yvette's eyes lingering on us both, watching, *judging*.

"Good girl," Alexandre murmurs, the tips of his fingers brushing the edge of my lower lip. I feel the sensation of it all the way down, tingling between my legs as his blue eyes fix on mine, holding my gaze as I swallow hard, the croissant sticking in my throat as I do.

Yvette clears her throat. "Don't let the coffee get cold," she says, her tone sounding as if her teeth are set on edge.

I cast a sideways glance at her, part of me wanting to rebel against Alexandre's treatment of me and another part enjoying it sheerly because it seems to be annoying her. I fold my hands in my lap, waiting for Alexandre to tell me I can touch the coffee, and he smiles indulgently at me.

"Yvette is right, *poupée*. Go ahead and enjoy your coffee before it gets cold."

I take a sip, forcing myself not to make a face. It's stronger than any coffee I've ever drunk before—and I haven't had coffee often. I've never been able to stomach black coffee, and flavored coffees and lattes weren't exactly in a ballerina's diet. Alexandre is clearly enjoying his, sipping delicately at it as he and Yvette begin to converse in French again.

I drink the coffee slowly, a dozen thoughts swirling around in my brain until Alexandre and Yvette stand up suddenly, the rest of the pastry forgotten as he motions for me to get up as well. My stomach rumbles as I look at it longingly. Still, I get up too, feeling like nothing so much as a dog called to heel as I start to follow Alexandre and Yvette back to the apartment.

The earlier feeling of lightness is gone, replaced with a deep-seated anxiety about this new woman, who is coming back to have dinner with us. My feet feel tight and painful, my chest equally as much so. I don't say a word as we go up to the apartment, feeling wound tighter and tighter by the moment as we step inside.

Before Alexandre can say anything to me, I turn to go down the hall to my room, only to hear his voice cut through the air behind me, sharp and commanding.

"*Anastasia.*"

I freeze in place, my heart leaping into my throat.

"Yvette, wait for me in the kitchen." Alexandre's accent thickens, his voice wrapping around me like the edge of a knife, smooth and sharp.

She makes an irritated noise, but I hear her disappearing, a moment before I feel the heat of Alexandre's body behind me, his hand gripping my arm tightly as he spins me so that my back is against the wall.

"You are not to disrespect me in front of Yvette." His voice is low and dark, wrapping around me like smoke—smoke that could choke me, hold me down, kill me. My heart is racing in my chest, leaping into my throat as his hands grip both of my arms, holding me against the wall as he looks down at me with those piercing, angry blue eyes.

"Who is she?" I whisper. "Who is she to you?"

Alexandre's mouth tightens, a muscle in his jaw leaping. "A friend," he says shortly. "But you have no right to ask me questions like that."

Inexplicably, I feel tears spring to my eyes. "I'm sorry," I whisper. "I—"

He lets go of one of my arms, his hand reaching up to stroke my jaw. "Shh, *petit*," he murmurs. "You must remember your place here, or I will start to think I've been too gentle with you."

I can feel myself starting to tremble, but at the same time, I'm suddenly, intensely aware of how close he is, of the lithe, muscled lines of his body looming over mine, the tension of his hand on my arm. He could take anything he wanted from me right now, force anything he desired, and a part of me suddenly wants him to. *Get it over with, so I can stop dreading when it will happen,* I think, but it's not that, not exactly.

I shouldn't want a man like him. But there's something in him that calls to something in me. Maybe it's just that he's been kinder to me than almost anyone else has in a long time, but a part of me doesn't want him to stop touching me—doesn't want him to step away.

But of course, he does.

"Come into the living room," he says sternly. "And mind your manners. I know your feet hurt, and you should rest, but Yvette will have you kneeling on the floor instead of sitting on the couch if you don't."

Who is this woman who can make decisions like that in his house? I want to say it aloud, but I know better than that now. He said she was a friend, but I feel as if she's more than that.

The thought sends another burst of jealousy through me, hot and bitter, and though I know I shouldn't feel it, I can't help myself.

I follow Alexandre mutely out to the living room, taking a seat on the couch where he motions for me to sit. "I'll be in the kitchen with Yvette," he says. "Stay here."

I feel like a dog ordered to stay, but I have a sinking feeling that's what I'm meant to feel. Yvette had called me a pet, and something tells me that she hadn't been joking when she'd suggested the collar and leash.

Just the thought makes my skin crawl with a claustrophobic sort of panic all over again.

Mind your manners.

A part of me instantly, hotly rebels against that. There was a time, wasn't there, when I would never have let a man speak to me like that? *Wasn't there?* It feels so long ago that I can't really recall it. Everything before Franco had come and snatched me from my new apartment, the one I'd leased after Sofia had moved out of the apartment we'd lived in together, feels like a life that belonged to another person. When I try to think of that girl, I feel like she died. Like her body is somewhere in the warehouse where Franco had chained me to the ceiling, like she'd suffocated in the smells of burning flesh and tears.

All I can hear in my head anymore are the voices of the men who have hurt me. *If you don't talk, little girl, I'll make sure you never walk again. Forget dancing. You'll never even stand up.*

Maybe I could find the kind of man who likes girls who can't run away to buy you. But you're too damaged for anything else.

What are these fits? Mind your manners.

Mind your manners.

Mind your manners.

I squeeze my eyes tightly shut, balling my hands into fists so that I don't panic again. I try to ground myself, to feel the smooth, cool leather of the sofa under my palms, the soft cushion of my shoes against my scarred soles, the brush of the silk dress against my skin. I smell something like frying onions and butter and garlic, and I breathe it in, reminding myself where I am. I'm still someone's captive, but I'm no longer in the warehouse with Franco or in the mountain chalet with Alexei. I'm not being tortured or beaten. Alexandre is strange and mercurial, and Yvette seems kind of like a bitch, but no one has hurt me yet.

It feels odd to just sit in the living room with nothing to do. It does make me feel like a pet, or a doll, left to sit quietly while the people who matter talk and spend time together in another room. I can hear hints of their voices floating from the kitchen, speaking in rapid, fluent French that I couldn't begin to hope to follow.

I don't like being left alone with my thoughts anymore. It's all I can do to keep them at bay, to keep them from crowding into my head so that I want to scream, and I know that will only make Alexandre angry.

It feels like an eternity before he comes to get me. "Dinner is ready," he says, motioning for me to follow him into the dining room. I get up slowly, dreading a meal sitting at the table with Yvette, but knowing I don't have any choice.

It smells delicious, and my stomach growls as soon as I step inside. I haven't had anything other than the coffee and bite of croissant since breakfast this morning, and my mouth waters as I see the platter in the center of the table with quartered lamb chops, a bowl of roasted carrots and another of fresh green beans, and another plate with the baguette sliced and toasted, glistening with butter. Yvette is seated on one side of the table, and her eyes widen as Alexandre pulls out a chair for me.

"What are you doing?" she asks, her eyebrows shooting up nearly into her hairline. "She's not going to sit at the table, surely?"

"Yvette—" Alexandre's voice takes on a warning tone, but Yvette is already shaking her head, her eyes narrowing.

"You'll spoil the girl, Alexandre. She'll think she can get away with anything. You need to teach her her place early."

My place? I hover near the chair that Alexandre is still gripping, my stomach twisting into anxious knots. *What is she talking about?*

"I don't think that's necessary—"

"What's different about her?" Yvette shakes her head. "Pets eat on the floor, Alexandre. You know better. She can't be allowed to eat at the table with us. She'll get all sorts of ideas in her head. She's your possession, not part of the family." She stands up, reaching for a plate and beginning to spoon food onto it—a small portion of carrots, slices of lamb, another of green beans. She holds it out to Alexandre, who stares at it for a long moment and then lets out a breath.

"Alexandre—"

"Alright." He rubs a hand over his mouth, taking the plate. "Here, *petit*. Next to me."

I watch in mute horror as he sets the plate on the floor, next to his chair. It dawns on me that he really expects this—worse still, that it's Yvette pushing him. He would have let me sit at the table if it were just the two of us, but she's insisting that he treat me like a dog. And from the way she's talking, this isn't the first time this has occurred.

Some other girl has knelt on the floor and eaten from a plate next to him while—what? While he sat here and spoke French with Yvette, barely paying attention to her? The thought makes me sick, and I don't know how I'm going to eat.

I don't want to do this.

"Anastasia." Alexandre's voice takes on that stern note again, and I feel my chin start to tremble.

I can't refuse. I can feel Yvette's eyes on me, waiting to see what I'll do. Slowly, feeling tears start to gather in my eyes, I sink down to my knees on the rug, swallowing hard.

"Good girl." Alexandre sinks into his own chair, stroking my hair. "That's very good, *petit*. See?" he says, turning to Yvette. "She's very well-mannered, especially considering what she's been through."

"They've all been through something," Yvette says, waving her hand. "I'll never understand your affinity for damaged things, Alexandre. This entire apartment is filled with junk, and for what?"

"There's a reason you don't understand," Alexandre says quietly, cutting his food and raising a bite to his lips.

"What is that supposed to mean?"

"Just that," Alexandre says, and then they switch back to French, spoken too quickly for me to follow.

I look down at my own plate, my stomach churning. Alexandre hasn't given me any utensils, and something in me rebels at eating with my fingers. I stare down at it for a long time until Alexandre catches me kneeling there with the plate still untouched.

"Eat, Anastasia," he says sternly. "Don't disobey me again."

My throat feels so tight that I don't know how I'll swallow a single bite. Still, I force myself to pick up a carrot, biting into it as Alexandre returns his attention to his own meal. The food is delicious, all of it fresher than anything I've ever tasted and cooked to perfection, but it's hard to enjoy any of it. Yvette's eyes periodically flick to me, and I can see something in them that I don't entirely understand—some animosity that almost looks like jealousy.

I don't understand why she would be jealous of *me*. But it also becomes clear as the meal goes on that her relationship with Alexandre is perhaps not what she wishes it would be. I can see the way her eyes rarely leave him, the way she leans forward eagerly when talking to him, the way her hand rests on his forearm occasionally as she speaks rapidly in French.

He doesn't touch her. He looks at her intently, occasionally, particularly when she makes some point that sounds emphatic from her tone—though I can't understand the words—but he doesn't look at her in the same way that she does him. And slowly, looking up at the two of them as I pick at my food and watch them have their meal while barely paying attention to me, I think I begin to understand their relationship a little more.

I somehow manage to clear my plate, and Alexandre strokes my hair as he picks it up with the rest of the dishes. "Good girl," he says again, and I feel a small, strange flush of pleasure. It feels dehumanizing to be here on the floor, my plate picked up like an empty dog bowl, but at the same time, his praise feels good. I squirm where I'm kneeling on the rug, feeling the tingling spread through me as his fingers run through my hair, down to the base of my neck, where they linger for a moment before he stands up.

I want to stand up—my legs are starting to feel numb, and my feet are aching from my weight being on my knees and calves and heels, but I don't move. I can see Yvette's appraising eyes on me, and something in me wants to please Alexandre, to be a good girl for him. To have him fight for me, whatever Yvette tries next. *If I'm good, maybe he will. Maybe he'll pick me over her.*

It feels almost as if I've been split into two different people, the lingering hints of the girl I used to be who wants to fight against thoughts like that, and the person that I am now, someone so starved for love and affection that a pat on the head and simple praise for obedience that I shouldn't have to give in the first place feels like a gift, like something I should be grateful for.

It doesn't help that Alexandre is so physically attractive, a genuinely beautiful man—the kind of man I would once have been attracted to, when I still thought about things like dating and sex for my own pleasure.

Alexandre returns a few moments later with a platter of cheese, honey, fruit, and toasted slices of the baguette, as well as a silver French press filled with coffee and two china cups. He doesn't look at me as he sits down, as if he'd assumed that I'd still be there sitting quietly, and something rankles inside of me at that. I want him to *appreciate* that I'm being good, that I'm still kneeling here when it seems frankly ridiculous that I should be required to at all.

His conversation with Yvette picks up seamlessly again in French, and I sit there struggling between the urge to cry and the urge to kneel in perfect silence, so that maybe Alexandre will reward me in some way later. I don't even know what that might be or what I might want, only that I've begun to crave the brief burst of happiness that I get from his pleasure.

A moment later, Alexandre reaches down, and I realize that there's a piece of cheese in his fingers, a sliver of something that looks fancier than any cheese I've ever eaten. There was a ballerina showcase at Juilliard once with a buffet that had cheeses like that on it, entire boards of them, but I wouldn't have dared take even a bite. Our teachers had watched us like hawks to make certain that none of us did.

My mouth waters as Alexandre holds it out to me, feeding it to me like a treat as I lean forward and take it out of his fingers. It feels less intimate than earlier when he'd fed me the bite of croissant, but even now, he lingers, his fingertips brushing over my lower lip as I eat the piece of cheese.

He keeps talking to Yvette the entire time, but I can feel her eyes on me as he feeds me—bits of cheese, little pieces of strawberry with honey on them. If it weren't for Yvette sitting there and the way I'm kneeling by his chair, it would almost feel romantic, the brush of my tongue against his skin as I take each small bit of food, the way his fingertips linger on my mouth. Gradually, bite by bite, I can feel my heartbeat starting to speed up, my breathing quickening as I feel that tingling spreading over my skin, like that night in the bath. It spreads over me, concentrating between my thighs, making me quiver and pulse as I swallow hard, trying not to let on how it's making me feel, especially not with Yvette's keen eyes on me.

It feels like the meal goes on forever, until I'm nearly squirming on the rug, fidgeting as Alexandre feeds me those small bites while he carries on his conversation with Yvette. At long last, he stands up, collecting the platter and coffee cups, and I kneel there trembling, hoping that she won't notice me.

But of course, she does.

"Stand up, pet," Yvette says in her smooth, richly accented voice. She crosses to the window on the other side of the table, opening it halfway so that the evening breeze and scent of flowers from the apartment terrace can come drifting in as her cigarette smoke drifts out. She leans against the low paneled wall as she looks down at me. "Hurry up, little one."

I can't "hurry up." My legs are half-asleep from kneeling so long, my feet aching from the long day, and I nearly stumble as I get up, pitching forward and catching myself on the back of one of the chairs.

"Hmph." Yvette snorts, one eyebrow rising as she looks me over. "Clumsy. Alexandre said you used to be a ballerina. You must not have been much of one."

That stings so deeply that I can't bite my tongue the way I know I should. "I was injured," I say defensively, still trying not to put all my weight on my feet. "I was very good, once upon a time."

"But not now." Yvette clicks her tongue. "Alexandre paid too much for you, but then again, he always has had a weak spot when it comes to pretty broken things like you. Turn around?"

I try to do as she says, even as I wobble on my feet, the pain shooting up my calves. Yvette makes another sound deep in her throat as I turn to face her again, slightly pale as she straightens, coming closer to me.

She takes another puff of her cigarette, red lipstick clinging to the end of it as her full lips purse around it, her fingers trailing through my hair. "You're pretty enough, I suppose," she says grudgingly. "A beautiful face." Her hand drops to the tie of the silk wrap dress, and my chest tightens with the knowledge of what she's about to do the second before she actually does.

But it's not as if I can stop her.

She pulls it loose with one quick motion, letting the dress fall open and pushing it aside so that she can see me, naked underneath except for the panties I'm wearing. "Hmm," Yvette murmurs, and I see the flicker of jealousy in her eyes again as they flick from my small breasts down to my concave belly and slim thighs. "A bit waifish, but I suppose all ballerinas are." She smiles tightly, but there's no humor to it. "Has he fucked you?"

I blink at her, startled. "No!" I gasp, and Yvette laughs.

"Well, there's that, I suppose." She leans closer, one long nail pressing into my stiff nipple. "You'd like him to, wouldn't you?" Her warm breath puffs against my ear, and I shiver, eliciting another sharp laugh from her.

"He's very handsome, isn't he? A girl like you should feel lucky to be owned by a man like him. He praised you so effusively at dinner tonight, but I think you're a very bad little girl." Yvette's nails press harder into my breast, enough that I think there will be a mark left behind as she scratches them downwards, over my ribs, and down my belly. "You should have been on your knees by the table before he had to tell you, like a good little pet. You wouldn't get away with such disobedience if you were mine."

Thank god I'm not then, I want to hiss, but I don't. It's taking everything in me to be still, not to let Yvette see how afraid of her I am. She makes me feel the way Alexei did, as if there were no telling what he might do next, as if I couldn't possibly comprehend what twist his psychotic brain would take.

She's in love with Alexandre. I don't know where the thought comes from, but it seems obvious once it springs into my mind. She wants him, not to be his pet the way I am, but she's jealous of the attention he gives me, especially because it's apparently different than the—others? The mysterious other girls who must have been here, and who I have no idea where they went. The thought makes me want to scream, but I hold myself perfectly still, my heart fluttering in my chest like a trapped bird.

"You want him to, don't you?" Yvette murmurs next to my ear. "To fuck you, I mean. I saw you in the hallway with him, the way you looked at him. I saw the way you reacted when he fed you at the café and just now, at dinner. I'm very perceptive, you know." Her nails scratch lower, down below my navel, and I shudder.

"If I touch you down there, I imagine I'll find that you're wet. Little whore. Alexandre thinks you're this sweet broken thing, but I know better. You're a little slut, like all the strays he brings home. But I'm not going to let you get the better of him this time."

Her fingers drag lower, pressing against my most intimate flesh through the cotton of my panties. It's not exactly sexual, just as Alexandre's touches haven't been, but hers isn't gentle. It feels like an examination, and I squeeze my eyes tightly because I know what she can feel.

I am wet, throbbing still from the sensations that Alexandre's fingertips on my mouth sent shivering over my skin, and I know she can feel it. I know from the way she laughs, deep and throaty, her fingers rubbing over where I'm aching the most, the damp patch on my underwear spreading.

She snatches her hand away, shaking it as if there's something filthy on her fingers, leaning back against the chair. "Little slut. Why don't you take care of it right now, while I watch, if you're so wet for him?" She nods towards the apex of my thighs, squeezed tightly together now. "Go on, touch yourself."

"Stop it."

Alexandre's voice comes from the doorway, sending a rush of relief through me so intense that I close my eyes, feeling almost dizzy from it. He steps into the room, his eyes narrowed and angry.

"She's mine, Yvette. Stop tormenting her."

Mine. The word should frighten me, but it doesn't. It feels safe. Protective. Like he won't let anyone, even this awful woman that he seems to like so well, hurt me.

"She could be a fun plaything," Yvette says with a tight smile. "We could both play with her, Alexandre. Imagine what she would do with a little—*urging* from me." She nods towards my trembling half-naked body. "She wants it already."

"No." Alexandre's voice is sharp as a knife, cutting through the air. "She's not yours to play with, Yvette. She's mine." His gaze whips towards me, and I shudder at the look in his eyes.

"Go to your room, Anastasia."

I don't make him ask twice. I hear him starting to speak to Yvette in French, quick and angry, but I don't bother even trying to parse it out. I grab my dress in my fist, clutching the fabric over my breasts, and despite the pain in my feet, I flee.

I don't stop until I'm in my room, just as he said, the door securely closed behind me.

And then I sink to the floor, my heart pounding as I start to cry.

LIAM

Our first stop is Russia, to meet with Levin's old boss. It's hardly a place I was eager to return to, and I feel a cold knot of dread in my stomach as we disembark from the plane, tension rippling through me. From the expression on Max's face, he feels similarly.

A driver is waiting for us, and I glance at Levin. "We're going to leave this place all in one piece, correct?"

Levin smirks, opening the door. "We'll all be fine. My old boss has a special arrangement with Viktor now. You'll be in no danger, I promise you."

I'd never thought of Levin as anything but Viktor's guard dog, his main enforcer and right-hand man, but as we approach the fortified mansion where we're meeting with his former boss, I begin to see him in a new light.

Max and I follow as we get out of the car; Levin strides towards the iron gates, his expression tense as we approach the armed men ten deep at the front gates alone. *"Smert elo milost,"* he growls to the man at the very front, a tall and muscle-bound guard all in black with a flak vest and a semi-automatic weapon in his hands.

"Vladimir is expecting you," the man replies, and the gates swing open.

Fuck. As we walk down the stone path towards the looming front doors, across the expansive green lawn—more green than I've seen anywhere else in Moscow thus far—I feel my skin prickle. The entire place is crawling with armed men, more even than I'd ever seen in Viktor's security.

"How many enemies can a man have to need an army in his front yard?" I hiss to Levin, who smirks.

"Vladimir does not have enemies," he says, nodding to the men guarding the front door as it opens. "He has men who do not yet know they are dead."

Well, fuck me. I glance over at Max, expecting a similar reaction on his face, but it's as hard and tense as I've ever seen it. Every line of his body tells me that he's not pleased to be here, and it makes me wonder how much of his story I still don't know. After all, I don't know him well, only that he's a former priest under Viktor's protection.

The foyer is black and white tile in a diamond checkerboard pattern, leading to a mahogany staircase that goes up to the second floor. There are more guards scattered upstairs, patrolling. It makes me feel skittish and on edge as Levin leads us upstairs, turning to the right as if he's been here a hundred times before, and down to a set of double doors overlooking the lower floor.

Of course, he has. He used to work for this man.

Here, away from Viktor, Levin seems different—more commanding. His blue eyes are flinty as he raps on the double doors, repeating the same Russian phrase he had at the front gates. His voice is rougher and more thickly accented than usual.

"*Smert elo milost.*"

I narrow my eyes as the doors open, looking curiously at Levin. "What does that mean?"

He glances over at me, his face expressionless. "Death is a mercy."

I think of our own words, the phrase spoken by the leading King. *I do not demand that you kneel, but I ask that you bow.* "And I thought our words were dark," I mutter as we follow Levin inside, the doors closing behind us with a heavy finality that makes my skin crawl.

This entire place feels like a monument to death and torture, and it makes me feel faintly sick. I've never been fond of the more brutal side of the life I was born into. I've never been a man like Luca or Viktor, who torture with ease when need be. I'd never ripped out a man's fingernail or cut off a piece of him until the night I helped them torture Alexei, and for all that, I don't regret my part in ending that man; I still wake in a cold sweat from dreams of it some nights.

Bleeding a man like that was a new experience for me, one that I'm in no hurry to repeat. I don't quite know what it was that came over me that night, beyond a sheer and palpable rage that he'd sold Ana before I could save her, that he'd consigned her to a fate that I might never be able to rescue her from. I'd helped torture him as much out of anger at myself as rage directed towards him, and I can't ever forget what we did that night. Every time I look at Max, I still hear his words echoing as he'd started to cut at the man's hand.

Aren't you afraid of your God?

I would, if I thought God was in this room.

I glance sideways at Max, wondering if he still has nightmares about it too, or if he ever did. This house feels like another place where there is no God, only the brutality of man against man, for crimes both real and imagined. This is the place that will be sending men and women to Viktor and Levin soon to train, and I wonder just how much better it is than what Viktor did before.

At least they'll be there of their own choice, I hope.

There's a long desk spread with papers in the center of the tiled room, art scattered across the walls in heavy gilt frames. Behind the desk is a tall, handsome man, perhaps in his early forties, with blond hair combed back and the icy blue eyes I've become accustomed to seeing in the faces of so many of these Russian men, his broad jaw set as he looks up and sees us.

"Ah, Levin." Although he looks mildly pleased to see the other man, his expression remains stern. "I'd heard you wanted a meeting. Is this about the business with Viktor? I sent word I'd have the first group of

IRISH SAVIOR

students shipped over in the next weeks, just as soon as their papers can be arranged—"

"It's not about that, Vladimir, although Viktor was pleased to hear it."

"Hmm." The man's thick pale eyebrows twitch, and he seems to notice us for the first time. "And who are these men you've brought with you? Not future assassins, from the look of them."

"No, sir." Levin gestures, and both Max and I step forward. "This is Liam McGregor, leader of the Boston chapter of the Irish Kings, and Maximilian Agosti, a priest."

"A priest, eh? We don't get many of those under this roof. Someone in need of last rites?"

Max's face is as impassive as a stone wall, and I can't help but wonder what he's thinking. He doesn't correct Levin, likely because leaving out the *defrocked* part of the equation offers him some additional protection here, beyond what his connection to the Andreyev name gives him.

"He's with us, on business," Levin says smoothly. "I'm here to ask a favor."

"A favor." Vladimir's eyebrows draw together. "A favor from the syndicate is no small thing, Volkov."

Neither Max nor I miss the abrupt switch to Levin's surname. I can see the tension in Levin's shoulders as well, though he doesn't let on.

"I did quite a few favors for the syndicate in my day," Levin says quietly. "I need a name, if it can be found."

"A name can be worth more than a life here." Vladimir frowns. "You were a valued asset to us, Volkov. I can't say I'm inclined to pass on information without a price attached to it, though."

Levin's face remains impassive as he reaches into his pocket. Every armed man in the room moves at once, all of their attention and weaponry aimed towards him, but Levin just smirks as Vladimir raises a hand.

"If I wanted your boss dead, he would be," Levin says coolly as he extracts his hand from his pocket. "One of the reasons I was allowed to leave is because he knew better than to try to have me killed. But that's not what I'm here for."

With one smooth motion, he flips something into the air above Vladimir's desk. It takes a moment before I realize as it falls that it's a coin—a heavy one, from the solid *thud* that it makes as it hits the wooden surface.

"A name," Levin says, his voice as hard as the coin sitting face up in front of Vladimir.

The blond man stares at him for a moment, as if he can't quite believe what Levin's done. The room goes very silent, so much so that even the slight ruffling of the papers sounds loud as Levin and Vladimir stare each other down.

I'm not sure what Levin's done, but it's clear that the coin carries some significance. At long last, Vladimir reaches for the coin, holding it up. I can see a woman's face etched into the side of it and letters spelling out something in Russian—likely, I would imagine, the same phrase that Levin used to access the mansion.

"You're sure this is what you want to use this on, *syn?*" Vladimir narrows his eyes. "Once done, it cannot be undone."

"A woman's life is at stake," Levin says, his voice gravelly. "I'm sure."

Vladimir turns the coin over in his fingers, considering. Another beat passes, the air thickening with tension, and then he drops his hand, abruptly pocketing the coin.

"Tell me who you're looking for," he says calmly, as if the entire odd exchange between him and Levin never happened.

* * *

W<small>E LEAVE</small> the mansion with a name—Adrian Drakos, a Greek assassin trained by the syndicate who apparently makes it his mission in his free time to hunt down the types of men who buy and sell women. While Vladimir himself had no knowledge of a Frenchman who would spend a hundred million dollars on a damaged woman—and he'd looked slightly green around the edges at the idea—he'd assured us that if anyone could point us in the right direction, it would be Drakos.

Which means we're headed to Greece next.

As we leave the mansion, I feel torn, heading back to the car and the hotel Viktor arranged for us. On the one hand, Levin seems to think it's a solid lead, worth whatever he handed over to Vladimir for it. On the other—I doubt Ana is in Greece, which means this is yet another pitstop on the way to really finding her, and more time that she's in the hands of the Frenchman that bought her.

More time that anything could be happening to her. The possibilities are endless, and I don't dare imagine them, or I'll go insane.

The hotel that Viktor arranged for us is an unsurprisingly lavish, five-star hotel in downtown Moscow. The three of us head directly for the bar. It's full of leather booths and mahogany tables with dim lighting and the smoky scent of whiskey filling the air, which makes it feel remarkably homey for being in the middle of Moscow. We find a booth towards the back, where there aren't many guests and Levin motions for a waiter as we settle in.

"Jameson on the rocks, a double shot," I tell the crisply dressed man who comes over to our table.

"Vodka, whatever you've got." Levin glances at Max. "And you?"

"I'll take an old-fashioned, a double as well." Max leans back in the booth. "I need a stiff drink after that experience."

"What was that back there?" I narrow my eyes at Levin. "Between you and Vladimir. The coin? What the fuck happened?"

Levin sighs, waiting until our drinks are in front of us to respond. "I used to work for the syndicate," he says calmly, taking a sip of his vodka. "I know Vladimir well, and what would be necessary to get a name out of him. Any name."

"That doesn't really answer the question."

Levin raises an eyebrow. "I'm not sure you're owed an answer to it."

I shrug, leaning back as I take a sip of my own whiskey. "Be that as it may, you can't fault me for wanting one. Especially when you say that Vladimir's enemies are walking dead men, but that he let you leave the syndicate on account of the fact that you'd kill anyone who tried to stop you."

Levin smirks. "There are a considerable number of excellent assassins that trained under Vladimir. And then there's me."

"Pride goeth before a fall," Max mutters, tossing back a slug of his old-fashioned.

"Who brought the priest?" Levin cuts a sideways glance at him. "That's a fancy drink to shoot back like that."

"Fuck me for not drinking straight rubbing alcohol." Max gives him back the same glare. "Liam wanted someone to say last rites over his dead body, I assume, when he gets himself killed going after Anastasia."

"You've got a filthy mouth for a priest."

"Enough, both of you." I shoot the rest of my whiskey in one gulp, motioning for the waiter to bring me another. "Are you going to answer me or not, Levin? The fuck was that coin?"

Levin sighs, tossing back the rest of his own drink and motioning for a refill as well. "It was a favor," he says, when the waiter walks away. "When I left, in consideration of my service to the syndicate, Vladimir gave me that coin. It was understood that if I were ever in need of a favor, I could trade the coin for it."

I stare at him for a long moment. "Anything?"

"Anything," Levin confirms. "Up to and including the life of anyone I might wish to take, no matter who they were. That coin was worth a great deal."

"And you traded it for a name?" Max sets his drink down, looking narrowly at Levin. "This Greek assassin?"

"If I hadn't," Levin says evenly, "Vladimir would have had us leave empty-handed. He's not in the habit of giving leads or exposing the inner lives of those who work for him. If this Adrian Drakos moonlights as a vigilante, hunting men who traffic women, he could well lead us to the Frenchman."

"And you considered it worth that?" I take a breath, leaning back against the booth. "You only had one coin, correct?"

"Yes."

"It seems like an uneven trade," Max observes.

"I'd agree." I look at Levin, still confused. "That coin for a name."

Levin takes another deep drink of his vodka, his handsome face pensive. He bends his head for a moment, his dark hair falling forward, and I see his shoulders rise and fall, as if he's deep in thought. He looks up, at last, fixing me with his gaze, intense and blue.

"You love this woman, yes? Anastasia Ivanova?"

I stare at him, taken aback by the directness of the question. "Yes," I say finally. "I can't explain why. I don't know her that well, but—yes. I love her. And I promised that I would find her."

"I loved a woman once, too." Levin spins his glass in his fingers. "I loved her, and she loved me, for all my faults and sins. She married me, despite the danger."

"What happened to her?" Max's voice is quiet, weighed down with some grief of his own, as if he knows what Levin is recalling and is remembering his own loss.

"She died." Levin tosses back the rest of his vodka. "As did the men who killed her, slowly, once I found them. After that, I was forced to leave the syndicate and seek other employment. But Vladimir gave me the one favor." He sets his glass down, fixing me once more with that piercing stare. "If trading that coin for a name saves the woman you love, Liam McGregor, then it was not an uneven trade."

Neither Max nor I speak for a long moment, the words hanging heavily over the table. I open my mouth, still unsure of what to say, when something else catches my eye.

Three stunning women, one blonde, one brunette, and one redhead, are headed in our direction, moving gracefully through the bar on heels that must be six inches high and legs a mile long, drawing every eye in the bar as they pass. The blonde is wearing a skintight, pale pink dress that stops just above her knees, her generous cleavage straining the neckline, the brunette is dressed in a jewel green cocktail-length dress that swoops low enough to show off her rounded breasts, and the redhead is wearing a dark blue slip that glides over her petite frame in the same way that every man in the room wishes their hands could, and probably some of the women too.

It seems highly unlikely that they're coming to our table, but sure enough, they stop in front of us, all three of them looking delighted to be there.

"Hello, gentlemen," the blonde says, pursing lips painted only a few shades darker than the pale pink of her dress. I can only imagine what other lips they must match.

"Hello yourself." Levin leans back, eyeing the three women. "Are you sure you're in the right place?"

"Vladimir sent us." The brunette smiles. "This is Nadia—" she gestures to the blonde. "I'm Katerina, and this is Natalia."

"Lovely names for three lovely ladies."

"Three lovely ladies for three *handsome* men." The redhead glances at me, her green eyes sparkling. "It's not often I find another ginger around these parts. Irish?"

"Aye," I say, stifling a laugh at the resigned expression on Max's face. I glance over at Levin. "A gift from Vladimir, I'm guessing?"

"A gesture of respect, I think, for the work Viktor and I are partnering with him on. I suppose he thought it would be rude not to include the two of you as well." Levin smirks, his eyes lingering on the blonde. "One each."

I can't pretend that it's not tempting. It's been longer than usual since I've been with a woman, and I've never been the playboy type. The redhead in particular who has her eye on me is gorgeous, exactly my type, petite and small-breasted with hair cascading everywhere, thick burnished locks that any man would die to bury his hands in as he buried himself inside of her.

But I can't bring myself to do it. It's clear the three women don't object to being here—they're undressing all three of us with their eyes, obviously eager to do Vladimir's bidding, and not because of some threat. But under the current circumstances, the idea of bedding a woman who's been paid to do so feels even more distasteful to me than it might otherwise. Beyond that, I don't feel any real desire for her. I'd have to be blind not to see how beautiful she is—how sexy all three of them are—but the woman I want isn't in this room. And if it's not Ana, I can't summon any genuine lust.

I might be able to go through the motions, but I wouldn't do her justice. And I'd rather spend a cold night alone in my bed than half-heartedly sleep with a woman for the sake of it. That especially has lost its appeal for me.

"I appreciate the gift," I say with an apologetic smile. "But I'm afraid I'm going to have to decline."

Levin eyes me. "Faithful to a woman who doesn't even know you're coming for her." His gaze rests evenly on mine, appraising me. "I think I was right to believe the coin wasn't wasted."

"I'll have to politely decline as well," Max says, tilting his glass back to finish his drink. "Man of the cloth, and all of that."

"Ooh, a priest." The brunette flutters her eyelashes at him, arching her back just slightly so that her breasts are on even better display. "I have a thing or two I could confess, Father. When my mouth isn't full, that is." She winks at him, and Max's jaw tightens. It's all I can do not to laugh—it wouldn't be kind, considering the predicament he's clearly in, but it's nothing if not amusing.

"A former priest," Levin says with a smirk. "I thought you'd broken your vows, *Father*."

"I do my best to keep to the ones I haven't forsaken," Max says stiffly. "I'm going to have to pass."

"What a shame." The blonde pouts. "We rarely get men as gorgeous as you three. And all different too—Italian, Russian, *and* Irish? I'd have been happy to take all three of you myself."

Now that's a picture I don't want to imagine. "I'm sorry, ladies," I say with a reluctant smile. "But I think the priest and I will be sitting this one out."

"Ah well, I think I can take one for the team." Levin tosses back the last of his vodka, setting the glass down and turning to the three women. "Ladies? I've got a bed upstairs with room for all four of us, not to mention the jacuzzi tub—"

"Jesus, Mary, and Joseph." I rub my hand over my mouth, motioning for the waiter to bring both Max and me another drink. "He's in for a night."

"You can say that again." Max takes the drink gratefully, sliding to the center of the booth as I take another sip of my whiskey. "I'm surprised you didn't take the redhead up on her offer. She was interested. It's not as if you're bound to Ana in any way."

I shake my head. "It wasn't her interest that was the problem. It's my *lack* of interest. And besides, I've got enough complications already."

"Is that so?" Max swirls the large ice cube in his glass. "Besides trying to find a girl who was sold to a man whose name we don't even know, let alone where he might have taken her?"

"Yeah." I glance down at the amber liquid in my own glass. "I had to sign a betrothal contract before I left."

"Fuck." Max's eyes widen. "Your meeting with Father Donahue?"

"Aye." I take another sip. "With Father Donahue, Graham O'Sullivan, and Saoirse, his daughter. The woman I'm meant to marry when I return to Boston."

"But that you don't intend to."

I tilt my glass in his direction, acknowledging the statement. "Aye."

"That's a hell of a thing." Max lets out a breath, considering. "You're right that you've got enough complications. I doubt this O'Sullivan fellow will take you breaking that oath lightly."

"He won't," I confirm. "But it was either sign the contract or come back to a civil war."

Max nods, considering. "And you didn't think of sending someone else after Ana?"

"I thought of it." I take another sip, glancing out of the bar window to the darkened city beyond us. "But I couldn't. When Alexei was taking her away, I swore to her that I'd come for her. I made two promises, and I know I can't keep both of them. But damnit if I'm going to break them both, either."

"And it's the one to Ana that you want to keep the most."

I nod. "Aye. That's the crux of it." I glance at him. "And you? Are you really so attached to vows you've already broken that you'd turn down that opportunity?"

Max smirks. "I've never been short of opportunities to sleep with women. If anything, they're all the more interested when they find out

I'm a priest, fallen or otherwise. But the vow I broke wasn't the one of celibacy, and I've done my best to keep to them, even if I'm no longer fully a man of the church." He takes another sip of his drink, letting out a long breath. "Besides, if Viktor makes good on his promise to me, that may not be the case for long."

"Ah. *Your* meeting with Father Donahue."

Max nods. "Viktor agreed to use what influence he has with the priest to see if he can have me reinstated, my former sins washed away and all of that. When we return, St. Patrick's will be my first stop."

"No inclination to sample the pleasures of the flesh while you can?"

Max smiles ruefully. "The inclination is there, sure. But I've done my best to atone for the path I've walked so far, and that's a part of it. Besides," he adds, finishing his drink. "You're not the only one who pines for a woman he shouldn't have."

I start to ask who he's talking about, though I'm sure I already know. But Max is already fishing out his billfold, laying cash on the table to cover his drinks as he stands up. "Have a good night, Liam," he says kindly. "I'll see you in the morning."

I linger there for a while longer after he leaves, swirling my whiskey in my glass and looking down into the amber depths, thinking about Ana. *A woman I shouldn't have.*

Tomorrow will see us back in the air and on our way to Greece. I can only hope that it will be one step closer to her and keeping the promise I made.

I'll find you. Wherever you are.

ANA

*A*lexandre doesn't come to my room. Long after I've cried all the tears I can muster, I pick myself up off of the floor. After a while, going to the bathroom to wash my face and stripping out of the silk dress, leaving it in a heap on the floor as I go to dig through the wardrobe for fresh pajamas. I find another silk set, this one black, and slip into it, climbing into bed with my entire body aching as if I've been run over by a truck.

I've run the gamut of emotions today, from happiness to panic and back and forth again. I slip into a restless sleep, a new ache in my chest as I wonder where Alexandre is, what he's doing. Part of me knows I ought to be grateful that he's left me alone, let me dress myself, and get myself ready for bed. However, the other part of me wonders if he's still with Yvette, what they might be doing together, what he might be saying to her and she to him.

She's mine. His voice echoes in my head as I fall asleep, my mind swirling with the images of everything that's crowded in throughout the afternoon.

I'm in the warehouse again, my hands chained above me, feet swinging a foot above the ground. The strain on my shoulders is immense, but worse still is the sight of Franco's handsome face, leering at me as he yanks off my shoes, running his fingers over the arches of my feet.

"I always did have a thing for feet," he says, sweeping his fingertip over my sole, so that my toes curl. "Not dancer's feet, though. Disgusting, what those pointe shoes do to you." Then, he grins, showing gleaming white teeth as he unsheathes a hunting knife, glinting in the light with a serrated edge. "Not as disgusting as they'll look when I'm finished, though, if you don't talk."

Cutting. Slicing. Burning. The hiss of a blowtorch and the smell of butane. My own screams, long after I'd given up everything that I'd had to tell him, and he'd started in on the rest of me, beating me for no reason but his own pleasure. I'd been unconscious long before he'd left me on Luca's doorstep.

The music again, but this time I hear it as I'm dangling in the warehouse, one leg tied up behind me as Alexei and Franco circle me together, merging and splitting, laughing at me as I hear the hiss of the blowtorch again, see the glint of the blade.

Their voices, merging together, telling me to talk, Alexei mocking me, calling me damaged, broken, threatening to sell me to men who will love that I can't flee.

And over it all, Alexandre's voice in my ear.

Mind your manners.

Mind your manners.

Mind your—

"Anastasia!"

Strong, long-fingered hands grip my shoulders, shaking me awake, and my eyes pop open to see Alexandre looming over me, his face barely visible in the dim light from the window. My throat feels hoarse and dry, as if I've been screaming in my sleep, and my face is streaked with tears again.

"I'm sorry," I manage thinly as I come back to my senses, and Alexandre lets go of me, stepping back with irritation written plainly across his face.

"You woke me up," he says, rubbing his hand over his mouth. "I like my sleep undisturbed."

"I'm sorry," I whisper again. "Really, I am. It was a nightmare—"

"Do you need me to start medicating you again? If it helps you sleep, I'll go and get it now." He turns away as if to leave and go to get it, and I start to cry despite myself, a sudden cold panic gripping me at the thought of being drugged to sleep again.

"I'm sorry if I interrupted you and Yvette—"

Alexandre turns back to me sharply. "Is that what this is about? Yvette went home. She's not—" He frowns, as if my comment is confusing to him. "That's not our relationship, Ana. She doesn't go to bed with me."

For some reason, I start to cry harder, my stomach twisting in cold knots. Alexandre looks at me as if he's entirely perplexed, running a hand through his hair.

"Anastasia, what is it?"

"I—I just—" I don't know how to put what I'm feeling into words, and especially not to this man, who is so strange in so many ways. "I'm all alone. I'm so tired of being alone."

The words slip out before I can stop them, hovering in the air between us, and Alexandre steps forward, turning on the light at my bedside as he sinks down into the wing chair by the window.

"You're not alone, *petit*," he says finally, his blue eyes resting on my face with obvious confusion. "You're here, with me. How can you be alone?"

"It's not the same," I whisper. "You own me. It's not—"

"It's not what?" The irritation returns, Alexandre's mouth tightening as he looks at me. "How does it matter, *petit*, if I own you? I house you, feed you, care for you and treat you well, so how can you be alone?" He repeats the question, and I can hear from the tone of his voice that he truly doesn't seem to understand. It confuses me as much as my statement seems to confuse him, and we stare at each other for a long moment, the silence thickening as it goes on.

Alexandre snaps his fingers suddenly, standing up smoothly. "A bath, *petit*. That's what you need." He strides towards the bathroom before I can say a word, flicking on the light, and a moment later, I hear the rush of hot water from the taps.

"I don't think—" I start to protest as he comes back, but he lays a finger against my lips, his hands already moving to undo the buttons on my pajama top.

"A bath will set you right." He strips off my clothes quickly and efficiently, picking me up as if I weighed nothing—and I barely do—and carrying me to the bathroom the same way he did that first afternoon when I woke up here.

It *is* oddly soothing, both the familiarity of it and the heat of the floral-scented water when he sets me down in it, and I can feel the panic of the dream receding. I hate to admit that he was right, but I can feel my muscles loosening, the heat sinking down into my bones as I relax into the tub.

"There," Alexandre says, his expression pleased as he sits down on the stool next to the tub. His eyes, as usual, don't linger on any specific part of me, and I find my mind wandering back to dinner earlier, the way his fingers had brushed against my lips, the way my body had tightened as he fed me, the sensations prickling over my skin.

It had reminded me of the way I'd felt the first time he bathed me in here.

"If Yvette doesn't spend the night with you, does anyone?" I ask cautiously. I can't get her references to other girls out of my head, other pets, and I can't shake the way she'd looked at him either. I could *feel* her jealousy when she'd examined and touched me, palpably. Nor can I forget the way Alexandre had said I was his as he stood in the doorway, saving me from her.

He'd saved me from Alexei, too. In an unconventional way, perhaps, but he *had* saved me. I have no idea what would have happened to me if I'd stayed in Alexei's hands.

"That's not any of your business," Alexandre says tersely, but something about the way he says it tells me no. I think of him upstairs in his bed, all alone. I think again of the way my skin had tingled as he'd slipped the bite of croissant between my lips, the taste of chocolate, and the brush of his fingertips against my mouth.

Before I can stop myself, I reach for his hand, my fingers wrapping around his wrist as I bring it towards me, pressing his palm against my breast.

Something shoots through me as I feel his hand brush against my nipple, a burst of warmth that heats my blood and makes my thighs squeeze together, my heart speeding up in my chest. Alexandre's hand lingers for a fraction of a second, a look of pure astonishment on his face. Then he jerks his hand back out of my grasp, water splashing up between us as he recoils.

Hurt instantly replaces the desire I'd felt, my chest aching with the feeling of rejection, even though I know I shouldn't feel that way. I shouldn't even want him, but I do, and I feel tears spring instantly to my eyes when he recoils from me.

"So she was right," Alexandre murmurs, his gaze fixed on my face. "You do want me. Or perhaps you simply feel you should repay me in this way?"

"But you don't. Want me, I mean." I wrap my arms around my chest, pulling back. "Why did you buy me if you don't want me like that? What did Yvette mean anyway, when she said you paid too much for me?"

Alexandre ignores my latter question. "It's not a matter of wanting," he says finally, after a moment of silence. "Beautiful things are meant to be looked at, not used."

I feel the tears still welling up in my eyes, hot and abrupt. He looks at me curiously, his gaze sweeping down the length of my body almost dispassionately, but I can see a flicker of heat in his eyes as they slide back up to my face.

"Are you so aroused, then?" he asks softly. "When Yvette touched you earlier, she said that it was obvious you wanted me."

I swallow hard, my face flushing. The last thing on earth I want to admit to this man is how turned on I really am, especially after being rejected. But his voice is soft, not accusing, curious.

He pauses, and for a moment, the only sounds in the bathroom are the soft rippling of water in the tub and our breathing, Alexandre's heavier than before as he looks at me floating naked in the bath.

"Touch yourself then," he says quietly, his voice hoarse and thickly accented. "If you need pleasure, *petit*, give it to yourself while I watch."

I blink at him, startled. Of all the things I'd expected him to say, it wasn't that. I can feel my skin flush even hotter at the thought. It's not that I've never masturbated for anyone—I can think of more than one hookup that got off watching me touch myself for him or while he fucked me. But this feels different, somehow. It feels oddly intimate, in the close hot silence of the bathroom, with Alexandre so close, fully clothed while I lay naked in the water.

But I want it. The ache between my thighs intensifies under the weight of his gaze, the sound of his breathing, and I swallow hard, feeling my hand drift downwards as if pulled by some other force beyond my control.

My other hand slides to my breast, where I'd wanted his, my fingers tracing over my nipple as my other hand drifts over my belly, down to the apex of my thighs. I can feel Alexandre's eyes on me as my fingers slip between my legs. It only intensifies my desire, my heartbeat throbbing in my chest and beneath my fingers as I spread myself apart, wanting him to see.

I can't look at him. I already feel as if I can't breathe, my heart racing in my chest, and I can't meet his eyes. But I can hear his breathing quicken too as my fingers slide over my clit, making small circles, feeling how wet and slick I am for reasons that have nothing to do with the water.

I want him to say something, to urge me on, but he remains silent. I can't stop now that I've started, though, my clit throbbing under my fingers as my hips arch upwards in the hot water, eager for more of the friction. I don't know what to fantasize about, what to think; I can't make myself linger on any one image or thought for too long. But Alexandre sitting there is enough, the mingled arousal and embarrassment of being so vulnerable in front of him pushing me to a height of pleasure that I've never previously achieved by myself.

I forget my hesitation, forget any quandary I might have over who he is to me, forget anything except the way he keeps making me feel, the way my heart beats faster when he's close to me, the mingled fear and gratitude and arousal that I feel every time I'm in his presence. I think of him saying *she's mine* when Yvette had stood in front of me, her fingers pressed where mine are now, and I moan aloud, my thighs spreading apart as I rub faster, my fingers making quick, rapid circles around my clit as I hold myself open so that he can see if he's looking.

I hope he's looking. I steal a glance upwards as my fingers slide over my slick, pulsing flesh. I can see that he's aroused, the thick ridge of him straining against the silk of the pajama pants he's wearing, his dressing gown open so that I can see his muscled bare chest, the dark hair that I suddenly want desperately to run my fingers through as he stretches over me, for his fingers to replace mine, his tongue, his cock.

"Alexandre—" I whisper his name as my hips arch upwards into my hand, my fingers flying now, my other hand sliding from my breast downwards to join it, fingers dipping inside of my clenching entrance as I moan his name again. "Please—"

I hear his sharp intake of breath, but he doesn't move, frozen in place. I don't look up at his face, but I can feel his eyes on me, can see how hard he is, how much he wants me. *Just touch me,* I think desperately, but I know he won't, and besides, I'm so close to the edge that there's no time anyway.

I think I hear him groan when I come. Still, I can't be sure over the sound of my own moans, my fingers thrusting into myself as I gasp aloud, the orgasm crashing over me as every muscle tightens. My toes curl, the water sloshing around me and over the edges of the tub as I thrash underneath the stroking, thrusting motions of my fingers, wanting so desperately for it to be his hands instead of mine.

It takes me a moment to come back to myself, panting, my entire body vibrating with the aftershocks of pleasure as I let my fingers slip out of my clenching, fluttering body, gasping for breath. I finally look up at him, wide-eyed, and I see that his handsome blue gaze has darkened with lust. But his eyes are locked on my face and nowhere else.

"You look very beautiful when you come, *petit,*" he murmurs, his voice low and hoarse. He reaches out, pushing a piece of wet hair away from my face, and I shiver under his touch. "You did very well. Do you feel better, *ma petit poupée?*"

My little doll. I lean into his caress even though I know I shouldn't, still trembling. I want to beg for him to touch me again when he pulls his hand back, but he stands up, reaching for a towel.

"I told you a hot bath would set you right." He reaches for me then, lifting me up with his usual businesslike efficiency, setting me on the stool as he begins to dry me off, wrapping the towel around me as he reaches for the comb. "More tea, and you'll have a good night's sleep. All will be well in the morning, *poupée*."

Even without the tea, I can feel sleep starting to crowd back in, my eyelids heavy after the hot bath and orgasm. The comb trailing through my wet hair is soothing, his hands on my head and neck equally so, and by the time he's braided my hair and dressed me in the pajamas again, I feel half on my way back to sleep.

I drink the tea he brings me anyway, even though I know there must be a sedative in it again. The thought doesn't frighten me the way it did earlier, and besides, I know there's no way around it. Alexandre sits on the edge of the bed as he watches me drink every drop, taking the chipped china cup away from me as he tucks me back into bed, his fingers lingering on my cheek as he smiles at me.

"*Bon nuit, petit*," he says gently, standing up to leave. Halfway to the door, he stops, silhouetted in the darkness, and I feel my breath catch in my throat, half hoping that he plans to come back to me. To slide into bed next to me and finish what I started.

"I've heard through the grapevine," he begins, then pauses. "*Monsieur* Egorov. Alexei. Do you wish to know what happened to him?"

My heart nearly stops in my chest. *Alexei*. The name sends a thrill of fear through me, pushing all thoughts of desire to the back of my mind.

"Is he dead?" I ask softly, my voice carrying through the darkness.

There's a moment's silence, and I wonder if Alexandre will answer at all.

"Yes," he says finally, and a feeling that I can't describe washes over me. It's not relief or happiness—it's something else, something close to elation. Happiness beyond happiness, a feeling of freedom, even though I'm still as much a captive of Alexandre's as ever.

Out of the men who hurt me, one unequivocally cannot. Not ever again.

"Do you want to know how it happened?" Alexandre asks, his back still to me, and I let another beat of silence pass, considering.

A part of me does. But at the same time, I don't know if I want more violence to haunt the nightmares that I already have. *Maybe it's enough, just to know that he's dead.*

"Not yet," I whisper, my throat closing around the words. "Maybe eventually."

"I'll keep that to myself for now then, *petit*," Alexandre says. He moves forward then, towards the door, only to pause once more with his hand on the knob. "I will tell you this much, *petit*, so that it may ease your suffering."

The silence between those words and the next feels weighted with meaning, and I feel my breath catch in my throat, waiting to know what he'll say.

"He died slowly, *petit*. Screaming."

And then Alexandre opens the door and slips out into the hall without another word, leaving me there alone in the darkness.

LIAM

Just before I'm about to finish my last whiskey and head up to my own room, my cell phone starts to buzz. I pick it up, certain that if anyone is calling me at this time of night, it can't be good.

It's Niall, which after our last conversation, makes me even more certain that's the case. Particularly after the first words out of his mouth.

"You should come back to Boston."

"Hello to you, too." I frown, leaning back in the booth. "You know I'm not going to do that."

"Graham O'Sullivan has heard some rumors swirling around. Rumors that you and a couple of Viktor's men went in search of a woman—a woman *not* named Saoirse O'Sullivan."

"And did you do your best to assure him those rumors were exactly that?"

Niall lets out a sigh on the other end of the line as it crackles from half a world away. "You know I did, Liam. I'd lie to the devil himself if it kept your balls out of a vise. But O'Sullivan is no fool. And he's already aware of how you've dragged your feet regarding his daughter. If he's given a reason as to why you might be doing that, he's hardly going to dismiss it out of hand."

"It's your job to get him to dismiss it," I say tightly. "You're my right hand, Niall. Your job is to handle these things while I'm gone, so *handle* them."

"I'm doing all I can, Liam." Niall's voice is terser than usual. "It's a right shitshow here, and all because you're not here to keep these men in line."

"They weren't in line when I was there. You were at the last meeting. They're itching for a reason to replace me."

"And you're giving them one." Niall lets out another exasperated breath. "Come back to Boston, Liam. Let Levin and the priest look for the girl if you're so worried. But for fuck's sake, come back here and do your duty." He pauses, a heavy silence lingering over the line. "Or else I'm not so sure what you'll have left to come back to."

"I'll take it under advisement."

"I know what that means." Niall grunts, the line crackling again. "I'll call you if I hear more."

"Do that. I'll check in soon."

I hang up before Niall can say anything more, every muscle in my body feeling wound tight. I'd expected difficulties to arise while I was gone, of course, but not so soon.

For a brief moment, I'm forced to consider the possibility of going back to Boston. I could leave a message for Levin and Max, take a commercial flight back and leave them the jet. I have no doubt, Levin, at the very least, would continue on to Greece and stay in contact with me. I could do what Niall is clearly asking of me and set things right back home.

I don't even have to have a hand in planning the wedding to Saoirse. All I have to do is show up on the appointed day. And as for Ana, once Levin has located her, I can use some of the considerable wealth my father left me to set her up comfortably. She'll be safe, protected, all the things that I said I wanted.

But she won't be *mine*. It's all I can think as I pay my tab and head to the elevator up to my room. I won't have been the one to find her, save her, and bring her home. I want to find her, to look into her eyes and tell her that she's safe, that no one will ever hurt her again.

I'd said earlier that I love her. The words linger in my head as I slide the key into my door, the sounds from Levin's room down the hall carrying. From what I hear, they're having a grand time, and I can hardly begrudge him that. But the feeling of bitterness lingers.

I hadn't asked for the position I'd been given. It was never meant to be mine, and now it feels like a noose around my neck, tightening and slowly killing me. What I want is as far away as ever, with only a name leading us to the next point, the next clue. And after that? I have no way of knowing if I'll find her in time. What she'll be like when I do—*if* I do.

I could go home. Marry Saoirse, like I'm supposed to. It would be so easy. It's all waiting for me, neatly planned out, the contracts signed, the arrangements already being made, a ring on her finger.

Saoirse is a good girl. A beautiful, sweet girl, the perfect wife for a man like me in every way except one—that she's not the woman I want. She's not the woman I dream of at night, not the one who makes me hard and aching, desperate to touch her again.

I've never fantasized about Saoirse, never felt as if I'd burn the world down just to hold her in my arms.

Fuck. I run my hand through my hair, my body tense and restless. I strip down to my boxers, the whiskey leaving me pleasantly fuzzy around the edges, but just the thought of Ana is enough to have me half-aroused. I can feel the throb between my legs, the rush of blood as my cock starts to stiffen. I groan as I adjust myself, sliding onto the bed with my fingers lingering on the thickening length of my shaft.

Think of Saoirse. I force myself to summon her face as I run my fingers down my cock, feeling myself swell and harden under my touch. I take my shaft between thumb and forefinger, jerking it in a few quick, fast movements until it lurches against my palm. I wrap my hand fully around it, groaning with pleasure as my hips tilt upwards.

I try to think of her, glowing and radiant in the emerald dress, and what it would be like to undress her, to peel the satin away and reveal the slender curves of her body. I try to think of the kiss she almost gave me on the balcony and carry it through to its logical conclusion, to the warm press of her mouth against mine and her breasts against my chest, her arms slipping around my neck as she moans my name.

If anything, my erection falters, the desire receding as I groan with frustration. I *want* to desire her, if only because it would make my life so much fucking easier. But what gets me hard, what makes me feel as if I'm going mad with lust, is the thought of Ana.

Fuck. Ana. I think of her delicate face, her soft blue eyes, the way her lips parted when she laughed at something I'd said in the garden, and I'm suddenly rock hard, my cock throbbing in my fist as I tilt my head back with a moan of pleasure.

God, I want her. I want to give her things she's never imagined, to touch and caress and lick her until she cries out my name, to make her beg for more, and then beg me to stop because she's had enough. I want to take away every terrible thing that's ever happened to her, to be her lover and her savior, to wipe it all clean and replace it all with more pleasure than she's ever dreamed of.

"*Ana,*" I groan out her name through gritted teeth, my fist stroking the length of my cock hard and fast, hips thrusting up as I imagine her astride me, under me, her body enveloping me with slick, wet heat as I bury myself inside of her. I imagine the softness of her, the warmth, the taste, the way I would bury my face between her thighs and bring her to climax over and over until she's wet and trembling for me, clenching around my cock when I finally drive inside of her.

I want her with a ferocity that I've never felt for any woman. I want to protect her and devour her all at once, to make love to her and fuck her wildly, to keep her safe so that I, and only I, can be the one who touches her.

I know it's madness, but I feel as if there's nothing I wouldn't sacrifice for that.

It's not a fantasy of taking her home from the bar or the illusion of her in her dressing room at the ballet that I think of as I tilt my head back, giving myself over to thoughts of Ana as I stroke myself. I picture her here, now, her blonde hair spilling out over the hotel pillows, her lips parted as she gasps my name, her thin body held in my hands as I thrust into her, claiming her for my own, whispering over and over again that I'll never let her go, that I'll never let anyone take her from me again.

That this time, I'll keep her safe forever.

I hadn't been able to save her the first time, but I won't give up this time.

"*Fuck—*" I grit my teeth as I come, feeling my cock swell and throb in my fist, my hips jerking with the fierce desire to be inside of her, to bury myself in her as deeply as I can as I spill myself into her. The pleasure is mixed with frustration as I spill over my hand, wanting more than anything to feel her body, her skin, her warmth, and not be clutching at a ghost as I come helplessly into my fist.

It feels hollow. The release eases some of my tension, but the uncertainty is still there, the feeling of being torn between two things and being unsure if I can do either of them justice.

I get up and walk naked to the shower, feeling the weight of exhaustion on my shoulders, and we've only just begun. I don't know how far we'll still have to go to find Ana, but I know one thing for certain.

I can't give up now. Whatever waits for me back in Boston, I'll face it once I've found her.

And I'll bring her home with me. Safe and sound—and mine.

ANA

*D*espite the sedative, my dreams are still thick and confusing, filling my head with images that make very little sense when lumped all together. The horrible, violent images of the warehouse and Alexei's chalet are gone. They're replaced with flickers of that day in the garden, of lying in the bath, of Liam's smile and Alexandre's eyes, his hands and Liam's, blending into each other until I'm unsure who it is that I'm dreaming of, who it is that I truly want.

When I wake up, I bury my face instantly in the pillow, the memories of the night before flooding back along with the dreams. Liam's presence in them was the most unsettling, mostly because of how pointless it seems. My attraction to Alexandre might seem unusual, even crazy, but he's here, with me. I'm here, in a situation that I desperately need to make the best of, so that I can survive it.

Liam is on another continent, in a place so inaccessible to me now that he might as well be on the moon, and for all I know, he's forgotten me. Even if I still hear his voice, calling out desperately as Alexei dragged me away that he'd find me, it doesn't mean he remembers it. It doesn't mean that he hasn't given me up as lost, a regretful casualty of Alexei's betrayal.

IRISH SAVIOR

I can't depend on Liam. I shouldn't even fantasize about him. I should never have—Liam was always beyond me, something that I couldn't dare to hope for, the kind of thing that I'd only torture myself with if I let myself linger on it.

But still, I can't entirely get him out of my head.

When Alexandre comes in with my breakfast, I have a hard time looking him in the eye. He doesn't mention last night, though, or what he'd said about Alexei. He just leaves the tray on the bed and tells me he'll be back, leaving the room without another word.

I can't help but wonder if he's upset at me, and it makes my stomach clench with anxiety. *Does he regret last night? Has it made him feel differently about me? Is it Yvette? Did he tell her what we—what* I *did?*

Those are all ridiculous thoughts to have. Alexandre owns me; I'm ultimately a pet to him—why would he regret being entertained by his pet? Why should I be jealous of Yvette? I'm not his girlfriend or his lover, and the anxious knots in my stomach that feel like the kind of anxiety I used to get in the early days of dating someone I liked can only lead down a road that will hurt me emotionally or worse.

Alexandre is unpredictable and mercurial, and he's never going to be more than what he is—a man who ultimately has absolute power over me. I shouldn't get lost in thinking of him as anything else—but I can feel myself faltering, hovering on the edge of being willing to let myself fall, if it means some pleasure and happiness in a world that feels determined to take it away from me.

When Alexandre comes back to collect my breakfast tray, he has a clean maid's outfit with him, the same style I wore yesterday. He lays it on the bed and peels back the blankets, finally looking at me as I swing my legs over the edge of the bed.

"Are your feet well enough to clean again today?" he asks, glancing down at them, and I swallow hard before nodding.

"Yeah—I think so. They don't hurt much."

"Well, rest if they start to hurt. You did a good job yesterday, but I abhor dust of any kind, so I'd prefer if the apartment were dusted and vacuumed daily. I'll be out for some time today, so there's no need to rush. You can take your time." He pauses, stepping back, and I realize he's waiting for me to get out of bed so that he can dress me.

After last night, though his touch isn't any different, it feels foreign to me. He still gets me out of my pajamas with the same swift efficiency, stripping me bare and then holding out the frilly maid's panties for me to step into without so much as a lustful glance at my pussy. But I feel shivery as he touches me, trembling with anticipation as if at any moment, his touch might change, even though I know it won't. *How can he not be thinking about last night?* I can't help but think as he buttons up the back of the dress, his fingers brushing against my spine, as I try desperately not to let him see that I'm almost quivering from his touch.

Deep down, I know what it is. It's a mixture of desperation for any form of pleasure or kindness, mixed with the desire for the unknown, the forbidden and taboo that Alexandre clearly represents. I *shouldn't* want him, so I know I've fixated on him, craving something that could give me a burst of serotonin when I've lost every other source of it.

But I want to believe it's more than that. That there's nothing strange or unusual about his treatment of me, that it's as altruistic as it could be in the best of circumstances, that he happened across me at Alexei's party and rescued me, a rich benefactor who swept me away to his eccentric Paris apartment, a Cinderella story.

Alexandre, the near-hermit prince, and me, the princess.

It's ridiculous, and I know it. Only a certain kind of person would have been invited to Alexei's party at all. Only a certain type of person would have known him well enough, or known *someone* well enough to be there. Alexandre's presence there alone means that he's not the man I want to believe he is. And yet—

In a short time, my world has turned so horrible that I feel like I could overlook it. If he wanted me to. If he wanted *me*.

His fingers through my hair feel like a caress; the nimble way he pins it up feels like a comfort, as he slips the last of the bobby pins into my hair and pins the maid's cap over the top of it.

If he's not paying me, I think as I look at myself in the mirror, *does that make me any better than a slave?*

He's paying you in food and a place to stay, the other small voice in my head argues, as I look at his calm, handsome face in the mirror behind me. *Is that so wrong?*

It is when there's absolutely no way you could leave.

It's foolish to argue with myself like this, and I know it. Alexandre doesn't seem to catch on to my internal turmoil. He just smiles pleasantly at me, tying my apron on as he looks at me in the mirror.

"You look quite lovely like this," he says, but there's no warmth to his tone, no intimacy. It's an observation, the same way someone might say that a statue or a painting is beautiful, if they had no emotional connection to it.

"Thank you," I whisper, but he's already pulling away, picking up the breakfast tray and heading for the door with the obvious assumption that I'll follow him.

He leaves shortly after that with a quick farewell, without saying a word about where he's going or what he'll be doing. I don't know why it surprises me—it's not as if I'm someone to him that would require an explanation. But it stings anyway—which is just another reminder of why I shouldn't let my imagination run away with me. For all I know, he's going to see Yvette, which leaves a knot in my stomach that I can't shake as I walk into the kitchen and start to do the dishes from breakfast.

No matter how hard I try, as I move around the apartment, take care of the various chores, and do my best to rest in between, I can't shake the memory of last night. I can feel his eyes on me as I touched myself, watching me like I was something beautiful, like he'd never seen anything like me. Even without looking at his face, I'd imagined that I was able to feel the reverence in his gaze—that he was looking at me the same way he touches me, as if I were something to be handled delicately. Something precious.

Alexandre paid too much for you. I can hear Yvette's voice in my head, smooth and rich like melted chocolate, saying it so matter-of-factly.

Which means that she *knows* how much he paid for me.

He told her.

That stops me in my tracks when it occurs to me. *How did that conversation go, exactly?* Was it like when I used to talk to my girlfriends about how much I'd paid for a new dress? *Oh, you paid too much for that, they'll have a sale next week.* What, exactly, is *too much* to pay for a human being?

What did Alexandre pay for me, anyway?

The thought sticks in my head until I feel as if I can't shake it loose. I look at the art around the living room, the statues on the side tables, the leather-bound books on the shelves. How much did he pay for those? Less, or more for me than the art on the wall? Less, or more for me than the first-edition, leather-bound copy of *Les Miserables* with the first page missing?

Less, or more for me than a set of Chinese vases, one with a base chipped and another missing a piece in the rim? The teacups? The silver in the kitchen?

It makes me feel sick the longer I think about it. I'd assumed at first that he must have paid next to nothing for me, that Alexei, after everything he said about me being worthless, must have been happy to make a profit at all. Glad to have me off of his hands. But Yvette's comment has changed everything.

I hover, more than once, at the door to the study, the feather duster in my hand, my nostrils filled with the scent of lemon cleaner and old books. Alexandre had clearly said that I wasn't to go in here or into his bedroom. There's no mistaking it, he'd repeated it twice. Those are the only two rooms off-limits to me in the house. Everywhere else, I can explore freely.

Generous, considering that I'm basically his pet and that he has an apartment filled to the brim with valuable, or at least semi-valuable items. Items that, if I wanted to, I could probably try to pawn. Attempt to get enough cash to get a plane ticket—but of course, I don't have identification. No passport, no driver's license, no birth certificate. Nothing to prove who I am.

In the eyes of the larger world, I might as well not exist. No bank account. Not a single piece of paper proving that I am anything but air, ephemeral and fleeting.

So why wouldn't he give me free rein of the house, excepting those two rooms? Stealing anything wouldn't do me any good.

Which means there are things he doesn't want me to see in those two rooms.

Things like maybe a bill of sale, telling me what he paid for me.

Alexandre paid too much for you.

I drop the feather duster, pressing my hands over my eyes. I shouldn't do it. I *can't*. Alexandre has been kind to me. Gentle. Maybe, if Yvette's attitude is to be believed, more delicate than he's been with others that were here.

And where are those others now?

Sold? Runaways?

Dead?

I can feel my imagination picking up speed, threatening to run away with me, my pulse rising up in my throat as my heart flutters in my chest. It's all too easy to let Alexandre warp from the slightly strange, gentle man who has treated me like a porcelain doll—mostly quite literally—to an eccentric serial killer who has the bones of his previous pets—dolls?—stored somewhere in this apartment.

Yvette could be his accomplice.

She could be fun to play with. We could play with her together.

She's mine.

The words tumble over themselves, rolling over and over in my head until I feel like I could scream. Did they play with other girls together? Did Yvette touch them the way she touched me, tormenting them, getting them ready for Alexandre? Did she hold them down while he did things to them? Pleasurable things, or painful?

I'd trembled with relief and something very akin to desire when he'd said I was his. I'd thought about it later when I'd touched myself in the bath. But now, with my imagination spinning out of control, those two words take on a much darker tone.

She's mine.

His to—do what with, exactly? *What does he not want to share with Yvette?*

I reach out for the handle of the door to the study and snatch my hand back just as quickly, as if it might burn me.

Would he really be angry if I went in?
He's been kind to me.
But what if it's all a lie?
What if this gives him the excuse to—

I can't even formulate an idea of what that could be. *Something must have happened to those other girls, if there really were others,* and it seems that there must have been. The women's clothes, the toiletries, the jewelry box, Yvette's comments, it all adds up to a truth that I don't want to face, but that is staring at me directly.

I am not Alexandre's first pet.

I am not the first girl he's owned.

And I am *not* special.

He didn't happen upon me at that party. He went to that party because he's the kind of man who buys a girl who catches his fancy. And I caught his fancy because I was a novelty. A damaged girl trussed up like a ballerina. Beautiful and broken.

I can choose to ignore it if I want because Alexandre has shown me some kindness in a world that has become, for me, very bleak. But I can't pretend that it's all a figment of my cracking imagination.

What do you think he did to them?

I can't picture Alexandre—graceful, handsome, eccentric Alexandre—hurting someone the way Franco hurt me, slicing open my soles, burning the wounds. I can't picture him trussing a girl up to the ceiling like Alexei did, beating me raw with a belt. All of that seems too cruel, too violent, too *indelicate* for a man like him.

Which gives me a new, terrifying idea.

If Alexandre wanted to hurt me, he wouldn't do it so brutally, so obviously. He'd find some way to do it elegantly, like a work of art. Carving something old into something new, a beautiful new sculpture out of something damaged and broken.

Like the cracked Japanese vase filled with gold.

There are plenty of serial killers who thought of their kills as art. Who thought their methods were elegant, beautiful, even.

I feel like I'm going insane. I don't even know how long I've been hovering in front of the door, waiting to decide if I should open it.

Alexandre could come home, and the moment will be lost. I'm not even sure how long he's been gone.

And this will eat at me, and eat at me, until I misstep anyway, and anger him. And then maybe I'll never know.

I reach for the handle again. *Maybe it will be locked. And then the decision will be made for me.*

But it's not. The door opens smoothly, without a squeak or a hitch. My stomach instantly plummets with guilt because that means that Alexandre trusted me not to go in here.

Or it's a trap. To see if you'll obey.

If that's the case, I've already failed. Would he know somehow, if I backed out now?

I take a step into the room, and then another.

I shut the door behind me, and the decision is made.

The room is cool and dark, and it smells of leather, faintly smoky. I see a fireplace on one wall, which must be the source of the smoky smell, and a long couch along one wall with a leather upholstered chair behind a desk. There's another of the expensive, faintly worn rugs on the gleaming hardwood floor, and the entire room is spotless.

I abhor dust.

I think of the things that Alexandre might be called if he were a less rich man, living in a less interesting place than Paris. A hoarder. Obsessive-compulsive. Germaphobe, maybe. Creepy, certainly, considering how he treats me, undressing and dressing me, feeding me from his hand, brushing my hair.

Here, he just seems eccentric. Romantic, even, in a fairytale anti-hero kind of way. The sort of man that you question if you really want the heroine to be saved from or not. The kind you almost want to root for, because he's handsome and rich and just has a few odd habits.

Alexandre paid too much for you.

Yvette's voice slithers into my thoughts again, reminding me of why I'm in here. Not to marvel over Alexandre's cleanliness or count the number of items in this room, taking up all the available surfaces. Not to think about what kind of man he is.

To get some kind of answers before he comes home.

I try to keep my ears pricked for the sound of the key in the front door, so that I can slip out before he catches me, if he comes home before I leave the room. The feather duster is where I left it, dropped right in front of the door. If I'm quick, I can scurry out, grab it, and pretend as if nothing ever happened. As if I were just dusting the bookcase to one side of the door. Lingering over the volumes.

Nothing Alexandre could find anything wrong with.

Certainly not snooping around his study

Part of me hopes that the drawers of his desk, the first place I think to look, will be locked. But of course, they're not. Alexandre seems to be a man who doesn't try too hard to safeguard his secrets— or maybe he simply is so isolated from others that there's no one to find them. It would explain why he's close to Yvette, if she's his only friend. If it's just her—and me.

The thought makes me sad, somehow, and guiltier. *What if there's nothing? What if he's just the eccentric rich Frenchman that you thought he was, and you're almost all he has? And you're betraying his trust?*

Alexandre paid too much for you.

Mind your manners.

The memory of his voice, hissing that at me in the hallway as he'd held me up against the wall, pushes some of the guilt back. I'd seen a hint of something different in him then, just like the night I'd refused to tell him about my feet in the bath, and he'd gotten angry with me.

Something that maybe, just maybe, I need to watch out for.

The first two drawers don't have anything interesting. Some old papers, spreadsheets, nothing that gives me any clue as to what he might have paid for me or that mean anything to me at all. But then, as I start in on one of the heavy wooden drawers on the left side of the desk, I come across something halfway through a stack of papers that makes my heart stop.

Alexei Egorov.

For a moment, I want to shove it back into the drawer without looking at it. *Maybe it's better not to know.* It had felt good, that one moment early on when I'd believed Alexandre had paid nothing for me, that Alexei had just pawned me off for whatever he could get, and that maybe there was something wholesome in what Alexandre had done, in a weird sort of way. Seeing the damaged and broken things around his apartment that first afternoon had made me wonder if it could be true.

But then Yvette had gone and fucked it up with just a few well-placed words.

She did it on purpose. And you're playing right into her hands.

I stand there for too long, holding the paper. I can't decide. If I don't look at it, I'll wonder forever, now that I know. But if I do, I'm doing what she wants. I'll discover something that will drive a wedge between Alexandre and I. And if he finds out—

I pace around from behind the desk, my heart hammering, the paper still clutched in my hand. I stop in front of the fireplace, the insane idea to light it and burn the paper before I can read it springing into my head.

But I look down at it. I can't stop myself. In the dim light, I make out my name and a number that I can't make sense of at first. There are too many zeroes. No number should have that many zeroes after it. It's impossible.

How much did he pay for me? A hundred thousand? No, too many zeroes. A fucking million?

But it's still not right. And I realize as I read it again and again, with a sort of dizzying disbelief that makes me feel as if I'm going to pass out, that Alexandre paid a *hundred million dollars* for me.

For *me*, a twenty-one-year-old damaged ballerina with no future, no name, and a wrecked mind. A girl prone to fits and panic attacks, who can barely stand up for an entire day, who certainly would melt down if forced into anything sexual. A girl who Alexei had clearly said, out loud, before the party, was worthless except to the kind of man who would enjoy a girl who couldn't run.

The kind of man who would enjoy helplessness. Begging. A girl he could torment and watch her try to get away, like a butterfly with her wings pinned down. The worst kind of sadist.

That doesn't seem like Alexandre. I can't make it fit in my mind.

I knew he was rich, but *that* rich?

Alexandre paid too much for you.

For once, I agree with Yvette.

I stare at the paper, reading it over and over, as if it might change. As if it's a trick of the light, some magic ink that will melt away, revealing that it's a hoax. A joke.

That he really paid a hundred dollars. A thousand, even. Ten thousand.

Not a *hundred million*.

But it doesn't change. And I stare at it so long, lost in the whirling thoughts in my head and my fevered imagination, that I don't hear the key in the door or the footsteps in the hall or the smooth swing of the study door opening up. I don't hear anything at all, until a heavy, long-fingered hand grips my shoulder painfully, and I hear Alexandre's voice say my name in a tone he's never used before. That chills me to the depths of my soul.

"*Anastasia.*"

LIAM

The next day, we fly to Greece, to Santorini. I've never been to Greece, but when we land and take a boat to the main part of the island in the early evening, it's everything I've ever seen in pictures. The endless, perfect blue sea, the cotton candy clouds as the sun begins to set, the winding roads and crisp white buildings topped with rich blue domes. It looks like a paradise, and I could almost regret that we're here on business and not on pleasure.

Maybe we'll find Ana here. I'll rescue her and sweep her off to one of these villas, and she can recuperate there. I'll wait to return to Boston, and we'll have a few blissful days alone, just the two of us, here in this romantic place.

It's a fantasy so ridiculous I'm embarrassed just thinking it.

Ana almost certainly isn't here. We're here to find and meet with Adrian Drakos, and he'll give us our next lead to chase, unless he for some reason has met the Frenchman himself, disposed of him, and can tell us what's happened to Ana. That is a one-in-a-million chance, and I don't dare pin any hopes on it. At best, he'll have met or know someone who has met the Frenchman and can give us a name to go on.

That's what Levin's coin bought us. A name, for another name, and hopefully the end to what could very well be a wild goose chase. Or the first stop of many. We won't know until we talk to Drakos.

It turns out that he's not hard to find. On an island like this, a man with a security detail tends to stick out, and it's easy enough to find out where Drakos is staying. The next step, of course, is getting to him without getting killed.

Unsurprisingly, Levin's password is the key.

"Smert elo milost."

Those words, spoken to the black-suited men in front of the villa, make them instantly step aside for us. I can feel their eyes resting heavily on Max and me as we follow Levin. Still, not a single threatening gesture is made in our direction as we walk up the white steps and onto the patio with billowing white curtains, lounge chairs scattered across it with a table covered in various foods and aperitifs in the center.

"Having a party, Drakos?" Levin asks dryly, and it's then that I see our target, standing on the far end of the patio looking out towards the water, in a slim-cut black suit tailored perfectly to his lean frame.

The man who turns to face us has the features of a model, with dark hair swept to one side, green eyes, and a shadowing of stubble across his strong jaw. He moves with catlike grace, but I'm not fooled in the slightest. I've seen men like him training in the boxing ring, the lighter-weight fighters. They seem like easy targets, but they move faster and hit harder than any heavyweight I've ever trained with.

"Levin Volkov." His voice drips with dry humor, as if he were expecting Levin. "Vladimir told me you were coming. I wondered how long it would take you to find me."

"Not long," Levin smirks. "You certainly stand out in a place like this."

Adrian Drakos shrugs. "Here? I'm not trying to hide. If I were, you wouldn't have found me until I found you—or until I let you."

What kind of men does Vladimir make? It makes me wonder about the future of this business Viktor is setting up, what his new enterprise will mean for the Russians, and what that, in turn, means for the alliance Luca and I have made with him. I'm not sure that I've fully understood what I've allied the Kings with, and I hope that I don't come to regret it.

Levin is a man I'd certainly be pleased to have at my side. But Vladimir makes my skin crawl, and Adrian doesn't strike me as the kind of man that I'd like to have knowing where I sleep at night.

I'd be likely to wake up to an asp in my bed.

"I hear you traded a great deal for Vladimir to give you my name, in conjunction with what you're looking for." Adrian raises an eyebrow, walking past Levin towards the table, where he picks up an opaque blue glass filled with some sort of sparkling drink. "Here. Enjoy."

"I'll pass," Levin says dryly, and Adrian snorts.

"What, you think I would poison an old friend? Take it. Don't insult my hospitality. And your friends, too. Drink and eat. You're in Greece, home of some of the finest food in the world." He narrows his eyes at Max and me. "You haven't introduced me, Volkov. I see you've lost your manners."

Levin frowns, taking the glass from Adrian, though I notice he doesn't drink from it. "Liam McGregor," he says, gesturing to me. "And Maximilian Agosti. Liam is the reason that we're here."

"Ah." Adrian turns his piercing gaze to me, looking at me distinctly as if he's deciding whether or not I'm worth his time. "Do you know what Levin traded for this information for you?"

"I do," I say stiffly, taking a glass from the table to be polite, but also not drinking from it. It doesn't take much instinct to know that I should follow Levin's lead here, and I see Max doing the same.

"There are men who would kill for a favor like that from Vladimir," Adrian says casually, twirling his glass. "And Levin traded it away for almost nothing."

"Not nothing," Levin says stiffly. "Vladimir says that you're familiar with a certain type of man. The type that buys and sells women. That you have a—predilection for putting an end to them, in your free time."

Adrian shrugs. "We all need hobbies." He glances towards me, his eyes narrowing. "What does that have to do with you?"

There's no point in beating around the bush. "I'm searching for a woman," I say bluntly. "A woman who was sold."

"Ah," Adrian says with a wry smile. "A woman. No wonder Levin traded his coin for information. You found his weakness."

"It was inadvertent." I return his gaze evenly. "I didn't know when I asked him for his assistance that it would hit quite so close to home. But I've since learned more about him."

"So he told you about Lidiya."

"Briefly." I don't flinch back from his stare, however unwavering. "Enough for me to understand."

"Levin has always had a soft spot for all women." Adrian tosses back his drink, setting the blue glass back on the table, where it catches the dying light as he turns back to the edge of the patio overlooking the water. "But particularly for her. He would have left the syndicate for her. Some of his associates thought that was inexcusable. Levin thought their actions were inexcusable. There was a great deal of blood shed."

"We're not here to dredge up the past," Levin says tightly. "It's long done and over with. Vladimir traded me a favor for me to walk away with no more lives lost. Yesterday, I traded that favor in for a name. Vladimir and I are even. And you have the information that I purchased with that coin."

"You purchased a name. *My* name. Whether I share information is up to me." Adrian turns back towards us, leaning against a pillar. "Who is this woman?"

"A former ballerina." I'm hesitant to tell him her name yet, though I will in an instant if I think he'll truly help us. "Kidnapped from Viktor Andreyev's safe house and sold by his traitorous brigadier to a Frenchman."

"Ah, so the plot thickens. The *Ussuri* lost his women, and you are chasing one of them down." Adrian smirks. "He always was good at sending others to clean up his messes."

"The woman means something to me," I say curtly. "I've come after her of my own volition."

"A romance!" Adrian's eyes narrow, and he grins. "Ah, there's not much of that in my world these days. Blood, yes, a great deal, and sex? Plenty of it. But a man who believes in love, there's a rare find in our world." He pauses, considering as he looks at the three of us. "You say a Frenchman bought her?"

"Yes." Against my better judgment, I feel a flare of hope in my chest. If there's a chance, even a small one, that this Adrian Drakos might know of the man who has Ana, I can't help but cling to it. It's the best shot we've had thus far.

He frowns, clearly thinking. The silence that follows is agonizing, broken only by the ripple of the warm breeze over the water below and through the gauzy curtains on the patio.

"I haven't encountered any Frenchmen," Adrian says finally. "Though I am glad to hear that Viktor Andreyev has given up his flesh trade. I wondered if the day would come that I'd be permitted to go after him. The man that kidnapped them, is he dead?"

"Very," Max confirms, his expression terse. "I helped see to it myself."

"All three of us did, along with Viktor, who did most of the honors." Levin's face is equally tense as he faces down Adrian. "I know you have no lost love for me now since I've worked for the Andreyevs and that you don't understand how I could, given my past. But things have changed in the Andreyev household now, and our search for this woman is a part of that. If you're withholding information from us on account of the *Ussuri*'s sins, I hope you'll reconsider."

"I'm not," Adrian says calmly. "Though I had considered it, if I'd had more information to give. I haven't encountered any Frenchmen buying or selling women through any channel." He frowns. "Is it possible that he might take pains to conceal his nationality? Or that he might have been faking it?"

Levin considers, but I shake my head. "The other women who were there said if anything, he was very flamboyant about it. He made no efforts to blend in with the other party guests. If anything, he seemed to enjoy making a scene. And I was told his French seemed very authentic, from someone whose mother was particularly fond of France and Paris and spoke the language."

"Hmm. A French accent *is* difficult to put on without approaching mimicry." Adrian considers. "Is there anything else beyond his nationality or appearance that might be a clue? Perhaps I could use that to steer you in the right direction." He presses his lips together, thinning them as his jaw clenches momentarily. "However I might feel about the *Ussuri*'s past, if he truly has turned over a new leaf, I commend him. And if this Frenchman is what you say, I would do all I could to help you find and put an end to him."

I glance at Max, who looks as frustrated as I feel. "I—" I stop suddenly, remembering what Viktor had told me in his office. "He spent an obscene amount of money."

"Oh?" Adrian looks at me with renewed interest. "What do you mean by *obscene?*"

Levin makes a noise next to me that might suggest I should be careful, but I can't hold back now. If there's a chance in hell that Adrian can even point us in the right direction, I have to pursue it, for Ana's sake.

"A hundred million dollars," I say flatly, and I see Max's stunned expression out of the corner of my eye. "For a girl that was physically damaged. She likely wouldn't have been expected to fetch a high price."

Adrian's eyebrow rises, and I can see that something has resonated with him. It's on the tip of my tongue to beg him to spill whatever he's just thought of, but I force myself to stay silent. Whatever it is, he'll tell us in his time, or not at all, and I'll only prolong it by trying to drag it out of him. It's clear that he's enjoying the back and forth.

"I haven't heard of a trade specifically in women, though it may have been before at some point," Adrian says slowly. "But I have heard, through the grapevine, so to speak, of a man who searches out damaged valuables. Art, artifacts, old books, the like."

"And you've heard his name?" This time it's Levin who presses forward.

"No." Adrian shakes his head, and I feel my heart sink again. "Not his name. Not even that he's French, so I can't ensure that it's the same man. But I have heard that he's willing to pay more than these items are worth to collect them. He's become something of a joke among the crime lords, that all they need to do is find some damaged good that might once have been worth something, and they can make a profit off of nothing."

"That sounds like our man," Max mutters, and I shoot him a look. I don't like to think of Ana as *nothing* or damaged goods. But it's true that it sounds like it could be the man we're looking for, if he thought of Ana that way.

"A man who purchases flawed art above the asking price," Levin says thoughtfully. "It does fit. But without a name—"

"Last I heard, he was in Tokyo, meeting with Noboru Nakamura, *oyabun* of the Yakuza." Adrian shrugs. "It would have been before this party when you say this Frenchman bought the woman you are looking for. I don't know what he was looking to purchase. If I'd heard then that it was a woman, I would have looked into it further. But the rumor was that it was another of his flawed purchases."

Levin's mouth tightens. "The Yakuza. You're sure of this? Nakamura, specifically?"

Adrian nods. "I'm quite certain. I didn't think it was anything worth my time. Just an urban legend, so to speak. But it's possible this could be the man you're searching for. In that case, Nomura or one of his *kobun* might be able to help you. They might even have a name for you. It could also be a dead end. But that's the best information I have, for the price you paid, Volkov."

"I appreciate it." Levin nods to him, taking a step back. "You've been very generous."

"I have my moments." Adrian turns to look out over the water as the sky darkens and the breeze picks up just a fraction, and despite the warmth of it all, I shiver slightly. "You should go. I have things to do tonight. My men will escort you out."

The black-suited men immediately start to move towards us, and Levin jerks his head hastily towards the entrance to the patio, suggesting we shouldn't linger. I can only imagine what *things* Adrian Drakos has to do tonight. Someone will suffer and bleed this evening, certainly. Someone deserving?

Who, exactly, is to judge that?

Not me, who barely a week ago helped to cut off the fingers of a man who hung from the ceiling screaming and who intends to end the life of another, just as soon as I can find him. My fingers are itching to curl around the trigger of a gun pointed at this Frenchman's head, or perhaps his balls first. Depending on what he's done to Ana.

It would give me more pleasure to beat the shit out of him with my own two fists. But that would take time that I don't intend to waste. My mission is to get Ana away from him, and a bullet is the quickest way to expedite that.

What Adrian Drakos does after we leave is none of my concern. What matters is that he's given us something. Not what I'd hoped for exactly—not the Frenchman's name, or location, or even knowledge of Ana's whereabouts or condition.

But he's given us another clue. A good one. A place to go, and another name of another man to speak to, one that hopefully will have another door opened by Levin's password.

Tomorrow, we'll get on the plane to Tokyo.

And I'll be one day closer to Ana.

ANA

When he says my name again, I can hardly hear it over the thundering of my heartbeat in my ears.

Stupid, stupid, stupid.

I was supposed to be listening for him to come home. Instead, I'd been so wrapped up in what I'd found that I hadn't heard anything, and he'd snuck up on me. Found me here, in one of the only two places he'd clearly said I shouldn't be.

Now, I know I'm going to pay for it.

I can feel myself starting to shake under his iron grip on my shoulder, the panic rising up thickly from my gut, making my stomach contract, my chest clench, and my head swim until I think I might pass out. Maybe I should—at least then I won't be awake to face his anger.

But I'll come to eventually, and who knows what I'll wake up to then?

Slowly, I turn to face him, his hand still gripping my shoulder so hard that it hurts. He's never hurt me before, and somehow that strikes me more deeply than the fear, enough for me to say something aloud despite my fear.

"You're hurting me," I whisper, my voice quavering, but it does nothing to change the black expression on Alexandre's face in the dim light.

"Good," he growls, his voice low and dark. He turns on his heel then, starting to stride towards the couch along one wall, dragging me along with him. He flicks on a Tiffany lamp next to it, the warm yellow glow bathing part of the darkened room in light, and I can see the expression on his face more clearly.

I wish I hadn't. The anger in his eyes is naked, palpable. His mouth is tight and hard, set in a thin line, and I can see the simmering rage.

"Give me that." He snatches the paper out of my hand so fast that it nearly tears and looks at it. He instantly sees what I've found, and his expression blackens even more.

"I gave you one simple instruction. Didn't I?" His voice is so cold, so hard. He's never spoken to me like this before.

I've fucked up. I've ruined it. Oh god. The terror is bone-chilling. I can't stop shaking; my teeth are almost clattering together. I don't think I can answer him, but I have to.

He shakes me so hard that my teeth clack together anyway, painfully. *"Didn't I?"* he roars, his voice filling the small room, and I let out a small cry of fear.

"Yes," I whisper, shivering. "Yes, you did."

"What was it?" He shakes me again, harder, like a terrier with a rat. "Tell me, Anastasia. What was my instruction to you?"

I swallow hard, but my mouth is too dry, and my throat convulses. "You said—not to—go in your study. Or your bedroom." The words come out halting, one at a time, and I don't know at first if he'll even give me the time to finish. But he does, as if he wants to hear it from my lips.

"Where are you, Anastasia? Are you lost? Or just stupid?"

"Your study," I whisper. "Alexandre, I—"

"Don't give me fucking excuses," he snarls. "You're no idiot, for all your injuries and fits. You're a smart girl, I know that. You knew which rooms not to go into. You went looking for something, and you found it." His hand tightens on my shoulder even more, pressing into the bone until I think he could almost snap it, and tears of pain start to drip down my cheeks.

"Stop sniveling." He glares down at me. "Yvette was right. I've spoiled you, and you thought—what? That I'd come home and laugh at your little misadventure? Forgive you for everything? You forget who you are, Anastasia. You are *mine*."

That word that had sent such relief and desire through me yesterday, that had fueled so many foolish fantasies between last night and a few minutes ago, sends another chill of pure terror through me. My worst suspicions feel confirmed. This man isn't the one who has so gently catered to me like a fragile doll or who had watched me with such controlled lust last night as he urged me to touch myself for the sake of my own pleasure. I'd dropped my guard, and this is where I've found myself.

Stupid. So stupid.

I should have known better.

"The evidence of it is right there. You've seen it yourself." He nods at the crumpled bill of sale on the rug. "A hundred million dollars, Anastasia. Can you fathom that much money?"

Mutely, I shake my head.

"Of course, you can't. But it should drive home that simple point, which surely even you can understand. You are *mine*. Mine to do with as I please." His lips pull back in a threatening, humorless smile as he backs towards the couch, sitting down on the edge of it and pulling me facedown over his lap with one swift motion that I'm helpless to even anticipate, let alone fight.

"And right now," he continues, "what I please is to punish the ungrateful little brat that I paid so much money for and have spoiled so thoroughly. No more, Anastasia," he warns, and then his hand is on my skirt, pushing it up over my ass and hips, his fingers curling into the frilled waistband of the ridiculous panties that go with this ridiculous outfit, pulling them down to bare my ass to his gaze and his hand.

His palm presses against my bare cheek, and before all of this, it might have still aroused me. Even the spanking could have turned me on under the right circumstances. In my old life, there was a time when I was the old Ana that I'd have jumped at the chance to play out a scene like that with a man like Alexandre. Hot, dominant, sexy, a little strange but kinky.

This isn't a scene, though, and Alexandre isn't someone I met at a bar or a New York sex dungeon.

He's a man with absolute power over me in every fathomable way. And right now, he's so angry with me that I can't begin to think where he might stop with this punishment, or what I might need to fear.

The possibilities are endless and too terrifying to consider.

He pulls the skirt up further, baring all of my lower back, ass, and thighs to his gaze, and I feel his hand pull away as if to strike me for the first time. But before the first blow can fall, I feel him hesitate, and then his hand does come down. But he doesn't hit me. Instead, I feel his fingers trace one of the lingering scars on my hip where Alexei beat me with the belt as I hung from the ceiling in his chalet, and then another of them on the curve of my ass, another on my upper thigh.

"Was this Alexei?" he asks, his voice dark, and I don't bother trying to hide my tears.

"Yes," I manage in a choked voice, sniffling.

"What happened?" His fingers are still tracing the old marks, and again, it could have been arousing in different circumstances. My bare pussy is pressed against the crisp fabric of his pant leg, and I can feel him hardening against my belly. He's not immune to having me across his lap like this, half-naked, any more than he was immune to watching me in the bath last night. It's just a matter of whether or not he'll act on it.

Not like this, I think desperately, though I don't dare say it aloud. Whatever Alexandre does to me, I hope it's not that. As recently as yesterday, I wanted him, and I don't think I can bear it if he takes that away from me too, if he violates me. If he hurts me in ways that go far beyond what he could do with his hands, a belt, or other implements.

If he hurts me like that, after what I've started to feel for him and the restraint he's shown so far, I think it will break me beyond repair.

I wonder if he knows that.

Unlike his questions about my feet, I don't try to avoid answering this time. I'm too afraid to withhold anything from him now, and even if I thought I could, all I can hope is that perhaps I can get some sympathy from him now. His pity isn't what I wanted, but I'm terrified enough to take whatever it is that I can get.

"Caterina made him angry," I whisper through my tears, doing my best to choke them back. "He scared one of the children—Anika, I think it was—and she fought back. He knew hurting her wouldn't stop her from fighting back. He was already raping her. So instead, he hurt the people she cared about. He knew that more than her own pain would make her fall in line. So he brought Sasha in and beat her in front of Caterina. And then me." I bite my lower lip hard at the memory, hard enough to taste blood, the tears dripping faster down my face and onto the leather couch and the rug beneath us. "She felt responsible for Sasha, and I'm her closest friend's best friend."

I wonder if I should have said that last part, but I don't think it matters now. Giving Alexandre information he could have easily found out on his own with a little digging into my past isn't going to change what he does to me now. Being truthful with him and clarifying that I'm not holding back is my best chance. My best chance to show him that I can be his *good girl* again.

Even now, facedown across his lap with his hand caressing my old scars, moments after he was close to blistering my ass with his hand, a part of me yearns for it. To be the girl whose hair he stroked and head he patted, the girl he fed treats and smiled at, praised, and cared for. The girl that he protected from Yvette, saying sternly, *mine. Mine,* in a way that felt possessive but not threatening.

Not like now.

"He knew hurting us would break her. He started with us and told her that her pregnant friend would be next, and then the children after that, if she still refused to behave. But Sasha and I were all it took." I remember what happened after that and squeeze my eyes tightly shut against a fresh wave of tears. "He tried not to scar Sasha. She was worth a decent amount. But he didn't care about me. I was already damaged. Ruined. *Worthless.*" The last isn't a plea for Alexandre's sympathy, though I know he might think that it is. They're Alexei's words, and they went deeper than even I realized. Lying across Alexandre's lap like this, crying and broken, caught snooping, my naked ass and all of my scars bared to him, I feel exactly that. Worthless.

At the mercy of whatever Alexandre decides to do to me.

He's silent for a long moment, his fingers tracing the scars. I can feel the tension in every line of his body, the hard ridge of him beneath my belly, straining at his fly. He's hard, aroused, angry. Just the thought is enough to terrify me. I know what aroused and angry men are capable of. Once I would have said *not Alexandre.*

But now I'm not sure.

"Get up," he says finally, his voice still cold and harsh, and I don't waste a second. I scramble to my feet, my ankles tangling in the black frilled panties caught around them. I frantically kick them free onto the rug, the skirt of the maid's dress blessedly sliding back down to cover me.

Alexandre's face hasn't softened. He still looks furious, his piercing blue eyes dark and angry, his mouth set in a thin line. His hands are gripping the edge of the couch on either side of him now, every muscle in his body tight and rigid. I don't dare look at his erection, pressing noticeably against the front of his trousers. I'm afraid to draw attention to it.

The tears are still streaming down my face, my breath coming in short, hiccupping gulps. I'm seconds away from a full panic spiral, the only thing stopping me the knowledge of how little Alexandre likes my *fits*, as he called them. He won't be picking me up off the floor and cleaning my face for me this time. He'll have far less patience, and I have no idea how that might manifest.

"Beg," he says, his thickly accented voice cutting through the air between us. "Get on your knees, *petit*, and beg my forgiveness. Do it now, before I change my mind."

And what? I'd never dare ask the question, but it hangs there. What would he do to me if I refused? If I summoned the old, stubborn, defiant Ana and raised my chin, refusing to kneel to a man, refusing to beg.

If it were Franco or Alexei, I would know the answer. With Alexandre, I don't. And somehow, that's even more terrifying.

"Beg," he says again, his voice rasping. "Don't make me tell you again, *petit poupée.*"

Little doll. Like a puppet whose strings have been cut, I fall to my knees, ignoring how the impact feels against my already bruised joints. "I'm sorry," I gasp, my hands on the rug, nails scratching at it, feeling the loose threads, the imperfections. The damage that Alexandre finds so endearing, so charming, so *valuable.*

A hundred million dollars. I still can't fathom it.

But now isn't the time to try.

Now is the time, if there ever was one, to obey.

Beg.

ANA

"I'm sorry," I whisper, with everything that I have in me. I don't know if it's entirely true—I'm glad I found that paper, happy that I know. I couldn't have imagined that would be the number I would find, but I would have driven myself insane wondering. I could blame Yvette and her comment, but I know that won't help me. Yvette didn't make me go into the study.

I did that on my own.

"Please." I look up at him, at his hard and angry face, my hands shaking so hard that I feel like my fingers might tear into the rug. All of me is shaking, terrified, kneeling on the floor in the ridiculous maid's dress. I do wish I could go back, even if it's just to listen more carefully and get the fuck out of the office before he could catch me.

Being sorry for getting caught isn't really sorry, but I'm hoping Alexandre won't be able to tell the difference.

"Please don't be angry. I shouldn't have snooped. I'm so sorry, please don't hurt me. Please forgive me, Alexandre, please! I didn't think you'd be so angry, it's my fault, I should have listened. I've been a bad girl, please, please—"

The words tumble from my lips once I start, one after another, until I'm speaking so fast I can hardly breathe. "I know you don't want to hurt me, Alexandre, please! I'm so sorry, I'm so sorry, I didn't think—"

I'm crying too hard again to speak, and my head drops forward, some of my hair escaping from under the maid's cap and falling around my face. Dimly, I see him stand up from the couch, and every muscle in my body tightens with panic and the need to run, to flee, to get away. But at the same time, I can't move, frozen to the spot, a rabbit caught in a trap.

"You're right that I don't want to hurt you, *petit*," he says, his voice slightly less harsh. "I don't want to be cruel to you. But you *must* learn to obey. You are mine, my *petit poupée, mon chouchou*, and you must learn to trust your master. You must learn to obey me in all things, without question. And then—" his hand touches my cheek, and I force myself not to flinch back. But he doesn't strike me. To be fair, he never has. Instead, his fingers slip beneath my chin, tilting my swollen and tear-stained face up so that I'm forced to look at him. "Then you will be my good girl again, won't you, *petit*?"

I nod speechlessly, relief washing over me like a drowning wave. *He hasn't hurt me. He's barely touched me. Maybe I overreacted. Perhaps it was all an insane overreaction, everything I did, coming in here—*

"You will have to earn my trust again," Alexandre says sternly, dropping his hand from my chin. He steps back, looking down at me, and I can see how intensely aroused he still is. He must be achingly hard, painfully so, but he doesn't so much as acknowledge it. He doesn't move to adjust himself or touch his rigid cock. Although I'm kneeling right in front of him, he doesn't give the slightest sign that he expects me to notice it, much less relieve him by sucking him off.

"Since you wanted to be in my study so badly," he continues, his voice lowering to its normal calm pitch, even and cool. In a way, the lack of emotion is almost as frightening as his anger. I want to hear him be pleased with me again, to praise me, to speak to me in that kind, encouraging way that he sometimes does. His indifference is almost as painful as his anger.

"You will stay here, kneeling where you are, until dinnertime. You are not to move, not to stand, not to change position. I will come and get you when it's time to eat. Am I understood?" Alexandre pauses, and I nod quickly, even as my heart sinks. Kneeling here for that long will be excruciatingly painful—but it could be worse.

It could be worse, I repeat in my head. I know how accurate that is. Kneeling on a rug as punishment is far from the worst thing that's happened to me.

"Yvette will not be here tonight," he continues, and I feel a flush of happiness at that, but it lasts for only a second. "I'd meant to have you eat at the table, as I'd planned on normally doing since she wouldn't be here to object. But since you've decided to act like a misbehaving pet, I see no choice but to treat you as one until you earn my trust and my forgiveness once more. So as a lesson in manners, you will eat on a plate that I will bring you, here on the floor. And for every meal hereafter, whether in your bedroom or in the dining room, you will do the same, until I say differently. Am I understood?"

Mind your manners. Even now, it grates on me, but if I had—well, I wouldn't be in this position.

I also wouldn't know the truth about what he'd paid for me. That, for some reason, I'm worth such an outlandish amount to him.

I still don't know *why*, though. And now is definitely not the time to try to find out.

I nod mutely, fresh tears sliding down my cheeks. In a matter of minutes, everything between us has shifted. He towers over me, his face still grim and set, even though his voice has returned to normal. He's still angry at me.

He plans to make me eat off of the floor like a misbehaving puppy. To leave me here. To force me to obey his commands.

And a part of me, even as I feel my eyes well up with misery and humiliation, feels that tingling spreading across my skin, down between my thighs. That shivering feeling as Alexandre looms over me, powerful and dominating.

My master. My *owner*.

"Answer me," he says sharply, and I flinch.

"Yes," I whisper. "I understand."

"Yes, what?" he barks, and I raise my eyes to his, seeing the implacable expression on his face.

"Yes, sir," I whisper.

I feel an inexplicable rush of arousal as the words slip from my lips, and without my panties, there's nothing to stop it. I can feel it, sticky on my thighs, and from the way his eyes widen slightly, I think he knows. I see his cock twitch in his pants, thick and hard and inches from my face.

But he doesn't so much as touch it through the crisp fabric of his trousers.

"I'll know if you move," he says sternly. And then, without another word or a hint that he's even noticed his own arousal or confirmation that he's noticed mine, Alexandre flicks off the light, turning and stalking out of the room as he closes the door behind him.

Leaving me in total darkness.

* * *

THE TEMPTATION TO touch myself is strong, almost overpowering. He hadn't told me that I couldn't. He said to kneel here, without getting up, without changing position. But I don't have to change position for that.

He hadn't even acknowledged the possibility, but he'd known. He'd known that he'd aroused me. I'd seen his eyes widen, as if he'd seen some shift in my body language, felt a change in the air. Smelled my desire.

My cheeks flush hotly in the darkness, so much so that I think if anyone were in the room, they'd be able to see the blush on my face. The thought is humiliating—and even more intensely arousing.

I can feel it slipping down my thighs, my bare pussy drenched with it. Between my swollen folds, I can feel my clit throbbing, aching to be touched, and I squeeze my thighs tightly together, shifting so that I can get a little bit of friction. I'm amazed that he didn't tie my hands behind my back, order me not to touch myself, and prevent this somehow. Tell me that I couldn't come. But other than last night in the bath, as a direct result of Yvette's baiting, Alexandre has never acknowledged anything sexual between us.

Still, it feels like a test. *I'll know if you move,* he'd said. Will he know if I do this? Even if I don't actively touch myself, will he know?

I can't help it. I squirm on the rug, kneeling there, my hands planted firmly in front of me and then clenched by my sides in fists. The desire, nagging at first, spreads through me. Denying it makes it worse. It makes it bigger, more demanding. Telling myself that I shouldn't feel this way, that his treatment of me shouldn't have turned me on, doesn't help. Telling myself that I shouldn't want him doesn't help.

He's protecting you. Keeping you safe. Preventing you from making mistakes that could get you in trouble. He didn't hurt you. As angry as he was, he didn't hurt you. Can you say the same about others? This punishment is uncomfortable, but it's for your own good.

Your own good.

Those last words sound like Alexandre's voice in my ear, as if he were in the room with me. I shift away from it, as if I can escape my own thoughts, almost daring to move from my position on the rug before I catch myself. There's a pattern in the rug, and Alexandre is keen enough to notice if I'm kneeling in a different place. I have to stay here, in this spot.

Kneeling, with my legs aching and my pussy dripping down my thighs.

He didn't say not to touch it.

I hold out for as long as I can, knowing that I shouldn't. Knowing it's a test or a trap. But I can't stand it forever. I don't know how long I kneel there in the darkness with my eyes streaming tears and my pussy aching before my hand drifts to my thigh, pushing up my skirt. Before it slips between my legs, my fingers delve between my slick, drenched folds, instantly finding my clit.

This isn't about teasing myself to a climax like last night. This isn't hesitant or unhurried or for Alexandre's eyes as much as my own pleasure. He could come back at any moment. This is about sheer, burning arousal, the hard throbbing clit under my fingertips,

IRISH SAVIOR

and my desperate need to orgasm. I press my fingers against it, pushing back the tiny bit of skin so that they're directly against my most sensitive flesh. I bite my lip hard to keep from moaning as I rub hard and fast, my thighs quivering as my hips grind against my hand.

I don't change position. I stay right where I am, my hand cupping my pussy as I massage my clit, my teeth sunken into my lip. My other fist clenched as I force myself to stay absolutely silent even as the intense pleasure crashes through me, taking my breath away.

It takes a matter of seconds. I come hard and fast, my hot, wet flesh pressed against my hand. At that moment, I don't care if he knows. I don't care if he finds out and punishes me. The pleasure is too much, too good, my clit hot and throbbing against my wet fingers, my entire body tense and quivering, and it's everything I needed. It's worth anything that happens. I want to plunge two of my fingers into my drenched, clenching pussy and fuck myself to another climax, but I don't dare. I can't shift my position enough for that. All I can do is grind against my hand, drawing out the pleasure as long as possible before my clit becomes too sensitive, and I pull my hand away, gasping.

It's not until the urgency of the need fades that I know what a terrible mistake that was.

There's no way he won't know. My fingers are sticky with my cum, my pussy and thighs even more drenched than before, my skirt crumpled up on my legs, my face and chest flushed and hot. I know exactly what he'll see.

A disobedient pet that came without permission, even though she knew better, simply because he hadn't explicitly said "no."

A bad girl.

His bad girl.

A flutter of excitement quickens in my chest, and I crush it as fast as I possibly can.

I kneel there in the darkness as the minutes tick by.

When the door opens, I smell food. Alexandre's brought me dinner, and my stomach rumbles. The light from the hall floods in, outlining him, and I see him stride towards the Tiffany lamp by the couch, reaching for the switch.

Oh no.

He turns to face me, and I see the flicker of realization on his face. His nostrils flare as his eyes flick down to my reddened chest, my wrinkled skirt, and very slowly, he sets the plate of food aside on the side table.

"Pick up your skirt, *petit*," Alexandre says calmly. "And spread your thighs. Show me what you've been doing."

His tone brooks no argument. My heart races in my chest. I know he's going to be angry. He'll punish me. But how?

I've pushed him again. Pushed someone whose limits I don't know, who hasn't hurt me yet, but could.

We could play with her together.

Mine.

Other girls. Other girls who disappeared.

I'm playing a dangerous game.

"Anastasia."

I'm learning that when he says my name and not one of my nicknames, the danger is approaching. That he's getting impatient, too angry to play games with me. That I can't stall any longer.

Slowly, I reach for my skirt, pulling it partway up my thighs.

"Higher."

I pull it up a little more, another inch.

Alexandre lets out a frustrated sigh. "I'm not playing a game with you, Anastasia." His voice doesn't sound aroused, just irritated. "You know what I want to see, and you know that I know what you've done. So raise your skirt up to your hips, and spread your thighs. If you were shameless enough to orgasm here in my study, you're shameless enough to show it to me."

I don't dare disobey him again.

My hands are shaking when I clutch my skirt and lift it up, all the way up to my hips, spreading my thighs wide. Wide enough for my pussy to open up, for him to see everything in the glowing light. The glistening moisture on my thighs, my folds, my flushed clit. Everything, bare and vulnerable to him.

Part of me wants him to react. To lose control. To be overcome with desire the way I was, and grab me, shove me back onto the rug. To eat me out, strip me bare, fuck me. To make me *his*, the way he keeps saying I am.

To stop being so detached, so cold. So dismissive even when he's clearly turned on.

I can see him getting hard again as he looks at my bare, exposed pussy. His cock is thickening as I watch, straining against his pants. He hasn't changed, still in the black suit trousers and white button-down shirt that he'd worn out earlier with the sleeves rolled up to his elbows. His hair looks messier now around his handsome, stern face.

His piercing blue eyes drag upwards, all the way up to mine.

"You've been a bad girl," he says, his voice cool, detached. As if it doesn't matter to him, all of the earlier anger faded. "I told you last night to touch yourself. I knew you needed it, and you deserved it. You were well-behaved, even when Yvette tormented you. Were you a good girl today, *petit?*"

I swallow hard, my mouth going dry. I shake my head slowly.

"Answer me."

"No, sir," I whisper. And there it is again, the flush of arousal, turning my skin pink and making me wet.

Alexandre looks down. "You've made a wet spot on my rug," he observes. "So horny that you've made a mess." His eyes narrow. "Did I tell you that you could come when I left you here?"

"No, sir."

"Do you think that I didn't know you were aroused?"

"No, sir," I whisper again. "I mean—I think you knew. I'm sorry—"

"Don't you think I would have told you if I wanted you to come, *petit poupée?*"

His little doll. His to dress and undress, bathe and comb, feed and pet and allow pleasure when it suits him.

His to deny, when it suits him, too.

It should make me angry, not aroused. It should make me want to fight back.

But all I feel is a desperate, aching need to please him and an even deeper ache that can't be satisfied with just my fingers. An ache for *him*. To please him in every way, so that maybe he'll be happy with me.

So that maybe he could love me.

I want so badly to be loved.

"I'm sorry," I whisper again.

"Not sorry enough to not still be dripping all over my rug." Alexandre waves a hand, sitting back on the couch. "Do it."

I stare at him, startled, my hands still clutching my skirt. *He can't mean it.*

His eyes narrow at me as he leans forward, fixed on mine.

He can't.

ANA

"Clearly, you need to come so badly that you can't control yourself. You need to understand the consequences of your actions. So instead of touching yourself in the dark, do it now, if you need it so badly."

"I'm—" I swallow hard, hoping his last words constitute a way out of this. "I don't. I don't, really, I don't need to—"

"Anastasia." His voice sharpens again. "You're making a mess of my rug. And you need to be punished. So spread your thighs wider, so I can see everything. And touch yourself until you come while I watch. That's an order." Alexandre's eyes narrow. "Exactly as you did earlier."

"I—"

"*Now.*"

His voice, deep and rough and thickly accented, feels as if it goes straight to my throbbing clit. I feel it pulse, my pussy clenching, and I gasp.

"Now, Anastasia. Hold your skirt out of the way so that I can see."

I nod mutely, my heart racing in my chest as I grip my skirt with my left hand, holding it up so that nothing obscures his few. My face and chest are flushed bright red with humiliation. I've never felt like this before. It's not as if I've never been on display for a man before.

I've had my legs over the shoulders of plenty of guys, had them spread me open so they could see every inch of my pussy while they fucked me, been fucked from behind with a clear view for them of everything.

But this is different. Just like the bath, this feels intimate, intense, controlling in a way that's vulnerable and terrifying and embarrassing and deeply, deeply arousing all at once. I can feel my pulse throbbing in my veins, my heart racing until I think he must be able to hear it.

My arousal slipping down my thighs, wetter than ever. Drenched.

There's no way out. And I don't even know anymore if I want to stop.

I need to come so badly.

He's so hard. I look at his cock as my fingers find my clit, spreading my folds with my thumb and ring finger so that he can see what he's demanded to be displayed for him. My index and middle finger are on my clit, already rubbing, circling the hard, sensitive flesh as I watch him straining against his fly, visibly twitching against the fabric.

But he ignores it. His eyes are fixed on me, watching almost hungrily as I rub my clit, faster and faster, my fingers even more drenched than before as I grind against my hand helplessly, needing it. Needing the pleasure, the release, somehow even more turned on than before by him watching. Knowing that he's so fiercely aroused too adds to it; knowing that he's denying it pushes me even closer to the edge. I don't understand it, but seeing Alexandre sitting there, tense and stern and rock-hard because of *me*, has me on the edge of climax even faster than before, when I'd done this in the dark.

"Stop."

His voice cuts through the air, and it doesn't register at first. My fingers are flying over my clit, my hips arching into my hand, my pussy clenching hollowly at a desperately needed cock that isn't there, *his* cock, eager and waiting for me, if he'd only give in, only fuck me the way we both want him to.

"I said stop!" Alexandre is on his feet, his hand grabbing for my wrist, yanking it away from my throbbing clit, a second away from orgasm. Even as he takes my hand away, I can feel the dying tremors of it through my thighs, a faint echo of what it would have been before he ruined it.

I cry out in frustration, half moan, half sob, looking up at Alexandre with tear-filled eyes.

"You're in here to be punished, not for your own pleasure. Not so you can sit here rubbing your pussy over and over." He shakes his head, almost in disgust, and it reminds me of his reaction to my outburst when I'd hallucinated the jewelry box. Even in my foggy, lust-hazed state, something clearly connects in my mind.

It's emotions that Alexandre doesn't like. Intense, deep emotions. My outburst had made him uncomfortable, and so does this, this raw naked lust. This *need*.

My guess is that his makes him uncomfortable, too. Which is part of why he hasn't touched me, why he's ignoring the clearly painful erection threatening to tear through his fly. Not just because *beautiful things are meant to be admired, not used.*

Because he's afraid of how it would make him feel to use me. To lose control.

To *feel*.

It's even likely why he got his anger under control so quickly, even as intense as it had been.

He steps back, dropping my hand. I don't dare move. My hand is frozen, clutching my skirt, everything still bare and exposed, but he's not looking any longer. He reaches for the plate and sets it down in front of me, taking a hasty step back as he runs his hand through his hair.

"You need to be punished, but I won't starve you." His voice is deep and rough, but the anger has drained out of it again. "Eat, Anastasia. Don't touch yourself again, no matter how badly you think you need it. I'll come back to collect your plate and put you to bed."

Alexandre stalks out of the room, and I look down at the plate. It's baked chicken with herbs, tender and fragrant and sliced so that I can eat it easily, thin crisp asparagus, and a slice of baguette with butter. Hardly bread and water in a prison cell. My stomach rumbles again—

I'd forgotten to eat lunch—and even though part of me wants to disobey him and refuse to eat, I can't bring myself to. It smells delicious, and I'm starving. There's a glass of water with it, and I drink it quickly, unable to even wait until I start eating.

I let my skirt fall back around my knees and eat the food with my fingers from the plate on the floor, and I don't care. Or I do, but not enough to stop me. I eat every last bit, knowing it will please him and because I want to. When the plate is clean, I stay there, kneeling, waiting for him to come and get me.

When he does, he doesn't say a word. He picks up the plate and takes it back to the kitchen, and then returns, picking me up in one swift, graceful motion like he's done so many times before now. It feels familiar, comforting, and despite everything that's happened since he came home, I feel myself curling into his chest, wanting his warmth. Wanting *him.*

My knees and calves are burning, on the verge of cramping, my feet are aching. Kneeling on the floor for so long was painful, but I push it out of my head because I can't stop myself from craving comfort from him. He's all I have, the only chance I have for affection, and he's proven he won't withhold it from me forever.

As long as I'm a good girl.

If only that weren't so hard to do.

Alexandre sets me down carefully in the middle of the floor, and it's a struggle to stay on my feet, but I manage. He undresses me swiftly and efficiently, leaving me bare and shivering, and disappears into the bathroom. When he appears a moment later, it's with two damp cloths in his hand. He stands in front of me, cleaning my face and hands with one. Then with an equally businesslike motion, my pussy and inner thighs with the other, wiping all traces of my transgressions earlier away.

He tosses them aside in the hamper and I stand there motionless as he gets me into my pajamas, buttoning up the front and lifting me into the bed. I could cry with relief to be lying down. I'm exhausted from the emotions of the day, but something stops me when he hands me the tea that I know is laced with a sedative—probably a heavier one than usual tonight. He won't want to be woken up by my nightmares or worry about me wandering around the house before he's up and prepared to instruct me tomorrow on how my day will go.

But I can't get the image of him earlier out of my head, tense on the couch, or standing by my head, his rigid cock inches away. He hadn't touched it. Hadn't done anything to give himself the release I know he must have desperately needed. Sneaking a glance now, I don't see any evidence of it. Had he taken care of it earlier while I was eating?

The thought of him in his room, fist wrapped around his aching cock, sends a hot wave of desire through me all over again. I want to see it. I want to see him naked. I want to see as much of him as he's seen of me.

When he gives me the tea, I drink it. But I don't swallow. I relax my mouth, holding the tea there, and look up at him innocently as he watches me.

"Goodnight, *petit*," Alexandre says finally, his mouth tight as he turns to switch off the lamp, taking the teacup from my hand.

I don't answer, but he won't think that's odd. Sometimes I'm already falling asleep by the time he leaves, and tonight he'll just think I'm angry with him. Which I'm not, exactly. I'm frustrated, confused, and exhausted—and curious.

The minute I hear his footsteps recede down the hall, far enough that I know he's not coming back, I slip out of bed and spit the tea into one of the houseplants, my jaw aching. I slide back under the covers quickly, my tongue tingling from the sedative, and wait until I know he's done with whatever nighttime rounds he makes in the apartment. Until he should be in his bedroom, the one other place I'm not allowed to go.

In for a penny, in for a pound.

He didn't hurt me earlier. He's shown a clear reluctance to be cruel, even when he's angry with me. Is it really going to be so much worse if he catches me sneaking near his bedroom?

Maybe. I'll just have to be more careful this time so I don't get caught.

I should stay in bed, but the curiosity is too much. I slip out and down the hall, pausing every few feet to make sure I don't hear him still downstairs or coming back down from his room. My heart is racing in my chest as I put one foot on the bottom of the spiral staircase, holding my breath as I hope that it doesn't creak. If he hears me—

It feels like it takes me forever to make it up to the second floor, one careful footstep at a time. That's excruciating, too, because once I'm about halfway up, there's no way to explain this if he should come out of his room for some reason and see me. *I didn't drink the tea, sorry. I know I was supposed to, that I was disobedient again, but I just—*

Just what? There's no logical reason for being on the steps leading upstairs at this time of night, the apartment dark and quiet all around me. *I wanted to read a book in the library. Yes, at this hour. No, I'm not lying. Why would you even think such a thing?*

It's not an exciting kind of danger. I've been at the mercy of too many men to find sneaking around and risking Alexandre's anger thrilling. My stomach is in knots at the thought of the risk, but there's another feeling there too, that quivering, trembling, skin-prickling desire. Not because of the danger, but because of what I might see. Because on the other side of the door, only a few feet away from me now, Alexandre is in the other forbidden room, and I don't know what I'll find there, what he's doing. The curiosity fills me, and it's a feeling almost like the one you get when you first start dating someone you *really* like, when you feel almost obsessed with knowing every little detail about them, even the smallest and least consequential things.

When one day, you go from not even knowing them to wanting to know *every* single thing, like what their routine is in the morning even if it's the most boring thing ever, just toasting breakfast strudels and sleepily making coffee and scrolling through their phone. Even if they take the same route to work every day, even if their nighttime involves reheating leftovers and watching Netflix, it all becomes fascinating, mysterious, all pieces that make up this person who has suddenly infiltrated your heart and bones and blood and certainly your better sense.

That's how Alexandre makes me feel. Not like I want to watch Netflix with him or sit while he scrolls through his phone—I haven't seen a television in the apartment. I'm not sure Alexandre owns a cell phone, or if he does, he must use it strictly for emergencies.

But something as simple as what he might be doing before bed—brushing his teeth or reading a book or, I don't know, doing shirtless pushups in the middle of the room—seems suddenly fascinating. Part of it is how eccentric and distant he often is; it humanizes him in a way, to think of him doing something as simple as flossing or trying to pick out a book to read in bed.

After what happened today, I'll take anything that makes Alexandre seem more human, more ordinary, and less like a terrifying billionaire who I've realized quite clearly I don't understand in the slightest.

But I *want* to. That's the part that I know makes even less sense than anything else, but I want to understand him. I want—I want so many things.

The broken parts of me all respond to him, aching to be wanted back, to be loved, to be cared for and protected. And that's what he wanted, wasn't it? Something beautiful and damaged.

I could be that for him.

I realize, as I step up gingerly onto the second floor, holding my breath as I try not to make any noise, that his door is partially open. *He must have really thought I wouldn't sneak up here.*

That flicker of guilt stirs in my stomach again, like when I'd realized the study wasn't locked. But of course, he wouldn't have thought I'd come up—he'd given me the drugged tea and hadn't realized that I hadn't drank it.

As far as he knows, he's alone in a silent house, with no one to bother him until sometime tomorrow morning.

My heart skips a beat in my chest at the thought of that kind of freedom—and at the idea of what he might be doing with it.

The light from his room is streaming out over the hardwood floor and the long rug that runs the length of the hallway next to it. As I stand frozen in place, trying to decide how to move forward without being heard, I hear a rustling from his room and then a strange, slick, heavy sound. I hear something else, something almost like a deep male groan, and something hot and primal flutters in my chest at the sound of it, a reaction that's almost purely instinctual.

I don't *think* about moving towards his room, exactly. I don't think about what I'm doing at all. I hear him groan again, the sound low and pleasured. My heart stutters in my chest again, my skin prickling and that tight, aching pressure settling down in my groin, spreading through my thighs in a way that makes me feel as if I'm getting wet all over again, even after two climaxes and without even really knowing for sure what's going on inside that room.

I just do it because of that part of me that is so inexplicably drawn to him, the part that is damaged or longing or just grateful that it's him I'm with now and not Alexei—maybe all of those things. The part that doesn't believe that there's anyone else coming for me, that there's anyone else who cares for me even as much as Alexandre does —not any man, at least.

There could be a certain romance to each being all that the other has left. If I depended on him, let him enjoy his fantasies and odd habits of treating me like a doll, and if I obeyed him, he might come to rely on me in some ways too, one day. He might love me. He would, at the very least, protect me.

If I'm his good girl.

But I'm pretty sure good girls don't lurk around the bedroom doors of the men who own them, trying to peek inside without being seen.

I don't regret it, though. Because what I see makes my breath catch in my throat, my pulse leaping as I catch sight of Alexandre, standing next to his canopied bed, left hand gripping one bedpost hard enough that even from here with the only light coming from his lamp, I can see that his knuckles are turning white.

That's not the first thing I notice, though. The first thing I notice, as if I could see anything else, is that he's *naked*. Completely, entirely bare, without a single piece of clothing or accessories or even a pair of fucking socks on him anywhere.

And I can't complain, because while Alexandre clothed is beautiful, while he's always an exceptionally handsome man, Alexandre naked is *glorious*.

He's all lean muscle, from the hard expanse of his back to the perfect curve of his ass, possibly the best ass I've ever seen on a man, and there was a time when I saw them fairly often. He has slim hips and muscled thighs, shoulders that are broad enough without being bulky, and leanly muscled arms. As he shifts back on his heels, I get a good view of his chest, strong and hard and lightly furred with dark hair that leads down to a trail of it across his flat abs, down to—

His chest isn't the only thing that's hard.

Seeing him aroused while clothed was one thing, but this is something else altogether. Alexander's rigid cock juts out from beneath his hips, long and thick enough to fill his hand, his long fingers wrapped around his shaft as he strokes it in long, quick movements that have him panting, groaning, gripping the bedpost. I stare at him from around the edge of the door, and I can't stop. I don't want to stop.

He's fucking gorgeous. And I want him more than ever.

ANA

I hang back, knowing I should take advantage of the fact that he's—*occupied*—and slip away, back down the stairs and to my room before he catches me. But I can't move. I'm frozen to the spot, my pulse caught in my throat, my own breathing coming quick and short as arousal washes over me, prickling my skin and making me feel hot and flushed as I watch him.

I don't think I've ever actually watched a man jerk off before. It could have been hot, probably, with some of the guys I've dated or slept with in the past, but it just never came up, so to speak. Guys my age were always eager to fuck, in a hurry to get past the part where they had to arouse me and on with the main event. I had asked a boyfriend once if I could watch him, even just as foreplay, and he'd looked at me like I was crazy.

If I wanted to jerk off, I'd just stay home. Then I wouldn't have to pay for dinner. He'd laughed then, like he'd said something really funny, and picked me up, tossing me back on the bed. *What's the point of jerking off if you've got a hot girl in your bed?*

I'd definitely had some good sex, too, back when I was going through men in New York City like the world might end at any second. But by and large, the men I'd met had been more concerned with their pleasure than taking the time to explore what I might like. Hell, *I* hadn't even gotten to fully figure it out. There are probably plenty of kinks that turn me on that I haven't even come across.

You found one of them today, didn't you? Maybe a couple.

I shiver at that thought, feeling my thighs squeeze together at the memory of Alexandre demanding I raise my skirt up and expose myself to him, the way he'd spoken to me.

I've slept with some very attractive men, encountered a decent number of excellent dicks, and had my share of interesting sex. But nothing, *nothing* had ever made me as wet as I'd been today, kneeling in the dark of the study and then being forced to repeat the experience for Alexandre's disdainful eyes.

And now, watching him stroke his cock, naked and out in the open like this, his feet spread and hand bracing against the bed as he starts to speed up, I can feel it all over again. It doesn't feel like any arousal I've experienced before. It feels like a bone-deep need, a longing that I can't satisfy no matter how many times I get myself off. I wonder if he's feeling the same thing as he fists his cock, gripping it as his hips thrust upwards into his hand.

Is he thinking about me? Is he picturing me on the rug of the study, my skirt pulled up around my hips, touching myself for him? Is he remembering the sounds I made? The way I smelled?

I'd been so embarrassed earlier, but here in this thickly charged environment, the air nearly crackling with desire as I crouch behind the door and watch him with a rapidly quickening heartbeat, I don't feel that hot rush of humiliation when I remember it. The only heat I feel is licking across my skin, beneath it, in my veins, making me feel as if I'm burning up as I watch Alexandre push himself closer and closer to the release that he must desperately need.

His hand falters for a second, slowing, and I see him let go of the bedpost, reaching over with his other hand to move something around atop the bed. It piques my curiosity again, and I raise up a little, daring to peer around the door a little further so that I can see what he's doing.

I can't see very much, but I manage to get a good enough view that

I can tell there are pictures scattered across the bedspread. Not drawn pictures—photos. They look like Polaroids, though I can't entirely be sure, and I can't really see details of who's in the pictures, though from the glimpses I get, it looks like photos of women.

My stomach flips, jealousy that I know I have no right to feel rising up with a hot, burning sensation that makes me want to cry. *Who are they?* I have an inkling, but I push it aside because I can't stand to think about that. Not right now. I'd rather think that he's looking at porn while he jerks off—an odd collection of porn, but that would fit with Alexandre's proclivities.

All men do that. I've never known a man who didn't watch porn or look at porn sometimes. But what Alexandre does, collecting broken things, possibly even other girls like me that are mysteriously gone now except for maybe, just maybe those Polaroids on the bed, isn't something all men do. It isn't something that *anyone* does, except for Alexandre.

I just wish I knew *why*.

His hand lingers on himself as he rearranges the photos, his fingers lingering on one as he starts to stroke again. The small voice in my head whispers that I shouldn't get distracted, that I should try to slip away, that all of this is a terrible, dangerous idea. But I can't stop looking at him. My mouth feels dry, desire pounding in my veins like a second heartbeat, and I want so badly to slip around the door, walk into the bedroom and across the hardwood floor to join him, to sink to my knees, and taste him. I can imagine how he would feel in my mouth, thick and hot, hard as iron sheathed in velvet skin, pressing against my tongue as I'd lick away the slick arousal from the head, moaning as I discover what Alexandre tastes like. *Salty*, I think, my hand straying to the front of my silk pajama bottoms without my meaning for it to. *Tangy. Hot on my tongue.* I can imagine him pushing himself into my mouth, his hand curling around the back of my head, his cock sliding into my throat as I look up at him from my knees, wanting to please him. Wanting him to be pleased *with me*.

Alexandre is stroking faster now, his shoulders tense, his hand gripping his cock in a vise as he stares down at the photos on the bed, his face unreadable as he clutches the bedpost. I know he's close, and I've barely even started to touch myself, my fingers sliding inside of my pajamas and over the already slick folds of my pussy, soaked just from watching Alexandre pleasure himself.

I know I shouldn't. If he catches me—but if he catches me here outside his bedroom, spying on him, the punishment will likely be severe anyway. This can't make it much worse, and I'm aching for it, my body crying out for a release from the tension that's crackling in the air of the bedroom, like a gathering electrical storm.

Everything I've seen Alexandre avoid, everything I realized he was attempting to control so tightly today—anger, fear, lust—I see in his face as he strokes his cock faster, his hips rigid now instead of thrusting. I can see him pick up a rhythm, likely the one that will make him come, and I feel a quiver of frustration because I want to come too. I want to come *with* him, and I've only just started to brush my fingers over my clit—

My body spasms as my fingertips find the hard, aching nub, and I have to clap my other hand over my mouth to keep from crying out with the sudden, intense pleasure of the touch. I'm so aroused that my pussy lips are already swollen and puffy, parted slightly so that my fingers can easily slide between them, trailing in the slick arousal until I reach the spot where I need the friction most. As it is, I can't stop the muffled moan from behind my hand, and my heart almost stops in my chest, certain that Alexandre is going to hear me and I'll be caught.

But he's too lost in the moment, beyond hearing or seeing or thinking about anything except the oncoming rush of his impending orgasm. His jaw is clenched, his piercing blue eyes fixated on the mess of photos on the bed, a dozen emotions flickering across his face as his hand twists around the length of his cock, his palm rubbing over the glistening head as I see the muscles of his perfect ass tighten, every inch of his body stiffening as he approaches the edge.

I realize dizzily that I'm almost there already, too, that watching him turned me on so much that I'm already primed, my body eager for a release after just a few seconds of pressure against my clit. I can feel it throbbing under my first two fingers, my body trembling with pleasure as I press the heel of my other hand against my mouth, forcing myself to stay absolutely silent as I race towards my own climax along with him, the immediacy and intimacy of it only intensifying the pleasure.

It's been so fucking long. Maybe that's why I crave him, why I want him, not because I'm so broken that I'm lusting after the man who bought me and keeps me captive, but because it's just been *so long.* So fucking long since I was touched with desire, kissed, held. So long since a man tried to get me into bed, flirted with me, asked me back to his place, or agreed all too quickly to come back to mine. It's been so, *so* long since I've had sex, felt someone inside of me, wrapped myself around someone else as the heat of their skin sank into mine, and it feels like a desperate, hollow craving like I'm starving for all of it. I never thought of myself as a nymphomaniac. I was pretty sure back then that I was having a healthy amount of sex for a pretty girl in her early twenties living in Manhattan. It might have felt a little skewed then, given that my best friend and roommate was a virgin who barely looked at guys, let alone did anything dirty with them, but it wasn't excessive.

I was just having fun back then. It hadn't meant anything, except that it felt good. Now I feel like I'm drowning, like my own touch is just enough to hold back the need so that it doesn't consume me, but a small voice in my head whispers that it can't last forever. That I can't spend the rest of my life sneaking around Alexandre's apartment, spying on him as he jerks off, and I hide and touch myself along with him.

Deep down, I don't think that it's just because it's been so long since I've gotten laid. I stare at Alexandre carefully from around the door, my hand still working inside my silk pajama pants, my breath coming in small, quick gasps as I watch him shudder, his cock straining in his fist as he groans aloud, a deep and visceral sound that tells me he'll come any second now.

Clothed and groomed for the day, Alexandre is eccentrically handsome, but naked and in the throes of pleasure like this, he's magnificent. I can see every inch of his leanly muscled body. I let myself take in the sight greedily, enjoying the sight of so much attractive male flesh on display—and that's not even considering the eight or nine inches of hard, throbbing cock between his legs. I force myself to forget who he is, what he's done, the conflict between us and what I am to him so that I can enjoy it, because it has been *so fucking long* since I've just gotten to appreciate a handsome naked man, since I've gotten to look and let myself be swept away with desire.

I'm close, I realize in the same second that I see Alexandre's hips shudder, his entire body going stiff as his head tips back, his hand suddenly a blur on his cock as he jerks it hard and fast, his teeth clenched as he bows forward suddenly, his hand slipping from the bedpost and catching on the edge of the mattress as he looks down at the spread of photos, his expression almost tortured as I peek a little further around the door just in time to see him shove his cockhead hard into his fist, the first spurt of his cum jetting out over his fingers.

He keeps stroking furiously, a sound that's almost a roar coming from his mouth as his head bows forwards, his spine curling forward as he thrusts into his hand, hot cum coating his hand as his entire body ripples with the fierce pleasure of his orgasm—and before I can catch my breath or do anything other than shove the heel of my hand against my mouth once more in a desperate attempt to keep quiet, I feel my entire body convulse in a sudden spasm of pure, electrifying bliss.

Oh god, oh god, oh god—I bite down on the heel of my hand, sobbing against my palm with the sheer pleasure of it, collapsing against the door as my knees give out. Watching Alexandre orgasm is the hottest fucking thing I've ever seen. I can't look away from his quivering body, tall and broad and masculine, his breath coming in hard pants as he groans, squeezing his fist around his cock as his thighs flex. More cum spills out from his cockhead over his hand.

The sight is so intensely erotic that I feel like I can't breathe.

Alexandre is almost animalistic in his pleasure, his entire being focused on his throbbing cock, not caring about the cum on his hand and wrist and floor or what it might get all over, only his desperate need for release. It's all the more intense because I've seen the other side of him too, the one that can't stand dust and insists on the apartment being cleaned top to bottom every day, the one that was both angered and turned on by my arousal soaking his rug.

I'm not surprised that even as his orgasm recedes, I can still see cum dripping from the tip of his cock, sliding down his shaft as he half-collapses against the bedpost, still squeezing and lightly stroking as the aftershocks ripple through him. He'd been hard for so long today that I can only imagine how intensely he must have needed to come, how many times he'd had to force it back, holding onto his control with an iron grip. His orgasm must have been blindingly good, and the thought of him fighting back that need does nothing to calm down the desire that I can still feel pulsing through my veins.

I want to go to him all over again, cross the room and drop to my knees in front of him so that I can lick away the lingering drops of cum clinging to his cock, take his softening length in my mouth until he's hard again, suck him until he's throbbing and solid between my lips, and then—

Then what? Are you going to fuck him? Do you really *want to do that? You can pretend long enough to get off and indulge your fantasies, but at some point, you've got to come back to reality, and—*

The photos are still spread across the bed, shattering some of the fantasy. I still can't see them very well, although I can definitely make out a few feminine shapes. They're all definitely Polaroids, some newer looking than others, with black ink scrawls across the bottom in various handwritings.

You know what that is. You know.

Maybe I'm being paranoid.

Or maybe I'm just gaslighting myself into thinking better of this man than he could possibly deserve. I snatch my hand away from my pussy, squeezing my thighs together as I feel the damp silk between my legs clings to my skin. I start to think rapidly about how to retreat before he decides he needs to pee or get some water or a midnight snack and catches me. He'll punish me if he does, and something tells me that, especially now that he's had his orgasm, it won't be as embarrassingly pleasurable as spreading myself open for him and masturbating for him.

You saw what you wanted to see, naughty girl, the voice in my head whispers, and it sounds alarmingly like Yvette, mocking me. *Go back to bed now, before he catches you. Run!*

I don't run. I know better than *that*. I do back up hastily, though, as I see him straighten, reaching for the photos with the hand that wasn't wrapped around his cock and is now drenched with his cum. I get one glimpse of him dispassionately scraping them into a pile, gathering them up as carelessly as he might a stack of papers, in distinct opposition to the way I saw him staring down at them as he stroked himself earlier.

Whatever he'd felt, whatever he'd *allowed* himself to feel while caught in the iron grip of his lust, he's locked it back up now. I saw it on his face just before I retreated, the animalistic need gone, his jaw relaxed, his face impassive and cool, as he usually is.

The Alexandre that I usually know. The one who caught me in the study today.

The one that I still want, just the same.

I feel strangely guilty for spying on him as I scramble quickly back down the stairs, moving as fast as I can while still trying not to make any noise, for watching him without his knowledge in his most vulnerable moments. I'd at least been aware that he was watching me earlier when he'd demanded I put myself on display for him. Still, as far as I know, Alexandre has no idea I was hiding behind the door.

If he had? I honestly don't know. The man I'd been watching had been so caught in the throes of lust and emotion that he might have ignored me, at least for the moment, rather than take a chance on losing the promise of his onrushing climax. But I'm not naïve enough to think that even if he'd tabled dealing with me in favor of an orgasm

—which is fair enough—that he wouldn't have turned his attention back to me the second he was finished coming.

And not in the way I'm craving it, either.

What are *you craving, exactly?* I ask myself almost bitterly as I slip noiselessly down the hall and back into bed, tucking the covers tightly around me as I slide down onto the pillows. *Love? Companionship? Affection? Safety? Pleasure?*

And out of those, what could Alexandre really give me if I chose to ignore the circumstances of our relationship and gave in only to pure longing? Safety, perhaps, as long as I didn't anger him, and even then, he seemed inclined earlier to force himself to temper his rage rather than hurt me.

Affection, probably. It's easy to remember how he'd fed me, carried me to the bath and bathed me, gently undressed and dressed me again, petting my hair and patting me on the head before leaving me for the day. When I please him, he's more than affectionate with me, even if it's with the clear detachment of an owner to his possession—his pet. His little doll.

Companionship? *I doubt it.* I swallow hard, trying to imagine Alexandre being my *friend*. Maybe in time, if we got to know each other well enough, but even in this brief time, it's become clear to me that Alexandre keeps to himself. I don't even think Yvette knows more than half of him, perhaps, which I privately think is why she's so desperate to keep any other woman away from him—probably in hopes that in time, he'll fall for her.

Alexandre says that Yvette is his friend, but I suspect that a "friend" to Alexandre is different from what it means to others.

Love? I bite my lower lip, forcing myself not to cry at the thought. I *miss* being loved, and not just romantic love. I miss Sofia, the way we laughed together, the way we finished each other's sentences, the way we knew each other, down to our bones. *The best worst roommate I ever had.* My best friend and the truest example of love I've ever had. I know it must be killing her to have lost me, to be a world away, married and pregnant and unable to come after me. If she weren't pregnant, or maybe even just out of her first trimester, I think she might actually have come after me.

Fat chance. Luca would handcuff her to the bed permanently before he let her run off into danger like that.

The thought brings me up short. I hadn't liked Luca at first—I'd thought he was arrogant, overbearing, and cruel to Sofia. But in time, he'd softened, and I'd gotten to know other sides of him. I'd come to appreciate what he had done for Sofia and was willing to do for her, and even begun to care for him, like a brother that I'm on tentative good terms with. Now it would be something of a joke that he'd lock Sofia up rather than let her risk herself for any reason, regardless of how she felt about it or her opinion.

Alexandre had wanted me to stay out of his study and his bedroom for a reason. What that is, I don't know—but I'm certain he hadn't wanted me to find the bill of sale. He could be hiding things, or he might be protecting me—from knowing too much, from something that might hurt me. While cruel in their own way, his actions might possibly come from a place of caring.

So why is he worse than Luca, or Viktor, even? Viktor definitely hadn't been kind to Caterina in the early days of their marriage. He'd all but bought her, as Alexandre bought me, except Viktor had bargained with peace instead of cash.

I struggle with it, lying there in the dark–with what the real differences are between the men that my closest friends love; the men who, I hope, arrived in time to save them even if they were too late for me. Deep down, I want to find a reason that they're the same, that Alexandre is no worse than any other white-collar criminal I've known—just an eccentric billionaire instead of a mafia boss or Bratva beast.

But my thoughts keep drifting back to the other girls, if they really were here. What Alexandre might have done to them, what might have happened. *Who was here before me? Whose clothes am I wearing? Whose things am I using? Did she sleep in this same bed? What about the ones before her, whoever she was?*

I squeeze my eyes tightly shut, driving the thoughts back before they can drive *me* insane. I don't have any of those answers, and I can't ask Alexandre for them. Which, coupled with the fact that I now know he paid a *hundred million dollars* for me, means that I should be keeping my distance from him as much as I can. Obeying him without question. Putting up walls around my heart and everything else I can lock down emotionally, rather than letting myself be overrun with desire.

Pleasure. The last thing I'd thought of, the last thing I need. That I *crave*, aching for it, but not in the way I used to, for the sake of it. Now I crave it because I feel so lonely all of the time because I want something to fill that space inside of me, to feel like another person cares about me, if only because they're taking the time to give me pleasure.

Alexandre is not that man. He'd given me permission to touch myself in the bath, and he'd ordered me to as a punishment, but he's never touched me with desire. In fact, today, it was *very* clear just how strictly he intends to *not* touch me sexually. He'd had a raging, throbbing erection for most of the time that he'd been in that study with me, yet, he'd studiously ignored it—all the way up until he'd gone to bed, alone, and relieved that need—also alone.

I should be grateful, but I just feel hollow. I close my eyes, almost wishing for the drugged tea, if only so it would be easier to fall asleep. *He owns you,* I tell myself firmly, rolling onto my side and curling into a ball. *You can't fall for a man who owns you. You just can't.*

But as I try to breathe evenly, wanting desperately to fall asleep and get some much-needed rest after the events of the day, I can feel in the depths of my soul that it's becoming a losing battle.

I should forget any romantic ideas of the broken parts of him being drawn to the broken parts of me, or that my relationship is anything to him but something somewhat better than a slave's to their master and, at the moment, somewhat worse than a lapdog's to its owner. *If he paid a hundred million dollars for me, a number I can't even imagine, then it must have been for a reason. A* real *reason. And if it's not sex, then it's something else.*

No one pays a hundred million dollars to have a crippled maid clean their apartment. There's some other reason I'm here.

And instead of longing for Alexandre, I should be trying to uncover it.

I should be trying to get free before something terrible happens.

Instead, I feel like a frightened rabbit, cowering in corners, scurrying from place to place.

And worse yet—I'm a rabbit beginning to fall in love with the very trap that holds me in its teeth.

LIAM

We leave in the morning for Tokyo. Or at least, the plan that the three of us had assembled was to fly to the nearest private hangar and from there meet a driver who would take us to Tokyo, where we could then inquire as to how we might speak to the *oyabun* of the Nakamura faction of the Yakuza.

On paper, it seems simple enough. Levin's password has opened several doors for us now, but as we board the plane, I can see that his expression is terse and set, edged with worry.

I eye him as we take our seats on the plane, Levin, directly across from Max and me on the other side of the aisle. Unlike a commercial flight, there's no worry about cramped legs or screaming children here, no flustered flight attendants or too-cold air, and the whiskey is top-notch.

Though the Kings are as rich as any of the crime families, we don't flaunt it the way the Russians, and especially the Italians, do. My father never owned a private jet, and just the mention of it would have earned him a good deal of censure from the table. The older and even more conservative members of the Kings, wouldn't have faltered at letting him know how they felt about that sort of wastefulness. Why fly private when commercial gets you there just fine?

In fact, one of my brother, Connor's worst fights with our father was over exactly that.

He'd gone to a conclave on his own, in our father's place on account of illness—and I had thought privately then, as a test. Our father had enjoyed doing that—testing Connor to see if he continued to embody the leader that our father was trying so industriously to build him into, and he'd done it often. Connor might not have resented it so much if our father had treated it like a necessary evil, a part of the burden of fatherhood and the process of raising a leader of Kings. But instead, it was always clear that he enjoyed keeping Connor on edge, making him guess as to what the consequences of any given word or deed might be. He would praise him effusively, make him feel as if there were nothing he could do to lose our father's love and pride, only to viciously cut him down over nothing minutes later.

Sometimes, I think that it's not a surprise that Connor left, so much as that he didn't do it sooner.

It was our father's fault, too, that Connor and I weren't closer. While the pressures and burdens and responsibilities of being the future heir were heaped on Connor early on, weighing him down by the time he'd only barely become a teenager, our father largely ignored me. I was left to do what I wanted, to pursue whatever took my fancy at any given time. If I'd acted out or disobeyed or even caused trouble, our father hardly noticed. Even if I'd doubled down, wanting some of our father's attention for myself—positive or negative—I usually got nothing at all.

Connor, on the other hand, couldn't make so much as one misstep without our father raining down the fires of hell and brimstone on him, as if the slightest mistake on Connor's part would mean the instant end of the Kings and life as we knew it, the culmination of hundreds of years of tradition and rules passed down, turned to dust because Connor had—what, exactly? Been a few minutes late to a meeting? Kissed the daughter of the wrong man innocently enough? Made a friend from a lower-ranking family?

He'd ended up alone, for the most part. And now he's gone, likely for good.

You were wrong, da, I think grimly as I look out the window of the jet. *He's been gone a while now, and nothing's crumbled to dust. In fact, if the Kings fall, it won't be Connor Mcgregor's fault. It'll be mine, the one you ignored because you thought I was incapable of causing trouble damaging enough to be worth noticing.*

Well, I'm causing it now, and I can't help sometimes wondering if the nagging, gnawing guilt I feel is just our father heaping it on from beyond the grave, making up for lost time.

I let my hand drift over the buttery leather of the seat next to me, knowing *exactly* what my father would have to say about this.

At that particular conclave, one of the Italian bosses had invited several of the attendees, including Connor, onto his private jet. When Connor had come home, he'd done something he very rarely did—pulled me aside excitedly to tell me all about the experience. I'd never even imagined setting foot on such a thing. As a second son and a largely ignored one, there wasn't the expectation that I would ever rub elbows with the kind of men that our father and Connor did, the kind with private jets and summer villas.

I'd eaten every bit of it up, listening to my older brother wide-eyed and eager to hear as he'd described it in vivid detail. But unfortunately, I wasn't the only one listening to Connor's tale.

It *had* been a test, according to my father, to see how Connor reacted to the excess of some of the other families, if he stood true to our values in the face of such gross material wastefulness and ostentation. The fact that Connor had enjoyed it so much, been awed by it—envied it, even—was evidence of yet another moral failing on his part, just another way that, if not strictly guided, his future leadership would be a weak and pitiful one, leading to the downfall of all that our father had worked so hard to build.

And as to the fact that I'd been equally excited to hear about the private jet, the leather seats and pretty stewardess and expensive wine served?

My father didn't give the first shite about whether or not *I* might grow up to be materialistic and shallow. Only my brother, the one on whom everything would one day rely.

Ironic, isn't it? I think dryly, as if Connor can hear me somewhere. *All that, and it was da who almost destroyed it all with his traitorous machinations.*

But ultimately, he hadn't. And that was the second half of the irony, that it fell to me and not Connor to keep it all together.

Me, the misfit, ignored child, the one my father called a changeling because my mother had died giving birth to me, as if I could have somehow stopped it from happening.

As if I hadn't grown up wanting my mother, just as much as he'd wanted his wife.

More, maybe, since he hadn't had any trouble planting seeds in Francesca Bianchi while his wife was still alive.

I do my best to shake the thoughts away, to banish the ghosts of the past. They won't help me here and now. My father, for all his insistence that the excess of the other families was reprehensible and wasteful, had failed to apply the same lessons to himself when he'd seen the opportunity to grab more territory. He'd been just as greedy as anyone else, at least for power and blood, if not for money.

And as for my brother, he's long gone. I'd often longed to be able to rely on my older brother as a child, but as an adult, I've come to see that there is rarely anyone in this life that you can rely on at all. Even in the short time that I've been truly paying attention to the machinations around me, ever since my father begrudgingly brought me under his wing to replace Connor, I've seen how quickly others will put their own self-interest above those they're meant to stand shoulder to shoulder with.

It had never occurred to me that I could have something that I've never seen any man of my acquaintance have—someone closer to me than even a brother or a right-hand man. Marriages in the crime families aren't about love or even partnership—they're about alliances and children, bringing families together through comingling of blood and sometimes simply the threat of loss if someone in the other family puts a foot out of line. It's all politics—it has nothing to do with the man and woman joining in matrimony at their core. *Since I was a child, that has always been my impression of marriage.*

But I've seen something different since getting to know Luca and his wife, and now even Viktor and Caterina. I'd never thought too long for a wife that I could *love*, a woman who could be more than just a homemaker and the mother of my children. You can't long for what you never even knew existed.

I see the potential for something different, though, now. Something *more*. And when I try to envision it, the only person I can ever see by my side is Ana.

I swore to her as Alexei took her away that I'd come for her. I don't know if she could hear me, if she remembers, if she even believes in anyone's promises anymore.

But I want her to know that she can rely on mine. That I won't abandon her, no matter what anyone else urges me to do, no matter what it costs, no matter what it takes from me.

That out of everyone in the world, she is the one I want to keep my vows to, more than anyone else.

To death.

Given Levin's expression as we start to descend, *death* is the last word I want to think of right now.

"You look like someone walked over your grave." His face hasn't changed much since we got on the plane, tense and dark. "Not a fan of Tokyo? Or just flying in general?"

Levin's eyes narrow as he presses his lips together, glancing out of the window. "Actually, now that you mention it, I've never been a particular fan of airplane travel. Man was meant to keep both feet planted firmly on the ground."

"Ah, I don't mind it." I shrug. "Besides, who can argue with traveling in style like this?"

Levin raises an eyebrow but just tears his gaze away from the window as we start to descend, his expression still heavy. "It's not that," he says finally. "What do you know about the Yakuza, Liam?"

I frown. "Not much. I'm not sure the Kings have ever done business with them."

"None of the families on the Eastern Seaboard have. I know that the Bratva bosses still in Russia do, from time to time. But they're not to be taken lightly." Levin frowns. "I've never personally met Nakamura, but he has a reputation."

"Don't we all?"

Levin glances at me. "That Irish levity won't get you far here," he cautions. "Nakamura is as likely to slice your tongue off for insolence as find it charming."

Now it's my turn to narrow my eyes. "The Kings may not be as feared as the Bratva or as rich as the mafia, Levin. But we're no gaggle of knitting grandmothers, either. We've got our own reputation for violence—"

Levin smirks. "Oh, I'm well aware of what happens when you get an Irishman's back up. But Nakamura is likely to be as threatened by you and yours as a band of roving potato farmers."

"Now that's just offensive."

Levin shrugs, his mouth still twitching, and I can feel the tension in the air lighten just the slightest bit, though he still looks concerned. "Be that as it may, Liam, all I'm saying is that once we get into Tokyo and start to inquire, caution and discretion are important. The Yakuza defend their territories fiercely. They don't care much for outside interference unless *they* choose to make a business proposition or alliance. The syndicate password will open a great many doors for us in Europe, but here if spoken to the wrong person, it could be a knife in the back as easily as an outstretched hand—and that hand could have a knife in it, as well."

"So you're saying they're without honor?"

"Not at all. The honor of the Yakuza is paramount to them. I'm saying that a dragon doesn't particularly care if the sheep thinks he's honorable. Only the other dragons."

Levin pauses, and I see something flicker across his face, some memory that darkens his expression before disappearing once again. "The Nakamura family, in particular, is known for being both the wealthiest of the Yakuza families and the most violent. If we accomplish arranging a meeting with Nomura Nakamura, tread carefully.

Let me speak first. I, at least, have had dealings with the Yakuza before, and neither of you have."

The thought of hanging back, of not taking every opportunity to grab at whatever leads we can to find Ana, rankles with me. But at the same time, I'm well aware that I can't save her if I'm dead.

And I've certainly never dealt with Yakuza. I'm fairly certain no one in the Kings ever has. I brought Levin along for a reason, and this is exactly it.

A cool head on your shoulders will get you further in this world than a smoking gun in your hand. The words echo in my head out of nowhere, and it takes me a moment to remember where I heard them last. Certainly not from my father.

It comes back to me a moment later, an overheard conversation as a child between my grandfather and father, in a hallway where I'd glimpsed blood on my father's hands for the first time. I hadn't realized that the words had stayed with me, but they must have.

My father hadn't learned that lesson, but perhaps I did, even if I hadn't realized it quite so clearly. I've never been a man prone to hotheaded violence in the way my father was, or even Connor, who had a temper despite his outwardly calm demeanor. Even in the boxing ring, I make certain to keep that cool head, to take the measure of my opponent rather than instantly lashing out.

Look at me, da, I think half-bitterly as the plane comes to land. *Your misfit son, the changeling, stepping where maybe no King has stepped before, at least not one that I've heard. Are you proud of me?*

I doubt he would be, but it's long since stopped mattering to me. But as we stand up to head down the aisle and disembark, there's another face lingering in my thoughts—one that does leave a hint of an ache in my chest, a faint wish that he could see where I am and what I'm about to do.

I do miss you, brother.

"The driver should be here waiting," Levin says as the door to the steps out onto the tarmac opens. "We'll head into Tokyo and find a place to stay tonight, and I'll start making inquiries—"

His voice dies off as his feet hit the ground, and I don't see why at first, as I duck and take three quick steps down the stairs. But as I straighten and get a good look a the tarmac in front of us, my own pulse quickens, a knot of dread forming in my stomach.

"Shit," I hear Max swear behind me, a quick and heartfelt curse.

There's a black car there, alright. But I don't think it's the driver Levin mentioned.

Spread out in front of it is a line of black-suited Japanese men, armed and impassive, blocking our path to leave. Not a single one of them moves as Max jumps down to stand next to me, his face looking as uncertain as I feel.

This wasn't what we were expecting at all.

But I'd bet a pot of leprechaun's gold they're here for us.

ANA

When Alexandre walks into my room the next morning with the breakfast tray, I don't know what to expect. A part of me hopes that maybe yesterday was just all some terrible dream or that he'll have decided to forgive me after a good night's sleep. *Maybe he'll even sit down on the edge of the bed like he sometimes does while I eat and explain what I found in the study. Or perhaps that was a part of the dream too. It's unbelievable enough.*

All it takes is one glimpse at his face as he pushes the door shut behind him to see that's not the case.

He doesn't look as angry as he had yesterday, but neither does he have the usual pleasant smile on his face as he walks into the room. His eyes don't quite meet mine, and he sets the breakfast tray down on the vanity instead of bringing it to the bed, turning to face me with his lips pressed tightly together.

"Good morning, *petit*," he says stiffly, as if this is making him as uncomfortable as the tension in the air is making me. Or maybe this is his way of trying to conceal his anger.

For some reason, that last thought makes me more sad than frightened.

"Come and have your breakfast." Alexandre reaches for the plate and glass of orange juice next to it, and I have a moment of pure confusion. I eat breakfast in bed every day. He brings me the tray, and I eat while he fetches the maid's outfit, and then I get up and allow him to go about undressing and dressing me—

My stomach knots as I realize for the first time that I've actually begun to depend on my routine here. However unconventional and strange this might be, however much I know I should be bucking against it at every turn—it's brought me some comfort. The sameness of it, the way Alexandre has repeated the same motions day after day, was a comfort that I hadn't even realized I had until right this second when it disappeared.

I used to have a routine—a strict one. Up at five a.m., without question. A breakfast of a hard-boiled egg and black tea, or sometimes avocado toast if it was a particularly demanding schedule, and out the door for my first class of the day. That schedule might vary from semester to semester, but the days didn't, and I'd gone through them like clockwork, never missing a class, never missing a practice. I had been wholeheartedly devoted to ballet, what I'd believed to be the great love of my life, more than any man could ever be. My nights might have been unpredictable and wild, but I'd had my days down to a science.

That had been ripped away from me suddenly, without warning. And now I see that as borderline concerning and certainly morally grey as Alexandre's possession of me and behavior with me has been—it's also been a source of stability that I hadn't seen how desperately I'd needed it until right now, as I'm watching it dissolve all over again.

When Alexandre clicks his tongue at me, his eyes narrowing with a growing annoyance, my fingers curl around the bedspread, and I try not to panic as I realize what he's doing. I figure it out in the second before he bends down, placing the plate with my usual eggs and crepe and the glass of juice on the floor, stepping back.

"Now, Anastasia," he says, and my heart sinks down into my stomach.

It's not disgust or anger that I feel as I realize that when he'd said I'd lost his trust yesterday, he'd treat me like the pet that I'm meant to be until I earn it back. It's a sudden, yawning desperation to do exactly that.

To earn it back.

To regain the stability and safety that I hadn't realized he afforded me until just this second.

All the other things I'd laid in bed and thought about last night, realizing that he'll likely never offer me and couldn't do so with any real equality anyway—love, companionship, pleasure—fade away instantly in the face of the sudden, stomach-clenching uncertainty of where I stand with him and what will happen next.

"*Anastasia.*"

I nod quickly, my mouth going dry as I slide quickly out of bed, my silk pajamas catching a little on the rug as I sink instantly to my knees a few inches away from him in front of the plate, looking down at it with sudden nausea that makes me wonder if I'm going to be able to eat at all.

Even though I needed to know, even though it would have eaten at me continually if I hadn't after Yvette's comment, a part of me suddenly, viscerally, and deeply regrets having gone into his study. If I could go back and do it again—

But I can't. There's no changing what happened yesterday. All I can do is try to figure out what I'm going to do now.

My appetite is completely gone, but I know he will be upset if I don't eat. It always does.

The last thought startles me a little, enough to make me pause. It feels too intimate—to know a thing like that about a man like Alexandre. *It always does.*

But it's also comforting. The sameness of it. The surety. *This is something I know. He wants me to eat.*

I'll please him if I eat. Even if it's on the floor.

I manage to glance up at him under my lashes as I reach for the crepe, going to tear a piece off of the end. I hate eating with my fingers more than anything, but if that's what it takes to please him and make things the way they were before again, then that's what I'll do.

IRISH SAVIOR

He doesn't look pleased, though. If I didn't know better, I'd think that he looks as if he's hating every second of this, watching me eat off of a plate on the floor as I kneel in front of him.

But that wouldn't make any sense.

I hear the sound of the front door opening and closing, light footsteps in the hallway, and my stomach clenches with dread. *Please don't be her,* I think desperately as any fledgling remnant of an appetite I might have had instantly flutters away, leaving nothing but a cold knot in my gut.

"Alexandre?" Yvette's richly accented voice drifts down the hall, and I have to clench my jaw to bite back the protest that threatens to escape.

Who else did you think it was going to be? The Easter bunny?

"In here," Alexandre calls out, and I realize with mounting embarrassment that she's going to come in here.

Into *my* room.

While I'm on the floor like a dog eating breakfast.

Your room. What a joke. As if anything here is really yours. It's all his, and anything you have is at his whim, nothing more. So you'd better start behaving.

I hate that the voice in my head is starting to sound more and more like *her* every day.

I can feel my face already starting to heat as the doorknob turns. I keep my eyes fixed on my plate, not out of deference but out of a need to keep Yvette from seeing the expression on my face. However, I'm sure Alexandre will think it's the former.

"Why, Alexandre." Her voice is full of surprise, and I swallow hard as I see her feet, clad in narrow black leather flats, drawing closer. "I'd hoped that you'd come around to my way of thinking about this one, but I hadn't thought it would be so soon. Look at her on the floor like a good little pet. I'd thought for sure you were going to keep insisting on treating her like—" she trails off, and I can't help but wonder with bitter distaste what she was thinking of saying.

Treating me like I'm human? God, what a concept.

Part of me wants to blame her, completely and fully. She'd planted the thought in my head about what Alexandre had paid for me, and I don't think it was unintentional on her part in the slightest. She'd done her best to drive a wedge between us from the start, to remind him that any closeness or intimacy between us was—wrong? Inappropriate? Ill-advised? I'm sure she would have and might have, used any of those words to describe it, but I also know she's just a jealous woman who wants a man that doesn't love her.

That should bring me comfort—that he doesn't love her or want her in that way—but it doesn't. It's just going to make my life that much harder, especially because my antics yesterday are only confirming for him what she's been saying.

That I can't be trusted. That I need to learn my lesson. That I need to learn *manners*. My *place*.

But she hadn't forced me to disobey Alexandre and go into the study. I can't blame that on her. I doubt she was even trying to plant the idea in my head to go snooping—if anything, she'd probably meant to get me to start nagging Alexandre about it directly, so he'd become more and more annoyed with me.

Instead, I'd decided to take matters into my own hands. I'd set off a tinderbox of explosive reactions that have everything I hadn't realized I'd come to rely on, on the verge of exploding.

I feel sick. I want to curl up in a ball and cry, give myself over to the panic and the widening sinkhole of dark, heavy feelings, but I can't. Alexandre hates my outbursts, my fits of emotion, and besides, he's going to want me to eat. Any second now—

But he's turning away, speaking to Yvette in quick, quiet French before stepping towards the door. "Eat, Anastasia," he says firmly. "I'll be back for the plate."

And then he steps out into the hall, holding the door for Yvette before shutting it firmly behind them both.

My eyes well instantly with hot, jealous, angry tears. Jealous of Yvette, angry at myself. I'd ruined everything because I couldn't be happy with what Alexandre had offered me—a safe and comfortable roof over my head, his cautious affection, a place to even possibly try to heal some of my wounds, external and internal. He hadn't hurt me.

He hadn't touched me with anything but respect. And I'd fucked it all up because I don't trust him.

How could I, when he bought me from a man like Alexei?

I know what Sofia would say if she were here, if she could hear my own internal dialogue. *"Not hurting you and not violating you is the bare minimum, Ana. Not something to fall on your face and be eternally grateful for. Look at where you are now, eating on the floor like a puppy or a housecat."*

But isn't it my fault?

I wish, desperately, that I had someone to talk to besides the inside of my own brain. Ever since Franco and the deep, dark depression that had followed, I haven't felt sure that I could trust my own mind anymore. Sometimes, the things I had thought, especially right after, had shocked me. Dark, horrible things that terrified me because they'd never occurred to me even in the slightest, before Franco.

Thoughts about hurting him, slowly and painfully, revenge for my mutilated feet and my lost life. Thoughts about hurting myself, if only to escape the hell that he'd thrown me into, and for what?

Trying to help my best friend. Being loyal to her. Being willing to do *anything*, whatever it took, to help her.

BUT THERE *IS* no one else for me to talk to. I'm all alone, and that hits even harder in this particular moment, kneeling on the rug with my cooling breakfast on a plate in front of me, Alexandre and Yvette's voices trailing down the hall in French that I don't even bother trying to understand.

I'm a thousand miles from home, and I'm alone. The thought hammers itself into my head, over and over. The two warring sides of my mind can't stop fighting between the thought that I'm an idiot for ever believing that Alexandre could be anything other than my captor and my owner, and the thought that if I could just be good if I could just obey him and not take advantage after he's given me so much, I wouldn't *have* to be alone.

That side, mixed with the lingering desire for him and longing for his approval, wins out. Because no one is coming for me, and I don't want to be alone.

I scoop some eggs into my mouth, wanting to finish the food before he comes back. It's delicious, even cold, and I eat it quickly, washing it down with a glass of water. When Alexandre comes back into the room, I'm kneeling back on my heels, my fingers wiped clean on the napkin that's piled on my empty plate, my hands folded in my lap.

"Good girl," he says with surprise evident in his voice. "Maybe you learned your lesson from yesterday, then."

I want to tell him that yes, I did, but I stay silent instead. I think maybe he'll like that better. I keep my eyes on the rug as he scoops up my breakfast tray, setting it on the vanity and getting out the maid's outfit. Something in my chest leaps a little at the sight of it. *If he didn't trust me at all, then he wouldn't allow me to clean the apartment, would he?*

"Up," Alexandre says curtly, and I scramble to my feet, a little unsteadily. I feel his hand on my upper arm, keeping me from tilting forward, and a rush of sensation washes over my skin, the hairs prickling under his touch.

All I can see in my head is him last night, gripping the bedpost, his straining cock in his fist as he stared down at the pictures and groaned aloud as he came, his hips pumping—

Fuck. I can feel the blush threatening to creep up my neck and into my cheeks, and I bite my tongue, trying to force it back with the sharp pain. Now that I've seen Alexandre naked, how handsome he is, now that I've seen something so blatantly sexual that I know I wasn't supposed to, I can't look at him the same. I know what's underneath his crisply starched clothes, his carefully groomed exterior, his cool demeanor. Remembering that barely leashed passion while he touched himself makes me wonder what he would be like with a partner. It's impossible not to imagine his muscles flexing above me, his teeth clenching as his hips thrust forward, driving his cock—

"Anastasia, are you alright?" Alexandre looks at me, his eyes narrowed with what looks like concern. "You're flushed. And you're breathing heavily. Are you ill?"

"I—ah—no," I stutter, shaking my head. "I just didn't sleep well."

His brow furrows. "Even with the tea?"

It's the closest he's come to actually admitting that the tea contains a sedative. *Fuck*. Of course, he can't know that I didn't actually drink the tea. "Um—just some bad dreams." I bite my lip, hoping that he'll buy it. If he starts to get suspicious, I won't be able to get away with not drinking the tea again. And even though I know I should stay in bed tonight and every other night, rather than risk his anger, I'm already aching to see him naked again. To watch him while he touches himself and imagine that it's me that he's looking at with such desire instead of whatever porn he had scattered across his bed.

"Perhaps tonight will be better." Alexandre's hand drops from my arm as he shakes out the dress, and I instantly miss the feeling of his touch on my skin. It's hard to know if it's *his* touch that I want, or simply to be touched at all, but it hardly seems to matter anymore. Who else will ever have the chance to touch me again? And who would I want to, other than him? My options are slim to none these days.

Better the devil you know—and I'm not always sure that Alexandre even qualifies as a devil. Some days I'm less certain than others, like yesterday. And then days like today—I just can't be sure.

He undresses and dresses me efficiently, leaving the tray for me to pick up as he strides out into the hall. At first, I think Yvette has gone, but my heart sinks when I see her sitting on the living room couch, examining one of her long, manicured nails. She looks up when she hears our footsteps, her expression softening when she sees Alexandre and hardening again at the sight of me.

"I have to go out, as usual," Alexandre explains, glancing at me. I have a feeling that I know what he's going to say next before he says it, and his next words only confirm that. "Yvette will be staying here to keep an eye on you today while you work. I hope that she'll have only good things to report when I come home. And," he pauses, his eyes narrowing. "I shouldn't need to say this to you, Ana, but keep your hands occupied, and not between your legs."

Yvette smirks, her lipsticked mouth turning up in a cruel laugh, and I feel my face flame, more humiliated than I've ever been in my entire life. Even at Juilliard, where the ballet masters and mistresses would sometimes call out our flaws and mistakes in front of the whole class, I don't think I've ever felt so embarrassed. I wish the floor would open up so that I could disappear, and yet—I think I see a flicker of heat in Alexandre's eyes when he says it. I could be imagining it—I'm *sure* that I'm imagining it. Still, just the thought that he might be in some way aroused by the thought of me pleasuring myself or by instructing me not to sends a throb of sensation between my thighs that makes me grit my teeth and clench them together.

It's quickly mitigated by the realization that not only has he embarrassed me in front of Yvette, he's also leaving her here in charge of me. Which means I'll have to be here with her, alone, all day.

Cleaning Alexandre's apartment has been, up until now, a pleasant enough way to pass a day with no television or anything else to do. Now it feels like nothing but misery.

"Mind your manners," he says sternly to me, returning Yvette's delicate wave goodbye before heading to the door, and I don't think I've ever hated a phrase more.

If I ever leave this place, I never want to hear the word *manners* again.

"Well, well," Yvette smirks as the front door closes. "Just the two of us, little pet. *Petit animaux.*" She taps her nails on the knee of her tailored cigarette pants, looking me up and down with her dark, keen eyes. "It's a shame you're not mine. We'd have such fun. For one thing, you'd be cleaning *my* apartment naked. And the first thing you'd attend to, I'd require the use of your tongue." Her own pink pointed tongue trails over her lower lip, and I repress a shudder. It's not that Yvette isn't beautiful or that I couldn't ever be convinced to experiment with a woman—but she's so patently cruel and rotten to her core that I can't stand the thought of touching her, even if she were a man. She hates me, and not for any reason other than the man she wants has taken a liking to me, that he's amused by me and treats me better than she thinks he ought to.

Or he did *anyway.*

"What do you usually do first?" she asks, lighting a cigarette and taking two long puffs from it.

"Um, the dishes," I say in a small voice, and Yvette waves her hand.

"Well, go on then."

Alexandre must have given Yvette instructions about how she can and can't treat me because she's not *as* horrible as I'd feared. But neither is she kind. She waits until I've cleaned the rug in the living room before "accidentally" flicking ash on it, makes a point of nearly tripping me or getting in my way more than once, making it difficult for me to keep my balance, and then remarks on how ungainly and graceless I am for a supposed former "star ballerina." When I finally escape to the library alone to clean, she leaves me alone for a little while, only to pop in and tease me cruelly about how she needed to be sure I wasn't disobeying Alexandre's orders to keep my hands out from between my legs.

"I knew you were a little whore," she says casually from the doorway, smoking yet another cigarette. "And I know you're thinking of Alexandre's cock when you're fingering yourself in the dark. But he's not going to put it in one of his little pets, *Cherie*. You could never do anything to earn that, and he knows you're beneath him, even if he sometimes tries to pretend otherwise."

One of his little pets. I try not to think about it, but it's impossible not to hear the words, not to wonder what other pets he's had, what happened to them, if he paid a hundred million each for them too—which is impossible. No one has that kind of money. No one *could*.

I'm caught up in my thoughts when Yvette flicks ash on the floor again and giggles. "Clean it up," she says. "And get your mind out of the gutter."

She eats her lunch at the table, forcing me onto the floor to eat the bread and cheese she gives me—French baguette and brie, but it might as well have been cardboard for all that I can barely choke it down. Eating at Alexandre's feet is awful, but eating at Yvette's is so miserable that I can't stop a few tears from leaking out of the corners of my eyes, hoping all the while that she doesn't see them. But of course, she doesn't care enough to notice.

When Alexandre comes home, he tells me that I've done a good job cleaning, then has me go back to my own room while he and Yvette prepare dinner. I eat on the floor again while they eat at the table and chat in French, and I can feel the beginnings of a new routine starting —albeit one that I don't want to get used to. After dinner, Alexandre draws me a bath once Yvette leaves, and he goes so far as to gently massage my feet in the tub, asking me if they're sore from cleaning.

"A little," I tell him, and he gently rubs around the scar tissue, avoiding the spots that are the most sensitive. He doesn't ask what happened again, thankfully, and I have to blink back tears at the gentleness of his fingers on my skin. I want to ask him if he forgives me yet, if I have to keep eating off the floor like a dog, if Yvette will be here tomorrow, but I don't. Having him touch me like this feels too good, and I don't want to make him angry. So instead, I just close my eyes, sinking down into the steaming water, until he finally sets my other foot down and starts to help me bathe.

I use the same trick to get out of the sedative tea, holding it in my mouth until he leaves and then spitting it into a different plant this time—I'm afraid of killing only one and him figuring out my game that way—and wait until the lower floor of the apartment is quiet before slipping out into the hall and carefully sneaking up the stairs again.

I don't know if I'll see anything tonight. After all, he'd had one of the most intense orgasms I'd ever witnessed just last night—for all I know, he's going straight to bed. But I catch him partway through undressing this time. I watch in fascination as he takes off each item of clothing and folds it perfectly before setting it in the laundry hamper, rather than—oh, I don't know, *tossing it in* like a normal person. He strips all the way to his bare skin that way. I feel my heartbeat speed up in my chest as he turns. I catch sight of his half-hard cock between his razor-sharp hipbones, swelling steadily as if with anticipation of what comes next as he strides towards the bed and his side table.

I've never seen a man get erect without touching himself or being touched unless he was already hard when I got his pants off. But as

Alexandre takes out the photos and spreads them across the bed, his cock steadily thickens, getting harder and harder as if the process is as arousing to him as a touch. *He must do this the same way every night, like a ritual,* I realize, and the desire to keep coming back, to keep watching only intensifies as I watch him grow rock hard without ever touching his cock, his thick length nearly touching his flat belly as he looks down at the photos, his face tensing with growing need as he finally reaches for a bottle on his bedside table, letting the liquid drip from it onto his cock and slide glistening down the length of it before he *finally* takes his shaft in his hand, and begins to stroke.

I let out a breath that I hadn't known I was holding, the anticipation of waiting for him to touch his cock so intense that I can feel that I'm as wet as the lube coating his skin, my panties soaked from watching him. He looks like a marble statue, pale and lean and muscular, his hand gripping the bedpost like before as he strokes himself long and slow, his palm coming up to rub over the head of his cock before gripping and sliding all the way down to the base. Only his hand moves for several minutes before I can see his breathing quicken. He moves some of the pictures around the way he did before, as if looking for specific ones as his hips start to thrust into his fist, fucking his hand as if he's imagining a mouth or pussy, his jaw clenching as he groans with pleasure.

I've waited as long as I can. My clit is throbbing, my panties soaked and my thighs sticky, a wet spot forming on the gusset of my pajamas as well. I shove my hand inside, biting my lip hard to stifle the gasp of relief as my fingers find my clit, the pleasure only amplified by knowing that I'm disobeying his instructions to me earlier.

The danger doesn't turn me on, but how forbidden this is, does. Watching Alexandre pleasure himself without him knowing I'm here, rubbing my clit as I watch, trying to time my orgasm with his as my toes curl against the hardwood, it's hotter than any hookup I ever had back in New York. I know that it's wrong and unhealthy and fucked up in so many ways, just like my relationship with—*to?*—Alexandre is. Still, I'm slowly caring less and less with every passing day. It feels *good*, and I've had so little that's felt good in the past months. Whatever happens, right now, my heart is racing. My clit is throbbing against my fingers and pleasure is racing over my every nerve. At the same time, I watch one of the hottest men I've ever seen furiously stroke his cock a few feet away—and it feels good.

My life is measured from day to day now. I don't ever know what's coming next. So how can I not grasp what pleasure I can get while I can get it?

He doesn't last as long tonight. I don't mind—I don't know how long I could have held out, either. My hand is soaked with my arousal, my clit swollen and aching, and I need to come so badly that I have to shove my hand against my mouth to keep from moaning with relief when I see him tilt forward, his hand speeding up on his cock in the way that I now know means he's about to come. I rub my own clit faster, hoping he can't hear the slick sound of my arousal, but I imagine that it's impossible to over the sounds of his own wet flesh, his groans as he approaches his climax. His jaw is clenched, every muscle in his rippling thighs and perfect ass going rigid as he thrusts forward hard into his fist, ropes of his cum jetting out over his fingers as he moans and grunts, shuddering as he comes hard into his hand.

I let go at the same moment, gasping against my own palm as I shudder, struggling to stay upright as waves of intense pleasure wash over me. I thrust two fingers inside of myself without thinking, grinding the heel of my hand against my clit as I feel my pussy clench around my fingers, imagining that it's his cock, that he's coming inside of me right now, filling me with that thick heat as he groans and thrusts. I feel almost dizzy with need, aching with the desire for that to be a reality.

Like the night before, it's over too soon. As I see him start to gather up the photos, I yank my hand out of my pajamas, scrambling away from the door and carefully making my way back down the stairs before he can catch sight of me or leave his room.

My entire body is pulsing from the aftershocks of pleasure and adrenaline as I shut the door carefully to my room, sinking against it as I close my eyes. *This isn't normal.* I know it's not.

I *know* it isn't. But what else do I have?

LIAM

Fuck.

One of the black-suited men starts to walk towards us, flanked by five other men, and I begin to step forward, but Levin holds out a hand. "Let me deal with this," he says through clenched teeth, and as much as I don't want to obey, he did caution me about—well, if not this exact scenario, something like this happening.

"The *oyabun*, Mr. Nomura Nakamura, is honored to have such esteemed guests arrive in his territory," the man in front says, smiling to show pearly-white teeth. "If you'll come with us, please."

"I thought we were in Tokyo," Max mutters, and Levin shoots him a look out of the corner of his eye that could freeze steel solid.

The man smiles. "Just so. Mr. Nakamura's territory. He has sent us to escort you to his compound. This way, please."

Levin nods. "My companions and I are here on behalf of the *pakhan* of the Eastern Seaboard in the United States, Viktor Andreyev, and—"

"We know quite well who you are. Levin Volkov, brigadier to Viktor Andreyev. Liam McGregor, head of the Boston Irish Kings. Maximilian Agosti—priest?" The man smirks. "Well, it's good to keep the faith, especially when you walk into such danger."

"Then you know that there will be consequences if we are harmed."

The man smirks. "Mr. Nakamura is above such things. But there's no need to worry. The *oyabun* does not seek your blood, not yet, anyway. The night is young."

Every inch of Levin's body is tense, but he steps forward regardless, which tells me what I'd hoped wasn't true—we don't have any option but to follow them. If there was one—negotiation, fighting it out, just plain refusing to go and taking our own car into Tokyo, wherever it might be—Levin would have opted for it.

Going with the men is bad enough, but when they bring out the black sacks to put over our heads, even I can't help but balk.

"Do you treat everyone who visits Tokyo with this hospitality, or are we just special?" I ask tightly, eyeing the man holding it with distaste. "I prefer to see where I'm going."

"And the *oyabun* will find a special use for your eyeballs, if you would prefer that I take your sight permanently rather than utilizing this temporary solution."

Well shit. "Fine," I manage through gritted teeth. "But the *oyabun* should know that the head of the Irish Kings isn't pleased with his hospitality."

"For fuck's sake, Liam," Levin hisses from behind me in the car that we're unceremoniously shoved into. "Shut the fuck up."

He had told me to keep the Irish levity to a minimum. But I also hadn't been expecting to be blindfolded and carted off to the Yakuza headquarters before I'd even had a chance to sniff the Tokyo air properly.

The ride is a bit longer than I would have hoped, especially considering that I know the hangar where we landed isn't far from the city. I do my best to keep my mounting fears at bay, but not being able to see and being in a place where I don't speak the language, in a car with the goons of a notorious gang that I've never had dealings with before, doesn't exactly lend itself to feelings of calm.

I have to trust that Levin hasn't gotten us into something he can't get us out of. And beyond that, I have to believe that whatever happens, it's worth it.

As long as it gets me closer to rescuing Ana, it is. I mean that, with everything in me. I'll endure a terrifying car ride, an interrogation, whatever I have to.

I just have to survive it, with enough pieces intact to get to her. And based on what Levin said on the flight, that in and of itself might be a feat.

Not to mention the fact that from the brief time I'd spent with Adrian, I'd gotten the distinct impression that he might have sent us here just because he'd get a kick out of knowing we were stupid enough to go blindly stumbling into Nakamura's snake pit.

Well, there's nothing we can do about it now but go forward. We're here, so chin up. Prove that you're better than your father gave you credit for.

He'd certainly never faced down the Yakuza.

The car finally rolls to a stop, and cool air smacks me in the face even through the dense cloth of the bag over my head as the door opens. The bag is unceremoniously yanked off, and I see in the dim light of the torches in the courtyard that we're in front of a two-story, L-shaped Japanese-style house with the traditional shingled roof and paneled doors. I barely get a chance to look at it before I'm dragged out of the car by one shoulder and shoved forward into the hands of two of the armed men, with Max and then Levin being given the same treatment. Max looks pale as death, but Levin looks somewhat nonplussed, as if being manhandled by armed Yakuza is just another Tuesday for him.

Hell, maybe it was, back in his syndicate days. I'm starting to have a new appreciation for the man.

"The Nakamura clan welcomes you," the tall man who greeted us says, those same pearly white teeth glimmering in the dark as he smiles insincerely. "Follow me."

It's not exactly as if we have a choice, but I wisely opt to keep my mouth shut this time. As the three of us are hustled forwards through the courtyard, past the red-paneled front door, and down a dimly-lit hallway to another set of red-paneled doors, where we're abruptly

M. JAMES

pushed inside into a huge room lit with recessed lighting in the ceiling and a fireplace roaring at one end, the centerpiece of it a velvet lounge divan with cushions scattered all around.

"Shit," Levin mutters under his breath, and my skin prickles as I look at the man sitting on the divan. "That's not Nomura."

"Is that bad?" I ask through my teeth.

"Worse." Levin presses his lips together. "It's his son."

It would have taken me only a second to figure out that the man sitting there, surrounded by some of the most gorgeous women I've ever seen in my life and holding a chain attached to—a *fucking tiger?*—isn't Nomura Nakamura. The man can't be more than my age, if not younger, dressed in tight black leather pants and a black silk kimono left to hang open so that his muscled chest is bare, silver and gold chains layered on his skin. His hair is long, well past his shoulders and dyed blonde, with the black roots showing in a way that's intentional rather than lazy. His nearly black, almond-shaped eyes are half-lidded, sleepily bored despite the women draped over him, all in various stages of near-nudity, one between his legs with her head pillowed on his thigh and her fingers tracing the outline of his cock through the leather pants.

Oh, and the fact that he's holding a *fucking tiger* on a chain.

Just that.

Levin bows instantly at the waist, his voice full of grudging respect. "Kaito Nakamura, it's an honor to meet you in the flesh. Your father—"

"I'm not interested in hearing about my father." Kaito's eyes flicker open a little wider, taking us in for the first time, and his hand shifts, the chain moving. The tiger, which I'd deeply hoped was stuffed or animatronic, moves as well. Its yellow-gold eyes turn towards us in a way that tells me it is most definitely both real and alive, if perhaps a bit drugged. "I am, however, interested in hearing why my evening has been interrupted with…you three."

"My apologies, *kobun*." The man who had greeted us on the tarmac steps forward, bowing deeply. "I received word that these three were arriving in Tokyo with intent to arrange for a meeting with your father. I thought it best to intercept them before—"

"Before they could cause trouble. And with my father out of town, it falls to me to deal with it." Kaito sits up fully, pushing his hair lazily out of his face with one hand and dislodging one of the girls. "Someone get me sake. Enough for my guests and me—if they prove to be guests, rather than nuisances."

The tiger lets out a low grumble, and it's all I can do not to take several steps backward, partially because the men behind me are preventing it. *What do you feed that thing?* seems like an obvious question, but it's not one I'm about to ask—mostly because I don't think I want to know the answer.

"We don't intend to be a nuisance," Levin says politely. "Nor do we intend to take up much of your time, Nakamura-san. We received a tip from Adrian Drakos regarding some business that your father had done that might aid us in finding someone."

"I don't know any Adrian Drakos." Kaito looks increasingly bored, and something tells me that a man of Kaito Nakamura's wealth and youth doesn't take well to being bored.

I have no desire to find out how he might turn us into his entertainment.

"He's a former associate of mine at the Moscow syndicate. I once worked for them as a—private contractor." Levin says the last meaningfully, and Kaito's eyes spark with the tiniest bit of interest at last.

"Sake," he says sharply and jerks his head towards the low table in front of the divan, where more cushions are scattered. "Come, sit, while one of my women pours for us. Just you," he adds, narrowing his eyes at us. "So far, the two of you have done nothing to interest me."

Levin glances at us, but moves forward quickly, taking a cushion as far from the tiger as he can before Kaito Nakamura has a chance to change his mind.

The girl bringing the sake is tall and slender, dressed in nothing but a sheer gauzy kimono that shows her rose-pink nipples and the shaved apex of her thighs clearly, her slim thighs parting the fabric as she moves towards Kaito and Levin with a gilded tray containing four porcelain cups and a bottle of sake. She's one of the most covered of the girls. A few of them are wearing nothing but gold body chains connected to pierced nipples and, ostensibly, a piercing between their legs, while another pair are wearing only pasties and thong panties. The room smells like feminine flesh and perfume, with the underlying scents of fur, burning wood, and male sweat.

They're all extraordinarily beautiful. The one between Kaito's legs is one of the girls wearing only body chains, and she flattens her hand over his crotch, her eyes rolling up anxiously towards his face. He swats her hand away, saying something sharply to her in Japanese, and she pouts before rolling away, far too close to the tiger for my comfort. But instead of lingering near Kaito and Levin, she starts to sway towards us, circling Max and me with a sort of sultry curiosity that tells me that she's going to be the means with which Kaito toys with us next.

I'll take it over some other methods he could come up with, but still, I'm in no mood to be faux-seduced by a crime lord's woman, no matter how gorgeous.

"So." Kaito tosses back his shot of sake while Levin sips his, holding out the cup for the kimono-clad girl to pour another. "You've taken an interest in my father's business. Risky. My father doesn't like strangers taking an interest in anything that the Nakamura clan does."

"Not his business, precisely," Levin says calmly. "And might I say, this is excellent sake, Nakamura-san. Unmatched by any I've had elsewhere."

"You might." Kaito looks at him with narrowed eyes. "My father's business."

"Yes." Levin takes another sip. "We're seeking someone—a Frenchman who is in the habit of paying large sums for damaged items. Art, artifacts, rare books, perhaps—women." He pauses. "My contact in Greece, Adrian Drakos, suggested that your father might have done business with such a man."

"So he suggested that my father cheated this Frenchman?" A flush of red appears on Kaito's high cheekbones. "I should cut out your

IRISH SAVIOR

tongue and send it to this Adrian Drakos, for sending you here to speak such—"

"No, Nakamura-san," Levin says quickly. "Rather, I was told that it's the Frenchman who is a laughingstock, both among your clan and other crime bosses who have dealt with him. That he is an idiot who willingly pays a higher price than these items should fetch." Levin shrugs, taking another sip. "It's hardly your father's fault if a man throws money at him. Should he turn it down? A wise man would say no."

Kaito relaxes a fraction. "You mentioned women," he says stiffly. "The Nakamura clan does not sell women. We have several brothels, yes. But we do not sell women outright."

"No, of course not," Levin says agreeably. "But—"

"But this Frenchman has purchased one." I can't keep my mouth shut a second longer. Levin's words warning me to let him take charge echo in my head, but I can't stop myself. Listening to them banter is excruciating. Waiting for Levin to get to the point so that I can find out if this is just another dead end or if Kaito Nakamura might give us some hint, at least to get me closer to Ana, is driving me insane.

Kaito's gaze whips to me instantly, his dark eyes narrowing, and I see Levin go immediately tense, his fingers squeezing the porcelain cup until I think he might actually shatter it. *"Liam,"* I hear Max hiss, but it's too late now.

I take a step forward, painfully aware that there's a live tiger within a few feet of me, and I have no idea when—or *who*—it's eaten last.

"Is that so?" Kaito asks dryly, and I nod.

"I'm trying to find this woman. The Frenchman bought her for a massive sum—a hundred million dollars—from a man named Alexei Egorov. I don't know where he took her."

Kaito smirks. "And you think I do? Why not ask this Egorov if he's the one who sold her?"

"Because he's dead," I say stiffly. "I would know; I watched as my associate took him apart, piece by piece. In fact, I removed a few of his fingers myself."

223

Kaito tosses back another shot of sake, raising an eyebrow. "Is that so? I wouldn't have thought you had it in you, to look at you. I never heard that the Irishmen had much bite, to tell the truth. Just a lot of bluster and—what is that word you use? *Blarney.*" He snorts. "Such a stupid word."

I shrug. "Be that as it may, I don't shrink at violence when it's necessary. And I'm determined to find this woman."

"Is that a threat?" Kaito leans back, and I can see Levin wincing. "I'm afraid I don't take threats lightly, Irishman."

"Not a threat." I shake my head. "A fact. I *will* find her. We were told you might have information to help us do exactly that. If that's not true, then rather than continue to waste your time or ours, the three of us will take our leave so that we can continue to search. You can continue to—" I wave my hand towards the girls, a few of whom are looking more than a little pale at the way I'm speaking to Kaito and the tiger. "Do this."

The silence that hangs over the room for a moment is thick and heavy, charged with the uncertainty of what's going to happen next. I can see Levin cursing me silently, feeling Max's tension at my back, waiting for Kaito to unleash his men on us.

But then, out of nowhere, he starts to laugh.

He flops backward onto his divan, tossing back more sake as the black silk kimono falls open further, the picture of decadence and carelessness. "You," he says, pointing a finger at me as he tries to catch his breath from laughing, "are not nearly as boring as I thought you would be, Irishman."

I can *feel* the collective breath that all three of us let out as Kaito finally sits up again, leaning forward with his elbows on his spread knees as he considers. "I was there when my father spoke with this Frenchman," he says finally. "You're right. He spent a ridiculous amount for a *kintsugi* vase. My father ordinarily wouldn't have entertained such a thing. Still, the man was insistent, and after all, isn't someone who turns down a windfall as stupid as one who cheats to gain it?"

"I suppose." I narrow my eyes, watching him. "So what? He bought this vase and—"

"That's it." Kaito shrugs. "He dined with my father and me, we took him to watch some of our girls perform, offered him a girl for the night out of courtesy that he declined. Odd, but not every man has those proclivities. He left in the morning with his vase."

"And does your father keep records? Would he have noted where this Frenchman lived? An address?"

Kaito smirks. "Do you really think a man who purchases items for an amount far more than their value, who deals with the underworld and even purchases a woman gives out his home address?"

I let out a breath, running my hand through my hair with frustration. "No, of course not. But while I'm glad to know that the Frenchman has, in fact, been seen by someone else—this doesn't help us find the woman. We're no closer to knowing his name or where he might be keeping her—"

"Oh, I know his name. I told you, we dined with him. He mentioned the location of his apartment as well, once he'd been plied with enough sake. He wasn't a careful enough man, in my opinion, for one who does business with such dark corners of the underworld."

For a moment, I think my heart is going to stop in my chest. "What is it?" I blurt out without thinking, and Kaito smirks.

"You don't think I would tell you that for free, do you?"

I blink at him. "Name your price. The Frenchman's name and where he lives. I'll pay whatever you like."

Kaito laughs. "I am the *kobun* of the Nakamura clan, Nomura Nakamura's son. I don't need money."

"What then?" I know better than to hand a man like this a blank check, but I'm verging on desperation. If I thought that his men wouldn't kill me faster than I could reach him, I'd be across the room in a moment, my hands around his throat until he spat out the information that he has, information that I *need*.

He can lead me to Ana. *Finally*. Every second that ticks by is another that she's in the hands of that Frenchman, a second that I'm not using to get to her side and rescue her. And Kaito Nakamura is sitting there surrounded by his women, laughing at the expression on my face.

"Pet my tiger."

I stare at him, dumbfounded. "What?"

He shrugs. "You heard me. I don't need money; I need amusement. You want to find this woman so badly? You say you'd do anything to get to her? Pet it. Then I'll tell you."

He's insane. I look at the beast lying next to the divan, a jeweled gold collar around its neck. It's drugged—it must be, I can't imagine that it would lie there so quietly otherwise. But that doesn't mean I want to touch it.

"Liam—" Levin's voice is a low warning, and I see Kaito cut his eyes towards Levin with clear irritation.

"Stay out of this, Volkov," he says. "Your Irish friend spoke out of turn, so let him negotiate now. He wants the information. He pays the price." Kaito's dark eyes flick back to me, and there's less humor in them now. "Pet the tiger."

Fuck. I'm wasting time arguing, and for all I know, if I refuse, he'll come up with something even worse.

I take a step towards the tiger. I hear Max suck in his breath behind me, but I take another, forcing myself forward. My heart is hammering in my chest, but it's for Ana. *It's all for Ana.*

I'd said to myself getting off the plane today that I meant to keep my vow to Ana—*to death*, if need be.

I just hadn't thought this was how it was going to end.

ANA

The next few days are a strange sort of blurred routine, one that I don't love but that gives me something to cling to anyway. If obedience is what will earn me back some measure of happiness here, if that will earn me back Alexandre's affection, then that's what I'm determined to do. I've always done well with goals if I set my mind to something, and while this is something so much smaller than what my life used to be, just having something to focus on helps me quiet the noise in my mind.

I wake up each morning telling myself that this is what my life is now. It doesn't matter if I was once a ballerina, if I was once a free woman, if I once had an entirely different future stretching out in front of me. That's all changed now, in a series of steps that have built on each other—Franco destroying my feet, my collapse into depression, Alexei kidnapping me, Alexandre purchasing me. *It could be worse,* I tell myself and silence the voice in my head that wants to remind me that it also, once upon a time, had been so much better.

I get up, kneel on the floor before Alexandre tells me to, eat my breakfast quickly and silently from the plate that he puts down for me, stand up to be dressed in the maid's outfit. I ignore Yvette's jibes and the way she likes to make more work for me right after I've finished cleaning something, forcing myself not to think about how much I hate having her watching me while Alexandre is out for the day. I clean the apartment, I stay away from the two rooms I'm not allowed in, eat my dinner on the floor while he and Yvette share their evening meal—she's over almost every night now—and then go to my room for my bath.

And then, every night, I allow myself my one small disobedience, my reward for doing everything Alexandre wants of me, no matter how much I hate eating off of a plate on the floor or being around Yvette so much.

Every night, I pretend to drink the tea, slip out of bed, and crouch behind the door watching him. Every night, we come together while he looks at the photos on his bed, and he doesn't know it. I can't even imagine what he would do if he did know. It's the strangest sexual relationship I've ever had—completely one-sided and entirely secret from one-half of it. Yet, it's erotic and taboo in a way that I've never experienced before. Those orgasms, with my fingers pressed feverishly against my clit while I watch Alexandre strain towards his own release and listen to the sounds of his groans shivering over my skin, are some of the best I've ever had.

I also notice how ritualistic it is for him the nights I watch him. I manage to get there earlier and earlier every night, seeing how he takes off his clothes and folds them into the hamper in the same way, the order in which he does it all, the way he always refuses to touch himself until the photos are prepared and he's already fully erect, as if the anticipation is part of it. And it makes it better for me too, watching his arousal grow, waiting with my breath catching in my throat for that moment when he'll finally wrap his hand around his cock, and I can slip my hand between my own legs, and we can start the race to orgasm together.

My commitment to obeying Alexandre works, too. A week passes, and one morning when I walk down the hall with him, I see that Yvette isn't waiting in the living room. "Are you not going out today?" I ask him curiously, and he glances at me sideways.

"No, I am. You'll clean as usual."

That's the end of it. I don't dare ask where Yvette is, as if just saying her name might summon her like some awful she-demon, but she doesn't appear anyway. Nor does she show up the next day or the next, and I realize that slowly, I'm earning some of Alexandre's trust back.

"Don't get up," he says the next morning when he brings me breakfast, and my heart leaps in my chest a little as I realize that he's going to allow me to eat it in bed, like he used to.

That tiny voice whispers that it's ridiculous that I should be so pleased that I'm going to be allowed to eat in bed and not on the floor like a dog, but it gets quieter and quieter every day, easier to ignore. What's the point of entertaining it, anyway? Being dissatisfied with what I have here will only make my life miserable. There's no escape, no way out, and with every day that passes, I wonder more and more if there's any reason to wish for one.

What did I have back in New York, anyway? A best friend, but other than that? I don't doubt that Sofia would always love me and do her best to find time for me, but she has a new life now, a husband, and a baby on the way. That's even if she got away from Alexei before he sold her. I can only hope she escaped, that Luca found her. I had nothing other than that. Nothing but a bland apartment and depression, no boyfriend or hope of dating again or future career.

I'd had a glimmer of hope in Russia when I'd met Liam, but that had been foolish. That wasn't real.

At least this is a better reality than some others I've lived through now.

Yvette doesn't come to the apartment that night. Instead, Alexandre comes home with an armful of bags full of fresh food, and I come into the kitchen to smell the rich scents of butter and herbs and frying onions. When Alexandre serves up a dinner of a whole roast chicken on a slightly chipped porcelain platter, bowls of potatoes and fresh vegetables, and a sliced baguette, he stops me before I can sink to my knees on the rug and await my plate.

"None of that," he says calmly. "Go change, and then eat at the table with me."

Inexplicably, tears spring to my eyes, though I'm careful not to let him see. I hurry down the hall, undressing and dressing myself for the first time since I've been here. I pick the blue silk wrap dress again, wanting to remind him of that lovely sunny afternoon when we walked through Paris together.

He's waiting at the table when I walk back in, glasses of red wine poured for us both, and after so many days of eating off of a plate on the floor, kneeling until my knees ached, silently paying the penance for sneaking into his study, being able to sit at the table is almost overwhelming.

"Is the food to your liking?" Alexandre asks crisply when I take the first bite, and I nod, blinking back tears again at how *good* it all is.

"It's incredible," I whisper, and I mean it. I sip the wine slowly—I haven't drank alcohol in so long now that I don't want to get drunk and embarrass myself—but it's amazing too, rich and dry and paired perfectly with the crispy, buttery, herbed roast chicken.

I eat every bit of the food Alexandre serves me. He's quiet throughout the meal, asking me occasionally about tidbits of my day, which doesn't exactly offer up much in the way of conversation, considering the fact that it was spent cleaning. But I do ask him about some of the items in the house, venturing to ask about the statues in the entryway and some of the art and where he acquired them. He actually tells me, regaling me with a story about a trip to Italy to meet with a particularly intransigent art dealer who had a few pieces that Alexandre was determined to acquire, however difficult the dealer made the transaction. There's no way to know really how much of what he tells me is true and how much is exaggerated—and I've long since gotten the impression that Alexandre is a man who might be prone to exaggeration, but it doesn't really matter.

It's the conversation that matters, the sound of his laugh as knives and forks clink against plates, the way he refills my wine glass without asking, the way he doesn't stop me when I serve myself more chicken and crusty bread, enjoying being able to eat as much as I want for the first time in my life. It feels like we're—I'm not entirely sure what. More intimate than friends, not quite a couple, but just the sudden freedom to sit at the table with him and talk and laugh and eat and drink feels so heady that I don't even need the wine to feel tipsy.

We clean up afterward, side by side, Alexandre carrying dishes into the kitchen while I fill the farmer's-style stone sink with hot water and suds that smell like lemon peel and sunshine. The twilight is starting to gather outside. The birds are still chirping outside the open window where Alexandre's herb pots are budding. It feels sweet and simple and calm, and as he brings me the dishes, it's easy to imagine this being our every night, easy to picture us growing closer, slipping into the familiar routine of a couple, living together, falling in love.

Easy to forget the power he has over me, that he could take this all away at any time.

I expect him to tell me to go to my room after, for my bath and the tea that I'll pretend to drink. Instead, he looks at me when the last of the dishes are dried, an expression on his face that I haven't seen there before.

"Let's go up to the library," he says, and I'm so startled that I don't even think to question it—not that I would have, anyway.

I follow him up the spiral staircase to the upstairs, trying not to think of all the nights I've crept up here in the darkness to spy on him, how I know every spot that creaks now and how to avoid it, all the planks in the floor that I shouldn't step on. He leads the way to the library, pushing open the heavy old door and walking straight to the fireplace.

"I know it's getting a bit warm for a fire," Alexandre says. I can't help but notice the flex of his forearms as he picks up a few pieces of wood, the fine smattering of dark hair there, his white shirt rolled crisply up to his elbows. "But there's a certain ambiance to it that just can't be beaten, don't you think?"

I nod speechlessly, unable to think of what to say. I sink onto one of the velvet armchairs in front of the fireplace as he builds it and then walks to the gilded bar cart on the other side of the room, pouring two more tiny glasses of some sort of wine and returning to sit in the leather armchair opposite me.

"It's port," he explains when I take the small glass curiously. "A good after-dinner drink."

It's sweet and thick, and I take another sip immediately after the first, enjoying the syrupy taste on my tongue.

"It's really good," I manage, and Alexandre smiles, reaching for a leather-bound book next to his chair.

I watch him as he flips it open, the way he slouches slightly in the chair, shifting until he gets comfortable, finally resting one ankle on the knee of his other leg and settling the book against his thigh, flipping through the thin pages until he lands on whatever it is that he was looking for.

I expect him to read in silence, but instead, he startles me as he starts to read aloud, his smooth, silkily accented voice drifting quietly towards me over the warm crackle of the fire.

"Demain, dès l'aube, à l'heure où blanchit la campagne,
Je partirai. Vois-tu, je sais que tu m'attends.
J'irai par la forêt, j'irai par la montagne.
Je ne puis demeurer loin de toi plus longtemps."

He pauses, glancing up at me, and then smiles ruefully. "You don't speak French, do you, *petit?*"

The familiar nickname makes my chest tighten. "Not much," I admit. "I took some classes in high school, and you have to learn some as a ballerina, but I'm not fluent."

"Ah." Alexandre shrugs. "Well, perhaps you'll learn here. At any rate, I'm quite well-spoken in English."

I can't tell if he's being sarcastic or not, but a moment later, he turns his attention back to the book and reads what I think is the same poem over again, this time in richly accented English.

"Tomorrow, from dawn, at the hour when the countryside whitens,
I'll leave. See, I know you're expecting me.
I'll go through the forest, I'll go through the mountains.
I can't stay away from you any longer."

The words of the poem hang in the air between us, floating heavily, and I don't know what to say. It's too romantic a poem for us, for him to be reading it *to* me, or is it? Am I meant to think that's what this is? I meet his eyes shyly, flickering my gaze up quickly to see his sky-blue eyes on mine, but I can't read what he's thinking.

"Victor Hugo," Alexandre says quietly. "Did you know he wrote poetry?"

I shake my head, grateful for a change in subject. "No," I say quickly. "All I know of his is *Les Miserables*."

"That's most people," Alexandre says with a laugh. He flips through the pages again, reading in French when he stops.

"*L'amour s'en va comme cette eau courante*
L'amour s'en va
Comme la vie est lente
Et comme l'Espérance est violente."

And then without my asking him to, again in English:
"*Love goes away like this running water*
Love is leaving
How slow life is
And how Hope is violent."

"Apollinaire," Alexandre says, glancing up at me. "Though I suppose you're not overly familiar with the French poets."

"No," I admit, drinking the last of my glass of port. "But—I think I might like to be?"

"Ah." Alexandre looks pleased. "Then perhaps we'll have to do this again. But for now, I think a hot bath is in order. Your feet must be sore."

He tosses back the last of his port, and I follow him down the stairs to the bathroom, where we go about our nightly routine. Once I'm tucked into bed, I pretend to drink the tea, and once the downstairs is silent, I creep back upstairs the way I have every night recently.

But tonight, the door to his room is closed, the light inside turned off. I freeze in place, wondering if I've fucked up and beaten him to his room, but the rest of the apartment is dark and silent, too, not a sound stirring anywhere. I hover outside, wondering if the light will flicker on, if I've missed something. After a few minutes, it becomes apparent that Alexandre has simply—gone to bed.

I feel a pang of disappointment as I sneak back downstairs to my room. After the intimacy of the dinner and the wine and poetry in the library—more romantic than any actual date I've ever been on, if I'm being honest—I'd craved the only physical intimacy that I've been able to have with Alexandre.

But clearly, he hadn't craved the same, even alone.

I slip back into bed, and despite my churning thoughts, I fall asleep quickly. The wine made me tired after not having drank in so long, and I sink into a deep, dreamless sleep that's only disturbed by sounds in my room that, at first, I'm not entirely sure *aren't* a dream.

My eyes flicker half-open to see Alexandre standing near my bedside, in the silk pajama pants and open dressing gown that I see him in every morning, his hand moving furiously. It takes me a split second to realize what he's doing—looking down at me as I sleep, stroking his cock in the frantic, urgent motion that I know by now is his rhythm as he gets close to the edge.

My heart leaps into my throat. I should be scared, creeped out, disturbed—any number of things that I'm *not*. What I am is instantly wet, my pulse racing as I try not to let Alexandre see that I'm awake, afraid of startling him into stopping before he finishes, desperately wishing that I could join in—touch myself, touch him. Instead, I lay frozen, wishing for more than the dim moonlight allowing me to see a glimpse of his thick, straining cock in his fist, his taut expression, his clenched jaw as he furiously strokes himself closer to a climax.

"A-ahh!" He groans deep in his throat, biting down on his lower lip in an effort to silence himself. I see the white spurt of his release over his hand, his hips jerking and cock throbbing as his toes curl into the rug, and I feel like I can't breathe. I want to taste him, to touch him. It feels like torture to lie there in silence as he comes in his fist in jerks and shudders, finally going very still as the last drops of his cum slide over his fingers.

The guilt on his face is instant and obvious, even in the dim moonlight, and my heart clenches in my chest. I can see the regret written all over his expression in an instant as he backs up, still clutching himself, fumbling for the doorknob as he slips out of the room almost as quickly as I woke up and saw him there.

I want to go after him. I want to tell him how I feel, beg him to stop keeping this last part of himself separate, to let us really be together.

But I don't. I lie there in bed trembling and aroused, and as my hand slides down my belly towards the waist of my own pajama pants, I know one thing for certain.

If anything more is going to happen between Alexandre and me, I'm going to have to be brave enough to make a move.

And I also know that I can't wait much longer.

LIAM

I had thought a tiger's fur would be softer than this.

It's coarse under my fingers, and it takes a second for me to register that I'm really doing it, that my hand is really resting on the top of a tiger's head, between its rounded ears, and that I'm still alive and in possession of all of my fingers.

Once I start, I don't actually want to stop. It's nice, like petting an oversized housecat, and weirdly calming and thrilling all at once.

I wish my father could fucking see *this*.

"*Yoi shigoto nakama!*" Kaito calls out, stretching, and the tiger shifts, making a noise deep in its throat that makes me pull back instantly, taking a large step back. "Good job, bro. You've got bigger balls than I gave you credit for." He grins. "Maybe I should make the priest do it next."

"That's not what the deal was," I say tersely, moving to stand in front of him again—and also blocking Max somewhat from his view. "You said if I petted the tiger, you'd give me the information. I've done my part. Now do yours."

"Honestly, I didn't think you would." Kaito chews on his lower lip, tossing back more sake as he looks at me appraisingly. "But you're right, Irishman. I won't have anyone saying the Nakamura *kobun* has no honor. So here you are. The man's name is Alexandre Sartre, and he lives in the fifth *arrondissement* of Paris. I'm unsure of the exact address, but Volkov here ought to be able to find the man's nose hairs with that much information. He could probably have done more with less, from what I've heard of him."

"*Arigato*," Levin says dryly. "Nakamura-san."

Kaito barely looks at him. "Well, I suppose the fun is over then. Unless you'd like a trip to one of the brothels?"

"Don't you have enough women here already?" Max asks dryly.

"Spoken like a true priest." Kaito grins, pinching the nipple of one of the girls closest to him, wearing only a body chain. "There's never enough women. Trust me on that, Agosti." He glances back at Levin and me and then at the man who brought us here, who has been standing silently throughout most of Kaito's dramatics. "Take them to the ryokan. They can rest there, free of charge. Leave Tokyo in the morning," he continues, narrowing his eyes at us. "Or else I'll have to reconsider the hospitality of the Nakamura clan."

"Of course." Levin stands, bowing at the waist, and I do the same. "*Arigato*, Nakamura-san. Your hospitality is much appreciated."

The lodging that we're taken to is rustic but pleasant, old-fashioned Japanese architecture with a sprawling garden surrounding it and a huge *onsen*-style soaking pool that we're directed to, none too gently by the old woman who runs it, who makes it plain that we're meant to get clean before we lay down for the evening.

Max and I both balk at the idea of stripping down—I'm not exactly accustomed to bathing in a hot springs pool, indoor or outdoor, naked in front of other men—but Levin seems to have no such concerns. He shucks his clothes quickly, and when he catches our raised eyebrows, he just shrugs.

"When in Rome," he says simply, sinking into the steaming water. "Or Tokyo. You know. Whichever."

The bath *is* good, the hot water sinking into my muscles and relieving the tension in a way that I hadn't realized I needed until just that moment.

"All in all, I think I like Tokyo," I say ruefully, leaning back against the stones of the pool. "Not a bad place."

"You almost got us killed," Levin says with his eyes narrowed. "I told you to keep that Irish mouth of yours shut."

"I got us the information, didn't I? Who's to say he would have given it to you?"

"No one," Levin says crossly. "But that wasn't skill on your part, just luck. He could have had you killed or tortured for your insolence just as easily as been amused by it."

"Well, it's about time the luck of the Irish started working in my favor," I say, tipping my head back. "And we have the information we need. Tomorrow, Paris."

She's so close. I can feel my anxiety building as we head to bed, dressed in cotton pajamas the *ryokan* staff has provided for us. With each step, we've gotten closer, just as I'd hoped. Now, with the Frenchman's name and the location of his apartment, Ana is practically at my fingertips, the ability to save her only a flight away. I can't bear the thought that it might slip from my grasp now, that I might fail her.

I wonder if she's been holding out hope for me, if she's thought about my coming to rescue her, if she believed that I would. I wonder if she's dreamed about me the way I've dreamed about her, fantasized about the moment that I would arrive and rescue her from the Frenchman like some knight in a fairytale, her defender, her savior.

Alexandre Sartre. I can't begin to put a face to the name. Still, I picture someone old and leering, someone, who couldn't possibly get a girl like Ana in any way other than by illegal, deplorable means. The thought that he might have hurt her in some way makes me sick, but I have to hope that for a hundred million dollars, he wouldn't have laid a finger on her in violence.

Of course, there are other ways to hurt someone that doesn't have to draw blood. But I can't think about it. I have to keep that cool head that I've always done my best to maintain, if I'm going to have any hope of saving Ana.

And after all this time, after I've come this far, I can't believe that I'll do anything else.

I certainly can't entertain the thought of failure.

I dream about her that night, the way I have every night since I returned to Boston, since I left New York, since I've been searching for her. I dream of her in my bed and out of it; I dream of her by the window in my apartment, her blonde hair shining like a halo around her head, her blue eyes light and laughing. I imagine her walking across the hardwood floors, twirling, dancing, without a care in the world. I imagine her spinning right into my arms, her delicate body arching backward, her breasts against my chest, her pointed chin tilting up for me to kiss her full lips, for her to melt into me.

I dream of finding her in a Parisian apartment, of her face lighting up when she sees me burst in, of her mouth forming the words *finally, you found me, I knew you would.*

I dream of her whispering that she loves me, that she believed in me, that she never gave up hope. I dream of her being *mine*, at last, my girl, my lover, my wife even, if I can find a way to make it happen without destroying everything I've been placed in charge of.

And I'll do it, somehow. I believe I can. If I can find Ana halfway across the world with nothing but a description and a dollar amount, I'll find a way out of the betrothal contract. I'll find a way to mollify Graham O'Sullivan, and I'll make Ana my wife.

I'll have the life I didn't know I could imagine for myself until I met her, and everything changed.

I'll save her, and after that, nothing else can ever hurt us, ever again.

I'll make sure of that.

ANA

I half expect Alexandre to be strange with me again the next morning, after waking up to find him in my room. But he isn't. He brings me my breakfast as usual—in bed, as if the entire ordeal of having me kneel on the floor never happened at all—and dresses me in the maid's outfit. There's no sign of Yvette, and after our meal together last night and the poetry in the library, my heart feels lighter than ever. *Yes, him coming into my room and watching me while I sleep and pleasuring himself was strange,* I tell myself as I do the breakfast dishes, *but I've spied on him often enough. I can't judge.*

A small part of me wonders if he knows I've been outside the door and if last night was a way of him turning that back on me. But the abject guilt I'd seen on his face makes me think that's not the case. It makes me all the more sure that he would have been angry with me if he'd ever caught me, but that's not enough to make me not daydream about going up there again tonight, hoping that I won't find the light turned off the way I did the night before.

Halfway through the afternoon, as I'm dusting the books, there's a knock at the door. It startles me because no one ever comes to Alexandre's apartment except Yvette, and she would hardly knock. She'd just come in like she owned the place. I put down the feather

IRISH SAVIOR

duster gingerly, my heart racing in my chest because Alexandre hasn't ever told me what to do in a situation like this. Am I supposed to ignore it? Answer it? Will I be in trouble if I choose the wrong one?

The knock comes twice more while I'm shifting from foot to foot, trying to decide, and I wind up dithering in the foyer for so long that I hear the footsteps of whoever it was start walking away. I give it a few more minutes, even more anxious about going to the front door now and finally opening it.

There's no one there now of course, but there is *something*—a long white box tied with a huge silvery ribbon, like a pre-wrapped present from a department store, and a smaller box on top of it, and then one smaller still, like Russian nesting dolls outside of each other.

It must be a delivery for Alexandre, I think, reaching for them. I can't just leave them outside in the hall. They might get stolen. *Or Yvette. Maybe she had something delivered here.*

But as I pick them up, the tag on the biggest one flips over, and I see my name in an elegant script.

For Anastasia.

From Alexandre.

My heart starts to race in my chest and I almost trip, nearly dropping the boxes. I carry them into the living room, feeling like I can't breathe as I set them down on the couch, unsure of what I'm supposed to do. Should I open them now or wait for Alexandre to come home? I haven't forgotten his reaction to my disobeying him about the study, but surely this is different? I don't have explicit instructions for this, so will he really be so angry if I do the wrong thing?

I don't want to end up eating my meals on the floor again, but I'm also not sure I can wait until he comes home. And if I *am* supposed to open them before he comes home, he might be upset with me for wasting his time or think I'm unappreciative.

Unappreciative of what *exactly? You don't even know what they are.*

I start with the smallest box. When I open it, my mouth drops open when I push aside the silvery tissue paper filling it. What I'm seeing doesn't make sense—a gold bangle bracelet studded with sapphires, a pair of drop sapphire earrings set in gold, and a matching necklace that's a thin gold chain with a bezel-set teardrop sapphire hanging from it. They look expensive, and I gingerly set the box down, thinking there must be some mistake. But I open the next box anyway, my pulse leaping in my throat.

The next box is shoes—shoes with the ubiquitous red bottoms, but not heels. They're flats made of the softest leather I've ever touched, and the inner soles are thickly padded, as if Alexandre had them made custom. I feel my eyes start to burn as I set them down and reach for the ribbon on the largest box, unsure of what I'm going to find inside.

There's a card on top of the silvery tissue, and I open it first. It's written in a sprawlingly elegant hand, and there's no doubt that it's from Alexandre.

Anastasia,

Please get dressed in these items that I've chosen for you, and be ready to go by eight p.m. exactly. Don't be late, petit. *I have a special evening planned for us.*

--Alexandre

Dumbfounded, I move the tissue aside to find a dress nestled in the paper, and when I lift it out, I can hardly believe what I'm holding in my hands. It's a cocktail dress that comes to just below my knees, made out of the softest, slipperiest sapphire-colored satin I've ever touched, with a sharp v-neckline that will come down to just below my breasts and corset-style ribbon cutouts on the sides. I can't imagine how Alexandre would know my size, but when I scoop all the items up and carry them to my room, holding the dress up to myself in front of the mirror there, I think it might actually fit.

I take a bath on my own for the first time, wanting to make sure I'm sparkling clean before I even think of putting that gorgeous dress on. I wash my hair and comb it out, letting it air-dry as I go through the dresser for what I should wear under it. The satin is so fine that I can't find any panties that won't show, and I don't need a bra, so after several minutes of trying to make up my mind, I decide to go for the most daring option—nothing.

Which means that when I slip the dress on, the satin slithers over my bare skin, cool and sexual in a way that I never imagined a dress could be, clinging to the delicate lines of my body in a way that both hints at everything and shows very little. I don't have any cleavage to speak of. Still, the neckline looks sexy anyway, hinting at the soft swells of my small breasts on either side. The corset ribbons on either side of the dress give my waist a curve that it doesn't currently actually have. The dress fits me perfectly, as if Alexandre had my exact measurements. The shoes are more comfortable than anything I've worn thus far, so that even after being on my feet cleaning, I think I might actually be able to walk tonight without too much discomfort.

When my hair is fully dry, I comb it out again so that it falls straight and soft and silky down my back and put on the jewelry last of all, which is so much finer than anything I'd ever thought I would wear.

I'm ready at five minutes to eight, walking into the hall just as I hear the front door open. When I come out to greet Alexandre, my mouth drops open at the same moment that his eyes widen.

He's wearing black suit pants, smoking loafers, a black cashmere turtleneck, and a burgundy velvet jacket with black satin lapels, a look that most men wouldn't be able to pull off. But Alexandre does it handsomely, his blue eyes shining as he looks at me, and I feel like nothing so much as his perfectly dressed china doll—and I don't hate it.

The pleasure in his face as he looks at me is enough to make me not care that I didn't pick any of this out, that I'm following his instructions. I can't even imagine how much all of this must have cost or what kind of place we must be going to in order to warrant all of this. Although—knowing Alexandre and some of his eccentricities, he might have dressed us both up to go to a dive bar, for all I know.

But that's not where we end up. He takes my hand and leads me out of the apartment. We walk out into the cool, fragrant Parisian night and down the cobble streets until we find an elegant restaurant where he has a reservation. We're swept back to a dimly lit corner with candles burning on the table and champagne already on ice.

"What is all of this?" I ask softly as I slide into the circular leather-backed booth, and Alexandre just smiles.

"I wanted to spoil you a little, *petit*. You've been such a very good girl. Don't you think you deserve it?"

It feels like a loaded question. After all, I've been sneaking around his room for over a week now, and I don't know for sure whether he knows about it or not. But I opt to assume that he doesn't—because if he really *doesn't* know, as I suspect, then I don't want to ruin the night.

"I don't know," I say softly, instinctively feeling that's the best answer. "But it's absolutely lovely, Alexandre. Thank you."

He slides in next to me, and a server appears almost instantly with a tray of oysters on ice with lemon and a vinaigrette in the center of the tray. "Have you had raw oysters, *petit poupée?*" Alexandre asks as the server pours our champagne.

I shake my head, and he smiles.

"You're going to love it," he assures me, squeezing lemon over the chilled oysters and then using the tiniest teaspoon I've ever seen to sprinkle some of the herbed vinaigrette over one of them before picking it up and bringing it to my lips.

I let him feed it to me, and the tang of the vinegar and saltiness of the brine fills my mouth, cold and clear and crisp. I swallow it down convulsively, feeling something throb deep inside of me at the intimacy of his fingers on my chin, the liquid clinging to my lips.

He feeds me almost every bite of our dinner. After the oysters that we share there's a soup course, a rich onion soup with baguettes that he lets me feed myself, but after that, there's a trio of entrees—duck with crispy vegetables, some delicate fish with a lemon sauce, and a cut of steak so tender that Alexandre cuts it with a fork, covered in a red wine reduction with onions and mushrooms and bleu cheese. He feeds me bites in between his own, and I want to moan with pleasure at every flavor. It's the best food I've ever had in my life, even better than what Alexandre has cooked for me, and I savor every bite. After years of depriving myself of staying in ballerina shape, eating like this is almost sexual. It feels as if Alexandre knows it.

Each course is served with wine or champagne, right down to the port that's served with our dessert of cheese and fruit and crème brûlée. I'm so full that I don't know how I'll keep eating. Still, I eat what Alexandre feeds me anyway, the juicy fruits and silky custard too delicious to resist.

I could get used to this, I think to myself, as we walk back in the cool night air. There are no cars, no smog, no rushing around, just slow routine days and delicious food and beautiful dresses and walks in the cool night air. The days of kneeling on the floor and Alexandre's anger and his threats seem so far in the past that they might as well be a bad dream, with the satin dress clinging sensually to my skin and champagne bubbles still on my tongue.

It could happen again, as easily as a change in his mood, but right now, it's easy to believe that it won't. Especially when his hand moves down my arm as we walk, finding mine, our fingers intertwining. My heart leaps into my throat when that happens, pounding as my skin prickles, burning from his touch, and I feel like I can't breathe. I feel like that every step of the way home, all the way to my bedroom, where he starts to undress me as detachedly as he ever has, stripping me bare and setting the jewelry aside in the jewelry box that had caused my hallucination that one afternoon, and then helping me into my pajamas.

It feels selfish to be disappointed in anything after such a night, but it feels like such an abrupt change. From a romantic dinner and walk holding hands through the streets of Paris back to his old detached self, his hands carefully staying away from anything that could even be deemed remotely sexual as he dresses me in my silk pajamas.

I want more than this. I want his hands on me, to tumble naked into bed with him, to *know* that the romantic dinner out is a date. I want the twilight evenings washing dishes side by side, the smell of herbs and sunlight in my nose. I want the city to wrap its arms around us and for this to be our place, our haven, Alexandre and I. He might own me, but how does that matter? Tonight was better than any night I ever had when I was dating men independently. If anything, I can feel safe that he'll cherish and care for me always, because I cost him a sum of money so large that it's unthinkable to me.

The small voice in my head tries to whisper to me to hold out, to keep some distance, not to fall for a man who can never view me as his equal because he'll always own me, but it's easier to silence now. *No one is coming for me,* I whisper back. *There's no leaving, so why be miserable? Why not make the best of it and find happiness where I can? Isn't that what everyone told me to do back in New York, when I lost everything and wanted to die?*

A small, fading part of me knows that's not what they meant, but it doesn't matter. I pretend to drink the tea like always, slip upstairs and to the cracked bedroom door like always, the light spilling out. Though this time, when I see Alexandre walking nude towards his bedside table, his cock thickening without him touching it, I don't hang back. I walk into the room, my heart in my throat, before he can get the pictures out. And when he hears my footsteps and sees me, his mouth dropping open with shock even as his cock stiffens to a full, rigid erection at the sight of me, I don't give him time to get angry or yell or tell me to get out.

I drop to my knees in front of him, reaching for his hips. The fine muscle underneath my hands, the softness of his skin, is enough to make me soaking wet in an instant, his cock hovering an inch from my lips.

"Anastasia, no." Alexandre reaches for my arms and pulls my hands away. "You can't do this. What are you doing? I told you not to come in here. No," he repeats, pulling me up to my feet, his rigid cock still bobbing between us as he looks down into my flushed face. "No."

I should leave. I know I should. He's never given me any reason to believe he wants a sexual relationship between us—except…last night, in my room, as he looked guiltily down at my "sleeping" body while he feverishly stroked his cock.

I want him, and I know he wants me too. I don't understand why he won't give in to it, but I don't want to leave. I don't try to drop back to my knees, though. Instead, I push myself up on my tiptoes, my hands against his chest as I tilt my chin up, looking up into those piercing blue eyes.

"What about this?" I whisper, and I kiss him.

His lips are soft and full and warm, almost feminine, and I feel his chest swell and heave with a deep, shuddering breath under my hands as my mouth touches his. He doesn't move, doesn't kiss me back, but he doesn't stop me either, and so I keep going. I run my tongue over his lower lip and suck it into my mouth, moving forward as his hands tighten on my upper arms so that I can feel his throbbing cock pressed between us, the heat of it burning through the silk of my pajama shirt. I push my tongue into his mouth, slant my lips over his, and I can feel him struggling not to respond, struggling to fight it until the moment that I rock my hips against his, feeling his cock slide over the satin against my belly as I tangle my tongue with his and bite softly at his lower lip. I hear a groan spill from his mouth that's almost painful.

"*Petit*," he moans, and then the hands on my arms aren't trying to push me away any longer. They're pulling me closer, his mouth eating at mine too, sucking at my lower lip, biting, his nails sinking into the flesh of my upper arms as we stumble towards the bed. We topple onto it, ending up with him on his back and me straddling him. I nearly tear off my clothes in need of closer to him, feel his skin, and have him inside of me before he changes his mind.

His hands are on my bare hips as I strip naked, searing hotly into my skin, his cock is between my thighs, my arousal slick on the straining velvet flesh, and I kiss him again, hard, as I guide him between my legs. He's thick and long, and it's been such a long time since I've had a man inside of me that I feel impossibly tight, so much so that Alexandre groans aloud again as he feels his swollen cockhead trying to pierce me, trying to push inside. I want him so badly that I'm already clenching, pushing him out, and trying to pull him in all at once, and I shove myself downwards, wanting to feel him. He's lying rigid beneath me, perfectly still. He stops kissing me when he feels his cock impale me, the wet heat of my tight, fluttering pussy enveloping the first inch of him, and then another, and another until I've managed to push myself all the way down his throbbing length, burying him inside of me as I sit atop him.

His eyes are wide and glazed with lust when I sit back, his hands lax on my hips, and it's me that starts to move. I feel dizzy with need, unable to believe we're actually doing this, that Alexandre is inside of me, his muscled, handsome body sprawled on the bed as he looks up at me dazedly. "Anastasia—" he moans as I rock atop him, sliding up and then down again, my body adjusting to the size of him as I feel every hard inch caressing the inside of me.

It feels like the tables have turned, like I'm suddenly the one in control, holding him down, riding him as he lies there, almost as if he's in shock that it's happening. I don't give myself time to question how right or wrong this might be. I can feel him throbbing inside of me, his hips twitching, his chest heaving as he gasps against my mouth, and I feel my entire body tightening as I hurtle towards an orgasm.

When it comes, I feel as if I'm splitting apart at the seams, my body convulsing so tightly around him that I feel as if I could break him, my fingers digging into his chest as I grind down onto him hard. I hear Alexandre gasping my name, his head tilting back. The tendons of his throat standing out in the same moment that I feel him swell even more inside of me, and then the sudden hot rush as his thighs tense and shudder. He explodes in a burst of pleasure that has him groaning deeply, his fingers clawing at the bed as he thrusts up into me hard for the first time, his cum filling me as we both shudder together in a deep, satisfying orgasm.

I'm shaking when I roll off of him, panting for breath, nerves suddenly swamping me as I realize what we've just done and how Alexandre could react to it. He might regret it, might blame me for "forcing" him into it, for making him fuck a pet. It takes several seconds before I can even bring myself to look at him, my heart hammering in my chest, but then I hear a soft snore and look over to realize that he's already asleep.

Oh my god. I want to laugh, but I don't—I don't want to disturb him. I grab a soft blanket from the end of the bed and pull it over his naked body, then hover there on the edge of the bed, unsure of what to do. *Should I stay? Should I go back to my room? Will he be angry if I stay? Will he be hurt if I go?* It's like my indecision over the person at the front door all over again, except this time even more meaningful.

IRISH SAVIOR

Finally, I get up and go to the bathroom to clean myself up, very aware of the stickiness of Alexandre's cum on my thighs and the realization of what we've done. I can't help but worry about how he'll react in the morning, but all I can do now is try not to panic—something that I *know* will upset him.

I do my best not to mess up anything in his bathroom, cleaning up as best as I can and then coming back to the bed. I don't want to leave—I want to curl up next to him naked under the blanket and fall asleep, skin to skin. It's been so long since I've gotten to have that, to experience it. And I'm sure it has for him, too—

Unbidden, my gaze flicks to the drawer of the side table, the one where I know the photos are hidden. *Don't do it,* that tiny reasonable voice in my head whispers. Still, my pulse is already speeding up, the same aching curiosity that led me to go into the study and to spy on Alexandre in his bedroom in the first place rearing its ugly head, tempting me to do something that I know I shouldn't.

He's sleeping hard, faintly snoring, his head turned to one side. He's not going to wake up, not if I'm quiet. And I want to know. What kind of man looks at Polaroids for his porn, and what kind of porn is it? Is it some kind of amateur fetish? I tell myself that I'm only looking so that I know what turns him on, so that I can make it better for him next time. So that there can *be* a next time.

Not just for my own selfish curiosity, I tell myself as I open the drawer and reach for the stack of photos.

But when I look at them, *really* look at them, I wish I'd just fucking left well enough alone.

My breath catches in my throat. There's a different girl in each one, some older than others, all of them seemingly of legal age, but just girls—not models or porn stars. They're in ordinary clothes, hair down or pulled back or atop their heads, smiling or laughing or serious.

There's a name at the bottom of each Polaroid—*Chelsea, Liesel, Beth, Grace, Marie,* and on and on.

Every single one of them is very, very beautiful.

And every single one of them has a flaw.

One is blind in one eye. One is missing a hand. One has a cleft palate, another has a missing tooth. One is in a wheelchair, another clearly deaf, from the way she's signing to the camera.

Every. Single. One.

I'm crying before I realize I am. Not for the girls, but for myself, because I'd been stupid enough to think I was special. To tell myself that Yvette was making it up about the other girls. That she was talking about *actual* pets. That this wasn't something Alexandre just *did*, collecting damaged, beautiful girls the way he collects damaged, beautiful china and books and art and rugs.

I wish I hadn't seen. I wish I didn't know. Or if I had to find out, I wish I had before we'd slept together, before I'd started to fall for him, because now all I can see is each of these girls in bed with him, riding him, feeling him hard and thick and solid for them, his gasping moans as he gives in to his body's urges despite himself, fucking him to a fast, desperate climax after weeks of wanting, wanting, wanting—

I forget where I am, that I shouldn't wake him up, that I'll make him angry. I forget everything except my heart breaking inside of my chest. A heart that never should have been even the slightest bit his in the first place, and I feel as stupid as I did the day he caught me in the study, as stupid as I did when he made me eat off the floor, as stupid as I ever have.

I was never special. There were always other girls, and I *knew* that; I just pretended I didn't.

And now I've made it so much worse for myself.

I don't hear him wake up. I don't feel him sit up. I'm clutching the photos, tears dripping down onto the pictures that I've watched him jerk off over a dozen times, girls he owned, girls that are gone, girls that he clearly still wants since he gets *fucking hard just thinking about the pictures*, and I want to scream. I'm completely insensible to anything except the sudden, bone-chilling sound of Alexandre's voice behind me, still thick with sleep, and I know I've fucked up horribly once again.

But this time, I'm too heartbroken to care.

"What the *fuck* are you doing, Anastasia?"

ANA

"*What the fuck are you doing?*"

He shouts it again, louder this time, and I feel real fear for the first time since he caught me in the study.

"I didn't *fucking* tell you you could touch those, *Anastasia!*" He screams this last, snatching the photos out of my hand and throwing them back into the drawer. I barely have time to react before his hand comes back around, striking me across the face so hard that it sends me flying off of the bed and sprawling across the rug on the hardwood floor.

"I'm sorry—I'm sorry—" I don't know if I'm sobbing it aloud or not, but every inch of me is shaking, curled naked on the rug as my face flames and throbs, and I'm crying, frozen, panicking. I hear the mattress creak as he gets up, and I cry out in fear, every inch of me shuddering with terror as I feel the heavy, warm weight of his body coming to kneel next to me on the rug. I wait for a fist in my hair or the crack of a belt or his hand again, more abuse, more pain, because this was always how it was going to end up. I was just stupid enough to pretend otherwise.

"Oh god, *petit, petit poupée,* I'm so sorry, I'm sorry—"

Alexandre reaches for me, and I flinch away, trying to squirm, panicked, out of his grasp. But he doesn't let me, and it takes me a moment to realize that he's pulling me into his arms, onto his naked lap, petting my hair as he tries to soothe me.

"I'm sorry I struck you, *petit*, I'm sorry—"

I can't stop myself. The back and forth is enough to give me whiplash. Still, I curl into his chest anyway, laying my cheek against his smooth skin as he strokes my hair, whispering my nickname over and over as he apologizes.

"Who are they?" I whisper. I know I shouldn't ask, but it's gone this far—too far. "Who are those girls."

Alexandre's hand goes very still on my hair. "That's none of your business, *petit*," he says, his voice stiff and angry, and I can feel him tensing, the fury starting to return as his hand tightens on the back of my neck. "You shouldn't ask such questions—"

I don't know where the courage comes from, really. I should know better by now. I should squirm out of his lap, grab my clothes and, run back to my room, go back to being his pet. I should forget that tonight ever happened, forget wanting more, forget *everything*, but I can't.

I pull back instead, looking up at his heated blue eyes, and I try for once to speak to him as an equal. Not as the girl he owns, not the girl he paid a *hundred million dollars* for, not one of his pets, not his little doll.

As a girl who is falling for him, a girl who just fucked him, a girl who wants to know *why*, as her heart breaks into a million pieces.

I remember him asking about my feet that first day when he bathed me and how angry he was when I wouldn't answer. I remember, too, that he's never asked again.

"I'll tell you about my past," I whisper, my voice hardly audible. "If you'll be honest with me."

Alexandre goes very still. I can see him thinking, deciding. And then, as if he's made up his mind, he sweeps me up suddenly in his arms, standing gracefully as he holds me against his naked body, carrying me back to the bed as he pulls the duvet back and sets me on the mattress, crawling in next to me and pulling the blankets up so that he's covered to his hips and I'm able to pull the sheet up around my breasts, covering me while he looks at me evenly.

"Very well," he says quietly. "But you first."

I lick my dry lips nervously. I'm not sure I like that arrangement—he could hear my story and then go back on the agreement to share, but I suppose he could be thinking the same thing about me. At any rate, I'm lucky I've gotten this far. I'm not exactly in a position to really negotiate with him. He's allowing it.

"I was tortured," I say softly. "My best friend was in trouble, and she was pregnant. The Russian Bratva wanted her, and she didn't trust the man she'd married to escape them yet. I went undercover and slept with some of them, trying to get information to help her, to help her find a way out of her marriage and the city. Her husband's underboss found out and tortured me without his knowledge or permission." I take a breath, swallowing back the memory of the fear and panic and agonizing pain, the crackle of burning flesh, and the feeling of a knife slicing into the soles of my feet. "He cut my feet up and then burned them with a blowtorch. He said I'd never dance again, and he was right. My ballet career ended that day. As you know, it's difficult to walk some days, from atrophy and scar tissue. I got very depressed and didn't care for myself the way I was supposed to, either. My life—hasn't been the same since. *I* haven't been the same."

I can see Alexandre's expression darkening as I speak, his eyes narrowing and a look of pure, hateful rage filling them. "Where is this man?" he asks tightly when I go silent. "He ought to have the same done to him. *I* should do the same to him, for you—"

"He's dead," I say quietly. "My friend shot him. He's been dead for some time now."

Alexandre goes silent for a moment. When he speaks, at last, his tone is solemn and low, his eyes not quite meeting mine.

"I've been hurt too, Anastasia," he says finally. "Perhaps not in the way that you have, not so—physically. But my father was a cruel man. I will go to my grave swearing that my mother died of his neglect. His second wife was a woman as cruel as he was, and he hurt me often, in many ways. She enjoyed my pain because I was a reminder that she was not the only woman he'd ever taken to bed or made his wife."

He takes a deep, slow breath, his fingers twisting in the duvet. "I have, over the years, tried to rescue other broken things. Other broken girls, like my stepsister, who my father hurt so badly that she eventually died." Slowly, Alexandre raises his gaze to mine, and I can see the depth of pain there, that he's remembering something that he tries very hard not to think about often.

"Alexandre, I'm so sorry—"

"Just listen. I've never spoken of this to anyone, but—" He takes a deep, shuddering breath. "I try to find all the beautiful things in the world now that no one else will love because they are flawed in some way. My stepsister was flawed. She had a club foot that she was born with; she couldn't walk right for all her beauty. My father hated her for it and claimed she would drain him for all her life, that no one would ever marry her. And yet—" Alexandre shakes his head, his face going very pale. "I know what you're thinking when you saw those photos. After what we did here tonight—but I never touched any of them. I wanted them, *god* I wanted them, every single one, but I wouldn't touch them. I thought if I kept my hands off of them, if I only ever fantasized, if I never touched them or made them touch me, they would stay with me. But they didn't."

To my horror, I can see tears starting to fill Alexandre's blue eyes, his voice choked. "They all left me," he says, his voice rasping and hoarse. "No matter what I did, no matter how well I cared for my little pets, they grew ill, or they ran away, or they killed themselves. I tried so hard to make their lives easy, beautiful, to feed and dress and care for them, to ensure that no one would hurt or use them ever again, but they all left anyway. And now that I have—" he gulps, his hands shaking in the blankets. "Now, you will leave me too, however you choose to achieve that."

I stare at him, something dawning on me. "Alexandre," I murmur softly, reaching out to touch his hand. "How long has it been since you've had sex with someone? Before tonight?"

He stares at me for a moment as if he doesn't quite grasp the question, and then he looks away. "More years than I can count," he admits finally.

"You weren't—" I stare at him, wide-eyed.

"No, I was not a virgin, Anastasia. When my stepsister and I were teenagers, I fell in love with her. We tried to deny ourselves for a very long time, but teenage desires are difficult things to fight. We had an affair—I lost my innocence to her, although my father had stolen hers well before that. I was the only man who ever touched her that she wanted, though. The only one she loved." He shudders, and I see tears dripping down the bridge of his nose, dampening the blanket. "My father flew into a jealous rage when he found out. He—took her—in front of me. He abused her until she died, while I was forced to watch. He told me, very clearly, that it was my fault. That if I had not touched her, if I had not given in to my *filthy* desire, that she would be alive. And I have not touched another woman since, until tonight. Not a single one of my little dolls."

Oh god, it all makes so much sense. Every last piece clicks into place, and I feel sick and horrified, not at Alexandre but at his father. A man who had managed to take a son with a good soul and twist him into this, a man who is still good at heart but so damaged down to the very depths of himself that he only knows how to express it in the strangest of ways. A man who, as a teenager, had been convinced that having sex with a woman he loved was the cause of her death, and as a result repressed his natural desires for years, his ways of showing love and care becoming more and more warped as the years passed.

I believe that he never hurt any of those girls that he bought. That he only wanted to give them something as beautiful as what he saw when he looked at them, to protect them from men like his father. And yet, they'd all been so damaged too, probably used and abused in ways that I don't want to begin to imagine, that they'd all found some way to escape him, believing him to be warped and twisted and dangerous.

"You'll leave me too now," he whispers. "I shouldn't have touched you, shouldn't have let—but I *wanted*—more than any of the others, more than—"

"Did you go into their rooms too?" I ask quietly. "Did you watch them while they slept, and—"

Alexandre looks up at me, startled. "What? No. Only you, Ana, since Margot, you've been the only girl who I wanted so badly that I—I couldn't stop myself. I'm sorry that I've made you dirty, I'm sorry—"

"Alexandre." I grab his hands, squeezing them until he looks up at me. "You haven't. Your father was a cruel, awful person, and he lied to you. There's nothing dirty or wrong about sex if both of us want it. You wanted it, right?"

He swallows, nodding slowly. He's never looked so young or boyish as he does at this moment, looking at me through dark tear-drenched lashes, clinging to my hands. "Yes," he whispers, his voice thickly accented. "Yes, I wanted you, Anastasia. So badly, I could have come the moment I was inside of you, you felt so good—"

"And I wanted you. You didn't make me do anything. I wanted it. I talked you into it. So there's nothing dirty or bad here. Just two people who desire each other." *And one who owns the other*, I think, but I don't say it. I don't think it matters right now—maybe it won't ever matter. I don't feel like Alexandre's possession right now. I feel like the only thing keeping him from spiraling, which is a strange position to be in, after everything.

"I'm not going to leave you," I whisper, clinging to his hands. And then, before he can say anything, I lean forward and kiss him.

He freezes for a moment, and I think he's going to push me away. But he doesn't, and after a moment, he softens, his hands moving, wrapping around mine. Then suddenly, before I know what's happening, he's spilling me onto my back, pushing my legs apart, stretching over me. His dark hair flops rakishly into his face, his expression soft and vulnerable, his blue eyes searching mine.

"Anastasia," he whispers, and then he kisses me again.

He's inside of me before I realize what's happening, rock-hard, his cock sliding between my folds and piercing my sore body, but I don't mind. I wrap my legs around his hips, pulling him in, deep and then deeper still, winding my arms around his neck. "I love you, Anastasia," he whispers brokenly against my lips, and a thrill of uncertainty and fear ripples over me, but I hear myself whispering back to him.

"I think I love you too," I murmur, arching against him, feeling my nipples brush against his chest as he moves against me, thrusting slowly, so that I feel every inch of his thick, throbbing cock, how aroused he is for me, how much he wants me.

"You can't leave me," he groans, kissing me again. "Don't ever leave me, Anastasia, don't—"

"You own me," I point out, tilting my chin up to look at him. "How can I—"

"It doesn't matter." He shakes his head. "The others left me, but you can't. You can't ever leave. You're the most valuable thing I possess, Anastasia, the best piece of my collection. I can't bear to lose you, I love you—I couldn't bear it if you left me—"

I can hear the desperation in his words, the obsession, feel the way he thrusts faster with each statement, harder, as if he's possessing me with his cock now too, taking a new, deeper kind of ownership of me, and somewhere deep down I know I should be terrified. I know I should be afraid of this new level of obsession, but I can't find it in myself to be. Alexandre is as broken in his own way as I am in mine. I want to believe that it's the broken pieces of each other that fit together in this way, that we can find each other, heal each other, that I can fall for him safely.

That I don't have to feel guilty about the pleasure rippling over every inch of my skin, the way he stops fucking me long enough to slide down between my legs and lick me to a screaming orgasm, his tongue circling my clit as if he hasn't been celibate for probably more than a decade, making me clench my thighs around his head until he comes up and kisses me with the tang of my own arousal still on his lips, thrusting into me again hard while I'm still fluttering around his cock. That I don't have to feel bad that I cling to him, arching against him, that I think the words *making love* when he thrusts into me hard, triggering my third orgasm of the night as I feel him start to shudder, his cum filling me hotly, spilling out onto my thighs while he's still vibrating inside of me, still fucking me, that I can feel myself falling for him.

That I think I love him.

He's been kinder to me than any man has in a long time, I think defensively as I lie there afterward, curled naked in his arms, held against him tightly as he falls asleep again without letting me up to go clean myself in the bathroom. I know this isn't right in so many ways. *Or maybe it's just unconventional,* I tell myself. *Maybe it doesn't fucking matter if we're both happy.*

I know I'm conveniently forgetting so much that he's done to me, even just tonight. But I can't stop myself. I want this. The pleasure, the happiness, the feeling of having found someone who understands me and who I understand in return.

Alexandre is broken, but so am I.

Maybe that's what I'm meant for, now. To slot the broken pieces of myself against someone else, and if we cut each other until we bleed?

At least we'll bleed out together.

* * *

THE NEXT MORNING, it's his bathtub that Alexandre carries me to in order to clean up, and he slides into it with me, a copper tub big enough for both of us. When we're both scrubbed pink, he brings me back to bed, dressing and bringing me breakfast, and then he puts me in the maid outfit as always. "I'm having a dinner party with a few friends tonight," he announces as I eat. "Yvette will be there—I know that doesn't please you," he adds, frowning. "But she is my friend. I'm going out to get some things while you clean, but I'll be back earlier than usual. You can clean this room too," he adds magnanimously, as if he's given me some kind of gift. "The only room you can't go into now is the study, *petit.*"

There's a slight warning to his tone, but I don't take it too much to heart. I know better to go in there by now, and anyway, there's not any reason left for me to do so.

"Okay," I say softly. "Do I have to eat on the floor while your friends are here?"

Alexandre looks horrified. "Of course not, *petit!*" he exclaims. "You are not my pet any longer. You are my lover, and you will eat at the table like anyone else. Yvette will keep her opinions to herself."

Can I be your lover if you own me? The question flickers in my head, but I ignore it. Instead, I let him dress me in the maid's outfit as always, carrying the tray downstairs to wash the dishes and feeling a sort of warm, pleasant domestic-ness about it all, even if it's all somewhat strange still. There's a certain ownership I feel about the apartment after last night, that it's mine in a way, now that Alexandre and I are really together. Even if none of it really is, even if it's all his, just like I'm *his* in the most strict sense, the feeling matters to me more than anything, and I think it's the same for him.

I have to *believe* it's the same.

I feel lighter than ever as I go about my daily chores, my heart hammering with excitement at the thought of meeting Alexandre's friends or perhaps even being introduced as his lover. *Lover* sounds so much better than *girlfriend* or *partner*, I think as I dust the art and statues, much more European, more French. Sophisticated.

The hours fly by until he comes back with food and wine for dinner and another package for me. He takes me back to my room, and this time when he undresses me out of the maid's outfit, he lets his hands wander. I can feel the desire in them, see it in his eyes as his fingers trail over my breasts, between my thighs, parting me so that he can stroke my clit, until I'm panting softly. Alexandre sinks to his knees, fastening his mouth between my legs and sucking it into his mouth, rolling the tight, hard nub between his lips until I clutch his hair and cry out with a sudden, intense pleasure that makes my knees buckle. He scoops me up, laying me stomach-down on the bed as he frees his hard cock from his pants and thrusts it into me, gripping my hips until he finally comes with a cry, biting and sucking on my neck as he fills me with his cum. I shudder around him, too, clenching and moaning as I come for a second time.

I feel limp and blissful as he goes to get a cloth to clean me up, more like a doll than ever, but I don't care. Why would I? I've had more orgasms in the last twenty-four hours than I have in months, and if a man owns me, it's a rich, handsome man with a huge cock and a penchant for cooking me delicious meals and dressing me in pretty clothes. Why would I fight it, even if he treats me like a doll?

You've gone full Stockholm Syndrome, the small voice in my head whispers as Alexandre cleans his cum off of my thighs, but I ignore it. It's so easy to ignore now.

"I brought you a new pretty dress," he says, smiling at me as he unwraps the package he'd brought home along with the food and wine. And it *is* pretty. It's soft lavender linen, another wrap dress like the silk one I wore on our first afternoon out. Alexandre puts it on me with nothing underneath it, the delicate linen brushing over my skin as he braids my hair over one shoulder and then shows me the jewelry he purchased, a simple rose gold bangle with a raw amethyst set in it and a matching set of earrings. "No necklace this time," he says, dragging his fingers down my slight cleavage. "I like seeing your breasts unobstructed."

I shiver at his touch, looking at myself in the mirror, pink and flushed and smiling, and I barely recognize the girl looking back at me. I haven't looked this relaxed or happy in a long time.

There's a knock at the door, and we go out to the living room. To my disappointment, the first person to arrive is Yvette. "You can help me start preparing dinner," Alexandre tells her, but her gaze goes immediately, laser-like, to my neck.

"What the fuck have you done, Alexandre?" she asks in her thick accent, her voice rasping for once instead of soft. "Have you fucked the pet?"

"That's none of your business," Alexandre says stiffly. "Help me in the kitchen, please? The other guests will be arriving soon."

Her upper lip curls as she walks past me, and my pulse leaps into my throat. *"Whore,"* she whispers as she slides past, low enough that Alexandre can't hear. "You'll pay for this. I don't know how or what spell you've put on him, but I'll make certain you pay."

"Alexandre won't allow that," I whisper, with a bravery that I don't feel. But she just laughs, whisking past me into the kitchen, and I feel cold fingers crawling down my spine at the venom in her words.

I'd forgotten about the threat Yvette posed, just for a little while. But now it's plain again, plain and terrifying, and I'm about to have to spend an entire evening with her. Tonight matters. I know it does. It's the first time Alexandre has had a dinner party since bringing me here. He's going to have me sitting at the table, with his bite mark on my neck, some of his cum still inside of me, his lover instead of his possession.

Yvette could ruin everything, and I know she wants to.

I just don't know how she'll manage it.

And I'm fucking terrified.

LIAM

I can't believe we're finally here.

After so many stops, so many twists and turns, we have the address of Alexandre Sartre's apartment. The place where he's almost certainly keeping Ana. And tonight, in just a few hours, I'm going to be the one to save her from him.

"You shouldn't go in alone," Levin says as I check my gun and then check it again, standing against one wall with his arms crossed. "It's dangerous. You need backup."

"For one man? We've already determined he doesn't have security. He lives alone—or at least, he did before he bought Ana. It's an apartment, not a compound. Three of us bursting in, even two, will be too much chaos. I'll go in on my own, deal with him, extricate her, and the two of you should be waiting with the car, so we can make a quick getaway. We get to the hangar, get on the plane, and it's straight back to Boston."

"Very tidy," Max says with a frown.

"Too tidy." Levin shakes his head. "It's not going to go off so simply, and you know that as well as Max and I do. Any man who has ever done a mission involving someone else's blood knows that, and all three of us have."

"I'm going in alone," I repeat stubbornly. "I don't want chaos, and I don't want her to be frightened or any chance of her getting hit in the crossfire. Just have the car running outside, so we can get away quickly. I'll handle Alexandre Sartre."

I can see from Levin's expression that he doesn't agree, but he stays silent. I'm not sure why exactly, when he's taken point for so much of this, but I expect that it's because, in the end, this is my mission. My goal is to save Ana, and he's not going to get in the way of that, if this is how I want to play it. Maybe he's remembering that long-ago day when he went in guns blazing to avenge his dead wife. Maybe he simply has grown used to being the second-in-command rather than the one in charge, but for whatever reason, he merely shrugs and double-checks his own weapons.

"The car will be waiting for you," he says simply, and that's the end of that. Max is armed too, and he watches me with quiet, dark eyes, silent as he's been for much of the time since we left Greece.

But as I step past him, striding towards the door as the clock hits seven, he rests his hand on my shoulder, his voice low and somber.

"The grace of St. Patrick of the Isles be with you," he says quietly. "And keep you safe as you go after her." He makes the sign of the cross, quick and sharp. I'm reminded of Father Donahue in the church after Saoirse and her father left, watching me with an intense gaze that says he's afraid for me, if I keep going down this path.

But we've come too far now. There's no going back. Ana is here, in this city, and I won't leave until I take her back home with me.

* * *

IT'S NOT hard to find the apartment. What is surprising is that I see a few people going up the stairs to it, men who look to be in their late twenties or early thirties, well-dressed, and a couple of prettily dressed, very French women. It makes it so much easier than even I had expected, though. I simply slip out of the car, tailing the last couple. Before they can shut the door behind themselves as I follow them up, I slip inside, closing the door myself as my hand goes to my gun.

Alexandre's guests—since that's what they must be—stop and stare at me in horror as I draw my gun, gesturing down the hallway. "Show me where he is," I say coldly, glaring at them. "Alexandre Sartre. Take me to him."

Most people aren't equipped to fight back when faced with a gun. I don't know exactly what to expect, but the guests at least do exactly as I thought they would—they move gingerly down the hallway, leading me through an over-decorated living room and through an arched doorway into a dining room with a heavy, long table set for a dinner party—and Ana, sitting to the right of the chair at the head of it.

For a moment, I freeze in place. I don't know what condition I had expected her to be in or where exactly I had thought she would be —*chained in his basement, maybe? Locked in a room?*—but it wasn't this. I hadn't expected to see her with her cheeks flushed, blonde hair flowing over her shoulders, dressed prettily in a lavender linen dress with expensive-looking earrings at her ears.

She looks—*happy*. Radiant, even. Glowing.

Until she catches sight of me, and her mouth drops open.

"Liam?"

Her voice is a breathless gasp, and I hear it as relief, happiness that I'm here. That I've come to save her. I see the man I must be looking for emerging from the kitchen, another beautiful if slightly severe-looking Frenchwoman at his side with a cigarette in her fingers, his brow furrowed with confusion as he catches sight of me standing in the middle of the dining room with a gun leveled at his guests.

"Anastasia?" His voice is confused. "Do you know this man?"

"I—" her voice trembles, but when she looks at him, I don't see fear. I see hesitancy and uncertainty, but not the fear I'd expected. And now I'm confused, too.

I'd expected to find her traumatized, terrified, panicking, and in need of rescue, not presiding over a dinner party like a lady of the house. Alexandre dusting flour off of his hands. It's all strangely domestic, and I have an odd feeling in my stomach, like I've walked into the middle of a rehearsal for a play that I wasn't supposed to see.

"Anastasia." There's a sudden warning tone to his voice, and she pales slightly.

"I—yes," she manages. "A little."

"And what is he doing here?" The tone darkens, thickens, Alexandre's accent growing deeper. His gaze turns to me. "Liam?"

"Liam McGregor," I say stiffly, raising my chin. "I'm here for Ana."

Her face goes bone-white in the instant that a red flush springs to his cheekbones. "Like hell you are," he snarls, striding forward, and then everything happens at once.

Levin was right, I have a moment to realize before Alexandre's guests close in around me, and the Frenchwoman standing next to Alexandre darts into the fray. I think she's the one who disarms me, but I can't be sure. I try to throw a punch, to wrestle free of the four men restraining me as the gun is lost. Still, I'm in too close of quarters to use my boxing skills, and the Frenchwoman is already backing up, my pistol dangling from her finger as she smirks at me.

"Liam!" Ana cries out, leaping up. Alexandre looks at her, his expression suddenly black with anger, and I see her flinch backward.

There it is. The fear that I'd thought I would see, but too late. She gasps as he swings at me, his fist connecting with my chin, and she cries out my name again as my head lolls to one side, the punch splitting my lip.

"How do you know this man?" Alexandre demands, rounding on her as his guests hold me with my arms pinned behind my back. "Is he your lover?"

"What?" Ana gasps. "No, I—I barely know him, I just met him in Russia! He knows my best friend's husband. I swear I've never—"

"I don't believe you," Alexandre snarls. "Lying little *chienne*. Bitch! He *is* your lover, or else why would he come here—"

"I don't know," Ana whispers miserably. "But I swear—"

"Why should I believe you?" he sneers, his handsome face twisting. "You've lied to me before."

"Alexandre." The Frenchwoman holding my gun comes to stand at his elbow. "I have an idea."

She leans up on her tiptoes, then, her free hand on his shoulder as she whispers something in his ear, and I see Ana flinch, paling even more. It's clear she knows this woman too, enough to dislike her.

Alexandre's mouth twists. "I don't like it." He shakes his head. "No one touches her but me."

The woman shrugs. "You might not like it, but you know I'm right. She won't respond *if* she loves you. His touch will mean nothing to her."

What the fuck is she talking about? I stare at her, but Alexandre is already nodding. The woman moves around the table, grabbing Ana harshly by her upper arms.

"Get your hands off of her!" I shout, but Alexandre is nodding to the men holding me.

"If you're going to disrupt my dinner party," he says coldly, "and make me question the loyalty of my *petit poupée*, then you might as well entertain my guests while I put her to the test. Take him over to the table where Yvette has Ana," he instructs.

I don't know what the fuck is happening, but I'm not given much choice. The four men holding me manage to manhandle me towards where the Frenchwoman—Yvette—is holding Ana so tightly that her nails are biting into her upper arm. As I stand there watching in horror, she grabs Ana's skirt in her fist, yanking it up as she turns Ana sharply and backs her against the table.

"What the fuck is going on?" I shout, twisting to glare at Alexandre, but he just crosses his arms over his chest, shrugging.

"You're going to fuck her while we watch," he says, as casually as if he were telling me to take a seat at the table.

"What?" I stare at him. *He's insane.* "No, I'm fucking not—"

"You will," Alexandre says coolly, "or Yvette will shoot her." He nods as Yvette raises the gun, cocking it and pressing the barrel to Ana's temple as she turns bone-white, starting to shake.

"Liam—" she whispers my name, her eyes starting to well with tears as they flick towards Alexandre. "Alexandre, please, I swear, I've never—we've never—he's not—"

Alexandre shrugs. "Prove it," he says coolly. "Yvette is right. If you love me, and he's nothing to you, then he'll be nothing but a cock in a hole. You won't feel pleasure, and you won't come. But if you do—" his eyes narrow, blackening with rising anger again. "Then you're a lying bitch, and Yvette will deal with you both accordingly."

He looks at me. "You came here for her, so hurry up. Now's your chance. Don't make us wait."

The four men shove me forward, letting go of my arms as they push me in front of Ana, who is visibly shaking now. I frantically try to think of some way out of it as I look into her tearful pale blue eyes, of some way to get the gun back, but I can't. Yvette's finger is on the trigger, and if I try anything, she'll shoot Ana before I can stop her.

I'd come here to save Ana, but somehow I've made everything so much fucking worse.

"Hurry. Up." Alexandre growls it from behind me through clenched teeth, and I let out a frustrated breath.

"You're a fucking man," I growl right back, clenching my own jaw. "I have to be hard to fuck her, you fucking—"

"You wanted her. I'm running out of patience to find out the truth."

Fuck. Of all the times for my cock not to respond—this would be it. I want Ana more than I want to breathe, but in front of strangers and the man who owns her, with a gun to her head, isn't how I'd envisioned it. It isn't a good situation for getting a hard-on, and it's the worst possible one for the two of us that I can imagine.

I have to fuck Ana to get us out of this. That much is clear. But by doing that—by allowing Alexandre to force me to fuck her, I'm essentially killing any chance of us ever being together.

I don't know of any way we could ever come back from this. No matter what I feel or Ana feels, no matter what changes in the future —this will always be our first time. On a dining table in her captor's apartment, forced at gunpoint. Whether she comes or not, whether I enjoy it physically or not, none of that matters.

Alexandre is making me violate her, and for that, I hope I get the chance to kill him, above all else.

He took her from me once—and now, against all odds, he's taking her from me again.

"It's okay," Ana whispers shakily, clearly seeing my predicament. "It's okay, Liam, please—"

The male body is a hell of a thing. Despite our predicament, those two words, whispered in her soft sweet voice—*Liam, please*—is enough to send my cock rocketing into a full erection, going from embarrassingly soft to achingly, painfully hard in a matter of seconds. I've imagined her whispering that a hundred times, at least with my fist around it—*Liam, please*—and my body doesn't seem to know the difference between that imagining and the reasons she's whispering it now.

"Get your finger off the trigger," I hiss at Yvette. "Or I'll move her the wrong way, and you'll set it off by accident. I need to get her up on the table."

"Then hurry the fuck up," she snaps, shifting her finger slightly so that at least she's not in danger of killing Ana while I fuck her. With her other hand, Yvette drags Ana's skirt above her waist, letting me see her bare for the first time, with no panties beneath the linen dress and her soft pink pussy naked to my view, and everyone else's in the room.

I know Alexandre must have fucked her, but I can't think of that now. I force myself to only think of Ana, of her voice whispering my name as I grab her hips and lift her onto the table, the gun still pressed to the side of her head as Yvette stays close to us. I spread Ana's legs, unzipping my pants with one hand as I pull out my inexplicably rock-hard cock.

"Well, I see you've found your manhood," Alexandre says dryly from behind me. "Don't worry, *petit*, I'm sure you'll prove your love to me quickly enough."

It's the cruelest test. Ana can try as hard as she wants, but that doesn't mean she won't get wet or orgasm, especially since I *know* she wants me. She wanted me the afternoon we met, the afternoon we talked in the garden. I *know* how I feel isn't unrequited, even if I don't know the exact depth of her feelings. Tears are running down the sides of her face as she lies there, frozen, clearly terrified, a gun to her head. I feel like the scum of the earth as I guide my hard cock between her thighs, to the folds between them that are cool and dry, not flushed and wet and swollen the way I'd imagined they'd be the first time I slept with her. I've imagined this moment so many times, and exactly none of them have been like this.

And there's nothing I can fucking do about it. Alexandre is violating us both, and I'm helpless to stop it. I can see his bite mark on her neck, and I hate him viscerally more than I've ever hated anyone. More than I hated Alexei, in this particular moment at least.

Ana bites her lower lip hard as I push into her, her body resisting me. Her hands clench into fists at her sides, her eyes closing, and I hear Yvette make a noise low in her throat as she pushes the gun against Ana's temple harder, leaning up to whisper in my ear.

"Alexandre says he'll believe she loves him if she doesn't enjoy it, if she doesn't come. But I'm telling *you*, little Irish lover boy, that if you *don't* make her come, I'll kill her and tell Alexandre the gun went off by accident. He'll be brokenhearted, of course, but I'll console him. You fuck her good, Irish, make her come hard, or she's dead." Yvette chuckles. "Of course, if she comes, he might want me to shoot her, so she might be dead either way. But at least she'll get some pleasure before she dies. And Alexandre is a bit of a hard read—he might forgive her. But I won't forgive you, if you don't make her come. I *will* kill her. Believe me on that."

I do. Alexandre *is* a hard man to get a read on, and from the way he looked at Ana before he got angry, I'm not entirely sure that he would kill her. But I believe, to the depths of my soul, that Yvette will shoot Ana if I don't make her come and call it an accident. Which means I'm stuck between a rock and a hard place.

Make her come, and risk her life. Try to keep her from orgasming, and almost certainly be the reason she dies.

I know which choice to make. And I have a flicker of an idea that just might work if I can time it correctly.

"Ana," I whisper her name under my breath, stroking her hair. "I'm sorry it's like this, Ana. I didn't want our first time to be like this, but I wanted you so badly. You feel so good, even like this, it feels *so* good —" I whisper it low enough that Alexandre can't hear us, mostly for Ana's benefit, to help her. But it's true. Even under the current circumstances, her body feels glorious, her pussy tight and hot around my cock, her perfect delicate ballerina's body like an art piece sprawled on the table among the crockery, her hair everywhere, her pale face upturned as the last rays of sunlight spill across it in the dying evening, and I move faster, harder despite myself. My body wants pleasure, maybe all the more so for the imminent danger, and very quickly, I can feel that Ana's does too.

She's crying still, but it's not just her cheeks that are wet. I can feel her growing wetter around me, her hips starting to move, my cock sliding in and out of her more easily as I hold her waist, grunting despite myself with the pleasure of it as I keep fucking her, aware of the eyes on us, of the fact that as soon as we both come, I have to make snap decisions that no man should have to make in the afterglow of orgasm. Or—if I can hold mine back, as soon as *she* comes. If I can force myself to pull out of her when it feels so fucking good—

"Liam—" Ana whispers my name, opening her eyes, and I know she's close.

So fucking close.

Yvette smiles wickedly, and her finger slides towards the trigger.

So. Close.

ANA

I can't believe this is happening.
It's like something out of a nightmare.
Liam is *here*. Here with me, fucking *inside* of me, and it all happened so fast that I don't even know how to make sense of it all. One second I was sitting at the dinner table, waiting for Alexandre and Yvette to finish cooking as the guests arrived, and the next, Liam appeared, like some kind of white knight, to—what?

Save me?

How?

Why?

I'd imagined he was back in Boston, living his life, running his business, thinking of me with regret and guilt sometimes maybe, but certainly not *looking* for me. Certainly not coming to find me, to —*save* me?

I don't even know if I need saving.

I don't know if I want it.

Do I?

A few minutes ago, I would have said no. Alexandre and I were happy. We were lovers. Everything was good.

But now—he's given me to Liam. Ordered Liam to fuck me, to *test* me. All because Yvette suggested it.

Yvette has a gun to my head.

Alexandre is okay with that.

He's testing me.

If I don't come, he'll know I love him.

But Liam.

I wanted Liam.

It feels so good.

Alexandre felt so good.

Liam feels so good.

I—I—I—

The voices in my head are too loud, the sensations in my body too much. If Alexandre loved me, why would he do this to me? He paid so much for me, said I was so beautiful, the most priceless thing in his collection, his little doll. He said he couldn't lose me, he couldn't bear it, but now he's *testing* me again. Testing me like the meals on the floor, like Yvette watching me to make sure I don't go where I shouldn't again, that I could be a good girl, mind my manners.

Good girls don't come with other men.

Good girls don't want other men.

Will he even want me after this? The tears come faster at that thought, that he might think I'm filthy after this, dirty. But he won't if I don't come. If I don't enjoy it. I try to cling to that thought, but then I look up at Liam, and the confusion is so terrible that I want to die.

Liam, handsome and red-haired, his strong jaw clenched, his muscular body hovering over mine, broad hands on my waist, his cock that's every bit as thick as Alexandre's buried inside of me, moving, thrusting, and it feels so good. It feels right. I'd imagined it, back in Russia, fantasized about it, even though I knew I'd never have it. But now, here he is, inside of me, and Alexandre forced it, but I don't know if that makes a difference. Because I'd wanted him, and he came for me, and now he's going to—

Oh god. His cock feels too good, good enough to make me forget about the gun at my head, and he's whispering things, words that make my heart race. *Liam doesn't want to do this, but he's doing it to save me. Alexandre is hurting me, but Liam's trying to save me, he came to save me, Alexandre did too, but he bought me, or rescued me? He owns me, Liam is trying to rescue me, Liam—Alexandre—Liam—*

It's too much. I close my eyes tightly, but the pleasure is racing across my skin, the feeling of Liam's broad hands and the sounds of him groaning in pleasure too much, his cock thrusting into me, thick and long, filling me, and I'm going to come.

I'm going to come, and I can't stop it, I can't, I can't.

My hands are coming up, grabbing at his arms, my back arching as the wild pleasure washes over me, my pussy tightening around Liam's cock as I cry out, and I hear Alexandre curse aloud. I can feel my heart breaking, my chest clenching with pain at the same moment that my body is shuddering with pleasure. It's the strangest, worst, most beautiful thing I've ever experienced all at once.

"I'm sorry," I gasp out. "I'm sorry, I'm sorry—"

I'm still fluttering, clenching, when Liam pulls out of me. I don't know how he does it, how he has the strength of will to stop. Still, Yvette is caught off guard by the force of my orgasm up close, distracted by the sudden howl of anger that Alexandre lets out. Liam slips out of me, lunging for her. I see him disarming her out of the corner of my eye, see the blur as he strikes her in the head with the butt of his gun. I hear the *thud* as she hits the ground, and I'm sliding off of the table into a heap on the floor, crying and crawling towards Alexandre, who is sinking to the floor as well.

"Anastasia, I thought you loved me, Anastasia, Anastasia—" he's whispering it over and over, his hands outstretched, and I'm crawling towards him, crying. I want to get to him, apologize, and tell him that I do love him, that I didn't mean it, that it was my body and nothing else.

"I thought you loved me. How could you do that? How could you enjoy another man, how could you—" Alexandre switches to French, his words a blur, and I dimly hear the sound of his guests trying to get out of the dining room, Liam shouting for them to get the fuck out while they still can as he steps between us.

I see him lower the gun, pointing it at Alexandre's head, and I scream, clutching at Liam's leg.

"No! Don't kill him, please, please, no, don't kill him, I love him, Liam, please don't, please don't—" I'm shrieking now, panicking, crying, the words tumbling over each other faster than I can say them aloud. Somehow Liam has managed to get himself in order, his cock back in his pants. However, he's still hard, the gun leveled evenly at Alexandre's head, and the terror I feel that I'm about to see Alexandre die in front of me is unmatched by almost anything else I've ever felt, even when Franco trussed me up in that warehouse.

"Fuck." I hear Liam hiss, and then he bends down, scooping me up with his free arm as he keeps the gun leveled at Alexandre. "I'm taking you out of here, Ana. I don't know what the hell you're thinking. You can't stay here. Not with him."

"Fuck you!" Alexandre shouts it, lunging for Liam, but he steps back, neatly aiming the gun and shooting Alexandre squarely in the knee. "You can't escape me, Anastasia. I'll come for you. You won't leave me like the others. You'll never escape me—"

The cry of pain that Alexandre lets out feels like a dagger in the heart, but Liam doesn't stop. He shoots again, in the other knee and then in the shoulder, until Alexandre is crumpled on the carpet, his wounds not fatal but still bleeding, his body twisted with pain, and I can barely see past the tears streaming out of my eyes and down my face.

"You can't, you can't—" I cry, twisting in his grasp. "Please, Liam—"

"God, Ana, stop fighting!" I can hear the exasperation in Liam's voice. "The man wants to keep you prisoner, *fuck*, Ana—Jesus, Mary, and Joseph, please be reasonable!"

I'm fighting him so hard that we haven't even made it to the doorway of the dining room. I can see Alexandre bleeding, writhing; I try to go to him, but Liam has an iron grip on me.

"Fuck, I don't want to do this," Liam groans. "I hoped—*fuck*, Levin was right. Just calm down, I know you're panicking, Ana, please listen—"

But I can't. It's all too much, the voices crowding in. I don't know who to believe anymore, Liam or Alexandre, which one is really trying to keep me safe, which one I should want to be with, which one I should trust.

I know what my heart feels, at this moment, and it wants to go to the man lying on the floor, the man who just this afternoon brought me a pretty dress and called me his lover, who—

There's a cloth on my face, a thick smell filling my nostrils.

"I'm going to keep you safe, Ana."

It's Liam's voice, filling my ears as something else fills my nose, making me dizzy. Or maybe it's Alexandre. *I'm going to keep you safe, Anastasia.*

They blend together, overlapping until I don't know which man is which. Until I feel limp and heavy, and I don't know what's happening, only that once again, I'm losing everything I ever believed I could trust in.

And then, as I feel Liam lift me into his arms, everything goes black.

* * *

THE NEXT INSTALLMENT of the Irish King series releases 3/20/2022. Preorder here! **Want to find out more about the sexy and dangerous Russian Assassin Levin? Sign up for part one of the exclusive serial. Only available for FREE to M. James' newsletter subscribers here!**

Printed in Great Britain
by Amazon